BLEA

BLEAK MIDWINTER

PETER MILLAR

BLOOMSBURY

First published in Great Britain 2001
This paperback edition published 2002

Copyright © 2001 by Peter Millar

The moral right of the author has been asserted

Bloomsbury Publishing Plc, 38 Soho Square, London W1D 3HB

A CIP catalogue record is available from the British Library

ISBN 0 7475 5751 9

10 9 8 7 6 5 4 3 2

Typeset by Palimpsest Book Production Limited,
Polmont, Stirlingshire

Printed in Great Britain by Clays Limited, St Ives plc

ACKNOWLEDGEMENTS

I would like to thank the Bodleian Library in Oxford for renewing my reader's card and for my re-acquaintance with its magnificent facilities (which I sadly neglected in earlier times), Dr Alexander Green of Burnley General Hospital for his advice on some aspects of disease transmission (though I would stress that any departures from feasibility are my own responsibility) and Ingrid von Essen for her sympathetic and intelligent editing. Also the people of Hook Norton, Oxon, and my fellow parish councillors for their stalwart opposition to the concreting of what remains of the English countryside.

To Jackie, all the time

In the bleak midwinter,
Frosty wind made moan
Earth stood hard as iron,
Water like a stone
Snow had fallen, snow on snow,
Snow on snow.
In the bleak midwinter,
long ago.

English Christmas carol, Christina Rossetti, 1872

Prologue

Miami Beach, Florida, a week before Christmas

IT IS hot. Unseasonably hot, even for Florida. By the side of the pool a strikingly beautiful young woman, somewhere between the attainment of adulthood and the first intimations that perfection does not last for ever, is lying on a sunbed.

From the shade beneath the bottle-green awning of an otherwise deserted terrace bar, four men are watching her, in the way that men ordinarily watch the bodies of nubile females: hungrily. But their hunger has an edge. A cutting edge.

The temperature is close on 28 degrees, or somewhere in the upper 70s, as the locals would say. The young woman has been in the afternoon sun for several hours. But she is not worried about burning. For one thing, her supple skin is well oiled with a high-potency sun filter, carefully reapplied, out of long habit, after every swim. The moist sheen on the golden-brown skin of her inner thighs could be residual oil or pool water. Or sweat. It occurs to her that if she had a watch, she would be tempted to look at it. To check time elapsed. But there is no need. She knows how late it is.

At the bar, one of the four men is checking the time on the aviator Breitling chronograph which he wears discreetly on his left wrist. It is high time. He glances at his colleagues. But they do not return his look. They are concentrating on the body of the young woman, taking in every beautiful inch exposed to them and mentally filling in the rest. One of them, the youngest, although he must be at least five or six years older than the object of his obvious desire, is licking his lips. It is a habit he has. A bad habit.

Now is the moment. Now the man with the expensive watch, whose name is Harold Hammerstein, gets down off his barstool. This motion attracts the attention of his colleagues, who all do likewise, as if they are used to imitating him. Which they are. And they emerge, quietly, quickly, all at once from the cool, dark shade of the terrace bar into the heat of the Miami afternoon; as they swiftly cross the lawn, the minimal sound they make is masked by the soothingly repetitive swishing of the sprinklers that keep the grass green.

There are only thirty feet between the bar and the sunbed where the young woman lies oblivious to the approach of these men in their incongruous dark suits. They are there in seconds.

Had she opened her eyes at that moment, she would have seen the long, dull metal barrels of their silenced pistols, indicating that they were more than just pleased to see her. But she did not.

Cool, Harold Hammerstein thought. Or just stupid. Stupefied, he corrected himself.

'Miranda,' he said, in what he hoped was a suitably sinister voice. 'Time to wake up, baby.' And then, after just the right, practised pause: 'Time to die.'

He had planned this moment. If truth be known, he had always known it would come, in one way or another. Whatever her reaction, he was prepared. The poolside was deserted, as it was every day at this time. And Miranda had followed the same routine as she always did. The beautiful, perfect Miranda. With her auburn hair, her long legs, her perfect body and imperfect past. And no future. Killing time, down by the pool.

'Wake up, bitch!' he snarled. He wanted this to be quick. But not so quick that she didn't know about it first. He wanted to look into her eyes before the four magnum shells, fired simultaneously, reduced her golden suntanned flesh to steak tartare.

It was overkill, and he knew it. There would be nothing left that was recognisably human, except to a forensic scientist. A waste, really. But these things had to be done.

'Wake up, Miranda!'

He kicked the sunbed. Then again, harder, so that one of her long legs jolted and fell to one side, landing hard on the concrete of the pool surround. Miranda did not show the slightest reaction. Which was the first time that Harold Hammerstein realised that there might be something wrong. Seriously wrong.

The man who licked his lips looked anxiously at his boss, only to receive a fierce glance in return that said he should keep his eye, and his muzzle, on the target. Who knew what dumb trick the mad bitch might be playing?

Harold himself bent down, grabbed hold of the elegant, gold-chained ankle that was still on the sunbed and pulled it hard to one side. Viciously. Leaving her legs splayed open at an obscene angle.

'Goddamn!' he muttered under his breath. And he reached up, grabbed her wrist roughly and held it for a few seconds, letting his eyes run up the elegant, golden-skinned arm to the little puncture marks inside the crook of her elbow. 'Goddamn the bitch to hell.' He spat out the words. 'And back.'

She had cheated him again. Miranda von Taxenbach,

née Amanda Workington from Croydon, south London, was already as good as dead. Hammerstein felt a red rage burn behind his eyes as he looked up and nodded to his three companions, whose weapons of death were still trained on the corpse. They fired anyway.

Part One

Incubation

I say then that the sum of thirteen hundred and forty-eight years had elapsed since the fruitful Incarnation of the Son of God, when the noble city of Florence . . . was visited by the deady pestilence. Some say that it descended upon the human race through the influence of the heavenly bodies, others that it was a punishment signifying God's righteous anger at our iniquitous way of life. But whatever its cause, it had originated some years earlier in the East where it had claimed countless lives before it unhappily spread westward, growing in strength as it swept relentlessly on from one place to the next.

In the face of its onrush, all the wisdom and ingenuity of man were unavailing . . .

Giovanni Boccaccio, Decameron

And in the end there were none who would bury them, none who would mourn them and none who would pray over them, so we laid our dead in the fields like carrion, for the churchyard was full. We laid them in ditches, where ditches were dug, and where not, we laid them on the open earth, for the ground was frozen now too hard to break. And even in the depths of winter frost the stench of mortality was fearful. The dogs and the wolves from the forest would not touch them. And all who remained were sore afraid. Yet at the end of the world, what shall a man fear? Our Maker has unmade us.

From the testament of Edward Gray,
Rector, St Peter's Alone,
Nether Ditchford,
Oxfordshire, England
January 1349

Chapter One

Magdalen College, Oxford; Friday
19 December, 4.00 p.m.

D ANIEL WARREN shivered. He pulled up the hood of his duffel coat against the biting wind that swept in across empty Otmoor and was channelled down Oxford's stone streets: an icy blast that froze the blood of any foolhardy souls lingering in its path. It was a long time since he had felt this cold. His glasses had misted up – frosted over, more like. His nose was blue, he was sure of it, and he sniffled continuously as he scuttled across the quadrangle for the relative shelter of the archway that led into Magdalen College's fifteenth-century cloister.

This was the way the early ecclesiastical scholars had lived when the college was founded, more than half a millennium ago: scurrying along draughty stone passageways with Gothic windows open to the elements, clutching rough woollen garments tight around them to preserve the warmth of their bodies. It had all the historical authenticity a California boy could crave, and then some.

Still shivering, he fumbled in his jacket pocket underneath the heavy coat, produced his 'fellow's key' and opened the oak door that led from the exposed cloister up a flight of stone stairs to the Old Library. At the top of the stairs he unlocked a second door and breathed a sigh of relief as he entered the marginally warmer atmosphere created by the few radiators: inefficient pieces of hulking Victorian ironware, painted an institutional brown and bolted to the walls underneath the tall, narrow windows. He was in no hurry to take off the duffel coat.

Magdalen's Old Library was one of Daniel's favourite places in the world. To him it was more than priceless old books and ancient parchments, more than a reservoir of scholarship: it was a time machine. To see through the eyes of another, even a contemporary living in the same town, was a challenge. Across the gulf of centuries the challenge – and the reward – was all the greater. It required more than just words and their understanding. It required context. And here, in a building that itself spanned the centuries, in surroundings that had changed but little since the first Queen Elizabeth's grandfather, Henry VII, had fought his way to the crown, Daniel Warren felt that half the leap had been made for him.

How had he ever been able to study history in California, in the sterile atmosphere of Berkeley with its steel and glass and dependence on computers for almost all research? The English novelist L. P. Hartley had been right: the past really was another country. Here he could touch it, almost see it and hear it. And, shivering as his body gradually adjusted to the relative warmth of the library, he could certainly feel it.

Bravely shedding his duffel coat, which he hung on a peg fixed on the end of one of the floor-to-ceiling bookshelves that protruded in long rows from each wall of the great room, he rubbed his hands together, massaging his cold fingers, and walked up to the library's north end to warm them on the radiator underneath the window.

Great purple-black masses of cumulus were rolling across what only that morning had been an all too rare bright-blue winter sky. Now the line of shadow advancing across the frost-seared grass of the college lawns marked the dark clouds' inexorable progression like a spreading stain. Peering out through the dull glass from behind the thickness of the ancient masonry, Daniel felt goosebumps rise on his flesh as the golden Cotswold stone that lent Oxford its particular magic turned ashen grey. A long strand of auburn hair fell down across one eye, and he pushed it back. Glancing out of the window again, he shuddered as he watched the shadow creep towards the great Neoclassical colonnade of the early eighteenth-century structure that with typical English perversity they called New Buildings.

In early summer, so he had been assured, New Buildings were wreathed in fragrance from thousands of pendulous pale-purple wisteria blossoms from a plant nearly as old as the building itself. Now, however, the thick, gnarled and twisted trunk and long straggling branches looked to Daniel more like the hands of some subterranean troll trying to drag the building down into the earth with fibrous fingers. As if the architecture's classical Mediterranean lines were an affront to the Gothic soul of the soil. On a day like today, summer seemed a fanciful illusion of the foolishly optimistic.

To get used to this climate, he supposed you had to grow up with it. He wondered how other foreign students coped, particularly those who came from subtropical countries. Like Rajiv, for example, the Indian medic who was working on a doctoral thesis on tropical medicine, and had become Daniel's closest friend in the three months since he arrived in Oxford. Then he remembered that Rajiv was a native: British born and bred and proud of it. Despite his ancestral roots, Rajiv was no more Indian than . . . well, than Daniel was

English, for example. But then, he was English, wasn't he, albeit at a few generations' greater remove? At least as much English as JFK or Ronald Reagan had been Irish. Roots mattered, didn't they? Up to a point. That was what his mother had always taught him. Among other things.

Other things, indeed. It was time to get back to work, back to the collection of manuscripts he had unearthed relating to his own specialist subject. What he found remarkable was that these documents, fragments of worn parchment and paper, old, hide-bound ledgers, had not been gathered together from the four corners of the earth in the interests of academic learning. They were here because they always had been here. Or hereabouts. They were local history, preserved because no one had destroyed them, because preservation was what Oxford did best.

Sitting down at the big oak table, away from the light of the window, because even the feeble English winter sun could degrade the legibility of medieval ink, he lifted the thick velvet cloth with which he had covered the documents spread out in date order. Carefully, with the practised fingers of a scholar, he lifted once again the one that interested him most, the piece of old discoloured paper, dry and thin, that had exerted a fascination on him since he discovered it.

Like the whole collection of papers, it was extremely old – indeed had been as old as the USA was today when the stonemasons were putting the finishing touches to this library at the end of the sixteenth century. But more than all the others, this document was Daniel's time-travel ticket, the one that offered him a free ride back down the centuries to see momentous events through the eyes of a man long dead.

For amid all the ledgers, with their manorial accounts

and receipts, the notices of appointment and dismissal of prelates, this was personal: the last testament of a man who had lived and died in extraordinary times. Under extraordinary circumstances.

Chapter Two

*The John Radcliffe Hospital, Oxford; Friday
19 December, 11.40 p.m.*

NIGHT. BUT no time for sleeping. Tired and aching
from dozing in his tubular-frame chair, Rajiv
Mahendra got to his feet and stretched theatrically,
letting go a long lazy yawn that came from the depths
of his weary soul. Through the plate-glass window
he looked without interest out on the sleeping city.
Or rather its sprawling outer suburbs. Seven storeys
beneath him Headington and Marston merged together
in a maze of crescents, cul-de-sacs and avenues, yellow
sodium lights reflected on the thin layer of frost on
tiled roofs and tarmac roadways. He no longer stared
in vain for a distant glimpse of the dreaming spires as
he had done when he first started work at the JR2, the
modern hospital built when the elegant but crumbling
eighteenth-century original Radcliffe Infirmary in the
city centre was long since outgrown.

He stretched and yawned again. Dreaming spires,
huh? Dreaming was a luxury he didn't dare dream
of. Deep, dreamless sleep was what he wanted. But
he was only four hours into his shift. Morning and
his bed in college were still a long way away. What
would Daniel be doing, he wondered? Packing up his
books in the library and heading back to Cloisters for a
glass of whisky before bedtime? Or perhaps he had spent
the evening in the college bar, sipping English ale and

pretending to be a connoisseur but all the while eyeing the pretty undergraduates. The big, bookish American was too shy to ask anyone out on a date.

Rajiv sighed. If only medicine had more sociable hours! Happily there was not much to do, though just occasionally he longed for a night-time emergency, something that would get the adrenaline flowing.

But tonight as almost every night, wards 7c and 7d (known as Alexander and Rowney to those who preferred the human touch), his little fiefdom, were quiet: no more than half a dozen patients in either, and nothing more serious than a nasty case of gastroenteritis. That was if you excluded old Mr Watson in bed five who had advanced cancer of at least three vital organs. But even there, Rajiv reflected, there was little likelihood of a crisis. Mr Watson's prognosis was not in any doubt. There would be no drama there, just the quiet, grim inevitability of a slide into morphine-numbed oblivion.

'All right, love? Would you like a wee cuppa?'

Rajiv turned with a smile at the bright Scottish accent. Annie Craig was his favourite person in the world. In fact, anyone offering him a cup of hot tea in the dark, quiet hours of the night went automatically way up in his personal popularity stakes.

'Thank you, Nurse Craig, that would be most appreciated.'

'Sure you're dyin' on your feet. The way they work you lads, it's a wonder half of you don't end up as patients on the wards. That'd be a turn-up for the books, eh, me tucking you in at night?'

Rajiv couldn't be sure, but he thought she had winked. He was grateful she almost certainly had no idea he was blushing.

Annie Craig had already disappeared into the glorified broom cupboard that served as the nurses' private kitchen, where she and her companion-in-arms Mary Clarke brewed endless cups of PG Tips and exchanged confidences about their own and others' sex lives. Rajiv wondered what they said about him. He had caught them once tittering uncontrollably and then turning melodramatically straight-faced when they spotted him. The rest of the day he had worried that they had been talking about him, only to find out that the cause of their hilarity had been one of the senior consultants doing his ward round with his flies undone.

'There you go then. That'll help keep them peepers from poppin'.'

'Sorry?'

'Keep you awake, I mean.' She handed him a steaming mug and stood in the doorway, her hands clasped around her own tea.

'You no wantin' to get out on the razzle then? Wi' all the rest o' them? Big Friday night an' all. What with the Christmas parties goin' on? Oh, er, I suppose you don't . . . I mean . . .'

He smiled. 'It's quite all right, nurse. Even Hindus can be very tolerant of other religions' customs, you know. And anyway, Christmas is not exactly an alien rite. I was born in Leicester. But someone has to work, and I suppose I mind less than most.'

'Och, sure we're all heathens anyway these days.' She perked up.

'Well, some more than others, perhaps,' he replied.

And Annie, suddenly flustered again, beat a retreat. 'I'd best be back on the ward – take a look and make sure they're all OK, y'know.'

Watching her retreating back, Rajiv noticed the shape of her calf muscles in the black stockings and wondered if he might one day make Annie Craig's day by taking her out for dinner. And dessert.

Having decided, much to his own surprise, that it was a distinct possibility, he reattuned his mind to the other pressing question of the night: whether he should knuckle down and get back to writing up the first part of the research into epidemiology that he hoped would one day get him his consultancy, or switch on the television and lose himself in an early-morning rerun of *Battlestar Galactica* on the sci-fi channel.

He had just about made up his mind that the research was probably more entertaining when Annie Craig stuck her head round the door again, looking even more flustered than she had a few minutes earlier.

'Doctor,' she said. 'You'd better come quick.'

'What's the matter?'

Rajiv was on his feet, following the nurse through the door out of the day room and down the corridor to Ward 7c.

'I don't know. He just sort of started moaning all terrible like, as if he was in awful pain.'

'Who did?'

'The man in bed six. The new admission. The one who came in this afternoon.'

Trotting to keep up with her, Rajiv tried to recollect. He had gone round all the beds at the start of the shift. He remembered the new man, but the notes had said only 'for observation' and he'd been asleep so Rajiv hadn't seen any point in disturbing him.

Now, however, at least Nurse Craig thought there was something serious to observe. She was already pulling the plastic curtains around the bed for privacy, though, as Rajiv reflected with the grim sense of realism that came with his profession, Mr Watson in bed five was unlikely to pay much attention.

'He was like that just now, when I was doing my round.' Annie was obviously concerned. It occurred to

Rajiv that that meant he ought to be, too. Annie was just a staff nurse, but she was nobody's fool.

The man's head was lolling from side to side and every few seconds his low moaning rose to an anguished cry. Rajiv put a hand to the man's brow, expecting it to be hot. Instead it felt cold and clammy. Yet he gave all the signs of being in fever, rolling restlessly, eyes half closed with a thin film of mucus in the corners. He glanced at the man's chart, but apart from his name (Atkins, C.) and the fact that he had been admitted around 4.00 p.m. for 'clinical observation', it gave him no clues. There were no indications of what he was supposed to be watching for. No reference to any medication. Sloppy! But that's how the National Health Service was these days. Especially just before Christmas.

He felt the man's pulse. Racing. Annie Craig was looking at him the way he had noticed nurses sometimes did, half expecting him to perform a miracle, half wondering whether he had the faintest clue what he was up to. In this case, he hadn't.

'Do you know anything at all of his history?' he asked her, more in hope than expectation.

'Only that Mary who was on before me said he had taken a turn at work or something.'

'At work, hmm?' The man's arms were big and muscular. It was hard to imagine him sitting at a desk. 'Any idea what he does?'

'I don't know. Oh – a builder, maybe. Mary said he wasn't brought in by the ambulance. It was a builder's van – Riggs and something, one o' the big national boys, putting up a' them new houses in the villages. Up near Banbury, I think.'

'Banbury? Why didn't they take him to the local hospital?' What was it called?

'The Horton?' She shrugged. 'Maybe they thought it was something more serious.'

'Maybe they were right.' He was pulling down the bedclothes, untangling the man's writhing limbs from the starched hospital cotton.

'Is there anything I can do?'

'No. Yes.' Second thoughts. 'Check his temperature for a start.'

Annie took a strip thermometer from her breast pocket and held it to the man's clammy brow. He had stopped squirming, as if removing the sheets had been a physical relief. Rajiv pulled the loose hospital gown up, exposing the man's nakedness. He was heavily built but running to fat. Late thirties, probably, but it was hard to be certain. His skin had a regular tan, no doubt from working outside without his shirt in the summer. Once upon a time, Rajiv thought, maybe Mr Atkins had fancied himself as a building-site Adonis, showing off his Greek-god physique to the passing female population. Maybe he still did. But right now his body seemed robbed of its toughness, soft and malleable, glistening slightly, like damp chamois leather.

'Thirty-five point two,' Annie announced. Far from fever: low, almost the beginnings of a chill. Had he been working outside in this weather? And if so, for how long?

Rajiv put on a pair of thin surgical gloves and began gingerly examining the man's feverish body for a rash. Meningitis had been his first thought, first fear; there had been another scare at a school in nearby Abingdon recently. And although children and young people were the most common victims, too many doctors, particularly in general practice, forgot that it could strike at any age. You could never be too careful. Any sign of a rash could be a warning, particularly near the lymph glands. He lifted the man's left arm and felt with his right hand under the armpit. Slight swelling perhaps, but no reddening. The other side was the same, except that the swelling was more pronounced. Almost as if there were lumps growing beneath the skin. Here too there was no sign of the telltale red rash that indicated meningitis, though there was some discoloration. It was more of a purple colour, as if he had been bruised somehow. Though it was a funny place to get bruises, under the arms. Perhaps some building accident could have done it. Of course it looked like ... and then again ... He pushed away the thought as preposterous.

Nonetheless, almost despite himself, he worked his way down to the man's groin, pushing the flaccid penis aside as he separated the legs. Big, heavy rugby player's legs with short ginger hairs. He moved them apart, and caught his breath involuntarily.

The nurse had produced a towel and was pushing back strands of limp, sweat-soaked hair from the man's fore-head, thinking only of providing some comfort, leaving the medical bit to him. Rajiv blinked, as if somehow that would change what he was seeing, what he was now carefully feeling through the surgical gloves: the same swellings as under the armpits, but bigger, much bigger. And darker. Almost like overripe plums beneath the surface of the skin. These were hard, as if threatening to burst the skin itself. Exactly as they were supposed to look. Except not here. Not now. He had seen them before, in his three-month 'elective' overseas, taken, at his father's insistence, in 'the old country'. The old man's old country. But there you expected it, or at least were warned of the possibility. In the crowded, unsanitary hill villages of Uttar Pradesh, where conditions were, by European standards, almost medieval.

Not here, not in Oxford. Not in this day and age.

But the evidence of his eyes and fingers was incontrovertible. It would take tests, of course, careful tests conducted as soon as possible, to make 100 per cent sure. But Rajiv had been there before.

He had no doubt, not the slightest in the world, what the diagnosis would be.

Chapter Three

Magdalen College, Oxford; Saturday
20 December, 1.00 a.m.

D ANIEL WARREN lifted his head from his notes and turned back to his laptop computer. On paper he was doing his best to transcribe the original from the tortuous Gothic script. It was something he had done often enough in the past, but usually from more practised monastic hands. This was the script of a man writing under great duress.

The task was complicated by the fact that he had to assess repeatedly which language was being used. Some of the references, particularly to religion, were in the dog Latin that was the lingua franca among churchmen in the Middle Ages. But the rest was written in old English, almost the language of Chaucer but not quite, still more Anglo-Saxon than that, with here and there words and phrases that were lifted straight from Norman French.

It was not dissimilar to a historical literary jigsaw puzzle: satisfying in a scholastic way. But it was more than that. At least he hoped it could be. On the laptop he proposed to turn the words into modern English and to carry their meaning across time, so that someone reading it today would have an understanding of what it had been like.

If he could do it, it would not only be the basis for his thesis, it would be the basis for a book, one that might sell more than the standard academic treatises. A book to inspire people to think about history as something that they lived in rather than something that was past. For that you needed drama. And the story unfolding in front of him was filled with drama. Buried among the old records, ignored by generations of archivists who had simply not taken the trouble to decipher it, he had come across a rare chronicle of medieval life. The diary of a priest in a small Oxfordshire village.

Diary was the wrong word really. Although perhaps that was how it had begun, until the events overcame the author and it had become a last testament. The testament of Father Edward Gray, priest of the church of St Peter's, latterly known as St Peter's Alone, in the parish of Nether Ditchford, Oxfordshire. It had taken him a couple of attempts to locate the village. The gazetteer for the county had revealed no such village as Nether Ditchford. Under Ditchford, he drew another blank. Then, using a bit of oblique logic which he thought inspirational, he had tried Upper Ditchford, and there it was. A few miles to the southwest of Banbury, not far from Chipping Norton. He had got out the Ordnance Survey map from the large-scale Pathfinder range which gave the most detail.

Upper Ditchford was easy to locate. But the find that really excited him was the little box with a cross on it, indicating a church, down by the stream, halfway between the two villages. For all around it were the unfinished, shaded lines that did little more than suggest the traces of vanished streets, and the legend: 'Medieval village of Nether Ditchford (site of)'.

Since then he had discovered the church itself, all but abandoned in a field. Father Gray had not been chronicling day-to-day life in his village; he had been chronicling day-to-day death. Deaths of men, women and children. The death of an entire village.

*　　*　　*

Just as Daniel was surfacing from his morbid reverie, Rajiv Mahendra opened the door to the laboratory on the sixth floor of the JR2 and turned on the lights, blinking as the harsh fluorescence lit up the empty work stations and equipment. In daytime the laboratory was invariably busy, filled not only with chemists carrying out tests for the hospital but also with research students from the university. At four in the morning it resembled the deck of the *Mary Celeste*.

Come on, he told himself. You can do this. You know it has to be done. He swallowed hard. He had done it before, on his one and only trip to India, his father's country, the trip of a lifetime that had turned into a nightmare. He had expected to be shocked by the poverty, but found himself pleasantly surprised. Conditions were poor, often highly unsanitary, but there was something about everyday life in the villages of Uttar Pradesh that had more depth and honesty than his existence in the housing estates of Leicester. After a few weeks, to his own surprise, he felt almost at home.

That was until the sickness turned it into a living hell. At first he had been horrified, then sympathised with the local doctors. He had volunteered to help. Some of them tried to persuade him against it. Too risky, they had argued. It wasn't his place. Wasn't his country, he knew they were trying to say. But when he insisted, they did not try for long. Even good manners could yield to dire necessity. And the necessity had been dire indeed.

It was to them that his thoughts went back now, to those few brave medics working in that makeshift field hospital against overwhelming odds, against something he thought he had escaped from when he boarded the Indian Airlines flight at New Delhi two months later. Six weeks later than he should have done.

Now half a world away, back home in the unimaginably different surroundings of a modern British hospital, he felt somehow more frightened than he had then, as he searched the shelves of the store cupboard, then mixed together the fuchsin dye, methalene blue and ethyl alcohol that made the preparation known as Wayson's stain. Then he went back to the ward. That had been the easy bit.

On Rajiv's instructions, Annie Craig had applied surgical tape around the grey steel bedside cabinet in which the man's clothes were stored. If he was right, they would have to be destroyed. The figure on the bed was still feverish, his legs splayed as far apart as possible to prevent anything touching the swellings. Rajiv pulled back the loose sheet and swabbed the blue-black nodes, though the very touch seemed to cause the man pain.

'Nurse Craig, hold him down, please,' he said, forcing the end of a needle into one of the evil-looking lumps. The patient passed out. Rajiv pulled back the plunger and cursed. There was almost nothing coming out. He had feared as much. He would have to aspirate it.

'Annie.' The formalities were suddenly forgotten. 'Can you quickly fetch me a jar of saline solution?'

Two minutes later he was ready to try again. He had given the man a sedative to lessen the chances of his coming to. This time the needle went in more easily. Rajiv pushed and watched as the salt solution entered the pustule, then quickly pulled back. The syringe filled quickly with a noxious-looking broth of pale fluid laced with thick blood. Exactly what he wanted.

Back in the lab he transferred a few drops of the fluid to several slides and placed them on the shelf near the radiator to dry. After about ten minutes, during which he paced the lab, anxiously trying to work out how this could have happened and what he needed to do next, he applied the Wayson's-stain mixture to each, and put the first one under a microscope.

Rajiv was no chemist, but he did not need to be. It took barely twenty seconds for the different chemicals of the stain to react to the sample. And there through the lens was unmistakable proof of what he had been looking for. What he had dreaded finding. The little blue ovoids, darker at each end, stood out clearly from the pink background. The stain was infallible. It had been developed specifically for this purpose, to identify this one particular family of bacteria.

There could be no possible doubt about it: Charlie Atkins had somehow come into contact with *Yersinia pestis*, a bacillus best known to the world by the disease it caused: bubonic plague.

Chapter Four

Magdalen College, Oxford; Saturday
20 December, 8.00 a.m.

'Y OU'RE SERIOUS?'
Rajiv nodded, grim-faced. 'Deadly.'
'I want to see him,' Daniel Warren repeated.
'I'm sorry?'
'I'm sure you are. But really, I want to see him.'
'What I meant was that I do not understand what you are saying. Whom do you want to see?'
'Him. Your man. The plague victim, for God's sake.'
'For your God's sake indeed. Plague victim? What are you, some kind of ghoul?'
'It is the plague, isn't it? You said –'
'Yes, but –'
'No buts. Then I have to see him. Absolutely.'
Rajiv was looking at him as if he had volunteered for guard duty at Auschwitz.
Rajiv had battered on Daniel's door at 7.00 a.m., looking as drained as he had ever seen him. Which was saying something. The way the English treated their health-care folk was beyond comprehension.
Daniel had dragged himself to the door, bleary-eyed, and opened it to see an even blearier apparition confronting him. Rajiv was leaning against the doorpost with only a thin raincoat pulled on over the tweed jacket that he wore to work, the one that his friend endlessly ragged him about, saying it made him look

25

like a provincial GP. He had obviously not even been back to his own room yet. His collar and tie were undone and there was a haggard expression on his face.

'Hey, what is it? You look like you've seen a ghost. And shit –' looking at his watch – 'do you know what time it is?'

In response Rajiv had simply shaken his head, staggered past him and collapsed in the big leathercloth armchair, oblivious to the deficiency of its springs. Daniel was concerned. Normally Rajiv survived the gruelling hours he put in at the Radcliffe better than he would have thought possible.

'Are you all right? Can I get you anything? A cup of coffee? Tea, even? I have some.'

'A whisky, please. A large one.'

That was when Daniel knew for sure that something serious had upset him. He poured him a decent shot of Lagavulin, and over the next half-hour Rajiv gradually unwound as he told of the night's experience and the discovery, here in England of all places, of a disease he had thought confined to the Third World.

At first Daniel thought that Rajiv was looking for his opinion: you could say it was his subject, after all. It had taken some minutes before he realised that that aspect had never crossed Rajiv's mind. He had barged in out of the first law of friendship: he needed someone to talk to. The idea that his American friend Daniel might have any interest at all in a medical matter was something he had not only not considered, but found hard to cope with. Worse: he found it grotesque. Particularly when Daniel dropped his bombshell.

'What are you talking about? Why should you want to go and see a seriously ill man you don't even know?'

'I may not know him, but I know his suffering. What

the hell do you think I've been sitting up there reading about for months now?'

There was a look of puzzlement etched into the lines above Rajiv's big, brown, perplexed eyes. The details of other people's subjects – beyond their simple academic labels – had never occurred to him.

'Wait a minute. What are you talking about? You're a historian –'

'Yes. Of the Middle Ages. The plague, damn it, your plague, bubonic plague, a.k.a. the Black Death, the scourge of Europe! I've only spent the past two years delving into the murky details of medieval medicine trying to pull together a thesis on the crisis of fourteenth-century society in the face of disease. Now an example of that very disease is virtually under my nose and you wonder why it's twitching.'

'But it is not so rare. There are cases of bubonic plague in India every year. And in the Middle East. Even in some parts of the western United States.'

The comment seemed to stop Daniel in his tracks for a moment. 'I know, I know. Believe me, I know. But not in Berkeley, California, and not in Oxford, England, either. This is my opportunity to get a glimpse of what the disease was really like. I know it sounds macabre, but it isn't, honestly. It's what good history is all about. How can I have a feel for how people back in the fourteenth century reacted if I have no real idea how I might react myself?'

'This is like some sort of method acting?'

'No,' Daniel protested, though in a way that was precisely what it was. Writing about something after reading about it was one thing, but actually experiencing it – well, not exactly experiencing it, at least he hoped not, but witnessing it – could change the nature of a piece and put life into his historical thesis. And there was more than that. More than Rajiv needed to know. At least right now.

'You want to see him because you want to know how much he's suffering? I can tell you how much he's suffering: he is suffering very much. He could die.'

'Will he?' Daniel had assumed that as the man was already in a modern hospital and under treatment, he was not in serious danger. These were not, after all, the Middle Ages. Even in England.

'I don't think so. Not now that I have identified the disease. There are treatments. Drugs. Usually effective, if it's caught in time.'

'And it's not as contagious as its reputation. Right?'

'Not at this stage, no. The incubation period is anything up to ten days. We must assume he was infected abroad and has recently returned to this country. The chances of him carrying the parasites are remote – but not nonexistent. However, it is only the pneumonic phase of the disease that allows direct infection between humans. And that is very rare. Thankfully.'

'So there's no reason why I shouldn't get a look at him. I'm serious about this.'

'So it would appear, and I am seriously horrified. Anyway it's quite impossible. He will have to be isolated. I've already had him moved to a private ward.'

'Which, with your help, could make it all the easier.'

'You're not listening! The very idea is disgusting. I think you must be drunk. The answer – to a question I would like to pretend I have never heard – is no. N-O. Now we will please not speak of this again. But I would very much like another whisky.'

'Rajiv,' Daniel said as he reached for the Lagavulin bottle, poured another generous measure into his friend's glass and handed it to him, 'you owe me.'

The effect was astonishing. The medic's lips were

barely wet when he thumped the glass down on the floor beside him so violently that a few drops splashed over the rim on to the threadbare Persian carpet. Then he stood up and, breathing deeply, with an exaggerated show of calm, turned around and left the room, not even bothering to slam the door behind him.

Daniel picked up the glass, swirled the remaining whisky around the sides of it, then drained it.

Chapter Five

Millbank, London; Saturday 20 December, 8.30 a.m.

From his office windows high above the Thames, Neal Faversham looked out at the murky waters below, dark and oily and barely rippled by the drizzle that fell incessantly on the dirty city. How could anyone ever think London was attractive? An endless queue of cars snaked along the Embankment, red tail lights in one direction, white headlights in the other, useless even in daylight against the December gloom. Across the river a little pyramid of coloured bulbs made a brave but futile attempt at seasonal conviviality, suspended surreally in the opaque sky: a Christmas tree on top of a crane, somewhere in the darkest depths of Battersea.

The hiss of the ageing Kenco coffee machine announcing it had boiled dry the last of its water reserve disturbed his reverie. He poured himself a cup and turned back wearily to the pile of papers on his desk. Missing persons were not normally his thing. Local police sorted them into two categories. 'Category one' was provincial runaways who thought the bright lights of London would be better than stifling suburbia, and usually ended up sleeping in cardboard boxes under the bridges. 'Category two' was suspected murder victims. Occasionally the two categories overlapped. Neither was usually a matter for the likes of Neal Faversham, but this missing person was different.

For a start, he thought, looking at the photograph in the pool of light cast by his desk lamp, she was extraordinarily attractive. Moreover, she was known to be extremely well connected. Too well connected for her own good in the end. Of the end itself, he had little doubt. The girl who smiled up at him seductively from her passport photograph, eyes half closed as if she had been practising flirtatious poses in the Photo-Me booth, was stunningly beautiful. As well as self-confident. So very different from the shy, immature schoolgirl who had looked vacantly out of the photographs her mother had produced when he stood on her doorstep in the rain in the suburban wilderness of south London.

Or the girl she had described as they sat together over cups of weak tea on the velour sofa in her living room, behind the net curtains that hid away the woman's quiet grief from the quiet world she inhabited. The world that had been so wantonly abandoned by the skinny schoolgirl, good at gym and sums and languages but a terrible daydreamer, according to the form mistress who had never really liked her, never understood her. But then, who had? What was there to understand? What was there that had gone wrong? And what had her mother done to deserve it? To be left like that, without a word, without a goodbye. Just a postcard six months later, from somewhere in Germany. Not even written properly – and she who had been so neat in her schoolwork – just a scrawl. Look at it! And he looked at the scribbled line in green felt-tip: 'Dear Mum, just wanted to let you know I'm all right. Sorry.' No signature, as if she no longer wanted to acknowledge her own name. No return address. No telephone number. Nothing to identify its origin. Not even the photograph on the reverse – it was an old view of Piccadilly Circus. Just the German postage stamp and a watery postmark that he thought said Hamburg, though he could not be sure.

No, there was nothing more. Nothing he could tell her, he had said sadly as he put on his raincoat and took his leave. That at least had been the truth. Just routine. Missing-persons inquiry. No, there was no news. Of course, they would let her know if there was anything. Not that he could hold out much hope. Not really.

Not at all, if he had been honest. Though honesty was not an option. The girl who smiled up at him from beneath those provocative eyelashes was dead. Of that there could be no doubt at all. Even though there had not been enough left to bury.

Chapter Six

The newsroom of the Oxford Post; *Saturday 20 December, 11.00 a.m.*

'Hey, Theresa darling, give us a kiss!'
    'I'd rather kiss a frog.'

'There you are, Henry, told you she'd got continental tastes.'

'D'you think she's got frog's legs an' all?'

'Never lets us get a proper look, does she?'

With a sigh of long-suffering exasperation Theresa Moon put down the telephone receiver. There was, after all, only so much she could take of a disco version of 'God Rest Ye Merry, Gentlemen' playing between the prerecorded announcements that told her she was moving up the queue and an assistant would be with her shortly. Her attempt to book a holiday would have to wait.

'Don't you guys ever grow up?'

'Oh, come on, Theresa! If I stopped being Peter Pan, you'd have to stop being Tinkerbell.'

'If you think I'm the fairy in this office, then your powers of observation are even sloppier than I thought. And the name's Therry, as you very well know, with an "h" in the byline. OK?'

'Ooh, get her!' Henry Comfort did his Julian Clary impersonation, flopping a limp wrist in the air.

'For heaven's sake, Therry!' Jack Denton was playing the father figure now, putting an end to the boyish banter. 'You're a bear with a sore head today. What's up?'

'Boredom, Jack, boredom.' Theresa leaned both elbows heavily on the desk and closed her eyes. 'There's got to be something better to do than this.'

'Sorry, Therry.' The older man sighed heavily. There was just no getting things right where that girl was concerned.

'Well, I've always got one or two suggestions.' It was Henry again, in his worst nudge-nudge mode. But this time even Jack gave him a frown.

'Good job you're not in America, lad. They'd have you up for sexual harassment twice a day.'

'And three times on Saturdays,' the young woman opposite them finished archly. 'Seriously though, guys, I know you're only kidding.' Henry raised his eyebrows speculatively. 'But that's part of the problem. I'm just the token girlie in this office. You get to do the real stories. I get the wedding beat.'

'Come on, girl,' said Jack. 'This ain't the *Sunday Times*, you know. The best story I've had in weeks was that break-in at Brown's cake shop, and all they got away with was an empty cash till and a few stale buns.'

'Yes, I know, but at least it's real reporting. Take my schedule for this afternoon: St Peter's, Hook Norton, at 1.00 p.m., St Michael's, Cropredy, at 2.30 and St George's, Middleton Cheney, 4.00. The biggest scoop I'm likely to get is if one of the brides isn't wearing white. And even then, like as not, that old bastard'll stop me mentioning it.' She flicked a lock of thick blonde hair back from her forehead, casting angry eyes in the direction of the glass-walled office in the corner where John Harkness, the editor, could be seen absent-mindedly picking his nose.

'Yeuch,' said Henry, following her glance.

'I know what you mean,' said Jack, 'but the old boy's just old-fashioned. He probably thinks you enjoy weddings.'

It was Therry's turn to raise her eyebrows.

'That's the way it used to be, you know.'

'When, before the war?'

'Well, before the Falklands War anyway.'

'So what do I do about it?'

'Just wait. You'll get your chance.'

'Probably before I get mine, eh?' said Henry with a laugh.

'Oh, for fuck's sake!' And with that she was gone, striding away across the open-plan office in the direction of the coffee machine.

Henry looked in mock amazement at his older colleague. 'Did I say something?'

Jack Denton sighed. 'No, Henry old pal. Nothing at all.'

'Still.' Henry had swivelled round in his chair to watch Therry's retreating angry swagger in tight needle-cords. 'Nice arse, eh?'

It was just before noon when Theresa Moon looked at her watch and decided with a sorry-for-herself sigh that it was time to move, or she'd be late for the first blushing bride. The third wedding of the afternoon was the one that mattered, over at Middleton Cheney, the daughter of one of the big local publicans. *Le tout* Banbury would be there. She snorted. The idea amused her.

Theresa Moon was a second-generation Banburger, as she liked to say. Her parents had been part of the big migration from London, carried on in stages from the 1940s until the 1980s. In fact it was still going on, but now the market towns were overcrowded and their inhabitants in their turn were migrating to the surrounding villages. It seemed that the process would never end until the whole south of England was one endless suburb.

Journalism, Therry had told herself, would be her way back to the big-city heritage her parents had robbed her of. But so far all journalism had done was rub her nose into the suffocating detail of provincial life. Weddings were worst of all, watching one Samantha and Jonathan or Claire and Simon after another tie the knot. Next they would put down a deposit on a starter home, first step on the way to the three-bedroom detached houses that each year covered another field. Banbury had long since expanded to swallow Bodicote, Bloxham was next and Adderbury well on the way. And no one did anything about it.

Sure, there were the odd Swampy-style ecological activists in torn sweaters with straw in their hair prepared to dig tunnels under the building sites, to live in hedgerows or trees to protect what was left of the unmanicured countryside. But they were mostly batty professors or unemployable anarchists. Faced with the rape of their countryside, most people just lay back in their upholstered armchairs and thought of an England that increasingly belonged only to the imagination. The English countryside was doomed. Suburbia was winning. And Therry Moon wanted out of it.

She had thought the move to Oxford would be the first step. A move up the ladder, with the chance of doing something that would get noticed. It had turned out to be a sidestep on to a slippery slope. She had been pigeonholed as the 'North Oxfordshire girl' to do the milk round of the provincial weddings and village notices. It was driving her mad. What she needed was a story she could get her teeth into, a proper feature, an investigation even, something that would grab the attention of the nationals and get her out of there. To London.

'Theresa?' The sound of her own name jolted her out of her reverie. Coming towards her, in a rare excursion from his fishbowl, was old John Harkness himself. A former Fleet Street star – a legend in his own lunchtime, except that it had been a liquid lunch back in the days when a pint cost less than a pound – Harkness had taken the editorship of the *Oxford Post* when he was already in his fifties. After a couple of months of initial enthusiasm he had retreated to the fishbowl and let the paper run itself in the same way it had under his predecessor: into the ground.

'Mr Harkness?'

'Hmm? Oh, yes, you should call me John. Everybody does.' Nobody did. 'Are you busy?' As if he didn't know. Maybe he didn't. 'I was thinking.'

'I was just leaving . . . uh, I'm supposed to be at Hook Norton for 1.00 p.m. The Moorhouse wedding.'

'Yes, yes, the weddings. Mm, I was wondering if you'd like to do something else for a change.'

'Sir? I mean . . . uh, what?'

'A feature. Something with a bit of digging involved.' Therry could hardly believe her ears. 'The NHS, for example.'

A slight disappointment welled, but she quickly suppressed it. Whatever had come into the old man's head, she was not about to sniff at it.

'What sort of thing were you thinking of?' She already had visions of ringing around hospitals to ask how many staff they would have on duty over the holidays, noting the usual gripes and ending up turning out a piece on 'how wonderful our nurses are'. It might be true, but it wasn't news.

For once old 'honest John' did not seem as dim as his reputation.

'Oh, don't look at me like that! I know what you're thinking: a standard pre-Christmas piece about the poor souls who have to work while we're all stuffing our faces with turkey. Well, you're not wrong, of course. But I was thinking of a more *dramatic* variant on the theme,' he said, trying to sound dramatic. 'Descend unannounced. Like the archangel!' He beamed idiotically. 'On the Radcliffe, I mean. The new one. Not that it's that new nowadays, I suppose, but you know what I mean. Anyhow, see how they cope on a Saturday night before Christmas. Bound to be busy, you see. Just drift around, talk to people, patients and doctors, give us the feel, you know, of a big hospital coping with crisis, or indeed not, as the case may be. Don't be afraid to tell it how it is. If they're in the shit, let's say so. Lots of atmosphere. Good writing. Anyway. Might make something. Might not, of course. But see how you go. Your sort of thing? Is it? Maybe not.'

'What? I mean, yes, sir. John, that is. Please. Thank you. It sounds really interesting. I'll give it the best shot I can.'

'Hmm, really?' He was smiling at her as if her response had genuinely surprised him.

'But . . .'

'Yes?'

'What about the weddings? Middleton in particular, the Bancrofts?'

'Ah, yes, the Bancrofts. Our little local celebrities. Well, I shouldn't worry. One of your male colleagues was quite keen to do that, said you probably wouldn't mind.'

Therry's eyes glistened. Jack, the old saint! She owed

him one for this, a pint of the best in the King's Arms. Half a dozen pints of the best if he wanted.

'Well, you'd best be off then.' Harkness was wandering away already. 'Funny, hadn't really thought of young Henry as the type to do weddings.'

Chapter Seven

East Oxford; Saturday 20 December 4.00 p.m.

D ANIEL KNEW the route Rajiv normally took to the JR2 and followed it. He wheeled his bike out of college through the porter's lodge and, wrapped up warm in his duffel coat with a black-and-white college scarf tied tight around his neck, cycled east over Magdalen Bridge, past the Angel and Greyhound Meadow and down St Clements.

This was where Cotswold stone gave way to red brick and the city turned slightly seedy or at best suburban: here the streetlights were not powered by gas as they were in Merton Street, for example, where the colleges sponsored a cultivated quaintness, but by harsh sodium, now in the gathering gloom casting a sickly glow on the Oxford the tourists never saw. Left along the flat stretch of Marston Road lined with the houses he had come to recognise as 'thirties semis', the architectural expression of the last gasp of the British Empire, then right by the little line of shops where the heavy traffic came in from the ring road, and pushing hard he pedalled up the long, steep slope of Headley Hill to the mini-roundabout that marked the entrance to the hospital.

Unlike the charming but cramped old Radcliffe Infirmary, the JR2 looked like a training school for morticians or the headquarters of some Stalinist secret police. Cold and unwelcoming, the massive building squatted on the upper slope of the hill. Panting with a shortness of breath that made him think it was time to start visiting the gym, Daniel leaned on the pedals to manage the last few yards uphill to Car Park Number One, shared between the main hospital and the maternity block. He chained the bike to a railing. Why, here in a city full of bicycles, were there no proper racks? Perhaps it was assumed that students didn't get sick. A gust of wind caught his scarf with a flurry of light snow. As he walked towards the main entrance he checked his watch: 16.25. He had agreed to meet Rajiv half an hour after the medic had begun his evening shift. It was always possible, Rajiv had told him, that he would be put on another case. And for a minute Daniel had worried that he might try that as an excuse for not going ahead with their plan. But Rajiv was a man of his word. At exactly 16.30 he appeared from the direction of the lifts and nodded to Daniel, who followed him into a staff room off the main corridor. It was empty, as Rajiv had been fairly confident it would be at that time.

'Well?'

'Well, what? Here, put this on.' He handed Daniel a hospital tunic in a blue-green colour that could be described as either 'duck-egg' or 'disinfectant', depending on your frame of mind. 'No, not like that, you idiot! You must strip off your top first.'

'Really? Can't I just put on a white coat, like you? I thought hanging a stethoscope around my neck would be enough.'

'You would be recognised as not belonging to the team on the seventh floor. In this you will look like a junior doctor from one of the medical wards. Unusual to be up there, but not suspicious. Basically nobody will pay any attention to you. Believe me, I know. Now come on. Hurry up! I want you out of here again in half an hour.'

'OK, OK.' Daniel threw off his jumper and shirt, dropped his trousers and pulled on the loose-fitting cotton hospital gear. It felt strangely insubstantial, like someone else's pyjamas. As if he were checking into the hospital as a patient.

'What shall I do with this?' He indicated his bundle of 'civilian' clothes.

'Put them in here. It's my locker. At least the one I usually use. None of them have keys any more. Now, come on. Follow me and keep your eyes down. Avoid looking at anyone, especially the nurses.'

Daniel felt hugely self-conscious as they walked down the corridor past the florist's and newsagent's shops towards the lifts. It was as if he were in drag, or wearing a grass skirt: he felt strangely exposed. Perhaps it was the thinness of the cotton tunic and trousers. Yet, as Rajiv had predicted, no one paid him the slightest attention. Rather than sticking out like the proverbial sore thumb, he had donned camouflage and faded into the background. Where better to hide a sore thumb than a hospital?

Two more youngish men dressed in identical blue-green fatigues passed in the opposite direction. One of them nodded to Rajiv, and Daniel thought for a moment that he looked at him strangely. But the moment passed. And then they were at the lifts. In the lift, Daniel at the back, Rajiv in front. Going up. Floors two, three, four. Menswear, lingerie, Santa's Grotto, Black Death. Floor seven. They got out and Rajiv pushed the double doors that led from the central area down a long corridor with single red-painted doors on either side. Private wards, for the growing numbers of those on employers' private medicine plans: those who preferred to pay a little extra for privacy. As if anyone had privacy in a hospital, with their whole body open to invasion. Daniel was not good in hospitals. He had respect for the medical profession, but he still regarded hospitals as where, in the end, people came to die.

Rajiv was opening the second door on the left. 'Shh! You will not say a word.'

Daniel nodded assent.

He had never been in a British hospital before so he had no idea whether this was a typical private ward. It was clean but that was about all you could say for it. Not even a television set, just a couple of chairs on the far side of the bed next to the window. The man in the bed was asleep, breathing laboriously, rasping with each shallow intake of air.

Daniel glanced at Rajiv, who shook his head. Not good. Clearly Mr Atkins – he read the name scrawled in blue marker on the whiteboard above the patient's head – was not doing as well as had been hoped.

'Where are the . . . you know . . . ?'

Rajiv sighed and narrowed his eyes in a look of disgust at what Daniel knew he considered his ghoulish voyeurism. But this was what he had come for. What, he asked himself, would a fourteenth-century apothecary be doing now, faced with a man in this condition? Probably using leeches to suck his blood, to 'cleanse' his body of impurities, in fact drastically weakening him further. What modern medical practices, he had often wondered, would seem equally insane a couple of centuries hence?

Looking behind himself as if to be sure he was not being watched in this gross act of infamy, Rajiv pulled down the sheet.

'It's all right now, Mr Atkins, we're just going to take a look at you,' he said, the literal truth but also a lie. Mr Atkins was not listening as Rajiv lifted the hem of his hospital gown, feeling as if he were preparing to molest a child.

Daniel could not contain a gasp. The swellings around the man's groin were horrible, obscene, like something out of *Alien*: evil, purplish black eggs growing inside the body of a suffering host. No wonder they had thought it the work of the devil himself. Even in a world used to casual cruelty and untimely death, this must have seemed like proof positive of demonic possession.

'It has got worse.'

Rajiv was lifting the man's right arm gently, looking at two similar purple pustules welling up in his armpit.

'Do they hurt?' Daniel hoped his friend heard the genuine concern in his voice. This was no longer part of the exercise. He felt deeply sorry for the man on the bed.

'Oh, yes. I believe they hurt like hell, if that satisfies you. Seen enough?'

Daniel lowered his eyes. 'Yes. I'm sorry. But thanks. Is there anything I can . . . ? I mean . . .' He realised the futility of the question.

Rajiv lowered the man's nightshirt and pulled the sheet up again. He noticed beads of sweat on the patient's brow, as if he were almost feverish, and made a mental note to tell the nurse to check his temperature hourly. Any sudden change at this stage could be most dangerous. He had better mention it to Dr Redwhistle too. The consultant would be round about 6.00 p.m., by when the ghoul would be long gone.

'I think the best thing you –'

But before he could tell Daniel that he wanted him to leave, the man on the bed began panting loudly and moving his arms as if trying to sit up, though his eyes were still half closed.

Daniel made to go round the other side of the bed and help him. But the sick man's breath was coming faster now, with a horrid croaking sound from the back of his throat. And then suddenly he sneezed. It was a sneeze like nothing Daniel had seen before, a violent splutter, followed by a sharp hacking, retching cough. He looked away in disgust as the top sheet was spattered with discoloured mucus, here and there flecked bright red with blood.

'Get out! Now!' Rajiv almost shouted the words at him.

'But what . . . ? Should I . . . ?'

'Just go, for Christ's sake,' he hissed. 'Now!'

Daniel did as he was told. He had never thought to see such venom in his friend's face.

Chapter Eight

The John Radcliffe Hospital, Oxford; Saturday 20 December, 5.00 p.m.

D ANIEL WAS sweating. A thin, cold film of moisture coated his skin beneath the loose-fitting hospital tunic. His heart was racing. Adrenaline, he told himself. Not fear.

Now he had seen the horror for himself. That was what it had been like all those centuries ago. The grotesque swellings, the morbid black discoloration. The sense of death looking over your shoulder. Even today, bubonic plague could be a killer. The man Atkins would be all right, he assumed. The speed with which Rajiv had propelled him from the room must have been a panic reaction. Couldn't blame him really, not when the bloke had started spluttering like that. He was probably going to have to call nurses, and it wouldn't do to have an unexplained stranger present. Wouldn't do at all. He owed the boy one. A stiff drink down the King's Arms. Christ, he could do with one himself. Now.

'Watch it, mate!' Two orderlies with a patient on a trolley glared at Daniel. He had nearly collided with them. Wasn't thinking. Which way? Left at the end. There were half a dozen people standing around the lift lobby, mostly visitors. Was it visiting time? He didn't know. Did it matter? Probably not. A pretty young nurse looked across at him and smiled. Flirtatiously? Or inquisitively? Was he looking as nervous as he felt? He smiled back. She looked away. Too much. Don't overdo it, Daniel. She'll think you're trying to pick her up.

The lift arrived. A tall, stout woman with a clipboard got out and stared at Daniel as if she'd seen a ghost, but she walked straight past him. A young nurse was moving towards the lift. The big woman barked a question at her. The nurse began explaining something, looking frustratedly at the lift as Daniel and three of the visitors got in. Daniel shot her a sympathetic glance as the doors closed. The lift walls were shiny, white and scratched, like the service elevator in an old hotel. A sign read: 'Please respect patients' privacy. This is not the place for the discussion of patients.' Daniel imagined spotty clinical students comparing tumours to cricket balls and grapefruits while the nearest and dearest of those dying in the cancer wards bit their lips in silent grief.

Floor six; five; four. The doors opened and a sour-faced woman trailing a fractious toddler got in. Pediatrics, Daniel noted automatically. He moved back to make way for them. Three; two. Two tall men in white coats, talking noisily about handicaps. At somewhere called Oat Hill – a sanatorium, he assumed. And then the penny dropped: a golf course. Consultants, clearly. Daniel tried to think himself into anonymity. A junior houseman. Nobody they should know or notice. His shirt felt clammy inside. He wondered if the sweat showed. Or smelled.

Floor one. Exit level. All at once, the artificial intimacy of the lift was replaced by the hubbub of the concourse. Like a provincial airport. Which way now to the staff changing room? It wasn't supposed to be like this. He hadn't been paying attention. Rajiv was supposed to be here too, providing cover. Not like this: not knowing where to go. There, surely, down there on the right, past the bookstall.

'Excuse me.'

What? Who? No. Not now!

'Excuse me, just one moment, please.'

In the first moment of lucidity the man in the hospital bed had had for two days, he realised where he was. And suddenly he knew what was happening to him. He was dying. Then the gurgling began again, deep in his throat, like a dark well being stirred and sinking, sinking into his lungs before erupting in fire that surged up his throat, blinding him with pain, choking him. He hacked and was dimly aware of moisture running down his chin. Then he fell back, drained and dripping dank sweat, shivering. As he did, he felt, not for the first time, the discomfort in his groin, the dark, putrid eggs swelling beneath his skin in the tenderest part of his body. And then, blessedly, he lost consciousness again.

Rajiv Mahendra watched him with mute horror. Despite Daniel's supposition, he had not summoned a nurse. Not yet. There was no point in increasing the risk. He checked the mask on his face, then gingerly, with a swab, he mopped the bloody trickle of mucus from the man's stubbled chin, put the swab into a beaker and sealed it. He lifted the intercom telephone on the wall and pressed the button that connected him to the ward sister.

'Stacy, it's Dr Mahendra here, in private ward C. I want you to put a sign on the end of the corridor declaring the ward off limits.' A pause while he listened to the beginning of a flood of questions. 'Not now, sister. Just please do as I say. And summon Dr Redwhistle. Yes. Now. Yes. Completely. Containment level two.'

The moment Daniel stepped out of the lift, Therry Moon had spotted him. Exactly what she needed: young, good-looking in a gawky sort of way, and obviously overworked. Exactly the type to spill the beans on a health-care system in crisis. She could already imagine the classic litany of gripes he would offer in exchange for a sympathetic ear and, if he played his cards right, the chance to take her out to the pub afterwards. If he was worth listening to.

The idea that he might not listen to her had not even entered her imagination. Therry was used to young men paying attention to her. Yet this nervous-looking young medic not only ignored her but affected not even to hear her. Annoyed, she found herself breaking into a slight trot to keep up with him.

'Excuse me, I said.'

The young man, shoulders bent over in his pale-blue hospital fatigues, took no notice, even increased his stride. Therry hoisted her slipping shoulder-bag strap, reached out and grabbed him by the arm. Brusquely he shook her off. Just who did this guy think he was?

'Now just hold on a minute, doctor,' she said angrily, stressing each syllable. One or two people turned their heads, but the focus of her attention ignored her. Male arrogance really took the cake! She ran after him, over-took him outside the flower stall and stood, hands on hips, blocking his path, doing her very best Lois Lane impersonation: the big-time girl reporter in a tantrum.

Daniel looked down in shock at the vision in front of him: a young woman with a tumbling mass of unkempt straw-blonde hair in a flying jacket with a tear in it, standing defiantly, hands on hips, looking as if she was about to rip his throat out. He hoped he was doing his best to conceal his true emotion, which was something akin to panic.

'Yes?' he said as abruptly as possible, trying not to sound American. 'What do you want?'

'What do you mean, what do I want? Is that any way to address a member of the public in a hospital? This is still supposed to be a national health service, *if* I'm not mistaken?'

Daniel's throat produced a noise that could only be described as a grunt. It was an unsatisfactory response, he knew, but right at that moment, words failed him. Who was this girl? What did she want? At least she was clearly not a hospital official. Maybe all he had to do was brazen it out.

'I'm from the press,' she said, suddenly breaking into a sunny smile practised time and again in front of the bathroom mirror. She watched him whiten. 'The *Oxford Post*. I was wondering if I could talk to you. Get an idea of a typical Saturday night. You look like you could use a break. If it's convenient?'

But even as she was speaking, she realised that the subject of her best media approach was not even listening to her. His eyes kept darting past her as if he were looking for someone else. Or thought someone else was looking for him.

'Hello, anyone in? Are you OK, Dr . . . mmm?'

Daniel could see her looking at his chest, wondering where his laminated photographic hospital ID was.

'I'm sorry, miss, I have nothing to say.' Daniel had spotted the door to the men's staff changing room just beyond the little flower shop. In there, in Rajiv's unlocked locker, hung his duffel coat and his grey Levi Dockers. In order to discard the uniform of the spy and reacquire civilian status, all he had to do was get rid of this woman. He tried to push past her.

Theresa Moon was having none of it. Whether or not this weirdo wanted to spill the beans on the NHS, she was damned if he was going to push her around. Besides, there was something strange here. That accent.

An American in Oxford? Sure. Loads of them. All over the place. But not working as junior doctors in NHS hospitals.

'You're American?'

'Yes.' Shit. Play on it. 'It's not a crime, is it? Now if *you'll* excuse *me*, I really have to –'

'Where's your hospital ID?'

The guy's eyes were boring through her. Big eyes. Green. Sexy even, behind those little wire-rimmed spectacles. But mad. That's it, she realised. This is a nutcase! Monday's banner headline flashed before her: 'PSYCHO! Hospital prowler seized. Our reporter spots sicko.' Even the nationals would take notice. Maybe. But now the man was physically pushing her aside, his eyes fixed on some space beyond her.

She pulled back two feet and shouted at him: 'Stop! Right there!'

Daniel almost fainted. Several people stopped to stare. Any minute now she would scream or something and a dozen burly orderlies would arrive and cart him off. Call the police. He could just see it. Spending the night in a cell. Rajiv would be thrown off his course, out of the university even. So would he, come to think of it. Great! Old man McClure back in Berkeley would really love that. He had to get a grip on this.

'Who are you? What are you doing here?' The girl had lowered her voice. She was standing there blocking his way, her eyes as hooded as a cartoon rattlesnake's.

'Look,' he said, doing his best to collect himself, 'I can explain. Can we go somewhere to talk?'

Therry Moon looked across her plastic cup of National Health Service cappuccino at the young man in front of her, evaluating him. No, probably not dangerous.

When she spoke it was not a question.

'You're not a doctor.'

Daniel realised there was no point in pretending.

'No.'

'Not even a medical student.'

'No.'

She reached across the table and pulled away the surgical mask from his face.

'I'm not having you hide behind this.' She crumpled the mask and shoved it in a pocket of the flying jacket.

'But you are a student, at the university?'

'Yes. Postgraduate.'

She shrugged, not interested in his academic progress.

'What's your subject?'

'History.'

'History?' Her voice was incredulous. 'I know the NHS is a bit behind the times, but surely . . . Come on, what the hell are you doing wandering around the Radcliffe dressed as if you're about to go into an operating theatre?'

'You wouldn't understand.'

'No. I dare say. Nor will the readers. Look, sunshine, I want fifteen good reasons why I shouldn't shop you.'

Of all the people in all the world, I had to get nabbed by a bloody journo, Daniel thought. 'I came to see a friend.'

'What? To operate on him? What is this, method visiting? Dressing up in doctor's kit just to make him feel at home? Come on, you'll have to do better than that.'

Daniel looked at her. She was pretty, underneath that unkempt hairdo and the battered leather jacket. Should he tell her? If he didn't say something, she was going to put him on the spot. And that meant Rajiv too. Perhaps he could make a deal with her. And then the words were out before he had thought the idea through.

'What do you know about the Black Death?'

Therry Moon almost choked on her cappuccino.

It took half an hour of patient explanation on Daniel's part, of disbelief, then growing fascination on the part of his listener. The hardest part had not been persuading her that his story was true, but that she shouldn't jump up straight away and start quizzing the hospital staff about the patient upstairs with the notifiable tropical disease.

Both Rajiv and he would be in trouble, almost certainly sent down from their college, he stressed, if his little escapade became public knowledge. Surely it could wait, couldn't it, at least until the next day? She could ring up the hospital without directly implicating them. They would be bound to admit it, after all. It was hardly the sort of thing that could be kept secret. Tropical diseases did not turn up in Oxfordshire on a daily basis. Let alone the Black Death.

'It's not the Black Death,' Daniel found himself insisting. 'Not exactly.'

'But it's the same sort of thing?'

'Yes, well, sort of.' What else could he say? That was, after all, why he had blackmailed his friend into letting him come to the hospital. That was the argument that had got him into this position in the first place.

'You say this guy's a building worker?'

'Yeh.'

'So maybe they dug it up!'

'Dug what up?'

'The Black Death, of course!'

Daniel sighed. 'I don't think so.'

'I'm only joking. Maybe. But anyway, how do you know?'

'It doesn't work like that.' He was certain it didn't. Well, fairly certain.

'Hmph!' Therry sniffed sceptically. 'Still. You never know, though. Could be a good story.'

'You said –'

'I said I'd ring in the morning. Anyway, it's nothing for you to worry about. Draw attention away from "Mad Yankee psycho killer stalks JR", eh? Hey! Sounds like that old soap opera. *Dallas*, wasn't it?'

Daniel smiled. What had he let himself in for?

'Who was he working for, then?'

'What? JR? Oh, I see, the man.'

'Yes. The man. The patient. You said he was a builder so he probably works for a building company. Yes?'

'Yes. I suppose. It hadn't occurred to me.' The patient's occupation had hardly seemed relevant. But Rajiv had mentioned something. 'A firm of builders. Wigshill or Mill possibly? Something like that. Maybe?'

'Pig-Swill.' She spat the words out with an unexpected vehemence.

'I beg your pardon?'

But the expression on the face of the young woman opposite him had given way from disgust to irrepressible devilment. 'Pig-Swill – Riggs-Mill, that's who it is, I bet, and that's their nickname. Big developers. Stick bloody executive homes all over the countryside if you gave 'em half a chance. So it'll be Nether Ditchford then?'

'*What* did you say?'

She looked at him as if he had a hearing defect.

'Nether Ditchford. It's only the biggest new housing development in north Oxfordshire. None of it wanted. None of it necessary. All of it highly profitable. If you ask me it's . . .' But something stopped her. The look on her interlocutor's face. The relief that had become apparent since they had agreed she would not reveal his little excursion in medical attire had suddenly vanished, to be replaced by a confused frown.

'What did you say?'

'Nether Ditchford. Why?'

'But there's no such place. Not anymore.'

'There is now. It's some old name they've revived for the new development. What of it?'

'Nothing. No. Nothing. It's just . . . It's just that I've been reading about it. A long time ago.'

Yesterday.

Chapter Nine

Beaconsfield, Berkshire; Saturday 20 December, 6.00 p.m.

T HE THING about the sort of house Geoffrey Martindale lived in was that the drive really was something
you drove up rather than just parked the car on, Neal
Faversham thought to himself, as he turned the 'firm's'
deliberately nondescript Ford Mondeo off the road into
a gateway marked by two posts surmounted by stone
lions. There was something reassuring about the noise
the tyres made as they crunched over the gravel. It was,
to an English ear accustomed to the cadences of the
late John Betjeman, almost an audible signal of material
success.

The house itself was a visible symbol of that success. Self-confidently arrogant in its bright-red brick,
Denholm House was of no great antiquity, Edwardian
possibly, maybe even later. What mattered was that
it was a pile. A great big pile that said one thing
loudly and clearly about its owner: it shouted money.
Masses of it.

Faversham parked the Mondeo almost self-consciously
neatly, parallel to the front wall of the house, in awkward comparison with the more expensive motors left
littered like discarded sweet wrappers on the gravel
forecourt. He let his eyes run over them, less out of
envy than out of a professional interest in what they
said about Denholm House's inhabitants. The BMW

Z3 was just possibly the expensive plaything of an older man, but more probably the gift of an indulgent father to a girl-about-town daughter. The Land Rover Freelander, useful for shooting, was probably, given the gleam of its polish, primarily used for the weekly shopping run. The Jaguar XJ6 was a standard status symbol for a man who hobnobbed with cabinet ministers, even if they were from the previous government. This one showed a touch of taste: it was an old model, a series III, in mint condition, obviously lovingly and expensively maintained. There was also, incongruously, a Ford Scorpio, a less than new Volvo estate and – parked as neatly as his own, as far as possible from the front of the house – an ageing Nissan Bluebird. Guaranteed to be the gardener's. The other two, he surmised, as he locked the door and walked up the front steps, were either neglected runabouts or, more probably, evidence of other visitors.

He rang the bell. The door was opened, to his surprise, by Martindale himself. What had he expected? A butler?

'Mr Faversham,' Geoffrey Martindale said, and added, without looking at his watch, 'how very punctual! Do please come in.'

Faversham followed him down a hallway of thick Chinese carpets and tall, heavy-framed wall mirrors that ended in a great carved wooden staircase, complete with burnished brass stair rods to hold the carpet in place.

'I'm afraid you must excuse us. The place is in a bit of a state. My daughter has had some friends round. You know what these young women are like.'

The 'place', to Faversham's eyes, was perfect. No, he thought, I don't know what these young women are like. What I want to know is: do you?

Martindale showed him into a room which, judging by

the more subdued, masculine tones of the Persian carpet and the desk at one end next to a window, Faversham would have taken to be his study, except for its size: bigger than most grand dining rooms he had seen. And there was a long mahogany sideboard lined with spirit decanters. Perhaps this was where Martindale held meetings, business meetings, meetings with his political friends. There was certainly no shortage of alternative rooms in Denholm House. Or perhaps he was just drawn to the view: the desk faced a window that looked out over the back of the house. The formal gardens, those tended by the man with the Nissan, were at the front. Here the land fell away gently, revealing a vista of rolling countryside rising slightly towards the Chiltern hills. A pointed church spire, rising next to a copse of trees in the distance, was the only human intrusion in the landscape.

'Nice view,' Faversham said.

'Yes, isn't it? I'm rather like the man in the Remington razor advert, you know. I liked it so much I bought it.'

Faversham shot him an inquisitive glance.

'Not all of it, of course. But the few fields beyond our garden. About a hundred and twenty acres in all, actually. Reaching just beyond Windham – the little village over there, you can just see the church. Thought I might farm it at one stage. Go green, you know. But then I thought, why bother? Get enough back from the dimwits in Brussels in set-aside as it is.' And he flashed a smile that was obviously meant to be winning.

'Not tempted to build on it yourself, then? Must be worth a bit as housing land, that lot.'

'Come, come, Mr Faversham. Now you're teasing me. Some things are beyond money, you know. Even to me. But you haven't come out here just to admire the view. You were very mysterious on the phone.'

'Was I, sir? Sorry. Didn't mean to be. But I thought it was something we'd both prefer to talk about in person, if you know what I mean.'

'Unfortunately, for the moment, you have that advantage on me.'

'It's about a young woman, sir.'

'Indeed? Not one of my daughter's friends?'

'I rather think not. Does the name Amanda Workington mean anything to you?'

Faversham was watching the man's face carefully for any sign of recognition. Or any attempt to conceal recognition. Though in fact he expected neither.

'Sorry.' It was said with a quizzical flicker of the eyebrows. More as if Martindale was surprised not to know the name. Which was exactly what Faversham had been expecting.

'No, I dare say it doesn't ring any bells. Probably wouldn't with most people who knew her. Since she left Croydon, at any rate.'

Martindale smiled and deepened his show of perplexity, as if he was having to make an effort to recollect where Croydon was.

'How about Miranda von Taxenbach?'

Now the quizzical look remained, but it looked to Faversham to have acquired a fixity, as if the man facing him were trying to decide what to do with his face next.

'I think the minister knew her too.'

'Hmm? Oh, I mean, yes. Of course. Charming young woman. Came across her only a couple of times. German, I believe, or possibly Austrian. How does she relate to this . . . what was it . . . ? Worthington woman?'

'Intimately. They were the same person.'

For the first time in the interview, Martindale seemed genuinely surprised. Far too surprised.

'She called herself Miranda von Taxenbach because she thought it sounded smarter. Worked better with the snob set. Not including yourself, of course, Mr Martindale, but you know how it is with some people and a title.'

A thin smile. Yes, of course. Some people.

'You knew her quite well, though, didn't you? Didn't just come across her a couple of times, really, did you, sir? After all, she spent the weekend here on – let me see.' Faversham brought out a little ring-bound notebook and made a show of consulting it. 'At least half a dozen times. The minister was present on all but one of those occasions.'

Martindale had drawn himself up to his full height. He's wondering how much to admit, Faversham reckoned.

'I'd forgotten you people keep a tab on things. Quite right too, of course. Security aspect and all that. Yes, Miranda was here on several occasions. With other of my acquaintances. I am a busy man during the week, and at the weekends I do quite a bit of entertaining. Much of that too, I'm afraid, work-related. Contacts and so forth, you know.'

'Yes, sir.'

'But I'm sorry, Mr . . . ?'

Faversham was silent.

'Mr . . . ah? You haven't yet explained what this is all about.'

'All in good time, sir. But could you be just a little bit clearer about your relationship with the young lady?'

'What exactly do you mean?'

'Did you ever sleep with her?'

Martindale's face froze, but only for a split second. Then a smile stole across it.

'Curiously enough, no. But then Miranda didn't leave

much time for sleeping. She was rather more active than that.'

It was meant conspiratorially, man-to-man stuff. But Neal Faversham did not smile back.

Chapter Ten

The King's Arms, Oxford; Saturday
20 December 7.30 p.m.

T HE KING'S Arms at the corner of Parks Road and
Holywell Street in Oxford, conveniently located
for both Wadham and Hertford colleges as well as
the Bodleian Library, is an archetypal student pub. Its
floors are bare boards, its walls covered with pinned-up
notices for performances of Webster's *Duchess of Malfi*
or Stoppard's *Rosencrantz and Guildenstern are Dead*,
the stock-in-trade of undergraduate dramatic societies. It
serves real ale and chilled lager and wodges of shepherd's
pie or anglicised lasagne with pasta that curls at the edges
from having been kept warm too long.

In summer its customers spill out on the street. In
winter they stay warm behind the double doors, standing
in groups in the middle of the floor or leaning against the
walls. Seating space is kept to a minimum, in the interests
of maximising turnover. 'They may think on their arses,
but they can drink on their feet,' was the maxim of one
of the KA's former proprietors.

The exception is the Back Bar, which needs capital
letters because it is, or at least aspires to be, an Oxford
institution. The Back Bar is slightly run-down, by design,
has more seats and is invariably smoky. It is favoured
by those customers who prefer to be sheltered from
the bustle of the contemporary student world, those
who fancy perhaps that it was here that C. S. Lewis

dreamed up Narnia and J. R. R. Tolkien wove his tales of Middle Earth (though in fact the public house those two gentlemen favoured was the Eagle and Child, more colloquially known as the Bird and Bastard, some half a mile away in St Giles's Street).

It was in the Back Bar that, some two hours after Therry Moon had forced her way into Daniel's life, he found himself seated beside her over a pint of Young's Special bitter and a half of Foster's lager. The tables were occupied by a mix of donnish types with beards and pipes, earnest young men talking seriously and two pretty young women with astonishingly white skin and facial anatomical piercings that made them look like refugees from a Borg collective. The donnish types obviously longed to mix metal with the Borg. The Borg, by contrast, looked as though they wouldn't assimilate them if they were the last sentient beings in the known universe. In a cluster around the bar, getting in the way of waitresses, a gaggle of male students in corduroys and pullovers were acting out scenes from Monty Python sketches first performed before they were born. Tucked away at a table in the corner, the tall, angular young American and the girl in the tatty flying jacket might have been part of the wallpaper.

Ever since Daniel arrived in Oxford he had barely exchanged more than superficial pleasantries with the opposite sex. Somehow, it seemed, the English did things differently. The direct approach was frowned upon, but his alternative tactic – a conspicuous absence of effort – had so far produced only a conspicuous absence of results. So, even though he knew that he shouldn't be talking to this young woman, that the worst thing that could have happened to him at the hospital was being accosted by her, he had looked her up and down and couldn't help himself.

'I'm sorry, but I don't even know your name,' he said now.

She looked sideways at him as if the possibility had never entered her mind. 'Therry Moon, she said. That's Therry with an "h".'

'Really? Short for Theresa maybe? A beautiful name. Very spiritual.'

'Yeah. Maybe. But I'm no Albanian nun, so I don't use it. Let's stick to Therry, if you don't mind. The "h" is good in the byline; makes people remember it.'

Daniel nodded, embarrassed. Why did he always say the wrong thing?

'So tell me,' she said, flashing the sunshine smile again, 'all about the Black Death.'

Daniel smiled despite himself. At parties when people asked him what he was studying, they would always give him a wide berth – especially the girls – after he told them.

'It's, er . . . hard to know where to begin.'

'Well, how did you get into this in the first place?'

'Into what? History?'

'I mean the Black Death and all that. It's a bit gruesome, isn't it?'

'It all goes back to my mother, really,' he said with an audible sigh, like someone reluctantly obliged to retrieve a memory deliberately left to gather dust in a mental attic.

'Is she a historian too?'

Daniel looked up from his pint and held Therry's eyes, watching for her reaction.

'No,' he said. 'She was a witch.'

Chapter Eleven

*Beaconsfield, Berkshire; Saturday 20 December,
7.30 p.m.*

JUST AS Daniel Warren and Therry Moon were settling
into the Back Bar at the King's Arms, a telephone
began ringing in the panelled room referred to as the
library at Denholm House.

Normally Geoffrey Martindale hated being disturbed
in the evening. On this occasion, however, the interruption was welcome.

'Martindale,' he said, lifting the receiver.

'Geoffrey, it's Trevor.' The broad vowels of Birmingham
were an immediate giveaway to the origins of the caller.

'Trevor,' Martindale said. This was not going to be
the pleasant distraction he had hoped for. 'Why are you
calling me at home?'

'Yes, well, I'm sorry about that. It's just, I thought you
ought to know: one of the men's been taken to hospital.'

'One of the men? Is that any reason –'

'No. I mean, it's serious. One of the men from the site
near Banbury.'

'Near? Ohh, that site. I see. Is it . . . ?' He let the
question tail off, noticing that he had left the library
door open.

'Is it what?' The voice on the line was sharp, accus-
atory.

'I was just wondering. What exactly is the precise
nature of his complaint?'

'The precise nature of his complaint? The precise nature of his fucking complaint is that he's got the fucking plague.'

Martindale blanched, then, catching sight of his visitor in the doorway, turned his head away quickly.

'The bubonic fucking plague,' the voice on the line added in tones loud enough to cause Martindale to flinch. He turned and smiled apologetically at his visitor. Why the hell was the man still standing there? Once upon a time people in England respected privacy.

The man in the doorway had taken a step into the room and was affecting a polite examination of the bookcase. It was not that Neal Faversham had no respect for privacy. Quite the contrary: confidentiality was something he appreciated. More than many others, he often thought. It was just that what other people considered their privacy was part of his profession.

It was quite obvious that Geoffrey Martindale was uncomfortable about him overhearing even half of this conversation. Which did not surprise him, particularly as he was fairly certain he knew what it was about; in general, if not in detail. He advanced further into the room, turning his eyes, but not his attention, back to the bookcase, which only confirmed what he had suspected: that its owner bought his library by the yard.

'Where is he?' Martindale was asking. 'Well, I'm sure he'll get the best possible treatment. We must certainly hope so.'

A pause.

'What did you tell them?'

Another pause, fractionally longer.

'Yes, yes. Quite right.'

Faversham could sense the tension in the other man's voice.

'No, no. I'll . . . Iran. It must have been Iran.'

At that instant Faversham was glad he had his face turned towards the bookcase.

'Yes. That's why we take out such expensive health insurance for all our workers who go out there. Ah, perhaps you didn't know. Our friend Mr Atkins, yes, Charlie Atkins,' he repeated, as if trying to reinforce the man's name on his mind, 'had been on secondment to Iran, working on a new hospital project. Somewhere near Tabriz, I think you'll find.'

There was a long pause, as if the man on the other end of the line was having difficulty locating Tabriz.

'Yes, if you check the records I think you'll find Charlie Atkins returned only recently. Let me think. Yes, perhaps just six or seven days ago. Make sure you give all that information to Dr Redwhistle, Dr Simon Redwhistle. Professor, I think he is now. Tell him to spare no effort. The company will pay.'

Martindale made an impatient grimace.

'Yes, you were perfectly right to ring. Thank you very much.'

Geoffrey Martindale put the telephone down, walked over to the row of decanters on the polished mahogany sideboard and poured himself a large measure of vintage Armagnac. God knew he needed it. Remembering his manners, he turned towards his uninvited guest, who had now turned his attention from the bookcase, and gestured towards him with a glass.

Neal Faversham gave a polite nod of acceptance, and said, 'Not bad news, I hope?'

Chapter Twelve

The King's Arms, Oxford; Saturday
20 December, 8.00 p.m.

'I'M SORRY, do you want to say that again? Your mother's a witch?'

'Was. She died three years ago.'

'Oh. I'm sorry. I mean . . .'

He waved his hand. 'It's OK. Life's like that. Leastwise, that's what Mom always said.'

'When she wasn't casting spells?'

'Sort of.'

A wreath of smoke was hanging over the bar. The atmosphere was thick and muggy. Therry looked across their drinks at the young man opposite her, wondering if she detected the ghost of a smile playing on his lips, though it vanished almost as soon as she noticed it.

'Excuse me. I'm having trouble with this. This is England, you know: we're the ones supposed to have all that sort of stuff: ghosts in the dungeons, bats in the belfry . . .'

'Skeletons in the cupboard?' Daniel smiled weakly.

'But you, I mean, you come from America, for chrissake. California even. Right?'

'Right.'

'You have Hollywood and Beverly Hills and surfers and *LA Law* and riots and stuff. You don't have witches.' She paused. 'Do you?'

'Believe me, there are probably more wannabe witches

at this moment in California than there ever were in the whole of English history.'

'You're having me on?'

'California's a weird place. Even Americans think so. Mom didn't exactly wear a black hat and cloak or ride around on a broomstick or anything. Though, come to think of it, we did kinda take Hallowe'en seriously when I was a kid. But nowadays people would just have said she was eccentric, and not even that by California standards. She had a reputation as a healer.'

'Like a faith healer? Laying-on of hands? Casting out demons? Like those religious guys you have on TV, that sort of stuff?'

'Not really. She wasn't very interested in faith of any variety. It was a lot more down to earth than that – alternative medicine really, like Chinese medicine, for example. She knew all about acupuncture; used to laugh at the way people in the West pretended to have just discovered it, when she said we had known about it for hundreds of years, just been forced to forget. And she made potions out of herbs and flowers and things. Of course some of it involved things that were poisonous if taken in a higher dosage.'

'Like homeopathy.'

'Right. Exactly right.' Daniel smiled at her. 'Mom had a favourite saying; I don't think it was original but it was good. "Magic," she used to say, "is just science we don't understand yet." Take penicillin, for example: before Fleming discovered it back in the 1940s, people would have though you were mad to put mouldy bread on a wound.'

'Like rubbing a wart with a potato and burying it in the garden.'

'That sort of thing. Some worked and some didn't.

Because some had a basis in real science even if it wasn't properly understood.'

'Old wives' tales.'

'Or witches' brews. Eye of newt and spawn of frog.'

'Lizard's tongue and honeydew.'

'You know your Shakespeare?'

'What do you expect? Stratford's only just up the road, remember. But what's this got to do with the Black Death? You're not saying it was caused by witches?'

Daniel leaned forward, warming to his tale.

'Hardly. More the other way around, in fact.'

'I don't get you.'

'Mom didn't call herself a witch. Even in California it's not the best of advertisements for business. But she was serious about what she did. Serious about the history of women like her who had guarded old knowledge of folk cures down the centuries. My grandmother, she said, had been one too. But it didn't necessarily run in families. Just one woman passing on to another like-minded soul down the ages.'

'You make it sound like a secret society. A feminist equivalent of the masonic order or something.'

'In a way that's what it was. Mom always regretted, I think, that she didn't have a daughter. She said men had caused too much anguish down the centuries. Men in control had been jealous, refused to learn the women's lore or let them practise it. All because of the Bible.'

'The Bible?'

'Christianity's "good book" put women in second place,' Daniel explained, 'and told humanity to place its faith in prayer. So the old remedies were frowned upon and even when people started looking to doctors, they looked to men. Women who practised as healers were obviously heathens, they thought. Especially if the doctors didn't understand their cures.'

'And especially if they involved brewing up weird potions and sticking needles into the soles of their victims' feet.'

'Patients' feet. The victims were the ones the so-called doctors practised on.' He stressed the word 'practised' in a way that made clear what he really meant was 'experimented'. 'But you got it, all right. The best these guys could do was to have a go at "purifying" their patients with leeches, sucking their blood away and weakening them, just when they needed every last reserve of strength. They got them to heaven faster, OK.'

'And at the time of the Black Death it was particularly bad . . . ?'

'The paranoia reached its height. Men doctors didn't know what to do. Their science, their fat fees, the church's imprecations to prayer, all failed.'

'But the women succeeded?'

Daniel looked up wondering, Therry could see in his green eyes, whether she was mocking him. But she was not. She wanted to hear more.

'No, of course not,' he continued after a moment of silence. 'No one then had any idea about the cause of the plague. Most people just assumed it was a mark of God's anger, the Last Judgement, even: you know Pestilence was one of the Four Horsemen of the Apocalypse. The women healers – call them witches, wise women or what you will – might have had more solid knowledge and less quackery than most of their male rivals, but when it came to a calamity on this scale they failed just as abysmally. Many of them died in the attempt to cure others. Those who survived were blamed for their failure. The fourteenth century was when witch- burning started in earnest. Look at the English and Joan of Arc.'

'That was because she heard voices.'

'Bullshit. The English had her killed because she was the only competent military leader the French had. They burned her at the stake because calling her a witch was the best reason for explaining what she did –'

'Which was to beat the men at their own game.'

'I had to leave that line to you.'

Therry shrugged. 'So what are you doing, though? Writing a book about this?'

'In a way. I'm researching for a PhD – or DPhil, as they call it here. I did a history degree at Berkeley and now I'm working on a thesis. I'd like to turn it into a book, too: reach a wider audience.'

'But it's about the Black Death rather than witches?'

'Yes, though there's a lot of crossover. What I'm trying to do is get a new angle on how an epidemic on that scale affected ordinary people and their attitudes to the establishment of the day, the priests and doctors in particular.'

'Which is where your mum's influence comes in?'

'Right.'

'You're going to have to help me here a bit. History's not exactly my best subject. Is the Black Death the same as the Great Plague that hit London about the same time as the Great Fire?'

'In 1665 and 1666.'

Therry shrugged her shoulders.

'Yes and no. The plague that hit London in 1665 was bubonic plague, the same disease as the Black Death. In a way they were lucky with the Great Fire the next year – it destroyed any remaining centres of infection. But it had only been a small-scale rerun of the real terror, which swept the country three hundred years earlier.'

'You mean this thing keeps coming back?'

'In theory, yes. It still springs up today now and then, mostly in the Third World – presumably where this guy in the hospital contracted it. But modern drugs are better at containing it. Nobody really knows, though, why sometimes it just spreads like wildfire.'

'As it did way back when.'

'Right. Again nobody knows for sure, but it seems to have started in the Far East, probably China. The best estimates are that it got to Europe sometime in 1348, carried on board the ships of Venetian traders bringing back silk and spices from the Orient.'

'Ships' rats, wasn't it? The rats carried it, I mean.'

'Yes and no again. The plague was actually carried by fleas that lived on the rats. The rats came ashore and spread throughout Europe, taking the disease with them, though they now think the flea could even have jumped off the rats and survived for some time on clothing or on other hosts.'

'Yuck! It makes you want to scratch. But why was it called the Black Death?'

'That's not what they called it at the time. The Black Death label only got stuck on it a couple of hundred years later, to mark it out from all the other plague epidemics, not to mention all the other varieties of death that were available in the Middle Ages.'

'So what did they call it?'

'At the time, the plague was mostly known just as the great sickness. The Germans were more pessimistic right from the outset: they called it *das grosse Sterben*, the great death.'

'But just to be dying like that and not even to know why! It must have driven people mad.'

'It did. It brought out the worst in a lot of people too. In parts of Spain and Germany they accused the Jews –'

'They would.'

'. . . of poisoning the wells. Thousands were rounded up and stoned to death.'

'Nice.'

'They weren't nice times. Even without the plague. Then there were the flagellants.'

'Like that bondage stuff?'

'Not exactly. Though some scholars think there may have been a sexual element to it. If there was, it was pretty weird. These were fourteenth-century cult followers. Mostly they just wandered the countryside from village to village. Whenever they arrived somewhere, they would form a big circle and start beating the hell out of themselves with thonged whips. People came to watch.'

'People would. Just imagine if they'd had tabloid newspapers at the time.'

'I can't. But there's no lack of eyewitness stuff. Some of it from pretty good writers too. Boccaccio, for example.'

Therry squinted. The name obviously did not ring many bells.

'Italian. Author of the *Decameron*.'

'Oh, yeah, I remember. They made a movie. Years ago.'

Daniel sighed. Popular culture was better than no culture at all. 'OK, well, you remember there were ten people all telling the stories?'

Therry nodded. Less than decisively.

'Well, in the book, the idea is that they all come together because they are fleeing Florence to get away from the plague. The city was badly hit, as was most of Italy. Tens of thousands may have died. And you have to remember that the population of Europe was much smaller in those days, barely fifty million for the whole continent. France and Italy were the most populous nations. England was almost empty in relative terms, probably not more than three million in total.'

'Why was this plague so much worse than before or later?'

'Why? No one knows. Not really. Oh, there are theories. But it was bad, all right. The estimates are vague, but some of the more informed guesses reckon that anything up to a third of the population of Europe died.'

'God! But Boccaccio, your Italian, he survived and wrote about it?'

Daniel nodded. 'He describes it in pretty grim detail.'

'I thought the *Decameron* was all dirty stories. At least I'm pretty sure the movie was.'

'I'm sure it was. In Florence in particular, a lot of people decided that the best plan was to eat, drink and be merry.'

'For tomorrow we die.'

'Absolutely. The feast in the time of plague. A lot of them partied like there was no tomorrow. It was a huge jolt to the medieval concepts of chastity and piety.'

'I'll bet it was! Jesus Christ!'

Therry found the scholarly young American staring into her eyes as if she had somehow penetrated to the heart of the matter. In a quiet voice, for despite her casual blasphemy, Daniel Warren had no idea of her religious feelings, he said:

'Except that Jesus Christ couldn't save them. Or at least didn't. And for some of them, that was precisely the point. You see, I've found a document in the college library. It's why I was so taken aback when you mentioned Nether Ditchford. This is a chronicle of the Black Death in that village. Written by the parish priest. A man who found such evidence of damnation pretty hard to take.'

'You mean he lost his faith?'

Daniel nodded slowly.

'He sure did. But not just that. He lost everything. Everything in the world.'

Chapter Thirteen

The John Radcliffe Hospital, Oxford; Sunday 21 December, 01.00 a.m.

RAJIV WAS nervous. The man in front of him was not pleased. Not pleased at all. In fact, Dr Simon Redwhistle was downright bristling. But he waited for the nurse to leave the room before speaking.

'I suppose I should thank you,' he said tersely. Rajiv knew he was having difficulty containing himself. 'Yes. Thank you. Commend you, even, for acting so quickly. Another doctor perhaps might not have acted so pre-cipitately –' he pronounced each syllable with an exag-gerated clarity, and then spat out the next phrase – 'so presumptuously!'

Rajiv hung his head. He knew he had done the right thing. But Redwhistle had a point too. And Rajiv was not in a position to argue.

'Someone else might not have exceeded his extremely limited authority and started setting up containment procedures in a busy, overcrowded hospital, simply on the basis of one *unconfirmed* case.'

'But it's not –'

'Don't interrupt me, young man!' Redwhistle said, ignor-ing the fact that he was the one doing the interrupting. 'I know what you were doing. You were following your nose. Oh, you can give me all the guff you like about the World Health Organisation regulations, designed for wholesale epidemics in Bangladesh or wherever you come from.'

Rajiv was sorely tempted to tell him Leicester, but he was used to this sort of racist assumption.

'But let me tell you, young man, you have scared the wits out of half of my staff and spread panicky rumours that'll get into the local press, all because we have one sick man who is in fact exactly where he should be, right next to the tropical-medicine department of the best university in the country. All he needed was what he already had: a private ward and a sign on the door restricting access specifically to those medical personnel involved in his treatment.'

'But –'

'That's all. That's enough. All right?'

Rajiv nodded. He probably had overreacted, but that was no reason to humiliate him like this. Though at least the senior doctor had not done it in public.

'Yes, sir. Except that –'

'Good.' Redwhistle put a finger to his lips, indicating that a strict answer to his questions was all that was required. Inside, Rajiv was fuming.

Apparently placated by having achieved a state of obeisance in the junior doctor, Redwhistle seemed to mellow somewhat. He almost smiled.

'You were quite right to be anxious, though. Especially given the development you describe in the symptoms. As I understand, you were the only person to witness this. There was no one else in the ward at the time.'

'No, no one,' Rajiv lied, wondering if the double negative somehow negated the falsehood.

'And so far, since the change in his condition, no one but you and the duty nurse and myself have been in contact?'

'That's correct, sir.' Rajiv wondered whether he would eventually have to own up to Daniel's presence, in which case failing to tell the truth now would only make things worse.

Redwhistle was looking at his file. 'You alerted Sister Cooper over the intercom system, gave the *order* for the containment procedure –' Rajiv ignored the arch tone – 'and then had her summon me. Yes?'

Rajiv nodded.

'Well, as I said, I hope we have things under control. But I advise you to take the standard precautions. No doubt your experience in the field will already have suggested that course of action to you?'

Rajiv nodded again. His moment was coming.

'That is common sense, of course. But before we do anything else, at this stage, it is important that we get confirmation. You understand that, I hope? Your diagnosis of the symptoms was not necessarily faulty, nor your estimation of the gravity of the situation, although I will look into that in a minute. But we must be certain, absolutely certain, that this really is bubonic plague, before we can even begin to go into the ramifications of it having transmuted already into the pneumonic phase. I am sure your textbooks will have told you, there are certain quite specific tests that have to be done.'

'That's what I've been trying to tell you, sir. I've already done them.'

'You've . . . ?'

'Yes. I'm sure you'll agree, sir, I mean, all the experts say –' Rajiv recognised that it was a dangerous phrase the moment it slipped his lips: Redwhistle was not the sort of man who readily acknowledged others as having any expertise – 'to do the tests immediately. To be sure.'

Redwhistle was looking at Rajiv in a way he had not done before. If the younger man had not known better,

79

he would have said the expression on his senior's face was akin to respect.

'And the results?' was all he said.

'Positive, sir. Beyond any doubt.'

Redwhistle rocked back on his heels slightly, as if, despite the symptoms, he had not really been expecting this. A thin breath of air escaped his lips with a short, high-pitched peep.

'I see,' he said. 'Right, well, we must hope for the best as far as Mr Atkins is concerned. I can only say that it reinforces what I have been trying to get into the heads of British company directors sending their workers abroad to areas where there are serious health risks.' He tutted as if Charlie Atkins's plight was the direct response of the Confederation of British Industry's failure to hire him for another series of well-paid seminars.

'What is your prognosis, sir?'

'Hmm,' Redwhistle's mind, it seemed, was already elsewhere, probably contemplating the benefits to his bank balance of an increased programme of big-business advice forums, hosted at Christ Church, where he held his fellowship. 'Oh. Well, it's not as good as it could be, of course. Fifty-fifty, perhaps.' He delivered the bleak odds on Charlie Atkins's survival with all the interest of a bookmaker at a slow race.

At that point the intercom on the desk buzzed and the clear voice of Nurse Mary Clarke came over: 'Dr Redwhistle, it's Mr Atkins. I think you should come quickly.'

Chapter Fourteen

Jericho, Oxford; Sunday 21 December, 1.30 a.m.

T HERRY MOON glanced out only briefly at the frost settling on the low Victorian rooftops of Jericho before clambering into bed and pulling the quilt up tight around her neck. She shivered. Perhaps the damn central-heating boiler was on the blink again. Perhaps Josie, her flatmate, had forgotten to pay the bill. She reached out of bed and touched the radiator. To her surprise, it was warm; hot, even. Just showed how cold it had got outside. They hadn't had a winter like this for years. Or was that what people said every time there was a cold snap? What did you expect in December? Grey skies and damp drizzle. That was what the English always expected. Very different from the climate the California kid must be used to, she thought. Except that he seemed so oddly un-Californian. In fact, just odd really.

But not as odd as his pet subject. Therry grabbed the ring binder that she had laid on her night table. She had not been sure whether, after half a dozen pints of lager, she had any head for getting stuck into an academic's writing, no matter how popular he had insisted he was trying to make it. Still, the worst it could do was to send her to sleep. She opened the ring binder and was initially daunted by the thick wad of typescript. He had used a yellow sticky note jutting out of the paper to indicate the section he thought would interest her most. Though what had interested *him* most, she was certain, was the idea of getting her into his room. Flattering, of course, and he was not unattractive. But in the end he was just another bloke on the make. Then again, his story was interesting. The hated housing development up at Ditchford and the background of the Black Death had all the makings of classic feature material, the sort of thing that would make old John Harkness sit up. Though it would take some clever writing to make it hang together. But *if* it worked . . . She could see her name in the nationals yet. The fact that her horny California kid – whatever his ulterior motives – had been willing to lend her his precious research was a real boon. She supposed, with a smirk, she owed him one.

The bedroom light flickered. That was all they needed: a power cut.

'Come here, Tigger,' she said, reaching down from the bed to pick up a tortoiseshell kitten that mewed plaintively, then, as she stroked it, settled down to a contented purr on the quilt. Therry yawned and shivered again. Imagine how cold it must have been for those poor buggers back in the Middle Ages! She flicked through to the yellow sticky marker, but on the way her eye was caught by a passage of text he had highlighted a few pages earlier. The note above said the author was Boccaccio, the Italian bloke, describing the physical effects of the plague on the people of Florence. As she read, she was suddenly aware that this was real reportage by someone who had been there. Therry Moon's flesh began to creep.

At the onset of the disease both men and women were affected by a sort of swelling in the groin or under the armpits, which sometimes attained the size of a common apple or egg. Some were larger and some were smaller and all were commonly called 'boils'. Afterwards the manifestations of the disease changed into black or lurid spots on the arms, the thighs and the whole person. In many ways, the blotches had the same meaning for everyone on whom they appeared.

And the meaning was abundantly clear: death. Imminent, certain and painful death. Her eyes flitted down the page to another highlighted section, written apparently by a man called Villani, who had fled the north Italian port of Genoa at about the same time. His report was no less grim:

All who arrived in Genoa died and corrupted the air to such an extent that whoever came near the bodies dies shortly thereafter. It was a disease in which there appeared certain swellings in the groin and under the armpit and the victims spat blood . . .

She flinched involuntarily. Just what did the California kid say had happened in the ward at the Radcliffe?

. . . and in days they were dead. The priest who confessed the sick and those who nursed them so generally caught the infection that the victims were abandoned and deprived of confession, sacrament, medicine and nursing. Many lands were made desolate. And the plague lasted until —

The date was blank. Two lines below the American gave the reason in his own words: Villani had made the mistake of thinking Florence, the very city Boccaccio and his friends were fleeing, would be safer than Genoa. It was not. He had died in 1348, when the plague in mainland Europe was just reaching its height.

Grim, grim, grim, Therry thought, not at all sure that late at night was the right time to be reading this. She hugged herself beneath the blankets and was suddenly uncomfortably aware that she had been subconsciously examining her armpits for swellings.

Let's not be too silly, girl, she told herself, turning to the page marked by Daniel's yellow sticker. This was, he had confided with a mixture of shy embarrassment and pride, wholly new research which he had written up in academic form and annotated for his thesis, but he had also, with an eye to a popular history, tried his hand at presenting a translation into modern English of the document he had found in Magdalen Library, buried among old manorial records, fourteenth-century account books, dusty tomes that no one had bothered with for decades. It was quite remarkable, he had said, the only surviving account of the plague in English that in any respect came close to the memoirs of the Italians. And it had been written here in Oxfordshire, in Nether Ditchford.

My name is Edward Gray, son of John of Bicester, and priest of this parish by leave of his grace William, bishop of Lincoln [Funny, thought Therry, Lincoln was a long way away, especially in the Middle Ages, but she let it go], and I have held this office but a few months since the sudden passing of my predecessor, for the sickness had already made its appearance in the parish and claimed a man of God as its first victim, a fact which for many will no longer seem so strange as it at first might seem.

I was greeted kindly at first by the local folk

for none yet knew that the sudden death of my predecessor was the harbinger of doom for them all. I was to give them that message, though I did not then know it either as they showed me into the modest priest's quarters adjoining the splendid church of St Peter's now nearing completion after more than two generations of labour, and with the magnificent decoration of the nave mightily under way. Nicholas the Reeve, who collects tax for Peter of Castelnaud, lord of this manor and of several others in this part of the county, had met me at the end of my second day of journey from Oxford [Therry smiled to herself. Ditchford was barely twenty miles away, not half an hour at the speed she drove, even on country lanes] and bade me welcome among the villagers who did seem to me goodly folk, numbering some twelve dozen in all, with some sixteen families. A few were freemen with grander wooden homes, but most were villeins tied in service to the lord and inhabiting the wattle-walled dwellings common to country folk. Still, I was glad to be among them as for me, and for my maidservant Annie, as I introduced her to them, it was a living. What a wicked irony now lies in that word!

Already there was anxiety among the village folk since the sudden death of Father Nicholas, for rumours had been heard of the great sickness suffered abroad. And that it was also in England, though as yet only in such distant parts as Dorset and the port of Bristol. So it was with dire foreboding that I mounted the steps of the little pulpit to read them as almost my first act as their priest the episcopalian letter, my own heart sinking as I read out those doom-laden first words from the

Therry shivered. She hadn't a clue what a voice in Rama might be, or even where Rama was, though she had a vague and obviously inappropriate recollection of a science-fiction novel by Arthur C. Clarke. Nonetheless there was something chilling about the words themselves, made worse perhaps by the lack of obvious meaning, like those ancient prophecies of the oracle at Delphi, always somehow sinister in their opaque ambivalence. She turned back to the page; perhaps Father Gray would enlighten her.

He did not. For the next half-hour, Therry sat numbed as she read the priest's bleakly fastidious account of the decimation – no, the annihilation – of the parish of Ditchford. Of Matthew the Carter and his seven children, including two strong sons he had hoped would take on his trade, all of whom he watched die in wretched misery before he too succumbed to the black boils. Mistress Carter, she learned, was spared the evil only because she had 'mercifully' died in childbirth eight months earlier.

And the plague was no respecter of rank.

For even Nicholas the Reeve [a reeve, it turned out, was a sort of local tax collector working for the lord of the manor], he who welcomed me to this parish, fell over even outside the gates of the church, suddenly choking and coughing blood, despite having shown no previous signs of the disease. He was dead before nightfall.

Father Gray reported his row with the grave digger who abruptly refused to bury any more of the plague victims after his colleague collapsed and fell into a grave while they were digging it. He had shared the hole with its intended occupant. So the villagers were reduced to burying their own. If there was animosity against the surviving gravedigger, it had little time to manifest itself, for he died anyway, within a week of his colleague.

In no little time, even within three months of my arrival in the parish of Nether Ditchford, our churchyard which should have lasted for many generations was filled. Yea, more than filled, for plots destined to receive one family over many years, decades even, took their fill within weeks. It seemed as if my pronunciation of those doom-filled words from the pulpit of the Lord had only hastened His fury. Or was it the fury of the Angel of Death? With one quarter of our folk dead already, and it not yet Christmastide, there were not a few in whose souls, I fear, sacrilege had already been committed. Was this but one more test of our faith? Or was the Second Coming at hand and the final Pestilence upon us in anticipation? Or was there a still more cruel answer to our state of misery? That is, no answer at all.

A surgeon, or a man who called himself such, arrived but a few days before Christmas and took much charge of our villagers' meagre reserves: a few pence and the promise of a decent dinner (for it is sad to relate that in these terrible times the scant reserves of winter fodder went further than was usual, there being each day fewer left to share them). Yet all his science proved to little avail. Even those who had most to pay and on whom he let his leeches feast longest showed no obvious benefit. In fact, as if this curse was designed to thwart even the most vainglorious boasts of our scientific knowledge, they often died sooner, despite the copious letting of bad blood.

The Feast of the Birth of Our Lord this year of 1348 was a bleak and barren one indeed. It was as if the Lord of Misrule, that customary jolly soul whose pleasure it is to cause merry havoc in our order and give spirit to the feasting, had assumed an altogether blacker incarnation. In the end there was little regret over the doctor, for he himself succumbed to sickness on St Stephen's Day, though perhaps on account of his science, I do not know, he lasted longer than most, the black boils taking a week before they consumed him. He was the first death of this new and cursed year of 1349, which many now believe will see the end of the world. The monies he had taken were shared out again.

In their dismay more than a few of my flock did turn to older ways, when prayer and science had failed them. For there was an old woman, a crone called May, which some said was but a form of the name of Our Lady, but others whispered was her whole name, derived from the fertile month of blossoming spring, a name, therefore, as only a pagan might have given a child and which she could never have been christened. This crone lived in a crude wattle hovel which was said to be a filthy sty, though a few who dared admit to having been there said was indeed not so. It lay on the edge of the settlement, close to the Rop brook, and was hung with all manner of outlandish garlands made from plants plucked in the forests. They say she made potions out of them, boiled in a pot, with God knows what devilish enchantments.

But even her magic, whatever its inspiration,

failed. Those who had put their faith in her as a last resort were sorely disappointed, while those who had remained faithful to the doctrines of Mother Church said it proved she was a charlatan, even in league with the devil (for her charms, they said, had worked against other ills). This was a reasoning I followed only with difficulty and I was loath to condone the cries that she should be burned as a witch, as an act of atonement to Our Lord for doubting His mercy. Once I would have said His mercy did not demand such cruelties. Now I do not know. But as no one knew when or where again assizes would be held, nothing was done, and in any case human justice was not to have its way. The crone May too was taken. In much pain.

And even then the toll of death did not stop. The dead doctor too was blamed, for the numbers dying had risen rapidly since his arrival in our midst. As if he had brought a fresh dose of evil on his person. And in the end there were none who would bury them, none who would mourn them and none who would pray over them, so we laid our dead in the fields like carrion, for the churchyard was full. We laid them in ditches, where ditches were dug, and where not, we laid them on the open earth, for the ground was frozen too hard to break. And even in the depths of winter frost the stench of mortality was fearful. The dogs and the wolves from the forest would not touch them. And all who remained were sore afraid. Yet at the end of the world, what shall a man fear? Our Maker has unmade us.

Yet the fear remains. I know this for a fact. Take heed, whoever may read this, if indeed there will be any men left living. For I too have lost all that

I held most dear. The wages of sin, the Good Book tells us, is death. I have earned my wages in full, but they have been paid many times over. It is but six days, though it feels like the passage of years, since my Annie fell ill. When first she swooned in the vestry, it was as if a heavy anvil had landed upon my heart.

The appearance of the boils upon the sweet child's body was a desecration of a temple: the visible imprint of Satan's powers making a mockery of God's creation. For she was but a child, of barely thirteen years. And though I tended her once more as I had done on occasion when she was little after the cruel death of her mother, it was a wicked occasion to have to do so once again, to witness the foul pestilence spread its canker even to her most private parts, and she only beginning to flower into womanhood. A promise unfulfilled. No, a promise broken. God's promise. If it was ever made. I thought I had witnessed all the horrors already in the deaths of so many innocents, but now I know that I had seen them all but through a glass darkly, as one sees the suffering of others. And imagines to share them. But in reality, for all our pious and even goodly care for our brother, we are in our black souls rejoicing, even in our sympathy, that the evil which has struck him may have missed us as its true target.

I cannot write of her end, only with tears or blood, either of which are now more freely available than even the most expensive ink. I laid her to rest, along with the others, in the shallow ditch beyond the churchyard. Even for her, I had not the strength to crack the solid surface of the frozen earth. So she lies there, carrion like the others, to await a cruel springtime that indeed may never come.

Now I freely confess that it was at the moment of leaving her stiff and swollen body, deformed by disease and devoid of life, wrapped in a rough woollen sheet, that the anger took me. I went back into the body of the church of St Peter. Perhaps I should have prayed, fallen to my knees and begged forgiveness of the living God. But as I looked up at the crucifix and then all around me to the abandoned images of damnation I felt only an aching emptiness. In my madness I seized the fine white altar cloth with its delicate embroidery and lace and ripped it away, sending, as I did, the Holy Communion vessels clattering to the stone flags, where they rolled away, so many empty trinkets. And I took the cloth and stole with it to the burial ditch and draped it over my Annie's cold corpse.

For yes, she was my daughter, flesh of my flesh, and the proof of its weakness in every way. For I had broken my vow in her begetting, but thought the loss of her mother was punishment enough. But it seems that the Lord our God is indeed a jealous God. And as such I cannot love Him.

For God so loved the world that He gave His only begotten Son, but he resurrected Him. And for all the faith I muster I cannot see my Annie resurrected, nor any others among the putrid dead that lie in what once was Tinker's Field. And if they did rise again, would they not bring the evil with them? For the evil seems unassailable, and more immortal than our poor souls.

This then is my confession, though there is none qualified to hear it, scarce one who can hear any voice of reason among the little more than a dozen souls who remain alive – if that is the word – in this cursed parish of Nether Ditchford. I have a sore headache and feel swellings in my groin, and am sure my last torment is at hand.

This is, therefore, also my last testament, though I have no one to leave it to, and nothing to leave.

Not even hope.

Therry put down the pages on her bed quilt gently like a patient might set down a letter from a hospital that contained unfavourable test results. She looked for a moment at the neat typescript in its red plastic ring binder, so incongruous with its contents. Then, lost in thought, she closed it and set it aside on her bedside table, pulled the quilt tight around her and, with a heavy sigh, reached out and extinguished the light.

Chapter Fifteen

Heathrow airport; Sunday 21 December, 9.40 a.m.

FROM THE air, all big cities look the same. Even in Europe. Occasionally a distant glimpse of some landmark – the Eiffel Tower or the Sacré Coeur of Montmartre in Paris, the Houses of Parliament or St Paul's Cathedral in London, the Sagrada Familia in Barcelona, the Brandenburg Gate in Berlin – allows instant recognition. But mostly they look the same. The same sprawl of ribbon development along arterial roads. The infill of winding streets behind them. The clusters here and there that might be little local centres of activity, the remnants of small towns or villages swallowed up by the expanding metropolis at some earlier stage in its evolution, now digested and redeveloped as little more than traffic-congestion points. Like knots in wood.

But every now and then there are other features of the landscape that make identification easier for the passenger of the inbound aircraft who might have dozed off and forgotten his destination. In Barcelona or Copenhagen the dramatic proximity of the coastline to the runway, in Moscow the thick expanses of pine forest that surround Sheremetyevo. On the approach to London's Heathrow airport, no observant traveller can fail to note the great circular features that mark the edge of the airport area, as bizarre and improbable as alien crop circles. And as clearly artificial. On slightly closer inspection, as your 747 loses altitude on the approach run, they appear to be mostly water, perfectly circular man-made lakes. They attract waterfowl – herons and Canadian geese – though these make life so difficult for air-traffic controllers and airline pilots alike that there are constant attempts to discourage them from nesting in the area.

This is no wildlife preserve, at least not by designation. The landscape below is simply the location, sensibly remote from domestic housing, of the greatest collection of sewage farms in Greater London. For in a big city, mused Harold Hammerstein, passenger on the United Airlines flight from Miami to London, as the silver wings swooped low over the deceptively glinting surface waters, there is an awful lot of shit.

As he had done before, he wondered, as the wheels touched tarmac, how many passengers, aware of what they were passing over, had thought of the mixed blessing, in the event of a crash landing. What a way to break a fall! He smiled at the picture conjured up, and the woman beside him looked askance at him, wondering what the stranger was grinning at when he had barely said a word to her during the nearly eight hours of their transatlantic flight.

'Allow me,' he said, standing up as the plane came to a halt, and handing down her bag from the overhead storage locker. The smile was still on his face. He was estimating, had their plane fallen out of the sky faster than intended and hurtled into the cesspit, what the chances might have been of his emerging unhurt and smelling of roses.

After all, dung and death were what he dealt in.

Chapter Sixteen

Upper Ditchford, Oxfordshire; Sunday,
21 December, 11.00 a.m.

'A RE YOU sure about this?' Therry asked as her battered Range Rover lurched into another pothole.

'Of course I'm not sure. I told you the whole idea
was mad to begin with. I don't know what you hope
to achieve by coming out here,' Daniel replied, grabbing
the handhold above his head to avoid being pitched out
of his seat.

'So why are you with me? Eh?' Her face cracked into
a wide grin as she wrestled the steering wheel.

'Because . . . just because . . .'

'Because I asked you to. And it's very sweet of you to
come along for the ride and hold my hand. Anyway, I
mean about the history. That old manuscript stuff.'

Daniel shot her a sideways glance. Was she teasing
him or flirting with him? 'Of course I'm sure of it. It's
what I do.'

In fact he was not even sure what she was talking
about. After the King's Arms, he had persuaded Therry
to come back to Magdalen, a not unreasonable stagger
through the romantic gas-lit gloom of Holywell and
Longwall streets, on the excuse that he wanted to give
her part of the manuscript to read. As he knew he should
have anticipated, had he been sober at the time, she had
remained at the foot of his staircase. She had left the
Range Rover on a yellow line, she said. When he had

argued that the parking restriction was not valid at that time of night, she had replied that the parking wardens might well be out again before she got around to leaving, 'if we get into another deep conversation'. He found this remark so encouraging that he happily handed over his manuscript – the only copy he had, it struck him later; of course it was all on his hard disk, but unannotated – and to cap it all he agreed to accompany her next morning on this idiotic expedition.

When he awoke, wondering if he had the ingredients for Mom's magic hangover cure, he hoped she would forget all about it. Nonetheless, he had dragged himself out of bed in time, and she had duly picked him up outside Magdalen just after breakfast in a Range Rover that looked as if it predated the vehicle's success as a status symbol. Mud concealed most of the dents in the doors, and the engine roared like an angry walrus when she turned the key in the ignition.

'Nice machine,' he had commented wryly.

She smiled back coldly. 'It's called Rover. And it's never been to Sainsbury's.'

'Right,' said Daniel. It was what he said in England when he realised someone had scored a point off him for a reason he only dimly understood.

He also only dimly understood her enthusiasm. There was no possible link between the historical incidence of the plague at Nether Ditchford and a man suffering from a version of the disease more than six centuries later, even if he had been working on a construction site nearby. Was there? No. It was ridiculous. According to Rajiv, it was quite clear that the man had picked up the disease overseas, somewhere in the Middle East, where outbreaks still occurred from time to time. He had simply flown home within the incubation period. It was the sort of thing that with modern international working and air travel was bound to happen sooner or later. Most people thought bubonic plague was a disease of the distant past. They forgot that what century you lived in often depended on which continent you lived on. There had in fact been an outbreak in England as recently as 1910, in Suffolk, causing relatively few deaths – barely a dozen. No one knew quite how it had erupted or why it subsided so suddenly. But these things happened.

On the other hand, he had to admit it was something of a coincidence: here he was hanging the best part of his academic reputation on a document relating to one obscure Oxfordshire village at the height of the plague, and some building worker turns up with a form of the disease, having worked in the same damn place. There was only one word for it: weird. The historical scientist in him was not prone to superstition but somehow Daniel found it hard to believe in pure coincidences.

Therry, for her part, seemed to have had no doubt that it was fate handing her a story on a plate. The idea of an ancient curse, as she insisted on putting it, especially one dating from the time of the Black Death, had her salivating. Daniel found her enthusiasm disconcerting. Somewhere along the line, he felt, she was making one connection too many. And the last thing he wanted was to risk his reputation with involvement in some British tabloid-newspaper nonsense. That was why he had to go with her, he told himself. Having started this particular bandwagon rolling, he had better keep an eye on just where it was heading.

Of course he had been flattered by the praise she had heaped on his attempt to make his subject more accessible. He had been worried about his translation of Father Gray's medieval Latin, indeed still was worried, in case it fell between two stools: not formal enough for the academic lobby and yet too close to the original style for modern readers. But then he could hardly have the priest sounding like Clint Eastwood. One phrase in particular had fired her imagination.

'Where is Rama then?' she had asked as they swung around the Wolvercote roundabout, leaving the Oxford ring road heading north.

'Where?'

'Rama. "*A voice has been heard in in Rama*," it says there,' and she jerked her head in the direction of the red plastic ring binder that lay on the back seat behind him.

'Ah. It's the site of a synagogue somewhere in Judaea. It's a biblical reference, supposed to be the site of Rachel's tomb.'

'Who's Rachel? I don't get it.'

'It's from the book of Matthew; to be more precise, Matthew quoting Jeremiah prophesying doom and destruction: "A voice was heard in Rama, lamentation and bitter weeping; Rachel weeping for her children, she refused to be comforted for her children because they were not." Rachel was the wife of Jacob, and therefore traditionally the original mother figure for all Jews. The quotation has been taken to refer to anything from the captivity in Babylon to modern atrocities on the West Bank, where the tomb is supposed to be.'

Therry was staring at him sceptically.

'But Christians traditionally take it in the sense Matthew meant: that it was a reference to the children murdered by Herod after the wise men warned him about the birth of a "king of kings". As you know, he wasn't too keen on that idea.'

'I bet you're a wow at Trivial Pursuit. But seriously, the connection is . . . ?'

'The massacre of the innocents. It's a Catholic feast

day. I think the rest of Jeremiah goes on to tell people to "keep thy voice from weeping and thy eyes from tears". The bishop was warning people, in the clearest way he could – and it was better than you might think: people knew their Bible back then – that something pretty dreadful was about to hit them. Watch out!'

For a split second Daniel thought something pretty dreadful was about to hit them too. Without warning a tractor pulled out on the road ahead of them, crawling at barely 15 mph as opposed to their 50 mph. Daniel ducked instinctively and threw up his arm in a vain gesture to protect his face in the imminent collision. But without slowing down Therry threw the Range Rover on to the rough roadside verge and passed the tractor on the inside, still managing to flick a hand from the wheel to acknowledge what, to his astonishment, appeared to be a friendly wave from the tractor driver.

'You know that psychopath?' Daniel said when he had recovered and the Range Rover had bumped back on to the metalled surface.

'Sure. Dan Austin. Drove that tractor down Oxford High Street two years ago to protest about some EU farming reform. Him and twenty-six others. Snarled the traffic up for hours – coaches from London stuck back all the way beyond Magdalen Bridge. Great story.'

'Great.'

The elegant little town of Woodstock – ancestor of the one in New York State – and the straggling village of Enstone sped by as they headed north. Daniel found himself marvelling yet again at the contradictions of the English countryside: the warm stone of the old houses with their higgledy-piggledy roofs; the ornate splendour of Blenheim Palace with its vast park and lofty history. And then the housing estates of the 1960s and 1970s, incongruous little streets of identical homes, as if bought in a packet. But heck, people had to have somewhere to live.

'Is this the sort of thing they're building up at Ditchford?'

'And the rest. You'll see.'

Just beyond Chipping Norton, Therry turned left into a B-road and then an even narrower single-track road that was little better than a lane. The low, hilly countryside looked bleak and cold; the morning's frost had not yet completely lifted from the brown fields and barren hedgerows. What would it have been like six hundred years ago, when most people had no other fuel than what they could find in the forest? Even a horse had been a luxury very few could afford, so feet were the main form of transport. Cold feet wrapped in rags. Yet they had been enough to carry death the length of the country.

As the Range Rover crested the brow of a hill and turned down into the broad valley of the Swere stream, the view looked very much as it might have done in the Middle Ages, with a square stone tower sticking up defiantly from the brown earth. As it did six hundred and fifty years ago, when Edward Gray was appointed rector of Nether Ditchford, in the plague year of 1348.

'St Peter's Alone.'

'Is he?'

'The church. That's what they called it. Afterwards. Because most of the village had moved away, to be further from the graveyard. Just in case.'

'Did they? Well, it's not alone any more.'

'Christ, I see what you mean.'

In the few months since he had first discovered Ditchford, there had been a transformation. Beyond the church, the brown was not just that of ploughed fields but of an excavated construction site, littered with yellow earth-moving machinery. The old hedgerows had been uprooted and a vast expanse of countryside had been scoured and levelled.

'They're planning to build on all this?'

'Yep.'

'But it's vast. How many houses?'

'At least a hundred, maybe one hundred and fifty.'

'That's some development. It must nearly double the size of the village.'

'It'll destroy it, near as damn it. Turn it into another commuter suburb. How much employment do you think there is in Ditchford?'

'Ah . . . not a lot.'

'A few farms, but not many employ outside labourers these days. A small print works. The post office – and that's under threat – and the village shop, which mainly provides Saturday jobs for kids. There used to be a brewery, but that closed a couple of years back. Bought up and closed down by Whitbread or somebody, one of the big "nationals" who don't give a shit about the national heritage.'

'But I guess it's necessary. I mean new homes and all that.'

'Necessary? It's about as necessary as a historian in an operating theatre. All this is being done just because some arsehole in Whitehall ten years ago, probably with a wodge of some building company's dosh in his pocket, decided Britain was going to have a housing crisis.'

'I thought most European countries' populations had levelled off.'

'They have. Single parents and divorcees, that's what they were supposed to be providing for. Predict and provide: destroying the country to cover up the fact that they've already destroyed society. And what are they building? Small, affordable starter homes and rural flat blocks? Not that they'd look any better, but at least they'd be useful.'

'But they're not?'

'Too straight, they're not. No money in building houses for poor people. Executive homes, that's where the profits are. Pretentious fucking follies with plastic Georgian pillars, double garages and postage-stamp back gardens.'

'And are there enough executives to fill them?'

'They're all filled with people like me and my parents,' said Therry bitterly. 'People who fled London in one generation and took their problems with them; fleeing the county towns in the next for that very reason.'

'*Suburbs in rure.*'

'What?'

'Hmm? Joke, sort of. *Rus in urbe*, you know, bringing the countryside into the city, what the old planners tried to do. Now it's the opposite. Almost.'

'Yeh. You know, you are something. An American who makes jokes in Latin.'

'Stop! Wait! You're going past the church.'

'I didn't think you needed spiritual solace. The Pig-Swill office is up the hill.'

'You brought me here to tell you a bit about the history? Well, here it is.'

'OK, professor, you're the boss.'

Therry drove the Range Rover up on a bank by the side of the road and climbed out, glancing up at the tower, where a few rooks perched on pinnacles, cawing disconsolately.

'Cheerful place.'

'It has its excuses.'

'Are you saying this goes back to the fourteenth century?'

'Oh, yeah, it certainly does. Not all of it, of course.

The Victorians tidied it up a bit, trying to make up for centuries of neglect. Look at those windows.'

Therry squinted at the plain panes set in the stone mouldings of the rose window. 'Not exactly spectacular.'

'They're relatively modern. End of the nineteenth century, probably, when the superstition had finally died away and the neglect got on somebody affluent's Christian conscience. The original would have had stained glass. Given that the whole village had probably worked for half a century building the church in the first place, there were scarcely funds to replace it. Over the years, the parishioners drifted back. But they didn't move back.'

'Until now.'

Daniel looked at her. 'Yes.'

The church door was open and they entered. As soon as their eyes adjusted to the gloom of the interior, dark in contrast even to the watery winter sunlight, Daniel, walking ahead, found it. Right across the nave and extending down both sides of the aisle, the spartan whitewash yielded to darker, deeper colours, russet, ochre and copper green, chipped and faded from what he imagined must have been their original brilliance, despite the unmistakable darkness of the theme.

'What are you looking at?'

'Come and see.' He pointed high up where small windows let oblique shafts of light penetrate the dark. 'It looks like someone let their kids draw all over the walls.'

Daniel looked at her. It was the sort of stupid comment that he'd expect from a tabloid journalist. He wondered if she meant it. Therry came closer and looked up, squinting in the feeble light.

'What is it?'

'It's a doom painting.'

It was. Like nothing she had ever seen before in a Christian church, let alone the Church of England, this belonged to another era entirely, an earlier religion, one almost unrecognisable. Therry stood and stared, spellbound, at the two-dimensional shapes that emerged despite their antiquity and centuries of neglect, from the painted plaster, with a hideous surrealism: elongated bodies, pale and naked, hanging from the bloody beaks of two-legged crimson creatures with the heads of eagles, while others fell into what looked like great cooking pots suspended over roaring fires with leaping flames that seared dangling limbs. And all of a sudden she recognised what she was looking at: 'the abandoned images of Damnation'. The sight that six and a half centuries earlier had pushed Edward Gray over the edge. A religious iconography based on terror. A terror that the people of Nether Ditchford, in that dark, chill winter of 1348–49, must have thought had come to visit them on earth. Hell on earth. She shivered.

'Did you know this was here?'

'Are you kidding? Since I found the text I've thought of little else. I've tried to photograph it but it doesn't work.'

'Is it unique?'

'Almost. There are a few other – murals used to be as common in England as in Italy, but the Reformation changed all that in this country. This is a rare record of a terrible time. More people should see it.'

How many people had, Therry wondered? The local folk, of course. Probably so used to it they didn't even see it any more. If you could ever get used to the sight of something like that. But few others. Nether Ditchford was not on the tourist maps, though if the philistines up at Riggs-Mill knew anything about it, it would probably feature in their advertising 'literature': 'amidst the attractions of this charming village is a most original and amusing painting in the local church'. They would probably hire someone to complete it. To add a few pictures and give it a happy ending. For that was what shocked her most about the mural: the total absence of a benign deity, even in the background. This was a painting designed to inspire fear, but it lacked one critical element, one that was central to Christianity: there was no saviour.

After a long moment she looked around for Daniel, but he had wandered off down the aisle to the far end of the church, underneath the bell tower.

'Here's something else.' She walked over towards him and noticed an old, weathered stone font, engraved with what looked to Therry like distinctly pagan images. Daniel was looking up at a big wooden board lovingly inscribed in flowing handwriting, black ink on old oak, with a list of names and dates going back hundreds of years. He was pointing to a series that began, amazingly, in the early thirteenth century.

'Why does it say Lincoln?'

'Because that was the diocese. Oxford didn't have a cathedral until Cardinal Wolsey in the sixteenth century. Back then all this area came under the bishop of Lincoln. That's who the priests here owed their living to. Look here. Can you find Father Gray?'

Therry tried to scan the old-fashioned script.

'Where? I don't see any mention of a Gray.'

'No.'

'So?'

'That's just it. Look at the dates.'

'Which dates?'

'How about using your brain as well as your eyes? I thought journalists were supposed to be observant.'

Therry gave an exasperated shrug, screwed her eyes up and scrutinised the entries for the fourteenth century:

'John de Godefroy 1320–1324
Simon de Castell 1324–1339
John Gasson 1339–1345
Edward Delaunay 1345–1348
Nicholas Ford 1348
John Franscombe 1360–1369
Simon Venab– oh! I see, there's a gap.'

'Precisely. From 1348, the year the plague began to worm its way into the heart of England. Nicholas Ford almost certainly died of it. But where's his successor?'

'Not until 1360. That's twelve years later.'

'Full marks for math. And no mention at all of Father Edward Gray.'

'So either they forgot him or your old manuscript's just a story; maybe he didn't really exist.'

'Oh, he existed all right. Anyway, if he didn't, why the gap?'

'You mean he was left out deliberately?'

'That's what it looks like, doesn't it? Of course it wasn't that rare for places to be left empty for several years in the 1350s. There simply weren't enough souls to care for in some places. But for a priest to be excised from the register . . . well, it's exceptional. As if he was purged.'

'Like in Stalin's day, when they retouched photographs to remove Trotsky and people like that.'

'Sort of. Just funny to find no one has ever reinstated him. After all these years.'

'Can I help you?'

A tall figure in white surplice had materialised behind Therry's back without her noticing it, and she jumped.

'Oh, I'm so sorry if I startled you. My name is Father Grey.'

She stared at Daniel, expecting him to be as spooked as she suddenly felt. But he had turned that beatific American grin on the tall, bald priest.

'David Grey. I'm the vicar of St Peter's. I didn't mean to disturb you, but I do like to offer my services, such as they are, to visitors. You aren't of the parish, I think?'

'No, we're just passing through, just taking stock of your history here.'

The vicar followed Daniel's gaze to the roster of his predecessors.

'Ah, the American gentleman,' he said to Daniel.

Daniel gave him the smile again. Most of the time it irritated the hell out of him that the English only had to catch the faintest twang of a North American accent to start treating him like a retarded child. Even if most of his countrymen did deserve it. But sometimes it paid to play along. The vicar was obviously a natural-born patroniser.

'So nice to see you again. We get a lot of people from the good ol' US of A, particularly in the summertime, when the weather is fine.' The latter half of the sentence was spoken with an intonation that made Therry wince. Was he quoting a pop song?

Daniel ignored it. 'Nice to see you too,' he said. 'By the way, I've been meaning to ask: I don't suppose you're any relation?'

'I'm sorry?'

'To the missing man? On your list here.'

Father Grey turned his attention back to the board. 'I don't think I quite follow.'

'No? This list is not as complete as it might be. There's

a gap there, back in the middle of the fourteenth century, as I'm sure you know.'

But it was hard to tell from Grey's smiling countenance, now crossed with the ghost of a perplexed frown, whether or not he did.

'Ah, yes, I see what you mean. I suspect just a gap in the records. These things happen, even in England, I fear.'

'Do they?'

'Well, yes. Don't they everywhere?'

Therry was convinced that, whatever game Daniel thought he was playing, the latter-day Father Grey knew nothing of it.

'You don't mean to tell me, Father, that you have no idea of the missing name?'

'I'm afraid I . . .' The conversation was not taking the turn the vicar had expected. This pair were obviously not about just to drop a couple of quid into the church restoration-fund collection box and buy a few postcards of the font and the west front.

'Your namesake, Father: Father Gray. He ran into a bit of trouble with the authorities, and with the locals – those that came back, that is, after the plague.'

'The plague? Oh, goodness me! Yes, I see what you mean. That would have been the Black Death. Terrible times! A Father Gray, you say? How interesting. I'm afraid I know nothing of him. I'm not as well up in these matters as I suppose I ought to be. Might I ask where you get this information from?'

'I'm a historian.'

'Indeed. In America? How fascinating!'

Yes, fascinating, isn't it, a historian in a country with no history? For a moment Daniel felt like punching the guy right in his smug English parochial puss. 'I'm at Oxford at the moment.'

'Ah?' The cleric's face brightened measurably. 'At which college, might I ask?'

'Magdalen.'

'Indeed, indeed. My bishop was at Balliol,' came the reply, as if this conferred some sort of academic cameraderie. 'I was at Bristol. The usual place for those who didn't quite make Oxbridge.' It was said with a thin smile, and Daniel felt it was easier not to reply.

'Theology?' asked Therry, more out of that English awkwardness in a conversational vacuum than any real interest.

'Maths. I joined the church later.'

'Well, at least you should see some increase in numbers at church, what with all the new building going on.'

'Yes, isn't it exciting?'

'You think so?' Daniel winced at the aggression in Therry's voice, and wondered if the vicar noticed it too. If he did, he gave no sign.

'Oh, absolutely! We have to move with the times, you know. Not that one can count on too many of them being churchgoers, of course, not in this sadly secular age. But one can always hope, can't one? And in any case, it will be nice to feel the church is in the centre of the village rather than stuck out here on one's own. And at last we'll be able to get rid of that silly name – St Peter's Alone, indeed! It sounds so sad. I've already asked the bishop, and I think he'll agree. We'll probably just go back to being plain St Peter's, though I have to say I would have liked to replace the adjective with something that reflected a bit more community spirit – St Peter's Among Friends, perhaps. Well, that doesn't sound quite right, does it? It's so hard to strike exactly the right note –'

'St Peter's Junction,' Daniel suggested with a look at

Therry, who found it hard to repress a snigger. 'For when they put the motorway through.'

'Very droll,' the vicar replied uneasily. Now you must excuse me, please, I have business to attend to. Not just a one-day-a-week job, you know, despite what some folk say. Good day to you.'

'Have a nice one, vicar,' said Therry, and Daniel frowned.

'No need to antagonise him. I thought you reporters were supposed to be better at hypocrisy.'

'We are. It's a career failing in me. I can't do it. And anyway, you were the one who came up with St Peter's Junction.'

'I couldn't resist it. The idea of people sanitising history annoys me.'

'Silly old wanker! The vicar, I mean. Not you.' And she blew him a facetious kiss as she headed for the door. 'Come on, let's see a bit more of the place before it gets dark.'

Outside, it seemed as if dusk was already approaching, though it was scarcely past midday. A great, purplish cloud hung over the ripped-up fields, darkening even the bright yellow of the diggers. Robbed of their Tonka-toy primary colours, they seemed more sinister. Daniel had to tell himself they were just machines, at the service of the men who owned them. For better or worse. He glanced up at the darkening sky. It looked as if it could rain at any moment, but it might not; English weather frustrated him with its unpredictability.

Daniel walked a few yards up the little path that threaded between the gravestones in the neatly kept churchyard. Therry watched him, tapping her foot impatiently, glancing up at the gloomy sky.

'What are you doing now?'

'Looking for skeletons.'

'What?' She loped over to his side. 'Seriously?'

'Not human ones. All around here –' he waved an arm that took in not just the little graveyard but the field beyond, part of which had not yet been claimed by the digging machines – 'there are traces of the early medieval buildings.'

'I was wondering about that. I mean, you say the whole village used to be here around the church, and then they all upped and left and moved down the road? If they were so keen to leave, they wouldn't have taken everything, would they? I mean, it's not as if, back in those days, they could jack their houses up on a truck and take them with them.'

'No.' Daniel smiled at the idea. Once in Texas he had seen six or seven houses moving in convoy down the freeway: literally a whole community on the move. 'No, you're quite right. Though their houses were mostly wooden. That's why there are so few traces left. Anyway, you have to remember, most of the people here didn't actually leave.'

'They didn't? I thought –'

'They died. The new village was founded by a handful of survivors who were joined by other stragglers, perhaps escaping a devastated community somewhere else. It took decades to recover; the best part of a century in some places.'

'So what are we looking for?'

'Ridges. Furrows. I'm no archaeologist, but it's mostly the foundations of the bigger buildings, such as they were, that leave traces. The wooden houses just rotted away, but there would have been one or two larger structures: a village hall of some sort, a granary maybe. Straight lines in the grass.'

'You mean like that?'

Daniel looked where she was pointing, beyond an

ancient-looking yew tree next to the low dry-stone wall that edged the churchyard. Sure enough, for about fifteen feet in a straight line the grass looked as if an old, worn, thick-pile blanket had been thrown over a toppled tree trunk.

'Come on, let's take a look!'

Closer to, the line was less obvious. The way we all end, he thought, leaving barely a trace.

'What would this have looked like? Back then?' Therry was asking. 'Would the road have been in the same place?'

'The road? Hardly.' Daniel tried to focus his imagination. What would the scene have looked like in the fateful spring of 1348, when the horrors to come were still unimagined? 'They wouldn't have had a road, not to speak of. There hadn't been any since the Romans had left, nearly a millennium earlier. People who talk of "progress" have short memories. There would have been a mud track, worn by human feet and the hooves of bullocks pulling carts that left ruts in the soft, damp earth. Horses would have been a rarity, for the villagers at least – the privilege of the nobility. At best the local reeve might have had one'.

'The what? Oh, yeah.' Therry suddenly remembered, and wondered what the place was like then, on that cold December day six and half centuries earlier, when the reeve, the local taxman, who probably thought himself a cut above the peasantry, fell choking and spluttering on the hard, cold earth, and died within the day.

She tried to remember she was supposed to be a journalist.

'Just how many people died here? Does anyone really know?'

'Not for sure. It's hard to be precise. Nobody kept

records of the common people. Most of the estimates of death during the plague are based on guesswork from such things as turnover of priests or local officials.'

'Like the reeve?' said Therry, showing off the latest acquisition to her vocabulary.

'Exactly. Anyway, as I say, much of it's guesswork. Plus we know roughly how many people a piece of farmed land could support. And there are pretty good indications of that sort of thing in England in the early Middle Ages, thanks to the Domesday Book.'

'I've often wondered, why did people call it that? This was before the plague, right? Way back in William the Conqueror's time, wasn't it?'

'More or less. Actually it was drawn up for his son William Rufus, around 1086. But that still puts it some two hundred and sixty years before the plague. No, it was more of a joke really: people thought it had so much information in it that it would do for God at the Day of Judgement. That's why they called it the 'Doomsday Book', though the name was probably only thought of later.'

'Like the Black Death.'

'Right.'

'So there's no way of cross-checking your Father Gray's story against some accepted historical record?'

'No. But there's no need really.' Daniel had been expecting something of this sort from other academics, but not from some provincial newspaper hack. 'There would have been no reason for him to lie. Besides, what he says is broadly in line with what we think we know happened to some villages. Based on Domesday Book data and the general expansion of the population between the eleventh and fourteenth centuries, it's not unreasonable to imagine a place like this with about one hundred and fifty inhabitants.'

'And nearly all of them dying. Just like that? It's not just a story, then. It all happened here.'

'That's what history's all about. I would have thought a journalist would have understood that.'

Therry ignored the comment. She pulled her coat around her. Just thinking of it was enough to send shivers down her spine. Quietly, without a word to Daniel, she walked over to the little churchyard wall, so carefully repaired and restored, and looked at the dark shapes on the other side of it. Just grassy knolls to the casual eye, but one of them no doubt once the home of Matthew the carter and his strapping sons and tiny babies, and old Ned and mad May; and somewhere under the turf lay the remnants of their bones. Was this Tinker's Field?

Or was it one of those on the other side of the road, with the yellow bulldozers and diggers? She thought of the great iron teeth ripping into the soil and tossing it to one side, and with it the pulverised bones of little Annie perhaps still wrapped in the long-rotted fibres of her altar cloth.

Chapter Seventeen

London to Oxford mainline; Sunday 21 December, 11.40 a.m.

IN HIS mind's eye he can see them still, as clear as a movie show in the private theatre of his conscious recall. Even as the icy English rain hammers on the railway-carriage window, he is in another place, at another time.

The children are running. Downhill. In the bright sunshine. Through the long grass and wild coriander that scents the air. And he is watching them as they run. And thinking. Dark thoughts.

At the brink of the little stream that runs so clear and fresh across the corner of the field, the oldest, or at least the largest of them, a tall girl of maybe twelve or thirteen years, with long legs and hair that reflects the sun like burnished jet, stops abruptly. Then, as one of the smaller boys, unable to stop himself, splashes into the water beside her, she laughs. A high, tinkling laugh like the sound of glass pebbles poured from a bag. And the boy shouts in wounded pride at being tricked and splashes her. And she squeals. A delicious high-pitched squeal of girlish pique and mock terror. A squeal that even at a distance reminds him uncommonly of the squeal of a pig having its throat cut.

The children, happily, are unaware of that uncomfortable analogy. They are all laughing now. Kicking their feet in the little stream. And squealing with delight as the cool water splashes on their suntanned arms and legs. For a moment – *this moment* – their world is perfect. A bubble of bliss, sparkling in the sunlight. So unlike the real world. The world they live in. Their world in particular.

Watching them, he heaves a heavy sigh and shakes his head. And turns the key in the ignition of his Toyota Landcruiser. The rumble of its engine momentarily distracts the playing children, who look around them for the source of this intrusion. They spot him, high on the crest of the hill, and wave. Gaily. For a moment, he almost waves back.

'Innocents,' he mutters to himself. 'Holy innocents,' and he crosses himself instinctively, for his upbringing assured that there is a religious side to Harold Hammerstein's dark, corrupted soul. And then, like any strict Catholic forced to reconcile his life with the teachings of Mother Church, he comforts himself by taking stock of the concept of original sin. For are we not all fallen?

And now another squeal intrudes. One that is altogether more torturous to his ears, the high-pitched grinding squeal of worn brakes slamming on and steel wheels grating to a halt on iron rails. And he emerges from his reverie, sitting up and opening his eyes with a start. He has arrived in Oxford.

Chapter Eighteen

Nether Ditchford building site, Oxfordshire;
Sunday 21 December, 1.15 p.m.

THE LONG, thin, triangular flags fluttered from their poles like the heraldic banners of an army. Or, Daniel thought, of some second-rate battlefield re-enactment society whose members had doffed their Lycra chain mail and retired inside their Portakabin until the rain eased off.

A red Honda Civic stood on a stretch of hard tack gravel that led from the metalled road through a field of frozen earth that under the now persistent downpour was rapidly thawing back into quagmire. A large painted sign declared the battle slogan of the invaders: 'Riggs-Mill proudly presents: NEW HOMES for the NEW MILLENNIUM.' It was as if the old millennium, most of recorded human history, had been forgotten. But then there was nothing more inevitable than the arrogance of the new. And nothing more banal. The sign, beneath the letters R and M entwined in vermilion on turquoise on the banners above, had all the gravitas of an ancient movie advertisement: 'Cecil B. De Mille proudly presents *The Ten Commandments*.' Daniel told Therry, who laughed a harsh, bitter little laugh he had come to recognise.

'Yeah. Number One: Thou shalst not crap all over the countryside.'

'Right,' said Daniel. Because that was the only thing

to say. And smiled. Because he wanted her to smile back. She did.

Therry pushed open the door to the Portakabin, thrusting them both suddenly out of the natural drama of wind, rain and lowering dark skies into a brightly lit world of curiously cosy fluorescence inhabited by a woman in a lime-green suit with ice-blond razor-cut hair and the sort of minimalist spectacles Therry had only ever seen on television ads for Finnish mobile phones.

'Hi,' she announced, 'I'm Melissa. What can I do for you folks?' Smiling as if there was nothing she could not imagine doing. Daniel wondered, not for the first time, why it was that half the British resented everything American, while the other half appeared obsessed with emulating its tackiest aspects.

'We're interested in your houses,' said Therry.

'Homes,' the woman corrected, stepping forward from behind her desk. 'We like to think of them as homes, even before they're built. A Riggs-Mill house is a home from the day the very first brick is laid, to the day when the lucky family crosses the threshold.'

Therry wanted to say 'Don't you mean breeze block rather than brick' but decided to hear out her spiel.

'I can tell you straight away –' Melissa was warming to her theme – 'that what we are building here is a community for the twenty-first century, homes with every up-to-the-minute amenity, but in a ready-made village environment with roots that go back centuries.'

Daniel silently wondered how much of Nether Ditchford's history Melissa was familiar with.

'Nice,' said Therry.

The saleswoman's smile iced over for just an instant. Therry thought she was trying to work out which of them she should focus on in order to clinch the sale.

'How soon do you reckon your first properties will be available?'

Daniel's accent did it. Melissa turned a hungry look fully on him.

'By the end of the summer, sir. Or might I know your first names?' A beam at Daniel and a supplicatory smile to Therry. 'We do pride ourselves here at Riggs-Mill on the friendly approach.'

'I'm Da–'

'Jeff,' Therry interrupted. 'Jeff and Mandy.' Mandy was a name she had always loathed. She added, for the sake of a spurious authenticity, 'Jeff and Mandy Somerville. We're just married.' She did her best to ignore Daniel's stare, reaching out to grab and squeeze his hand. 'He's still getting used to it. Aren't you, dear?'

'Great.' Melissa was in her element. 'We think you'll find no better place to start a family than right here, in a New Millennium home, in Lodestone Hollow.'

'In what?'

'Lodestone Hollow. That's what our new community –' Therry noted that she avoided the obvious words like "estate" and "development" – is going to be called.'

'Why?' Therry put in.

'I'm so glad you asked!' The answer had obviously been well rehearsed. 'The ground around here is supposed to be rich in ore. A lodestone used to be an astrological instrument, you know. It pointed to the stars. We like to think that young families like yourselves –' Melissa produced a stage blush on their behalf – 'will follow their stars with us.'

Therry smiled back. Thank your lucky stars that I don't brain you, you silly bitch. It was certainly one up on Black Death Crescent, or Bubonic Plague Park. She squeezed 'Jeff's' hand again, reassuringly. 'Isn't that romantic?'

Daniel looked from one beaming Englishwoman to the other in mystification.

'If you like, I can show you what they'll look like.' Melissa was already fetching a glossy brochure from a drawer in the desk. 'You'll note the high standard of internal specification. We at Riggs-Mill pride ourselves on producing the best. Of course, the weather is not exactly at its best at present, but you have to use your imagination.'

Daniel used his, and saw what Therry meant – the organic, often tortured, legacy of centuries carpeted over by a sterile suburbia that was neither town nor country.

Half an hour later Daniel and Therry emerged with fixed grimaces from the cosily lit artificial cocoon of the Riggs-Mill site office into the cold and mud of a field where the colour green would return only in the form of trimmed and manicured lawns. They bade goodbye to the effusive Melissa with a promise that they would be in touch as soon as possible. The only blight on Melissa's day was the fact that neither felt able to leave a contact address. 'We're moving about a bit at present,' Therry had parried, though when pressed for a telephone number she had unthinkingly given the *Post*'s newsdesk.

'I only hope she doesn't call it too soon. I can just imagine the ribbing I'll have to take from Henry if he gets it into his head that my "fiancé" and I are looking for a new "home", let alone one of Riggs-Mill's jerry-built abortions.'

'I didn't think they were that bad.' Daniel tried to play devil's advocate. There was, after all, something disconcertingly American about the planned homes.

'Oh, for God's sake, those things aren't homes – they're packaging.'

'Right,' he said.

Daniel climbed into the Range Rover. Therry swung up and into the driving seat and turned the key that let loose the crotchety old walrus under the bonnet. 'I need a drink,' she said.

Two minutes up the road, between shoulder-height hedgerows in the process of being ripped out for the eventual installation of pavements and streetlights, a couple of ancient cottages loomed out of the dusk. The Cotswold stone would have been honey-coloured in another light. Today it was simply grey. Even the well-kept thatched roofs looked dark and damp. There was no light to be seen from within. What must it have been like when they were built, Daniel wondered, probably some time in the seventeenth century? During the Civil War, when Cromwell was Lord Protector, England was the most democratic country in Europe, but also one of the most miserable to live in. What it had been like there three centuries earlier was almost beyond even Daniel's experienced imagination.

'There we are.'

A hanging sign, swaying slightly in the lashing rain and painted – extremely badly, Daniel could not help noticing – with what looked like a bushy-tailed rat grinning at two cartoon dogs, indicated they had arrived at the Fox and Hounds. Therry swung the Range Rover through a gateway into a low, walled courtyard that served as a car park. There were five or six other vehicles already parked there. Probably they did food at lunchtimes. Daniel suddenly realised he was starving. He looked at his watch. It was 2.15 p.m., almost certainly too late. If he knew his English country pubs, the kitchen would already be closed. They would end up having to share a bag of salty potato crisps or, worse still, the knobbly little bits of toughened congealed cholesterol that masqueraded under the name 'pork scratchings'.

The interior of the bar was more welcoming than Daniel had expected, with old settles in darkened oak and a huge inglenook fireplace stacked with smouldering logs. A group of men talking noisily at the long, gleaming copper bar glanced around at them as they entered, but quickly turned back to the bar again and, much to Daniel's relief, did not lapse into the intimidating silence that too often greeted strangers in the British countryside. At tables in the middle of the floor, two families were finishing a meal. One had a child of about three squirming on his seat, face covered with sauce. The barman, a big, ruddy-faced character with an impressive, almost Victorian set of side whiskers, looked at them and looked at his watch.

'You weren't looking for food, were you?'

Daniel shook his head with a smile intended to camouflage his acceptance of the inevitable.

'Actually,' said Therry, 'I could murder a sandwich. If you've still got something left, that is.'

The barman beamed. 'Well, now, I dare say Mary could rustle something up for you, miss. What'll it be now, salad, cheese or a bit of ham? Comes from the best Gloucester Old Spots, it does. I cure it myself. Unless of course you happen to be a vegetarian.'

'Not likely. Old Spot sounds super. With mustard, please. English.'

'No problem, miss. And . . . ?' The glance in Daniel's direction suggested he was wondering if Therry was the sort who catered for her menservants. Daniel nodded dumbly.

'Right then, two Old Spot sandwiches it is.' He disappeared into a doorway, presumably to prevail upon Mary's good graces.

'What are you drinking?' Therry turned to Daniel as the landlord returned.

'Hmm? A pint of Hook Norton, please.' He recognised with delight the name of one of Oxfordshire's more distinctive local brews on the hand pumps.

'One of them, and a pint of Foster's for me.' (Therry was a lager girl, she had told him in the King's Arms the night before. 'A bit naff, I know, but I like the fizz. Anyway, it's what you Americans are supposed to drink. We're an odd couple, aren't we?' And he had had to agree that they were, wondering what, if anything, she meant by the word 'couple'.)

'Just passing through then?' said the landlord as he poured their beers.

'Actually, we were looking at the site for the new houses.'

'Oh. Them. I see.'

'You don't sound too keen.'

'Well, not really, you know. But it's not my business, I suppose. Thinking of buying, are you?'

'No.' Daniel was surprised at her directness. She took a sip of lager. 'Frankly, I think they're awful. But I'm interested in what people in the village think.'

The big man behind the bar glanced at his other customers. 'Well, go ahead, ask them. Why don't you tell her, Harry?'

A short man with dark hair and a sallow complexion turned round on his barstool and glared at the landlord.

'You tryin' to wind me up, Frank? You know damn well what I think. I think there's no harm in progress. And if a few people in this village are out to stop it, then they're damn fools. What's worse, they're mean-minded fools. More envy than anything. That's what drives you lot. And anyone of you'd do the same. Thank you very much, mate.'

He downed the last of his beer, pushed back his stool, grabbed a denim jacket from a hook by the back door and stormed out into the car park.

'Was it something I said?' Therry turned back to the barman, noticing a sly smirk cross his face behind the whiskers.

'Never mind, miss.' A tall man in a checked sports jacket, one of those who had been in conversation with Harry before the interruption, set his glass down on the bar and addressed himself to the man on the other side. 'You were a bit out of line there, Frank. You know how he gets.'

'Yer, maybe I was an' all. But it's about time he got a bit of what he's due. You know what folks around here think about them damn houses.'

'He's in favour of them?' Therry looked to the faces on either side of the bar. She hadn't intended to start an argument, but a row in a village community was always good copy for the *Post*.

'Aye, you might say that.'

'Well, he would be, you see, miss,' said the man in the checked jacket. 'You see, it's his land they're being built on. Made a nice tiny packet, has our Harry, and stands to make a bit more if the next phase goes ahead.' Turning back to Frank on the other side of the bar: 'He'll sell Lone Meadow too if he can, and it looks like he can all right. They'll buy whatever's going now that the plan to link the two villages is going to get the go-ahead.'

'Aye, Milton fucking Keynes it'll be. All roundabouts and one-way systems, Wordsworth Ways and Coleridge Closes inhabited by stockbrokers and such. An' their hooligan kids.'

'Maybe, maybe. You know the way I feel. Couldn't agree more. But he's got a point about the money, he has. It's a terrible temptation. Would be to anybody. Stands to reason.'

'How much will he make from it?' asked Daniel, entering the conversation for the first time.

'How much? What do you think, Frank? Six acres. I heard he got more than £75,000 an acre when he sold, this time last year. That comes to close on half a million nicker.'

'Aye, and the rest if he flogs off the meadow. Reckon it's worth even more now. He must be worth half a million easy, maybe a million if it all goes through. English money, mind.'

Daniel took the oblique reference as the customary indication that his accent had been recognised. He whistled under his breath. In dollars, what did that make? Close on a million. Yes, he could imagine Harry might be in favour. And he could imagine that one or two of his fellow villagers had indeed succumbed to the sin of envy.

'What'll it buy him, though? Happiness?' A third man, elderly, with a flat tweed cap and a grimy-looking waxed jacket, joined in.

'Well, it won't buy him the right to be rude in my pub,' said Frank.

Daniel wondered if he was the only one thinking that it had not been Harry's rudeness that started the row, at least not on this occasion.

'Might not need to. Might buy you out, Frank. Think of that,' said the tall man.

'Won't buy me out. Have to carry me out.'

'They just might do that an' all.'

Therry changed the subject. 'Is there much contact between local people and the workmen?'

'On the site, you mean?' Frank leaned over the bar, seriously considering the question. Therry nodded. 'Not much. Not really. Would you say, Ted?'

Ted, in the sports jacket, shook his head.

'One or two of them go into the shop from time to time, to buy a packet of fags or a copy of the *Sun*. Don't get 'em in here, though, but then I've that sign up, one on the door too.' He nodded up at the beams just above their heads, where Therry read: 'Sorry. No workclothes or dirty boots in the bar area please.'

'I won't say I put it up deliberate-like, but I don't want to encourage 'em. Not got anything to do with how I feel about the new houses, though I don't like 'em, I can tell you. And I don't mind the odd walker comin' in with muddy boots, as long as they give 'em a wipe, mind. That's what you expect in the country. But I didn't want the place turnin' into a navvies' local. Not before it has to.'

'You don't know a man called Charlie Atkins, then?'

There was a general shaking of heads.

'Who's he, then?'

'Worker on the building site. Now he's in hospital.'

'Accident?' There was more *Schadenfreude* than genuine concern in the big man's voice. As if Frank's only worry might be that Atkins had tripped over in the pub garden and was going to sue him.

'Not exactly. He's very sick.'

'Oh, well, I'm sorry to hear that. I always hate to hear of folks taking poorly.'

'He's more than poorly. He's got bubonic plague.' Therry dropped it into the conversation deliberately, like a stone into a goldfish pond. She wanted to watch the ripples and see if anyone darted for cover.

'Bloody heck!' said Frank. 'Plague? Like in the Bible? He hasn't infected anybody around here, has he? I thought that died out donkey's years ago.'

'Not in some parts of the world. They think he picked it up in the Middle East. There's almost no chance he could have passed it on to anybody here. He was only back on the site for a day, they say.'

'Oh, well, fancy that! Can't say I ever get much further than Spain myself. Went to Greece last year, though. Still, poor bloke. God help us!'

'That's what they said last time.'

'What's that, love?'

'The last time they had the plague around here. Only then they called it the Black Death.'

Daniel almost laughed. She had played the line for effect, and got it. Now the attention of the whole group at the bar was focused on her. Frank was staring.

'Isn't that a bit melodramatic, miss?' The elderly man in the cap and waxed jacket was looking astutely at Therry. 'Or is that why you're here, then?'

'What you on about, Bob?' Frank was clearly not an expert on local history. The man he called Bob, however, was.

'They've been down at the church. I saw their Range Rover down there earlier. You were having a bit of a look around, weren't you?' he said to Daniel. 'Where the old village was. *Nether* Ditchford, as was. Hundreds of years ago, Frank. Before your time.'

The others laughed.

'So, come on then,' said the man called Bob, focusing his shrewd eyes on Daniel, 'you weren't interested in buying one of the new houses. So what are you interested in?'

It was time to own up, Therry realised. 'Actually I'm a reporter, from the *Oxford Post*.'

She watched their faces close as she said it, except for Bob, who smiled a not unfriendly 'I thought as much' smile. She felt obliged, as she so often did, to explain further, to put them at their ease. 'But don't worry, I'm not going to quote anybody. At least not unless it's all right with them. It's not even for a story, necessarily. Just thought it was an interesting coincidence and all that. And there has been a bit of opposition to the new houses out here. Hasn't there?'

But it was too late. Already she sensed that she'd gone on too much. She always did. Never managed to worm her way into people's confidence, the way reporters did in the movies and some of her colleagues at the *Post* seemed to. But then they were blokes, mostly. Maybe it was a bloke thing.

The blokes at the bar were still looking at her and smiling, but with fixed politeness.

And then, unexpectedly, the man in the cap moved forward and took her arm. 'Oh, you're right, 'course you are. Just some of these folk are a bit bashful when it comes to the media, but I'll have a chat with you.' He pulled back, then held out his hand for her to shake. 'Bob Thatcher. And before you can ask, no, no relation. No more related to *her* than to the Queen. But then who knows, eh? Way back!'

Chapter Nineteen

*The Fox and Hounds, Upper Ditchford,
Oxfordshire; Sunday 21 December, 2.40 p.m.*

'WHY DON'T we sit down over here by the fire?
What remains of it anyhow.' This with an askance
look in the direction of Frank the landlord that suggested
an extra log would be an extravagance they could not
hope for. 'You tell me what you want to know, and I'll
help you if I can. I'm afraid we've lost most of the battle
here, but a bit of a good word in the press never did any
harm, eh?'

'No. Indeed.' Therry smiled. Nervously, Daniel thought.
Perhaps a welcoming reception was not what she was
used to.

They sat down at a round table by the edge of the
inglenook. The thick oak beam over the great hearth
was decorated with a few gleaming ornamental horse
brasses, the usual nick-nacks of English country pubs.
Daniel could not help wondering again what it would
have been like when the place was built back in the
seventeenth century. When this great walk-in fireplace
would have been the building's sole source of heat
and instead of glowing embers it would have been
filled with a roaring fire that kicked out smoke and
sparks in all directions, blackening the wood and searing the ruddy faces of the men who clustered around
it. Ruddy faces that he reflected were probably not
really all that different, come to think of it, from those

that watched them now above their pints of ale at the bar.

None of the others had offered to join them, as if going off with Bob to be inducted into the mysteries of the Ditchford anti-development movement was a dangerous process that they were reluctant to associate themselves with in public. Or maybe they had just heard it all before.

'From what you said, I gather that there's still some debate about how many houses they're going to build.'

'They'll build as many as they can, won't they?' It was said with a tone that struck Daniel as somewhere between bitterness, resentment, cynicism and resignation.

Therry shrugged. Yes, she thought, of course they will; the bastards are only in it for the profit. But I want you to tell me. 'Not much local support then?' she said.

Bob raised a sceptical eyebrow. 'What for?'

'Houses,' Daniel jumped in, much to Therry's surprise. 'I thought there might be some enthusiasm in the village for new homes. Somewhere for local kids when they leave home so's they wouldn't all move off to the towns.'

Bob sniffed loudly; snorted, almost. 'Bollocks,' he said.

'I'm sorry?'

'Bollocks is what I said, with apologies to your young lady here –' Daniel ignored the possessive – 'but what they's building is not for local folks. Three- four- and five-bedroom "executive" homes with double garages. Though God knows what they expect to execute around here. Hah!' He laughed at his own gallows humour. 'Hanging's too good for 'em.

'Look here, there's a few things you ought to know. First of all, most of the young folks around here move out anyway. Some 'cause there ain't the work, some because it's only natural – that's what kids do: fly the nest. But there's some too, particularly the girls, who might stick around but don't 'cause there ain't no affordable houses for 'em, like you say. But we went to the planning-committee meeting and said that, and you know what they told us?'

Daniel and Therry both shook their heads at the same time.

'That there was a provision in the plans all right for "affordable" homes for local kids. So we asked how many. Did they give us a figure? Did they bugger; they gave us a percentage. Thirteen per cent to be precise. But you know how many they build in reality? Bugger all. That's how many. And you know why? Because there ain't no money in it. Not real money, the sort they're interested in.

'You know how many new houses the government want to put up in the southeast of England in the next dozen years or so?'

Therry nodded. She knew only too well. Daniel, however, hadn't a clue.

'One bloody million. That's how many. Think about it.'

Daniel thought about it. He wasn't sure where this was getting them.

'How many folk in a house? Two? Three? Four? What's that give us? The population of southern England growing by a minimum of two million?'

'But if it is growing fast, then they've got to have somewhere to live, haven't they?' said Daniel, surprised to find he had taken on the role of devil's advocate.

'But it's not, lad, is it? The bloody population isn't growing at all. Not naturally. Ask yourself. You two, for example, got any kids?'

'No, no,' Daniel stammered, flustered by the assumption. He glanced at Therry but she had paid no attention; she was fixed on Bob. 'We're, uh, not –' he began.

The other man waved the interruption away. 'Don't matter none. Lots o' folks have kids what ain't married. Always have done. That's not the point. How old are you? Twenty-five, thirty maybe, I don't know. But I know one thing. Thirty years ago, you'd have had kids by now.'

Therry smiled politely.

'Now, you look at 'em. Women with careers, whatever – I don't say it's right nor wrong, mind, but they's not havin' kids afore thirty, even thirty-five. And how many do they have, at that age? One. Two, maybe. Am I right? Go on, miss, you have a think about it. How many of your friends have had babies? How many will? And how many will they have? How many folk do you know nowadays who have three kids or more?'

Involuntarily, not wholly sure where this was leading, Therry found herself doing the calculation. There was Louise who'd had an abortion last year; but that hardly counted. Babies were something other people had, except that, come to think of it, Therry didn't know any of her contemporaries who had any. They belonged in Neverneverland, some time in the future. A future that was too hard to imagine, in the perpetual present. But it was true what this old boy was saying, even if she couldn't see the relevance: even among her mother's generation, there were fewer big families than there used to be. The pill had changed all that back in the 1960s.

'I don't see how this relates –' Daniel tried. But Old Bob wasn't having any of it.

'The point, for crying out loud, is that the population not only isn't growing, it's shrinking. We're not even replacing ourselves any more. Not exactly a national disaster. Probably a good thing in the long run. Too many bloody people in the world as it is. But we don't need more houses eating up countryside that's scarce enough, if we haven't got more people . . .'

'But you have,' said Daniel. 'I mean, they aren't making these figures up exactly, are they?'

'Aren't they? You tell me then, if all these people aren't being born here, where the hell are they coming from?'

Whoops, thought Daniel. Here we go. That's what this is about: any moment now Bob is going to launch into a tirade, blaming all the country's woes on immigrants.

He was wrong. 'They're coming from up north, that's where.' He pronounced it 'oop nawf' in the familiar southern English imitation of a northern accent. 'Don't have no jobs up there. Worse than here. So those as is better trained or got the qualifications or whatever, they come down here, get commuter jobs in Oxford or Banbury at one o' them high-tech businesses, computer stuff and mobile phones and what have you . . .' Therry self-consciously reached out and withdrew her Motorola from the edge of the table.

'. . . and then buy one o' these here executive homes, commute in their big cars, clog up the lanes, demand kerbs and street lights, complain about horse shit and church bells, and before you know it – instant suburbia,' Bob concluded triumphantly, bringing his hand down on the little table with a crash that made their pint glasses jump. 'And it's not only the northerners, is it?'

Daniel knew better than to engage with the flow of rhetorical questions. He wondered how many village-hall meetings, how many planning committees, had been subjected to Bob Thatcher's practised outpourings.

'The government says we need more houses because the number of households is set to increase, what with all the divorces and unmarried pregnancies. Never mind the fact that single mothers are hardly in the market for four-bed executive homes. The true tragedy in what they're saying is that we're turning into a nation of sad, selfish, solitary gits. And what's the government doing? Encouraging it! The family's not "modern" any more, and "modern" is what those berks in Downing Street care about. As if whatever happened last was best. Nazism was pretty damn modern in the 1930s, and Winston Churchill, by contrast, was an old codger living in the imperial past; but we know which one we'd rather have in charge.'

Daniel nodded, despite himself. He hadn't thought about it like that, put it in so many words. But it was what he had been thinking when he saw the site contractor's mock-heraldic pennants and pompous sign: the arrogance of the new.

'An' what's worse is that they not only don't see that, they think they know better. That affluence is the answer to everything: central heating, two cars and who gives a hang that there's nowhere to go to because everywhere looks the same.

'Pretty soon we're all going to be living in a landscape that's about as exciting as a bloody visit to the super-market. Just like nobody wants to go to a proper butcher and buy proper meat, because it looks like it might actually be part of a dead animal rather than a piece of squared-off shrink-wrapped pink stuff, so we don't want the country to look like country any more, even our blessed overmanaged English countryside; oh, no, what we want is prepackaged, processed countryside, with all the richness and magic of bloody cheese slices.'

Bob sat back, his face flushed, whether from the fire of his obvious emotion or the heat of the fire was hard to tell. Frank had defied expectation by putting an extra log on after all, perhaps only for the chance to eavesdrop, and there was now a steady lick of flame darting up the inglenook.

'But there's still some land on the market?' Therry asked, bringing the conversation back under some semblance of control.

'Aye,' Bob conceded wearily. 'Lone Meadow. Another of Harry Turner's fields.'

'Funny name, Lone Meadow.'

'Aye. It is that. It's near the church, you see.' As if that explained everything.

'St Peter's Alone.'

'That's her.' Bob was eyeing her closely. 'But if you've been down there, it's my guess you already know a bit of our history.'

'You mean why the village moved?'

Bob nodded.

'The plague. The Black Death?'

He nodded again.

'That's why I wanted to speak to you. What you said about that man, one o' them builders, what was taken into hospital. Was that serious?'

'Very serious,' said Daniel. 'The man's critically ill.'

'No, that's not what I meant. Is it seriously . . . you know, the plague?'

Daniel nodded slowly, watching the effect of his confirmation on the man opposite. Bob Thatcher sat back and closed his eyes as if uttering a silent prayer, though from his expression it was hard to tell whether it was uttered in horror or thanksgiving.

After a minute he opened his eyes again and stared into the fireplace. Then, still saying nothing, he picked up a cast-iron poker and began to rearrange the burning wood, turning up the the half-consumed new log so that its burnt surface faced upwards, glowing incandescent red and orange like pictures Daniel had seen of lava flows. Or artist's impressions of the fires of hell. The older man stared into it.

'You know what they are, don't you? They're devils.'

'What do you mean?' asked Therry.

Bob turned back from the fire to direct a question to both of them. 'What do you know of Russian literature?'

To Therry it was a complete *non sequitur*, though the American was nodding strangely, as if he had some inkling of what the old boy was on about. Sensing the reaction, Bob was now talking to him.

'Have you read Gogol?'

'*Dead Souls*,' Daniel replied.

'That's it. Best bloody book in the world. One of 'em, anyhow. Remember what it's about?'

'It's a confidence trick. Something to do with accounting in the old Russian empire, when they still owned serfs – people measured their wealth in them. And if they died between censuses, they were still considered "on the books", as it were.'

'That's right, and what does our man do?'

Daniel was searching his memory. It was his mother who had introduced him to Nikolai Gogol, who, she had said, was not only a great writer but had a visionary's insight into the true nature of the world.

'He bought them up.'

'That's right. Rich folks thought he was crazy, paying good money for a list of names of the dead. But they weren't dead on the government's accounts. He made himself a wealthy man when he took out a vast mortgage based on this imaginary human fortune. It was an absurdity. A madness, dealing in the souls of the departed, like building houses for people who don't exist, creating an imaginary population explosion for the sake of profit. Like the madness that overtook old Gogol in the end. You remember what he called his hero, how he described him, I mean?'

Daniel nodded. 'The devil in a frock coat.'

Bob smiled triumphantly, as if he had been unexpectedly vindicated. 'Exactly. And what is our modern equivalent of a frock coat? Hmm? A bloody pinstripe suit, that's what. Just like the one worn by Geoffrey bloody Martindale.'

'Who?' asked Therry.

'The chairman of Riggs-Mill, that's who. The devil incarnate – just because he doesn't have horns and a forked tail, don't think he isn't. I had thought that wreaking irreversible damage on God's landscape was enough for him, that ruining the habitats of the Lord's creatures and carpeting the good earth with concrete would have satisfied him. But I should have realised. Oh, no, now he's brought back the great scourge of humanity! The plague prophesied in the Book of Revelations! A bit late perhaps, but then the Beast was never one to stick to a timetable. There will be more than one death to come out of this. Many more, you wait and see.

'And just remember, you heard it here first. You know where to find me. Good afternoon to you.'

Daniel and Therry sat stunned as Bob Thatcher got up stiffly and turned, without a nod even to his erstwhile drinking companions at the bar, and walked out. One or two of the men, Daniel thought, were shaking their heads.

Chapter Twenty

Oxford; Sunday 21 December, 3.30 p.m.

T HERE IS something inherently unpleasant about the
smell of latex. Especially when it has been treated
with a lubricant, even if, as in this case, it is of the
dry, chalky, carbon-based variety, rather than the more
common oleaginous alternative.

Such were the thoughts going through the head of the
occupant of room 12 in the Royal Oxford Motel, a dull
but respectable establishment just a few minutes' walk
from the station, as he stretched a surgeon's glove over
his left hand and then, with only slightly more difficulty,
repeated the procedure for his right.

He stood back and looked at himself in the full-length
mirror and could not contain a smirk of rare amuse-
ment running like an undercurrent through his general
irritation. The impression was somewhere between the
preposterously absurd and the elegantly sinister: a well-
dressed businessman sporting a new designer fashion
in evening opera gloves perhaps. Seen from a medium
distance, the latex moulded to his fingers like a second
skin, giving him all the appeal of an albino reptile.

He could almost have laughed, had he been the
sort of man who was used to seeing jokes at his
own expense. Many another, however, would have
shuddered. Especially when, for the sake of knowing
how it felt, he pulled the white mask across the lower half
of his face. Under other circumstances this might merely

have increased the surgical character of his appearance, but it was not made of soft fabric but hard, ribbed white cellulose, and in combination with his plain dark Armani business suit the overall impression was altogether different. No one would have been tempted to describe the vision that looked back at him from the hotel-room mirror as reassuring. But then dispensing reassurance was not part of his job description.

The mask was the best, he had been assured. Simpler versions were worn by cyclists in smog-laden cities; similar versions by men operating grass strimmers; and some, with more serious filters incorporated in them, were used by firefighters working in chemical blazes. In contrast to the facial coverings worn by surgeons, the purpose was not to keep germs from escaping the wearer's mouth, but to prevent them reaching it. Or any part of the skin it covered.

This particular version, he had been assured, had been developed for use in the most extreme emergency situations. The main customer for the product was the active deployment unit of the Centers for Disease Control, based in Atlanta, Georgia. It had been used, and proved 99 per cent effective, in the most recent, and quickly contained, outbreak of the lethal Ebola virus near the Liberian town of Vaijima. So successful had the containment exercise been on that occasion that the world's media, and even most of the local population, had remained unaware of the outbreak. The deaths of an entire village had been put down to just another clash between government and rebel forces. Politics, and common sense, had ensured that few questions were asked about the victims' speedy cremation.

The figure of 99 per cent should, of course, have been worrying. Anything less than 100 per cent, particularly in the circumstances, was less than ideal. But then the world was less than ideal. Always had been. Always would be. Miranda had proved that.

He stood back and looked at himself. The obvious advantage lay in total unrecognisability. All the more so when he donned the close-fitting protective eye goggles. From the special sachet within his crocodile-leather briefcase he extracted a latex hood, supplied by the same source and designed to cover the rest of his head and face, completing the total protection he had been advised was desirable. He decided against trying it on, however. The thing looked efficient enough, but would undoubtedly be extremely uncomfortable to put on and take off, let alone wear for more than a few seconds. He hoped that, when the time came, that would be all that was needed.

Some things were necessary in the line of duty. But he grimaced at the thought of it. When fully attired, it struck him suddenly, he would look as if he'd been fitted with a whole-body condom. It was an obscene but comical analogy. Harald Hammerstein had never worn a condom in his life. For one thing, it was against his religion.

Chapter Twenty-One

Upper Ditchford, Oxfordshire; Sunday 21 December, 4.00 p.m.

'Now I've heard everything,' said Therry, clambering into the front seat of the Range Rover. 'A lesson on Russian literature in the snug of the Fox and Hounds. What is it you do to people, Dan?'

He looked at her quizzically. 'All that stuff about *Dead Souls*, you mean? I haven't read it in years.'

Therry looked at him askance. 'Hey, don't knock it: you'd read it. You know, you're a real Renaissance man, Dan.'

'It's Daniel,' he muttered, though he knew she was teasing him.

'But what did he mean: "the devil in a frock coat"?'

'Hmm? Oh, just that evil isn't always what it seems to be. That as well as being something big and frightening, it can be something mean and nasty that corrodes the quality of life. Like greed, for example.'

'Yeah, for example,' she said, looking out the window at the digging machinery arrayed across what had once been fields.

'Was he right? I mean, about all these houses being built purely for speculative gain?'

'Pretty much. It's certainly not for the purpose of housing the homeless. The government and the developers wave statistics about – "predict and provide", they call it – but all anyone really knows is that the land is lost for ever. And a lot of people get very rich as a result.'

'How rich?'

'I dunno. I can find out, though. Agricultural land's worth next to nothing since the farming crisis, while house prices in the southeast just keep on rising. The people running this development stand to make a fortune. And probably not a small one.'

'Large enough not to let anything stand in its way?'

'Like covering up the fact that you'd accidentally unearthed dormant six-hundred-year-old plague bacteria? That, Dan my man, is, as they say, the sixty-four-million-dollar question.'

Therry started up the engine.

'Where are we going?'

'I'm taking you home, little boy. But first we're just going to stop off and take one last look at the site of our dream home.'

Daniel sighed.

'Right,' he said. Because, once again, it seemed the only thing to say.

The mock-heraldic pennants still fluttered in the growing dusk, their lanyards clattering against the flagpoles. The Portakabin was in darkness, but the big sign was still illuminated. The drizzle danced in the beams of the spotlights. Like Sleeping Beauty's castle at Disneyland, Daniel thought. The advertising hoardings a simplified symbol of an off-the-shelf dream.

What interested Therry was the rest of the site, the vista of devastation that extended across the fields and almost down to where the tower of St Peter's Alone stuck up like a broken tooth in the darkening sky.

'Shit! I don't believe this!'

'What now?'

'It's an electric fence. A fucking electric fence!'

Therry was standing a few yards away and Daniel could just make out the wire that ran behind her at the level of her waist.

'What? Well, don't touch it, for God's sake.'

'Too late, I already have. How do you think I know it's electrified? Don't worry, it won't fry you. It's just the level most bolshy farmers around here put up to keep their cattle in, but it's one hell of a cheek putting it up in an area where people are walking about.'

'Maybe it's just intended to keep animals from wandering into the building site. Anyway, I suppose we're technically on their land here. I mean, the site entrance is back there. And it does say –'

'Listen, sunshine, I know what it says. Well, at least I can imagine. But until they've bloody concreted over the whole countryside, I intend to walk where I will. Ever hear of the right to roam?'

Daniel had, vaguely. But he suspected that the law of trespass still applied. He reached out in alarm when he saw Therry produce a small torch and a pair of rubber-handled wire-cutters from the pocket of her bright-yellow waterproof.

'Hey, hang on a minute! Do you always carry burglarising equipment on you?'

'Tools of the trade. Come on, it's dark already, and we've got to get back to Oxford.'

'Exactly, so why are we . . .' But it was too late. She was through the wire, and beckoning him to follow her.

'For God's sake, Therry, this is trespass! What if someone . . . ?'

She shushed him with her finger. 'We're not stealing anything,' she whispered. 'Now come on, I just want to see if there's any sign . . .'

'Of what?'

'Of these bloody JCBs having dug up a medieval graveyard.'

Oh, great! Daniel thought. It's freezing cold, dark, and she's looking for a plague pit. There must be easier ways of getting a date.

'Ssshh,' said Therry, with a sudden urgency in her voice. 'Don't move! Do you hear that?' she whispered.

Daniel listened but could hear nothing, except maybe a rustle like a wind in dry leaves. Therry turned off her little torch and at first the absence of its narrow white beam cutting through the darkness blinded them. Gradually their eyes began to readjust. And pick out the eyes staring back at them. Not just one pair but four or five, no, a dozen or more. Tiny red eyes, almost luminescent in the dark. With a sinking heart, Daniel realised what he was looking at.

'Point your torch directly at them. And turn it on. Now!'

Immediately there was a frantic scuffling and a high-pitched squeal, matched only by Therry's own shriek as the beam played on the spectacle of a gyrating mass of fur, grey, brown and black. The one thing she had dreaded finding, yet, if she were honest, the one thing she had half been looking for: a swarm of rats.

'You there!' A voice, loud, masculine, aggressive, used to being obeyed, boomed out of the darkness. Daniel and Therry spun around, thrown off guard by the squeaking rodents scurrying past their feet.

Coming out of the newly fallen night were dark figures. Walking towards them steadily, purposefully, plague zombies emerged from the pit. And then a light. Bright. Blinding. Not so much a torch as a search-light, shone directly in their eyes. 'Stop! Don't go any further.'

Shading her hand with her eyes, Therry could make out, behind the powerful glare of the halogen flashlight, the shapes of two men in some sort of uniform, and a very large dog, snarling as it strained at its leash.

'What are you doing here?'

Therry bristled 'I might ask you the same thing.'

The moment of blind terror, when she had half fallen victim to superstition, and then the moment of more rational fear when she envisaged a pair of thugs on the lookout for some vulnerable sport, had passed. She knew what these characters were, with their mutt on a lead and their self-important attitude: private security guards. Private security guards and an electric fence? Riggs-Mill were pushing their privilege. And had something to hide.

'We're asking the questions.'

Therry tittered.

'Something funny, miss?'

'No. I'm sorry. I just can't believe you said that.'

The movement of the flashlights revealed that she had dented the macho armour.

'Anyway, take your damn searchlights out of my eyes. I can't talk to someone I can't see properly.'

Abruptly the beams fell. Therry found herself looking at the spectrally underlit faces of two hulking specimens squeezed into fetish uniforms. These were midnight blue with some sort of animal logo and the words 'Cerberus Security' emblazoned in gold on their shoulders.

'So what are you doing here?'

'Walking.'

'Very funny, miss, I'm sure.' Therry realised that this man was an ex-plod who couldn't shake the station-house dialogue. Therry knew the type. She'd had enough experience of it as a teenager, hauled into the station on a Saturday night after some fracas outside the disco: the phony politeness, the mock humility. The more genteel they got, the more the bastards were planning to stuff you. She gave him her best saccharine and strychnine smile through the rain and the torchlight.

'I meant, what were you doing here?' the man repeated.

'And I meant what I said,' Therry answered. The glue fixing her smile to her face was slipping. 'We were out for a walk. Having a look round. No harm in that, is there?' She felt Daniel's hand on her arm, reducing the aggression in her voice.

'I didn't say there was, miss. Just it's getting dark, you know. Don't see too many folks about. Especially on a night like this. And this is private property, y'know.'

The younger man at his side had let the expression on his face slip from a snarl to a sneer. More of a leer, really, his eyes sliding the length of Therry's body, taking in the tight trousers. Daniel was pulling at her sleeve. Time to go.

'That what the electric fence is for then?' Damned if the bastards thought they could get away with treating them like trespassers. 'It's illegal that, you know.' She wondered if it was. 'Putting up a fence like that, without a warning. Bloody dangerous.'

'There is a warning, miss. If you'd look.' He gestured with nod of the head off to his left, into the dark drizzle. Daniel glanced in that direction and saw a metal plate with some writing on it and the head of a particularly vicious-looking dog.

'Had some trouble, we have, you see, miss. Vandalism, theft of tools, that sort of thing. If you know what I mean.'

Daniel nodded. The responsible citizen. 'I understand, officer.'

Therry reeled back, gawping at him. Calling this jerk

an officer! Just because he had a Toytown uniform on. But she felt his grip on her arm. Avoiding an incident. Getting out of the situation. Wimping out, she called it. Bloody academic with no balls.

'We'll be off then, won't we?' he said, pulling her physically backwards, out of the torch beams.

'That's it, sir. Don't want you and the young lady catching your death now, do we. Mind how you go.'

Fuming and shivering, Therry allowed herself to be led back to where the bulk of the Range Rover marked the edge of the road. The torch beams followed them, lighting the way, and then vanished, their owners obviously preferring to continue their prowl in the dark.

Chapter Twenty-Two

*Magdalen College, Oxford; Sunday, 21
December, 7.00 p.m.*

DESPITE THE icy sleet that pelted him as he climbed
out of the Range Rover, Daniel was in remarkably
good humour as he waved goodbye and hurried into
the shelter of Magdalen's gatehouse. He was not put
out of it even by the surly glance shot him by the head
porter, who seemed to think anyone entering or leaving
the college a nuisance and distraction from his winter
pastime of toasting his toes by a small electric fire.

So what if she was going to make a newspaper story
out of it? She'd agreed to keep him and Rajiv out of
it, to ring the Radcliffe herself for official comment,
and, after all, as he had rationalised earlier, the hospital
would hardly try to cover up a serious illness, even if
they might be a bit reticent about giving out details of
a particular patient. Her far-fetched link to the building
works was just tabloid journalism and unlikely to do
any real harm, even to the building company's fortunes.
Besides, as she'd said, once the paper's lawyers had
trampled all over it, there was not likely to be much that
was controversial left. She was just using a coincidence
as an excuse to give her readers an all-too-rare history
lesson, and if the paper's leader writers wanted to take
it up to rail against overdevelopment in the countryside,
well, that was fair comment, wasn't it?

Daniel couldn't care less. His escapade at the Radcliffe

had turned out better than he could ever have anticipated: not only had he got his look at the patient –
he shuddered at the memory – but he had made a
friend. And with a bit of luck, more than a friend, he
allowed himself to imagine fondly. Unseeing, he gazed
up at the pinnacles of the Founder's Tower jutting into
the night sky, before making a run through the rain
from the gatehouse to the cloisters. It was the time
he loved best, despite the weather. No: because of it.
Walking through the dimly lit stone cloister in the dark
with rain lashing the bare wisteria through the open
mullioned windows on his left, he could imagine himself
back in the Middle Ages, hurrying back to a cramped
room, probably shared with three or four others, with
a lump or two of coal or a log of wood smouldering in
the grate.

So it was almost with a sense of *déjà vu* that he
stumbled up the stairs to his first-floor room and almost
fell over the figure asleep in the darkness on his doorstep.

'What the . . . ?'

The figure leaped to its feet with an equally startled
cry. Daniel found himself staring into the wide-eyed face
of Rajiv Mahendra. 'At last! Where the hell have you
been?' Rajiv exclaimed.

'What? Hey, easy on. What's happened? You forgot to
pay your battels or something? College bursar chucked
you out of your room? Wait a minute, you're not stoned
are you?'

'Chance would be a fine thing. A very fine thing
indeed,' muttered Rajiv almost angrily as Daniel got
out his keys and opened the door. The young medic
bustled him into the room.

'Take off your coat and drop your trousers, please.'

'Do what? Hey, Rajiv, kiss and make up is one thing,

but that's taking it a bit far, kid. I mean, I didn't even know you cared.'

But something in the other man's eyes – Christ, it wasn't a tear, was it? – made Daniel alter his tone.

'Say, what is this? You're not still sore at me? Listen, I'm sorry about yesterday. It was stupid, and I know how it looked, but I had to see the guy, you know? And anyway, it's over now. Friends? Buddies? OK?' Though all the while he was wondering exactly how he was going to get around to explaining that Rajiv's patient was going to find his name in the papers.

'OK, OK. This is not the time for arguing. Later. Now, please drop your trousers.' To Daniel's astonishment and no little horror, he saw that the medic had produced a green plastic box and was taking out a vial of clear liquid and a syringe. 'You're not paying attention. Please do as I say. Now.'

There was something in Rajiv's voice that made Daniel obey, but only as far as taking off his coat. When it came to dropping his trousers, the autopilot refused to function. If there was one thing in particular about the medical business that he hated – and he hated many – it was syringes.

'What is this, Rajiv? You have the serious look of a man about to practise some medicine. On me.'

'This is not a practice. This is quite possibly an emergency. Now do as I say or you may not live to regret it.'

'I don't understand. What is this stuff?'

'Streptomycin. What do you weigh?'

'Streptowhat? What do you mean, what do I weigh?'

'How heavy are you? It's not a complicated question, even for you. Come on, quickly.' Ravij was standing back looking at him clinically, like a butcher, or an undertaker. 'You must have some idea. Seventy, seventy-five?'

'Huh? What is this? I don't know. Yeah, I guess: a hundred and seventy or so.'

'What?'

'A hundred and seventy pounds, thereabouts. What is all this about anyway?'

'Pounds? Good grief.' He closed his eyes for a split second. 'Not far out. Approximately 77.2 kilos. Big bugger, aren't you?' He was eyeing the syringe carefully. 'There, that ought to do it.'

'Ought to do what? Look, just what the hell is that stuff? And what do you think you're going to do with it?'

'I've already told you. It's streptomycin and I am going to inject it into your muscle tissue. The buttock is the best place. Now, please drop your trousers.'

'You're serious, aren't you? Would you mind telling me why?'

The medic sighed. 'It's a precaution. But a very necessary one. Streptomycin is one of the few drugs that are both relatively safe and known to be effective against pneumonic plague. There is a chance – but a very remote one – that you may suffer some slight hearing loss.'

'WHA-AT?'

'Quiet, please. It does not happen immediately. In any case, the chance is minimal, almost nonexistent. Strentomycin is better than the alternatives. There are other drugs, sulpha drugs, which are more effective but can cause serious kidney damage. And anyway they are very hard to get hold of. Believe me, acquiring this was difficult enough. You might do me the favour of being grateful. If you recall, it was your own foolishness that created this situation.'

Daniel wanted to protest, but the facts were indisputable.

'You will also have to keep taking these for at least a week. I am doing the same.'

He held out a little brown plastic bottle of tablets. 'Tetracycline. It is a perfectly safe antibiotic. Used for acne, among other things, although in significantly smaller doses. You will take four tablets twice each day for the next ten days. All right?'

'OK, OK. But I thought the chances of infection were minimal? Wait a minute, you said pneumon– Shit!'

'Yes. Faeces indeed. I'm glad the penny eventually drops. I thought you vaguely knew something about this disease.'

'So did I. I thought it only rarely developed –'

'Indeed. Most cases of bubonic plague do not go beyond that stage. It is very rare. But you saw for yourself, for goodness' sake.'

'That cough . . .'

'That cough, precisely. We were lucky. We did not come into direct contact with any of the saliva or sputum. But even so, like that, the bacteria become airborne. You or I might have inhaled some.'

Daniel caught his breath.

'It is unlikely. Very unlikely. But as I said, the chance that it would turn pneumonic was very unlikely in the first place. Believe me, this is wise.'

Daniel nodded silently, the whole implication of what Rajiv was saying running through his head. The idea that he could be contaminated, could be contagious! He began to unbuckle his belt.

'Could we have passed this on?'

'Hm?' The medic was filling the syringe from the vial. 'Unlikely. Really. It is most unlikely that we are at any risk, and even less so that we are a risk to others. Even so, it is better to be safe. No?'

'Absolutely,' said Daniel, flinching as the needle plunged

into the muscle of his left buttock. And then, realising guiltily that it was an afterthought, he added, 'How's our friend up at the hospital doing?'

Rajiv pressed a little cotton wad against the puncture hole in Daniel's backside and motioned for him to hold it while he put the needle in a disposal pack and replaced the syringe in his box. Then he turned back and looked up at him, and Daniel noticed just how tired his friend looked. Drained. As if he had not slept properly for days. And it hit him for the first time that maybe he had not.

'Mr Atkins died this afternoon at about 2.00 p.m. I've been waiting here for you since shortly afterwards.'

Chapter Twenty-Three

Oxford; Sunday 21 December, 9.32 p.m.

D ANIEL HAD to wait for a good ten minutes in a biting cold wind outside the telephone box on the corner of Longwall Street before two obviously drunk girls finished a long and noisy conversation. The few snatches that emerged between howls of laughter held no interest even for eavesdropping.

'He never . . . oooh . . . Hahahaha . . . Noooo!'

Eventually the pair emerged, tangled in a six-foot string of tinsel. Daniel dashed into the relative warmth of the box, gagging on the stench of stale cigarette smoke, and took out the scrap of creased cardboard that was Therry's calling card. He looked at the number scrawled in pencil on the back and decided it was probably worth trying her home number first.

'Hey, if you know this number, you know the routine,' said Therry's recorded voice at the other end, before an electronic beep. Next he tried her direct line at the newspaper. Another machine, although with a more formal message. It included a mobile number.

Counting out pound coins and thinking that perhaps it was time he took out a British cellphone contract if he was going to be in this country for a year or two, Daniel dialled it. It rang six times before she answered, somewhat abruptly.

'Therry here.' In the background he could hear voices, music. Typical, he thought. Should have guessed, really.

Especially the week before Christmas. She was in a pub.

'Therry, hi, it's Daniel Warren.'

The voice softened slightly. 'Oh, you. How are you?'

'Fine. Just fine. How are you?'

'Well, I'm sick as a parrot actually, as we say in the trade.'

'You're sick?' A sudden cold clamminess seized Daniel's spine.

'Eh? What? Oh, no. Don't be daft. I'm not ill. Just fed up with the whole fucking pre-Christmas partying world.'

Daniel breathed a sigh of relief. For a moment he had thought . . .

'I've got something to tell you. There's been a development. It's serious –'

'No, it's not.' She cut him off. 'None of it's serious. A load of piss and wind. That's what John Harkness says. And he should know.'

'What? John who? What are you talking about? Listen to me –'

'I'd love to listen to you, darling, but now is not the time or place.' She said 'plaish'. The line was breaking up, then suddenly came back boomingly clean, and Daniel found himself uncomfortably curious about the identity of a male voice in the background. 'It's all a load of old cobblers, made up by a dizzy bird who couldn't hack the first proper feature she'd been given. It's a right fuck-up, a load of senationalist nonsense. According to His Holiness Sir John Harkness of Fleet Street Emeritus, editor incarnate of the *Oxford* fucking *Post*. Story spiked. Skewered.'

'Listen to me.' Daniel was insisting now, talking over whatever nonsense she intended to burble at him while the LCD display on the callbox indicated his fast-dwindling funds. 'Charlie Atkins, the patient, the man with plague. He's dead.'

There was a slight pause. As if she was taking in the news and then dismissing it. 'Really?'

'Really.'

And then she sighed, a long, deep sigh that spoke of resignation, disenchantment and too many lagers.

Daniel wanted to say something to encourage her. To tell her not to be so despondent. He almost said the death made a better story, until he realised just what it was he was thinking of blurting out. All he knew was that he wanted to see her again. For whatever reason.

Instead, she said, 'Well, that's that, then.'

'Right,' said Daniel. 'I guess so. Sort of. Maybe we could . . .' but as he didn't really know what he was going to say next, it was maybe just as well he didn't get the chance.

'OK, kid, that's it. It's all over. Dead and buried.'

Therry Moon was about to drift out of his life. For ever.

'We should meet,' he stammered.

'Yeah, one of these days.'

'How about tomorrow?'

'Tomorrow?' She sounded definitely drunk. 'Whatever.'

'I'll pick you up in the morning,' he said quickly and put the phone down before she could change her mind.

Chapter Twenty-Four

The Old School House bar, Oxford; Sunday 21 December, 9.38 p.m.

THERRY MOON clicked closed her mobile phone and then stood there stupidly looking at it, not quite sure what was going on or what she had just agreed to. If anything.

'And it's tidings of comfort and joy, comfort and joy . . .' A group of ruddy-faced businessmen in cheap suits and 99p Santa Claus hats from the market were moving into seasonal overdrive.

'Hey there, Therry girl, what's all this then? Stop brooding. Stuff the old fart and his story anyway! What do you say?'

Henry was a pain in the arse, but harmless really. And he had got her off the weddings. For all the good it had done her. She'd be back on the beat next week, now, without a doubt. The eternal bridesmaid at the weddings of strangers. She gave Henry a weak smile and took another pull on her pint.

Two hours later, and half an hour after closing time, the bright lights were turned on to snuff out with their cruel glare any late-lingering remnants of the party spirit. The drunk businessmen long gone, reeling into the bitterly cold street, weaving their way towards bus stops, taxi ranks and tomorrow morning's embarrassment, when the red faces would return.

Meanwhile, here she was alone with Henry. Even the other old hands from the *Post* had disappeared, Jack a few minutes earlier, after a painful half-hour's dithering, trying with a hopeless lack of subtlety to discover whether Therry wanted protection or discretion. In the end he had lost track of the question and left with a backward wave that could have meant good luck or just goodbye or even "go to hell". Therry didn't know and didn't care. She wasn't going anywhere. At least not with horny Henry.

'So hey, Therry, what about it, love?'

Was that it? Was he really going to be so crass? How's about a shag, love?

'Can I walk you home? Hmm?'

She almost burst out laughing. He lurched as far as the coat rack and took hers down first, attempting to offer it for her to put on. Inside out.

'Whoops! Sorry.'

'Just give it here, Henry. I can do it.'

She took the yellow raincoat from him, threw it on and walked to the door, not wholly steady on her feet herself. In the doorway she turned and blew him a kiss. And then she was gone, pulling the hood up and striding off, leaving Henry abandoned, with the look on his face of a child who has just awoken from a dream to find it is not his birthday after all.

Therry would never be sure at just what point she decided what she was going to do. At the time she told herself she was going back to the office to erase the story she had written, to leave no trace of her humiliation on the computer system. Perhaps she was even going to clear her desk. To leave a note that told them where they could stick their job, with their provincial manners and provincial morals. Perhaps she would have done too, had she not seen the bulk of her Range Rover lurking in the shadow cast by the car-park security light. Unless, of course, that was what had been at the back of her mind all along.

She had left the car there deliberately because they were going to the pub. Because she had had a drink at lunchtime anyway and at this time of the year, the police were liable to haul in anyone and turn the breathalysers up to hypersensitive. And Therry did not need the car to get home to the little house in Cardigan Street in Jericho, not even this late at night. She could get a cab. She could walk, come to that. The car would be there in the morning, should she need it. To get to the next bloody wedding.

But it was also there now. Its familiarity seemed welcoming in a world that had let her down. It was warm and dry, when the world was cold and wet. There was always the chance, of course, as her logic had told her earlier, when it was still fully functioning, that she would be stopped, even on the short run home. And she would lose her licence. She could hardly walk straight, let alone drive. But then driving was so much easier, she told herself as she unlocked the door and clambered up behind the wheel.

Even then, she had no intention – had she? – of doing anything other than getting home. Yet as she edged the Range Rover out of the car park, remembering just in time to turn on the headlights, she turned right, rather than left. This decision was made at a deeper level of her psyche, well below what passed for superficial consciousness. She was as surprised as anyone might have been, she insisted afterwards, to find herself staring into the falling sleet illuminated by the streetlights along the Woodstock Road and then flashing through the beams of her headlights on the dark and empty country road leading to the brave new world of Nether Ditchford.

The stunted tower of St Peter's Alone jutted out of the darkness, catching her by surprise as the Range Rover came over the crest of the hill. She slowed, then stopped to take it in. The village beyond it lay asleep, dark, the streetlights having been extinguished at midnight. She turned off the engine, killed the headlights and let the world settle back into darkness, only a glimmer of moonlight breaking through the heavy sky. 'Above the dark and dreamless sleep, the silent clouds go by.' The carol came to her unbidden, mercifully not in the tones of the drunken businessmen in the pub but as she had heard it in a church once with her parents, a long time ago, when Christmas was still Christmas.

It was with a sense of sudden loneliness therefore that she looked out through the windscreen at Ditchford in the dark, a surrogate Bethlehem in a heathen world. And all around, in the churned-up fields and ripped-up hedgerows: the camp of the Philistines. Waiting to attack. Or to unleash Armageddon.

She turned the key in the ignition, painfully aware of the violence the engine's roar did to the winter night, slipped the Range Rover into second gear and let it trundle down the hill towards the church and the encampment beyond. Just what she hoped to find, she didn't know: fields of corpses, zombies, the risen dead, marching in grisly armies across the mud, hands out-stretched, with black pustules under their skeletal arms. Or secret machinations: men in white containment suits like *Star Wars* imperial troopers erecting bubble tents with floodlights and instructions given by megaphone over the drone of helicopters overhead.

What she saw was a single bright light coming straight

towards her at high speed. Unstoppable. Shining right in her eyes. She jerked the steering wheel hard to the left, sending the Range Rover halfway up a bank. The vehicle's height left her hanging out of her seat at a ridiculous angle. She overcorrected, making things worse. Leaning like a rally driver into the nonexistent bend, she heard a screech and saw for a split second the snarling face of the driver of the van with only one headlight working that would have smashed straight into her, had she not reacted as quickly. Sure she had identified Riggs-Mill markings, she turned to scream at the van as its two functioning tail lights disappeared past the church and over the brow of the hill.

Then the steering wheel sprang to life in her hands, spinning against her in the opposite direction, almost snapping her thumbs. Half blinded, still shocked, Therry fought for a glimpse of the road, only to realise that she was no longer on it. The Range Rover teetered unsteadily, then jerked violently, nose downwards. She fell forward. Threw up her hand against the onrushing darkness. And joined it.

Part Two

Infection

> *Ring a'ring o'roses, a pocket full of posies*
> *A-tishoo. A-tishoo. We all fall down.*
>   English nursery rhyme

Chapter Twenty-Five

The High, Oxford; Monday 22 December,
6.30 a.m.

FROM DOORWAY to doorway the man lurched, from
Shepherd and Woodward's window display of college scarves and rowing colours to the Campus Shop
with its serried ranks of teddy bears wearing miniature mortar boards and gowns bedecked with seasonal
tinsel.

The shops were still shut, the High Street almost
deserted, the great stone walls of the colleges fulfilling
their medieval function of shutting out the world. If
you are not in here, they said, behind our buttresses
and old oak doors, then you are not one of us. Whatever your troubles, you must take them elsewhere. And
God knew he had troubles. The trouble was that God
didn't care.

Nonetheless, George Pirewski's half-forgotten half-
Polish background ensured that he fingered the crucifix
that hung around his neck. More like a pagan talisman
perhaps than a Christian symbol. Not that he cared.
He would accept help from any quarter. Though he
expected none.

The 'escape' from the hospital had been easy. Almost
too easy. Wasn't he supposed to be under special
observation? Did no one care that their lives were at
risk? And they only knew the half of it. He was not sure
how much he knew himself. He had to believe, hadn't

he? He had to trust, hadn't he? Trust. Ah, now there was a thing.

The chance had presented itself, and there was little likelihood that it would be repeated. That nurse, the wee Scottish one, had been distracted, red-eyed and tearful, and scared, he thought. Not that he blamed her for that. He was fucking terrified himself. He knew what they were dealing with better than they did. One of their doctors was already dead. And he suspected the death would not be the last.

The same thing had probably occured to the nurse. One of her mates, the one who was on alternate duty, had stuck her head round the door and beckoned her out. Off to huddle together and fret somewhere over a cup of tea. And maybe shed a tear or two for the Paki doctor. Well, he was fucked if they were going to have him to cry for too. For the first time since they had brought him in, unloaded him out of that bloody van like a sack of aggregate, he was on his own.

He had struggled out of bed, muscles aching, and pulled on a hospital dressing gown over the loose, washed-out hospital pyjamas. He found his shoes pushed under a chair in the corner, but no socks. The bedside cabinet, which he had hoped might have contained his street clothes, was empty. They had probably been destroyed to avoid contagion. He would have to find something else. Why they had forgotten his shoes, he did not know, but the opportunity was not to be missed. There was no way these people were going to save his life. They didn't even know what they were dealing with.

Amazingly, the corridor was clear. Before, he had had the impression that there was someone positioned outside his door, presumably as a precaution. Along the corridor, he could hear the nurse's Glaswegian twang on a telephone, although it sounded as if she was whispering, trying not to be overheard. She sounded worried. Not as worried as she would be when she got back. He wasted no time on the other doors. He had no idea behind which one his colleague lay, or whether he was still alive. He suspected not. Right now, that was not his problem. His mind seethed. The bastards! Had they known? How could they not have known?

The door at the end of the corridor was not locked; he pushed through, taking care not to let it bang behind him. On the outside, a sign read: 'Warning: restricted area. Highly contagious cases. Admission only to medical personnel with specific authorisation. All enquiries: contact Dr S. Redwhistle on ext 3548.' That was it. That was their idea of security. He tried to laugh, but his sense of humour failed him.

He made for the stairs, hoping not to be detected. Act normal, that was the thing. Even in the very early morning it was not unusual to see patients up wandering to the toilet or a day room. Two floors down, he realised that using the lift was more normal than using the stairs. He emerged on the third floor, relieved and amazed to see no one paid him any attention. Only a sudden shortness of breath and an agonising burst of acidic heartburn almost gave him away. He grabbed at a radiator, holding himself up until the worst passed. On the right was the men's surgical ward. He considered the possibility of going in to look for a locker that might contain some clothes. But at that moment a duty nurse came to the door and looked at him as if she was about to ask a question.

He pushed the lift button and was relieved when it arrived almost instantaneously, empty. Three floors down. It was barely dawn, yet already the ground floor was bustling: nurses and junior house doctors finishing shifts, cleaners nattering loudly and orderlies pushing carts of soiled linen. Down the main corridor on the left, there was a queue for the cafeteria.

Coats hung on a rack against one wall, next to a large and very visible sign declaring 'The John Radcliffe Hospital Trust takes no responsibility for loss or damage to property'. Quickly he scanned the overcoats. A grey checked one looked about his size. He lifted it as unselfconsciously as a man wearing a hospital dressing gown can and walked as quickly as he could, which was painfully slowly, back into the corridor, expecting at any moment to feel a hand on his shoulder. He did not. No more than, minutes later, anyone paid any attention when, with the coat wrapped as tight as possible, he lurched out into the freezing air.

The coat was slightly too big for him. But that was not something he minded as he pulled it closer over his bare chest, wincing at the pain in his armpits and the touch of the rough, unlined material on his tender, swollen skin. His sockless feet squelched unpleasantly against the leather inners of his shoes. Despite his inadequate clothing, he felt himself coming out in a sweat. Not the cold sweat of fear but the sticky hot sweat of fever. He tried, ineffectually, not to think about it.

Only now did he realise that he had no money. The stolen coat held no loose change in its pockets. A fact he rued bitterly as he watched a red Oxford city bus flash past him, raising a spray of dirty slush from the roadside.

He knew the city's geography only vaguely. The bus stops guided him, like a trail of crumbs leading a wounded bird to the slaughter. Down along Marston Road he staggered, oblivious to the drab suburban surroundings. The pain in his chest was growing. Would he make it? he asked himself repeatedly. And then realised he had not the slightest idea where he was going. He had to find a telephone box, and money to make the call. After that he could only hope. For a miracle?

On Magdalen Bridge another spasm shook him violently. Surely here he would be noticed, he thought as he clutched the stone parapet in the sickly glare of the pseudo-antique gas-effect streetlight. But the few passers-by showed no Samaritan inclinations; collars pulled high against the wicked weather, they hurried past. Barely ten yards away a tramp was also bent over the parapets, emptying the thin alcohol contents of his stomach into the dark waters of the river Cherwell.

With an effort of willpower that George Pirewski did not know he possessed, he staggered onwards. Into the all but deserted High.

It was now or never:

'Ten pence, guv, for a telephone call. It's urgent, mate, please.'

The man in the raincoat started back at the sight of the dishevelled figure with staring eyes that emerged from the doorway of the Campus Shop with a gaping overcoat revealing a glimpse of bare chest underneath. In weather like this! For an instant the spirit of chastened Scrooge almost caused him to break the habit of a lifetime and give the unfortunate a few coins. But there were only notes in his pocket.

Pirewski cursed the man's retreating back. Christ, that it should have come to this!

Across the road a young couple, presumably on their way home from some seasonal celebration that had gone on into the small hours, lurched arm in arm, giggling, out of the darkness of New College Lane. Summoning up his will and forcing down the pain, Pirewski limped across the road and repeated the spiel, the words coming belabouredly now. His chest felt as if it was on fire. The girl, unwinding her arm from that of her companion, looked at him with an expression that was very close to genuine pity and made as if to open her purse.

'No,' the young man at her side intervened, swaying slightly. 'He only wants to go and soak himself in booze. No doubt die in a doorway in this weather.'

Christ, thought Pirewski, if you only knew! He wanted to say something to make this smug little bastard know what he was feeling. But a wave of acid bile flowed up his gullet. He lurched forward, clasping the coat lapels around his burning, naked chest.

'See what I mean,' the young man blurted, pulling his girlfriend back, away from this retching apparition.

'Oh, Harry, the guy's ill. Give him something. It is Christmas, after all.'

'Ill? He's pickled, that's all.' But he turned to Pirewski with a knowing sneer on his face. 'A phone call, is it? Well, then –' and he dipped his free hand into his coat pocket to produce a wallet – 'this should sort you out. I'm sure there's at least 30p left on it.' And he handed over a BT phonecard, the smirk on his face fading rapidly as Pirewski snatched it greedily.

Thanks, mate, I won't forget it, if it's the last thing I do, was what Pirewski wanted to say, with as sarcastic a tone as he could manage. Instead, he felt fire behind his eyes and uncontrollable nausea. His lungs jerked violently within his fragile ribcage. Instinctively, uncontrollably, he opened his mouth wide to cough, to sneeze, to vomit. He didn't know which; didn't care; couldn't care. The couple facing him recoiled in horror, the girl shrieking as, with a sound like a train braking on rusty rails, the derelict emitted a fine spray of sputum into the air.

'Oh, my God, that's disgusting!' Harry grabbed hold of his trembling consort who recoiled with him, this time more than willingly. Brushing frantically at the front of their coats, they disappeared as fast as they could into the romantic lamplight of Catte Street, away from the horror still standing shaking in the bright glare of the High Street's stark illumination. Not until hours later would the young woman discover, with a revulsion that immediately outweighed the lingering nagging of her conscience, the small stains on her fake arctic-fox fur collar: little hardened grey splotches, flecked with red.

As his accidental saviours fled his presence, the wrecked form of George Pirewski fell to his knees on the hard flagstones of the High, crawled a few yards along New College Lane into an alcove in the ancient masonry, and fell mercifully asleep, the phonecard clutched tight in his cold hand.

Chapter Twenty-Six

*Cornmarket, Oxford; Monday 22 December,
10.00 a.m.*

B ITTER COLD pinched the cheeks of the Christmas
shoppers forced out into the tacky bustle of Cornmarket. The only warmth came from the fumes belched
out by the buses lumbering their way along the nomi-
nally pedestrianised thoroughfare. This was Oxford's
commercial heart. It was also the place in Daniel's mind
where Oxford was least like itself.

People crowded into Clinton's card shop, though it
was too late for sending Christmas cards. People with
parcels in their arms were pushing past one another.
Staring at cheap jewellery and watches in the window
of H. Samuel, piling in and out of Boots and W.H.
Smith, the chain stores that robbed any provincial high
street of the last vestiges of individuality. They seemed
even more of an abomination here in Oxford, clustered
like a cancer of the commonplace in a city that was a
temple to the achievement of the extraordinary. Now
in the week before Christmas particularly, with most
undergraduates gone home for the vacation, the old con-
flict between town and gown had entered into one of its
intermittent truces. The townspeople had reclaimed their
town and Oxford had temporarily ceased to be a city.

Three old men in shabby overcoats huddled on the
stone step outside the parish church of St Michael, passing a can of strong cider from one to another. A few silver

coins lay in the cap on the pavement in front of them, but it did not look as if the season of good will was doing them much good. The crowds flowing into Boswell's department store next door paid them little attention. St Michael's tramps were just another Oxford tradition, perhaps. They certainly looked medieval enough, with their weathered, roughly shaven faces, hollow cheeks and deep-set eyes.

How long had they been there, day after day? he had asked once. As long as anyone could remember, came the answer. Perhaps for ever. The thought bemused him: perhaps for ever. Not others like them, but the selfsame men. Guardians of the steps of St Michael's for the past six hundred years. He crossed the street, narrowly avoiding a Park'n'Ride double-decker, and tossed a 20p coin into the cap.

One of them looked up and fixed him with a rheumy eye and an expression that might have been gratitude. The one next to him hawked and spat a great glutinous globule of sputum on to the pavement in front of him. The third turned to examine it. Daniel swallowed hard and accelerated his pace. Past Boswell's, with its Christmas tat, and the ABC cinema showing the latest 007 extravaganza, and back into the world of carved stone and stately buildings. Somewhere beyond which lay his destination: Jericho.

Daniel had not ventured into Jericho since arriving in Oxford. The name was romantic, its biblical associations conjuring up some walled quarter with ancient Middle Eastern atmosphere. He knew its location only from the map: out west beyond the broad thoroughfare of St Giles and north of Beaumont Street, somewhere near the offices of the Oxford University Press. The Press, he realised as he wandered into the morass of grey Victorian back streets, was the key, the area first built up to house its workers in the early nineteenth century. The low rows of terraced houses were neat and tidy and grey and gloomy, at least superficially. As he started looking for Cardigan Street – named, she had made a point of telling him, not after the woolly item of clothing but after the Charge of the Light Brigade general who had improbably invented it – he could see a whole social history etched into the brickwork. The print workers were long gone, squeezed into the modern high-rises and council estates of Oxford's suburbs. Jericho had become gentrified and taken over by students, the houses probably rented once upon a time but increasingly, from what Daniel had observed of British society, bought up by rich parents as accommodation for their offspring and a sound invest-ment at the same time. As a result, former working-class corner pubs were now bistro-type restaurants or wine bars. Jericho had changed from Coronation Street into Oxford's Notting Hill. The students had been joined by the city's young professionals, one of whom was Therry Moon.

Daniel wandered up and down the little streets for nearly half an hour, always hoping that Cardigan Street would turn out to be just around the next corner, and more grateful than ever for his thick duffel coat against the biting wind. When at last he saw the name Cardigan on a street sign, he speeded up almost into a trot, as much in anticipation of being asked into the warmth as of seeing Therry.

He pressed the doorbell and then, when it gave no indication of functioning, rapped on the door with his red knuckles. He was just about to try again when it was opened.

'Oh, it's you.'

'Not exactly the welcome I'd been hoping – Jesus! What happened to you?'

'Oh, nothing much, just a second-rate assassination attempt. You'd better come in.'

'A second-rate . . . what did you say?'

Therry winced, chiefly from the pain of trying to smile. Or think, come to that. The cold compress taped above her left eye felt like a soggy handkerchief and was doing little to diminish the spread of purply yellow collecting beneath it. Her head was thumping as if she'd been existing on a diet of tequila slammers for weeks.

'Well, I don't know. What do you think? What does it look like?'

'It looks like you've been mugged. By a truck.'

'Not that far from the truth, if you must know. And spending the night in the Horton casualty hardly helped. Not to mention practically having to bribe a junior quack with what remained of my battered body not to report me to the police for driving "under the influence".'

'You did this in a car crash? Drunk?'

'No, I was up to my eyes on fucking cocaine and morphine! What do you think? Christ, I could do with a spot of morphine now. Either that or decapitation. You haven't got a guillotine on you by any chance?'

'What? Jesus, you ought to be more careful.'

'Listen, mate, I might have been pissed out of my head, but I didn't do this for fun. And it was no accident either. Those bastards ran me off the road deliberately. Scare tactics. I don't know. But it bloody well isn't going to work, is it, Tigger?' She lifted a cranky-looking kitten and kissed it on the nose.

'Scare tactics? What bastards? Are you trying to tell me somebody did this deliberately?'

Therry put the cat down. 'W-a-t-c-h my l-i-p-s. That's what I just said.'

'I don't understand. Who?'

'Pigs and bloody Swill, that's who. I was up at Ditchford last night.'

'You did *what*? Are you crazy? You drove all the way up there, with a head full of sauce, after the pub? Why?'

'For the hell of it. I don't know exactly. OK, so I was drunk. I was pissed off at having my story spiked by that other bastard, Harkness. I thought I might find something. No, I didn't. I told you: I don't know. It just seemed like the right thing to do at the time. Maybe I thought I'd find some proof they really had dug up the Black Death. What I didn't expect was to find some Riggs-Mill van hurtling towards me like a maniac in the dead of night.'

Daniel was silent.

'I'm telling you,' she continued, 'there I was sitting in the middle of the road – well, all right, not the most sensible thing necessarily, but those are quiet country roads, and Rover's a big boy – and this thing comes flying at me. Like they meant it. Serious. If I hadn't swung the wheel hard right, they'd have ploughed right into me. Full frontal? Hello, Danny boy, anyone in? You're not listening.'

'Sorry. I am. It's just . . . what time did you say this happened?'

'Mmh? Uh, I dunno. Late. Gone midnight anyway. Maybe one or thereabouts. Why?'

'Well, if it was a Riggs-Mill van, as you say –'

'Believe me, I should know. It nearly killed me.'

'OK, OK. It's just, well, they may have had a good reason for hurrying. I tried to get hold of Rajiv last night, just to buy the guy a drink – God knows I owe him one – but he was still at the hospital. Even when I rang the JR2, it took ages to get hold of him, they had to bleep him. I was about to ring off when he comes on the phone and tells me what's happened. A Riggs-Mill van came in during the night, shortly before 2.00 a.m. – said they couldn't wait for the ambulance. Another of their men.'

'What?' Therry was aware she was gaping.

Daniel nodded. 'The same thing. Bubonic plague. And this one hadn't been out of the country.'

'You don't think . . . I mean really think . . .'

Daniel caught her eyes. And held them.

'I don't know what to think,' he said, 'I don't know what to think at all.' For the explanation was unthinkable. Wasn't it?

Chapter Twenty-Seven

Broad Street, Oxford; Monday 22 December, 11.30 a.m.

'IT'S NOT possible. Leastways it's not supposed to be possible.'

Daniel Warren and Therry Moon were walking along Broad Street, past the lumpen stone mass of Balliol, Daniel for once ignoring, like everyone else hurrying by in the slanting rain, the little flat iron cross set in the tarmac that marked the spot where in 1556 Queen Mary Tudor had the Protestant bishops Cranmer, Latimer and Ridley burned at the stake. The day after he first arrived in Oxford, Daniel had stood on the cross itself, trying to feel across the centuries, get some sense of the pain of men who had been martyred for their beliefs. He had been shouted at by a traffic warden, told he would cause an accident.

Today they were using the pavement.

'But how do you know?' Therry was saying, tugging forward the yellow hood of her raincoat to protect the compress still taped to her forehead. 'I mean, you're not a scientist, are you?'

'No, I'm not. Well, not in the sense you mean. All I'm saying is that as far as I know it's not possible.'

'So let's find out from someone who knows more, right?'

'I thought that's what we were trying to do.'

'Yes, but Redwhistle won't talk to us, will he? I didn't

even get past his secretary. The minute I mentioned the word *Post*, she gave me the total brush-off. I mean, normally, right, these guys are dying to talk to the press.'

Daniel gave her a sideways look.

'Well, you know what I mean.'

'Yes, well, obviously the professor's got a lot on his hands. If there really are plague victims in there –'

'What do you mean "if"?'

Daniel didn't argue but went on. 'You can imagine he doesn't want to spark a panic, talking to some reporter who's going to splash "Black Death in Oxford" all over the front page of their newspaper.'

'Did I say I was going to do something like that?'

'Did you say you weren't?'

'Anyway, that's not the issue.'

'I think you might find it is, you know. People don't want to start a panic.'

'People don't want to die either, sunshine. We're not just doing this for fun, you know. What about your mate Rajiv, the doc bloke? Can't he help?'

'Probably, but I'd have to page him, and to be honest, it seems a bit self-centred to distract a man who's actually in there trying to save lives just because you want a story, which you admit yourself is probably just a wind-up. Bacteria do not live for six hundred years.'

'But you said yourself, the plague keeps coming back. All through history.'

'I said it used to. But the point is, when it comes back, it's not the same thing. It hasn't been lying dormant. It's a new strain, brought in from somewhere else. Usually somewhere pretty unsanitary. That's why it has more or less died out in the Western world. The only real chance anyone has of catching the plague is being unlucky enough to run into it somewhere in the Third World. Which is what obviously happened to this guy.'

'And now he's brought it back with him?'

'Yes.'

'And this other guy caught it off him?'

'Yes. Obviously. I mean, it's the only logical explanation.'

'Sure thing, Mr Spock. Unless we're kidding ourselves about modern medicine and the simple truth is that for the past couple of centuries we've just been in one of those windows of history that the plague has missed.'

'What do you mean?'

'You know, the way everyone thought the Cold War would go on for ever. And then suddenly it ended.'

'Yes.' Daniel was suddenly uncomfortable. There was no way she could have known it, but Therry Moon had stumbled on one of his pet theories about the relationship between people and their history. One he had been hiding from himself for the past week. History didn't repeat itself, despite popular belief. At least not exactly.

'Exactly,' she said, as if reading his thoughts but actually putting a full stop to the discussion and leaving him wondering why, or if, they had been having an argument in the first place. They dashed across the road past the great scowling stone busts of the Roman emperors that guard Sir Christopher Wren's elegant Sheldonian Theatre and into the shelter of the great Neoclassical slab known as the Clarendon Building.

The Clarendon, named for one of Charles II's ministers, is regarded by most of those who pass through it as little more than the gatehouse for the splendid fifteenth-century building that squats behind it, all vertical lines and pointing pinnacles: the old reading rooms of the Bodleian Library, which was also Daniel and Therry's goal. But for those using 'the Bod' for the first time, a visit to the Clarendon is essential. It houses the administrative department which issues passes to entitled readers: present members of the university, those old members who have taken their Master of Arts degree, and members of the public who can prove they are of good character and have legitimate need of its facilities. Depending on their circumstances, they may be required to pay a fee. Therry doubted whether the *Post*'s expenses would run to it, especially since the editor had spiked her story. So Daniel was signing her in, temporarily, as his research assistant. Although really, he was increasingly uncomfortably aware, it was turning out to be more the other way about.

Equipped with her reader's card, having taken the ancient oath not to 'kindle fire' within Sir Thomas Bodley's library, they walked through the great pinnacled courtyard, past Bodley himself in cast bronze effigy and preposterous Elizabethan pantaloons staring down sternly from his pedestal, and into the vaulted reading rooms. As Therry stared in mute wonder at the great ceilings and the vast arrays of shelving and the huge bound tomes that she realised were only the catalogue, Daniel made straight for one of the computer terminals that sat anachronistically along the thirty-foot refectory tables. And logged on to the Internet.

'This isn't exactly what I'd expected.'

'No? Thought we'd be poring over ancient archives and blowing the dust off mildewed volumes? Actually some of the old college libraries are still a bit like that, but the Bod's a national institution. And even you Brits entered the computer age towards the end of the last millennium, you know.'

Therry shot him a sarcastic smile.

A computerised catalogue I can understand. But why use the Internet?'

'Because that's where the catalogue lives. Out there in

cyberspace. At least that's where you find the doorway. This is OLIS, the Oxford Libraries Information Service. It includes not just the Bod but all the libraries in Oxford, most of which come under the Bodleian, but far from all the books are in this building.'

'You mean we can't just go and fetch something off a shelf?'

'Hardly. Well, not in most cases. There are actually quite a few history books on open shelving in the Radcliffe Camera.' He nodded towards the great window – like something in a cathedral, Therry was thinking, only without the stained glass – to where the magnificent dome of the university's chief history library dominated a square that rivalled St Mark's in Venice for the title of Europe's finest.

'If we'd been looking for fiction,' Daniel was going on, 'most of the stuff is kept on miles of underground shelving out at Nuneham Courtenay. Even most of the books in the Bodleian's main archive take several hours to retrieve. But I'm banking on most of what we want being in the Radcliffe Science Library.'

'Where's that?'

'Just up the road, past Wadham. But it's easier to check the catalogue here.'

Therry looked at the screen. Daniel was using Internet Explorer to access the OLIS website.

'You seem to know your way around this.'

'I should think so. I first discovered OLIS when I was at Berkeley. The only difference doing it here is that the books aren't six thousand miles away. Here we go. Look.'

Chapter Twenty-Eight

The Radcliffe Science Library Oxford, Monday 22 December, 1.30 p.m.

LITTLE OVER an hour later, Daniel Warren and Therry Moon sat hunched over one of the long, low reading desks on the second floor of the Radcliffe Science Library. At this time of the afternoon, right at the fag end of Michaelmas term, the library was nearly empty. Two rows away, between the open shelving, a pretty young girl with hair plaited into a long, golden braid lay slumped asleep over the unmistakable bulk of Gray's *Anatomy*. Who'd be a doctor of medicine? thought Daniel, thinking of the antisocial hours Rajiv worked and the lines on his forehead after endless sleepless nights. Another two rows down an oriental-looking man – probably a medical research student – was bent over an array of thin pamphlets, with the look of recently published dissertations. Otherwise Daniel and Therry had the room to themselves.

From the list he had accessed on the Internet in the main Bodleian, Daniel had ordered up most of the relevant texts. He had been impressed to see that the Science Library kept copies of most of the major historical books too, not least because Therry had been eager to fill in the blanks in her knowledge of the fourteenth-century plague, but also because anything ordered from its stacks could be got hold of within forty minutes. He had been annoyed, and slightly perplexed at first, to find that some of the most up-to-date papers on the plague were reserved by someone else. But it was probably coincidence: the books that were out were epidemiological studies that in several cases included other rare but highly contagious diseases; it was by no means certain that whoever had reserved them was interested in the plague. And in any event, the chance of either Therry or Daniel, with their limited medical and pharmaceutical knowledge, understanding them was slight.

'Jesus, what's that?' Therry pointed at a page where a book on the history of pestilence had fallen open in front of her. The sleeping medical student continued sleeping, but from down the library, the oriental man looked up in annoyance. Daniel shushed her, and then looked at the page she held open. The illustration was grotesque: a skeleton wrapped in rags but with a crown on its head, its limbs contorted as if frozen in some wild movement. The lipless teeth were bared in a gruesome grin.

'Dancing Death,' he replied calmly in a low voice, as if he had seen such grim spectres a hundred times before. Which he had. 'A sort of *memento mori* – a reminder of mortality,' he added in response to her quizzical look. 'They became commonplace during and after the plague. More pagan than religious really. The clergy didn't approve, but by then the clergy had lost a bit of their status.'

Over the next two hours, as the light through the windows grew paler and they clicked on the little individual desklights, they worked their way through separate piles. Therry skimmed introductions and picked out particular chapters for closer examination, stopping every now and then to scribble notes in her ring-bound reporter's notebook. Once or twice she whistled through her teeth, drawing dark stares from the Asian man four rows away, who was clearly of the old school when it came to rules about silence in libraries.

The 'Dancing Death' was the most sinister of the few illustrations, but not the only one, nor the most horrific. That title was disputed by a finely etched woodcut of the flagellants, groups of would-be holy men and women who wandered the countryside beating themselves in penance. It was elaborate, closely worked to detail the anguished expressions on their faces, the trails of blood from ragged cuts on their naked backs and the vicious-looking knotted thongs they wielded against themselves and each other. The caption said the artist was unknown but dated it to Nuremberg in Germany in the mid-fourteenth century. It was clear just from looking at the thing that the artist had been an eyewitness to the scene he depicted. In the future there would be photographs, video recordings, digital disks to preserve the horrors of more recent centuries. This was the nearest the fourteenth century came to a front-page picture.

Therry began to understand what Daniel's manuscript was trying to do. With a few notable exceptions, the histories of the plague were dry, indigestible material, attempts made to calculate probable death tolls centuries later from manorial records or church stipendiary reports; in an age when the life of the common man went unrecorded, the rate of death among his 'betters' was one of the few ways of estimating that of the population as a whole.

But even the statistics had a certain horror all of their own, if only because they illustrated the scale of a disaster so large that its effects were literally incalculable. What was clear was that the damage to medieval society was immense, that attitudes towards piety and the clergy changed radically, as if the terror of the plague and the seeming randomness with which it struck had instilled such terror as to – perversely – diminish the fear of God. Sanctity had proved to be no protection.

Daniel's material was also dry, and no less morbid: the reports of the Bombay Plague Research Council proving that, as Rajiv had told him, on the Indian subcontinent bubonic plague was more than a historical curiosity. Equally disturbing was *The Plague Manual*, a slim handbook for use in emergencies co-written by M. Bahmanyar of the Pasteur Institute of Iran and D. C. Cavanaugh from the Department of Hazardous Micro-organisms at the Walter Reed Army Medical Centre, Washington, DC, published by the World Health Organisation, Geneva, back in 1976. He smiled. In its way this too was a refugee from a different world.

It did not make for comfortable reading. 'The exposure of family members, visitors and anyone who does not take protective measures when approaching a victim is almost inevitable.' A *cordon sanitaire* was recommended to close off an infected village from the world, backed up if necessary 'by armed police and military'.

'Are you all right?'

'Hmm? Oh, yes, sorry. It's just pretty grim stuff, isn't it?'

'You said it.' She lowered her voice, noticing the oriental man scowl, then turn his attention to the loud scraping noise made as the young medical student wakened with a jolt, pushing back her chair on the parquet floor, and stood up, looking, Daniel thought, as delightful as the dormouse in *Alice in Wonderland*. Glancing around her in apologetic embarrassment, she gathered up a few notebooks, pushed the weighty Gray's to one side, shook out her long plait of hair and, pulling on a coat, got up and left. Daniel glanced at his watch. It was just gone 3.00 p.m. They had been there longer than he realised.

'OK. I give up.'

Therry clapped closed the book she had been reading and turned to look at the obtuse American beside her. For a moment Daniel stared at her, totally nonplussed.

'Well, what have you found? So far I've been grossed out in more ways than I ever thought possible. I'm beginning to understand that we're damn lucky any shred of civilisation at all withstood this bloody germ, but I still can't for the life of me make out if there's any chance that it could have survived over six hundred years buried in the mud of Nether Ditchford.'

'You're serious about this, aren't you?'

'Of course I bloody am. Somebody damn near killed me last night up near that site. I think they've got something they don't want people to know about. And I want to know why.'

'We need a second opinion. And I think I know who can give it to us. The man who thinks he should have had Redwhistle's job.'

Chapter Twenty-Nine

Oxford; Monday 22 December, 4.00 p.m.

D R ERWIN Gover lived in the sort of house Daniel Warren had grown up believing existed only in fairy stories: old, made of yellow stone, with rickety gables, a roof of ancient moss-covered tiles and a mill wheel that creaked under the pressure of water in a sluggish stream, a branch of the meandering Cherwell. The house was located at the end of a long alleyway off Parks Road that led between an old stone wall at the back of one of the colleges and a stretch of deceptively dense-looking woodland. Just a few dozen yards beyond the clump of trees, the 1960s-built university science area raised its hydralike head in rectilinear concrete and steel. But here at the end of the lane, the old house seemed to have sprung from another universe.

'Quaint, isn't it?' said Therry.

'You could say that, yeah.' 'Quaint' was the kind of English understatement Daniel had got used to. The place was fabulous.

'C. S. Lewis used to live here. You know, the guy who wrote those kids' books about the magic lion. Did you get those on TV?'

Daniel had never seen a television version but he had discovered the Narnia books as a child, and they had never lost their magic even when his mother had explained that they were all religious propaganda in disguise. She had succeded, as she intended, in putting him off them, but she had not managed altogether to destroy the magic of the storytelling. And suddenly he noticed the Victorian lamp-post. He was standing right next to it. The magic lamp-post in *The Lion, the Witch and the Wardrobe*, the link to another world. And he shivered. The world where it was 'always winter but never Christmas'. Altogether too apt.

He wondered what Dr Erwin Gover thought of his home's one-time inhabitant, and quickly decided not to ask. If there was one thing he had learned in his time in Oxford, it was that each generation took more pride in itself than in any of its predecessors. Besides, Gover was a scientist.

The man who opened the door, however, looked more like the eccentric keeper of some Dickensian old curiosity shop. He was wearing a faded crimson quilted coat, which Therry initially took to be a dressing gown but Daniel recognised as what was once referred to as a smoking jacket.

'Yes,' he said abruptly, with just the slightest trace of a German accent. 'What do you want?'

'My name's Moon, Dr Gover. I telephoned. From the newspaper.'

'Ah, yes.' Suddenly the gruff manner was replaced by an improbable smile, and the apparition in the dressing-gown affair shuffled backwards to admit them. Therry's quick phone call had worked wonders. There was nothing like the prospect of being quoted in the press as a 'top authority' to appeal to most dons, especially those who had a chip on their shoulder from being passed over for promotion.

They followed Gover down a dark hallway, lined with mahogany panelling and old prints of the Oxford colleges, which Daniel imagined came supplied with the accommodation, and squeezed past a coatstand weighed down with what appeared to be the entirety of Gover's wardrobe.

'We'll use the study, if you don't mind. It's probably less of a mess.'

Anything more of a mess than the crowded little room he led them into would have been hard to imagine. Two walls were completely covered by overfilled bookcases while the floor itself was only just visible between islands of stacked papers. It looked as if Gover had either just moved in or was getting ready to move out. Daniel suspected correctly, however, that neither was the case. Gover seated himself at an equally cluttered desk. On the far side, arranged so that its user would have the alternative of a view out over the slowly turning mill wheel, sat a trolley with a PC displaying a screen saver that looked like the spiral helices of the DNA molecule, alternating between livid orange and lime green. There was nowhere for either Therry or Daniel to sit, a fact which Gover seemed entirely to have overlooked. So they stood.

'I shan't offer you tea,' said Gover. It was a statement rather than an apology. 'Now,' he said, turning to Therry, with a glance at Daniel that suggested his presence was an anomaly he had only just registered, 'perhaps you will tell me what you want to talk about. You were not very precise on the telephone.'

As concisely as she could, given that she was inventing large parts of her story on the hoof, Therry told him she was working on a piece about the archaeological sites threatened by new housing development in the villages. In the course of her research for the feature, she had come across accounts of the Black Death and wanted to do a side bar on the disease itself. So of course she had come to Dr Gover, who was universally acknowledged as the leading scientific expert on the subject.

Her flattery was met with an undisguised but evidently not displeased harrumph. Daniel wondered how he would react to the name 'Redwhistle'. Gover had been the man whom university insiders had expected to take over the chair of epidemiology before the 'outsider' appeared on the scene.

'It's safe to say, isn't it, Dr Gover, that the last outbreak in Britain was the Great Plague that struck London in 1665, the year before the Great Fire?' It was a good question to start with, Therry thought, general but yet showing she was not a complete idiot on the subject.

Gover smiled as if he had been waiting for this one and had his answer ready: 'No, no, no, my dear. Nothing quite so remote, I'm afraid. The last recorded instance of bubonic plague in this country occurred in Suffolk. In 1913.'

'You're kidding?'

Gover's expression showed that he was pleased with the effect of his little bombshell. Therry was nonplussed but at the same time excited: 1913 was not even a century ago. If the plague had survived until then . . .

'But then what happened? Why haven't we heard about it? How many died?'

'Oh, barely a dozen, if I recall correctly. Despite its reputation, the plague does not always reach epidemic proportions. In this case, the vector was believed to have been rats that had come ashore from the Indies, but the pool of infection was relatively small, in a tiny village, and it died out quickly. It sometimes does, you know. If it runs out of a host population or encounters a pool of immunity.'

'It's the rats that spread it.'

'The rats are the most common means of its spread, though far from exclusively. The black rat is merely the most widely travelled little monster. Ground squirrels and prairie dogs in North America, even those cute little cartoon chipmunks, can in real life transport plague. And then there's the Siberian marmot – Genghis Khan forbade his men to kill them for food because the risk of infection was so great. But you must not think – as so many people in the popular media seem to – that it is these animals themselves that cause the infection. They merely carry the fleas.'

Daniel nodded impatiently and was about to interrupt. He had not come to Gover for a lesson in the basics. But Therry had long ago learned that the best way to get what you wanted out of an interviewee was to give them almost free rein and then slowly steer them in the right direction.

'And it's the fleas that carry the virus, right?'

'Wrong. There is no virus involved. You must not confuse a virus with bacteria. They are very different. A virus is, how can I put it for you, like a strand of DNA – you know what DNA is?'

Both Daniel and Therry nodded quickly. Although their knowledge was far from perfect, they did not want to be subjected to a complete biology lesson.

'Bacteria are different. They are, if you like, the most basic form of animal, microscopic. The original life forms to evolve in the primeval soup of earth's oceans were almost certainly bacteria. The first stepping stone on the evolutionary road. The bacteria that cause plague probably came into existence about the same time as those which eventually, over many millions of years, evolved into higher animals, including us. It is fanciful of course, but not incorrect, to think of the plague bacteria as earth's oldest original inhabitants, still battling it out with the usurpers.'

'You make it sound almost intelligent.'

The academic laughed thinly. 'We should not equate intelligence with the success of a species.'

'What do you mean?'

'Well, we think of humans as dominating the planet, which we do, in a way, but we cause more than enough harm to it, and to ourselves. Seen from a totally alien viewpoint, the most numerous, thriving and successful species on earth could be one of several types of ant, or even wheat. Intelligence is but one tool for survival. We have been at war with the plague bacterium for millions of years, and with not particular success, at least until the past century. Over history this one strain of bacteria has killed more people than all other diseases and all human warfare put together.'

Therry thought of the images in the library, of the Dancing Death, the flagellation and the hopeless prayers, of a population that knew nothing of the nature, even the existence, of its true enemy.

'The plague itself is a bacterium,' Gover continued. 'Yersinia pestis, named after a nineteenth-century Russian, one Alexander Yersin, who travelled to Hong Kong during the last major pandemic, in 1894. Thankfully that one never reached Europe, though it did get to California. Yersin was the first to isolate the bacillus. It lives in the digestive tract of fleas, particularly the rat flea, Xenopsylla cheopis, though it can also live in the human flea, Pulex irritans –'

'Latin for "irritating flea",' said Daniel, and was met with a glare that suggested he had, in Gover's eyes, described himself perfectly.

'Quite,' he said, getting up from his chair and making his way towards the bookcase next to the window. 'This, if I may just show you, is the little fellow responsible.'

He reached down a broad folder, like student's art

portfolio, which when opened out was revealed to contain a selection of extremely detailed anatomical drawings of insects. Gover rearranged the piles of papers on his desk and spread out an illustration of something that to Therry looked as if it had either escaped from the design studio for the *Alien* series of movies or some particularly challenging sushi kitchen.

'Yeuch! What is that?'

'A flea. Amazing, isn't it, how scale changes things?'

'Amazing,' said Therry. She didn't sound impressed.

'This flea is the host for our bacteria. They multiply in the flea's stomach to cause a blockage, threatening the flea with starvation. In order to survive, therefore, it regurgitates the bacteria into its victim while feeding.'

'I think I feel sick,' said Therry.

'Enough to make you throw up,' Daniel echoed.

'Not very pleasant, is it?' Gover smiled indulgently. The flea "throws up", as you put it, into the bloodstream.'

'But a flea bite isn't the only way to catch plague, is it?'

'Oh, not at all, not at all. The fleas only start the infection. The really virulent form of the disease is the pneumonic variation. It's only when the bacteria get into the lungs and begin to destroy the tissue that mass infection becomes a real risk. As the patient's lung tissue disintegrates, and the bacteria fight to get into the bloodstream, the patient lapses into coughing fits during which small droplets of his saliva, often mixed with blood, are ejected into the air. These droplets are of course laden with the plague organism. Anyone who comes into contact with them is almost certain to become infected. It's only when the plague becomes airborne that it really, er, takes off, if you know what I mean.'

Daniel ignored the infelicity. He was reliving the

horror of the man in the private ward on the seventh floor of the hospital suddenly lurching forward in his bed, his lungs exploding. No wonder Rajiv had virtually thrown him out of the room. Shit! He hoped the drug his friend had given him was as good as he said.

'By far the largest number of people who died in the Black Death succumbed to pneumonic plague. At its most extreme, it can be almost unbelievably virulent. People could contract it in the morning, almost without knowing it, become ill by lunchtime and dead before nightfall, either because of the destruction of their lungs or because the bacteria poisoned their blood. Septicaemic plague. No wonder people at the time thought it was a sign of the apocalypse.'

'How . . . how do you treat it? Antibiotics? Penicillin?'

Gover harrumphed again. 'Penicillin? If only! I'm afraid that against the plague it is totally ineffective. There are drugs, of course, but a lot of them have side effects that are almost as dangerous. All the sulpha drugs, for example.'

Both Daniel and Therry looked blank.

'Sulphadiazine, for example, has been shown to reduce mortality substantially, but . . .'

'But?'

'It also causes irreparable kidney lesions. Streptomycin injected directly into the muscle tissue remains the best bet, though there is a very slight risk that it can cause deafness if the dosage is not controlled.'

'What about tetracycline?' Daniel asked.

Both Therry and Gover turned to look at him, equally surprised.

'Mmh, yes. It works as a prophylactic, if properly administered. The dosage needs to be calculated exactly, depending on bodyweight, and it has to be taken consistently for at least a week.'

Daniel nodded to show he understood. Well done, Rajiv! he was thinking.

But Therry was thinking on different lines. She wanted to know how the disease was being incubated at Nether Ditchford.

'What about dealing with the, uh . . .' She searched for the word. '. . . the vectors, the rodents? How do people investigate suspected plague outbreak sites?'

'First trap a rat, of course, and test it for plague-bearing fleas.'

'Is it possible for an infected colony of rats to survive for a long time, a very long time, without the plague passing to humans?'

Daniel looked quizzically at Therry, wondering where she was leading.

Gover followed his look. 'Not really. The rats die of it too, you know. Eventually, when the bacteria run out of hosts, the plague subsides. Thank God! That is why even the worst outbreaks in the end run their course. Small communities are often totally eliminated. That is why the only way of being certain of controlling an outbreak still seems so cruel: isolating a community, by force if need be, until the disease has done its worst. At least nowadays we can treat those within the containment area, if we get there in time.'

'But could the bacteria survive on their own, without a host? In some sort of suspended animation? Like yeast – that's a living organism, isn't it? Which can be kept dried and later be brought back to life. Just add water!'

'We-ell, it's not as simple as that. But . . .'

'But what?'

Gover gave a sigh, as if about to concede something with great reluctance. 'But it has happened. In places like Iran, where plague is more or less endemic in some areas. I recall reading a year or two back –' his eyes momentarily scanned the great array of shelves as if willing the particular volume he had in mind to pop out on command – 'about an instance like that.'

'Go on, doctor, please.'

'Well, in some cases it appears that even when the hole has been sealed for months and there's no sign of fleas, the bacteria have re-emerged. As if they could somehow hibernate in the soil and then, with the recurrence of oxygen and insect life, make the leap back into a host.'

'How long could the thing survive without a host?'

'The evidence is slight and what there is, is not very clear. But there are recorded instances of six and nine months, certainly. In one case, it was thought that the burrow had lain undisturbed for over a year. And in another –'

'Yes, yes.' Insistently.

'In one case, near Tabriz, in Iran, in rat holes, they think they had been covered in for nearly ten years.'

'And still the bacteria survived!'

'And still there was a plague outbreak shortly after the holes were broken into. There was no definitive proof of a cause-and-effect relationship. But I don't see how –'

'What about six hundred years?'

Daniel had to hand it to her, the girl knew how to deliver a whammy.

'What? Oh, I see. I see what you're up to, young lady. Well, the answer is no. Definitively! And if you're thinking of indulging in sensationalist journalism, you needn't look to me to back up your wild ideas. It's not possible, I tell you. Simply not possible.'

Therry had coloured bright red, though whether from anger or embarrassment was hard to tell.

'I don't think you know that, Dr Gover. Six years or six centuries, it doesn't really matter, does it? It's the principle that counts. Are you saying that it is scientifically impossible despite the fact that there are comparable instances? What if I were to tell you . . .' She let her voice tail off. It was not quite time to play her trump card.

Gover was running his fingers through his thinning white hair in a gesture that might have been distraction or simply exasperation. '*I'm* telling *you* it has never happened.'

'With all due respect, Dr Gover, that's not the same thing.'

'Of course it's not. But –'

'But therefore there is a chance, maybe a remote chance, but a chance nonetheless. If it's not impossible, then it can happen, can't it? I mean, that's scientific logic, isn't it? It's maths, right? Like winning the lottery: the odds are millions to one against, so bad that common sense says there's no point in playing, yet there're enough jackpot winners out there who're glad they did.'

'Young lady.' Daniel could hear the frustration in the old man's voice. 'What you say is of course perfectly valid, but applied science unfortunately is not quite as clear-cut as you might imagine, and certainly nothing like as simple as mathematics. Medicine least of all. In any case, any mathematician will tell you that you can't calculate odds, no matter how astronomical, if there are unknown elements in the equation. And that's what there are in this case: too many unknowns. Far too many. And one of them is what exactly you are trying to prove. I am not in the business of providing quotes to order for journalists.'

That's exactly the business you are in, thought Therry, though she said nothing aloud. It was true: what she wanted was to hear him say that her theory was possible, not just for the paper – though it would put a spoke in old Harkness's wheels – but because she believed it. It was Sherlock Holmes, wasn't it, who said that when all other explanations have been eliminated, what is left, however improbable, has to be true. But when it came to anything that challenged their beliefs, she knew scientists could be as blind and bloody-minded as Christian fundamentalists.

'You haven't told me,' Gover was saying, 'what this is all about. Neither of you is a scientist. That is perfectly obvious. So why on earth are you working up such absurd speculations about a comparatively rare tropical disease that has not been known on any scale in Europe for centuries?'

'What would you say, Dr Gover –' the moment had come, as good as it was going to get – 'if we told you that early yesterday a man in the JR2 hospital died of the Black Death?'

Gover did his best not to look taken aback.

'I would say, in the first instance, that what you mean is that he died of bubonic plague, rather than the particular strain of it that visited these shores in the fourteenth century. And secondly I would ask you where this man had recently been travelling, for it is almost certainly there that he contracted this disease.'

'Maybe. Maybe. But if we were to add,' said Therry, using the plural to add moral weight Daniel hoped, rather than because he was her partner in speculation, 'that this man had been digging on the unexcavated site of a plague village –'

'I would say that you were letting your imagination run away with you.'

'. . . and that the contractor was trying to cover it up. And that Professor Redwhistle was helping him.'

Gover had been sitting with his eyes tightly closed, shaking his head. The mention of his arch-rival brought him up sharp.

'Redwhistle? He's involved?'

Therry and Daniel nodded together.

'How much do you know about Professor Redwhistle?'

They looked at each other, uncertain how to continue.

'He was ... is ... something of a rival of yours, isn't that right?' Therry blurted out, and Daniel closed his eyes.

Gover put his hands together in front of his face, almost as if he were praying, but his eyes were focused on the middle distance, a limbo somewhere in the empty space between them.

'I think I've said enough. You'd better go.'

'But Dr Gover –' Therry began.

'I said I think you'd better go.' He made a show of looking at his watch. 'I have an appointment. Please,' he said, gesturing them towards the door and the hallway.

'Just one thing,' he said, ushering them out of the front door into the icy cold of the gathering dusk. 'Be careful, be very careful. I know what I said, but you must understand that in the real world, anything is possible. Anything at all.'

Chapter Thirty

Oxford; Monday 22 December, 4.25 p.m.

NARROW MAGPIE Lane, which links Oxford's High Street with the quiet, cobbled Merton Street, has a long and dubious history. Once famous as a quick business retreat for ladies of the night and a venue for hasty knee-trembling encounters between students and local girls, it used to be commonly referred to as Gropecunt Lane. Recent years have not improved its reputation, although the footpads who long lingered in its shadows are now called muggers.

Happily for George Pirewski, he knew none of that. It had taken hours for the black-lined redness to fade from his eyes. When he drifted back to consciousness, his chest still burning as if his lungs were filled with lava, it had taken several minutes to remember where he was: lying in a cold stone alcove in an alleyway. A cardboard box left next to him and a few coppers by his head were the only testimony to the seasonal charity of passers-by.

But the phonecard was still clutched in his almost frozen fingers and a phone box, one of the nasty BT type that offers slim shelter from the elements of a British winter, stood only a few dozen yards away. Even so, as he staggered to his feet, he wondered whether he would make it. But as he moved, the fire in his lungs receded, if only temporarily. He reached the box, inserted the phonecard – there was exactly 30 pence credit left – and dialled the number. The number that he had memorised, that he had to believe would save his life.

It was a pager number. As he watched the precious pennies on his phonecard tick away on the digital display, he heard a recorded voice tell him to tap in the telephone number from which he was calling. He almost panicked before discovering that the box was indeed one of those that display their number. He keyed it in and the voice told him to replace the handset and wait five minutes. If he was not called back within that time, he should wait thirty minutes and redial. I only had 30p, he thought as he put down the receiver. I don't know if I have thirty minutes.

The phone rang within two.

This time the voice had been real. A man's. It was an emergency, Pirewski told him. He needed help. Yes. That sort of help. And fast. Where was he? the caller wanted to know. In Oxford. But the man already knew that. Whereabouts? In the city centre. The High Street. Good. Did he know Magpie Lane? Never heard of it. It was on the south side of the street. Yes, probably the other side. The same side as University College, but further along. He should be there. In twenty minutes. Yes, he could find it. Of course he could. It was going to be all right, wasn't it? He knew this wasn't supposed to happen, but it was an accident. They would fix him up, wouldn't they? Like they promised? Of course they would, the voice on the other end of the phone reassured him. They kept their promises. Unlike some people.

It had taken him most of the twenty minutes to find Magpie Lane, only a few hundred yards away on the other side of the road. It was already late afternoon, December's early dusk. The street was busy with last-minute shoppers, too busy to notice yet another derelict drift through their field of vision. Yet now in the dark and quiet of the alleyway, it seemed as if time had stopped moving. He hung, rather than stood, supporting his weight on a set of railings. He dared not let go for fear of crumpling to the ground and never getting up again. Somewhere, the minutes were ticking away. Somewhere else. His watch had a backlit LCD display but he did not press and illuminate it. He could not face proof that time was standing still. He felt that he had been trapped in purgatory on earth, a state of suspended animation, in pain that stopped just short of excruciating. Eternally.

The end of eternity took him by surprise.

Just a voice in the darkness. The two words: 'What happened?'

The voice was the same as on the telephone. He was certain of that. But he could not see the face of the man who was speaking, standing several yards away. A dark shape in a dark doorway. How long had he been there? Watching?

'Wha' – what do you mean?' Though he knew, of course.

'This. You. Him.'

'What does it matter? Come on, for God's sake. Give me the shot.'

'All in good time. You'll be OK. Don't worry.' The voice had a clinical calm to it. 'Tell me what happened. I . . . we need to know.'

'There . . . there was an accident, in the car. Taking Miranda to the airport. We were late. It, it was my fault. Driving too fast. Coming into Heathrow. We were late, you see. Drunk. We all were. A bit. I mean, we had done it, hadn't we? Pulled it off. Just after the tunnel under the runway, I pulled out on to the roundabout, through the lights. Swerved to avoid another car. Hit the barrier. No real damage, we thought. Miranda, she was furious. Screamed. You know how she was. Said we'd kill ourselves. Thought she was joking. Grabbed her flight bag and was gone. Called me for everything. Said she'd be in touch, though we didn't deserve it. But we didn't know what she was planning. Honest . . .'

'Never mind. Go on.'

'Well, I didn't know, did I, that anything had happened. It was only on the way back we stopped, on the M40, pulled into a lay-by to check the stuff. It was his idea, not mine. Don't be daft, I said, that's dangerous. But he said it would be a lot more dangerous if we lost it or let it leak away. So he opened the container. Not the glass one, mind, just the metal sheath. But we'd forgotten about the liquid nitrogen, see, inside, to keep it cold. And when he touched the neck of the glass vial, to make sure the stopper was OK, like, the frozen nitrogen tore the skin from his finger. And I guess it wasn't OK. The stopper, that is. It was just a few hours later that it started. I should have guessed, when he started coughing over me. Should have stayed out of the way, out of the goddamn, fucking way.'

A rasping, wheezing sob racked him. The effort of talking had taken more out of him than he had realised.

'Where is it now?'

'Where's what?'

'What do you think?'

'For Christ's sake! I don't know.'

'You have to remember, George, that was part of the deal.'

Like iced water trickling through his bowels, it came to him. Despite the fire raging in his veins, Pirewski's blood still managed to run cold. Was this a trade-off? Was that what this bastard was trying to tell him?

'All right, all right, I can find it. Now give me the drug, for God's sake! You don't know what it's like.'

There was a moment's hesitation. For he was right. The man in the shadows did not know what it was like. And he was curious. It was, after all, not just any illness. The figure hanging plaintively on the railings was suffering from a legend, a killing legend. And fatality, as they said in the movies, had its own attraction.

'Come on, for pity's sake! Give it to me.'

In the shadows, the man smiled. Although even if it had been light, the smile would not have been visible.

'Turn around. Face the railings, lift your coat and drop your trousers.'

'What?' For a moment Pirewski hesitated. Then he understood. In the arse. They always gave injections in the arse. Still, he was nervous as he did as he was told. And felt the man approach. Waited for the jab.

The man in the doorway emerged, removing the necessary instrument from within his coat, and walked slowly towards the trembling, shivering wreck hunched forward, holding the railings with one hand while the other rucked an overcoat up over pale buttocks that surreally, in the dark alleyway, alone reflected the distant lamplight.

'Hang on,' he said. 'This won't hurt a bit.'

Only at the last second, as if warned by some sixth sense, did Pirewski turn his head to see, with unbridled horror, the spectre that loomed behind him. Something fearsomely alien. Circular glistening eyes bulged from an impossibly white skin, hairless, smooth and yet grotesquely gnarled. Where the mouth should have been was a great white maw in the form of a grid. A mangled scream choked in his tortured gullet as the iron-cored rubber truncheon, deflected from its aim, smashed into his larynx. The second blow, delivered with an imprecation, compensated and hit him full on the base of the neck, instantly severing its connection to his spine. A judiciously extended left hand caught the weight of the crumpling body and lowered it to the pavement as the right hand delivered a final blow to the side of the skull, striking precisely on the soft spot between the temple and upper ear. But George Perewski was no longer capable of noticing the multiple haemorrhaging within his cerebellum.

Peremptorily, Harold Hammerstein searched the pockets of the loose-fitting coat. Empty. Save for a used, crumpled handkerchief which he extracted at arm's length with his latex-gloved fingers and regarded with distaste behind the protective mask. A quick glance up and down the alleyway assured him that Magpie Lane was still as deserted as could be hoped on a winter's evening in December.

He had chosen the location specifically. And the time. It had given him just enough time to get to the University Church of St Mary the Virgin, on the northern side of the High Street, and sprint up the 144 steps that led up the spiral staircase to the public viewing platform at the base of the spire. From there he had had a perfect view of George Pirewski entering the alley from the street below, and of the surrounding streets. Without a thought for the pain and discomfort of the man waiting for him in the alleyway, Hammerstein had delayed his descent until he was certain that Pirewski was alone and not bait in a trap. And then he got down to business.

He looked at the body at his feet. Good. There was little or no blood. Lucky really, as when the idiot had turned he feared he might have caught his jaw and splintered it, with all the unpleasant consequences of spreading blood and saliva that that would have occasioned. Instead the corpse of George Pirewski was virtually intact, as he had hoped. Perhaps a little too intact. On a whim he took the truncheon and rammed a good half of its two-foot length up the dead man's pale rectum. To the police it would like like a homosexual tryst gone wrong, a male prostitute robbed of his fee, or just another queer-killer on the loose. Either way, it would feed the salacious appetites of the investigating officers. Not to mention the media. And that was more than half the battle.

Stepping back briskly into his doorway, Hammerstein pulled off the goggles, face mask and protective head covering and crumpled them into a thick black plastic bag which he had kept in his coat pocket for the purpose. The gloves he removed last of all, gingerly, working with his fingertips only at the edge of the latex. He shivered as the last finger came free. Then the gloves joined the rest of his disposable outfit in the sealed bag which he secreted back in his capacious pocket. Hammerstein strode off briskly. All of a sudden, he realised, he could do with a drink.

Chapter Thirty-One

*The John Radcliffe Hospital, Oxford; Monday
22 December, 4.30 p.m.*

T HE PLAN was perfect. Almost. Janet Southby, the
front receptionist at the JR2, was normally due to
finish her shift at 4.30 p.m. Unfortunately that would
give her barely enough time to get down to the Westgate
centre to complete her Christmas shopping. However
Christine, who had come on as usual at 3.00 for the
evening shift, had agreed, provided things were quiet
enough, to hold the fort on her own for an hour longer
than usual and let her slip away early. The last thing
Janet needed, therefore, was an awkward bugger. And
this bugger was as awkward as they came.

Polite, of course; the worst of them often were. But
insistent. Tediously insistent. Chinese or more likely
Japanese; expensively dressed. She only wished she could
afford to buy clothes like that for her Tim. Bloody
foreigners! At least British people, by and large, had
the good grace to take no for an answer.

She was just explaining to the irritating enquirer for
the third and, she hoped, final time that there was no
one registered as a patient under the name McCormack,
and that if her computer could not find him, then as far
as she and the hospital were concerned, he simply did not
exist, when the doors were thrown open and two highly
agitated young people dashed in as if they were headed
for Accident and Emergency. Janet had prayed for an

interruption to get the stranger out of her hair. But she was not at all sure that this looked like the answer to her prayer.

The skies had begun to darken as the Range Rover climbed Headington Hill. Daniel had to force himself to believe that the thick blue-black cumulus lowering over them presaged nothing more sinister than a midwinter dusk. Freezing raindrops landed on the windscreen in smudges of dirty slush. Sitting staring out at the drab council houses and the yellow streetlights already flickering into dull life in the fast-gathering darkness, he was convinced of what they had to do: put their 'evidence' to Redwhistle in person. Despite Gover's misgivings, almost certainly based on the wounded pride of a jealous rival, the only way they could get their suspicion taken seriously – and action taken as a result – was if they could win over the professor of epidemiology.

All Redwhistle had to do was to agree that the possibility of plague bacteria being awakened from a state of dormancy longer than in any previous recorded instance could not be ruled out, and they would set off a storm of media interest. Therry would have her scoop, and Daniel Warren would have one hell of a peg on which to hang his thesis. The Black Death rediscovered would allow him to make the magic leap from scholarship to celebrity. And most importantly, he told himself repeatedly, they might also be saving lives.

If there was even the remotest possibility that Atkins had not contracted the disease in Iran, and that the two other victims had not caught it from him, but that all three of them had encountered the beginnings of a renascent colony of ancient bacteria-bearing fleas in the deep mud of Nether Ditchford – whether they had somehow survived down the centuries or been reawakened from some form of dormancy the scientists knew nothing of – then something had to be done. And fast. It had to be done before work resumed on the Nether Ditchford site after the Christmas holidays.

Therry parked the Range Rover outside the maternity wing in a slot reserved for expectant mothers. 'One of the advantages of being a woman,' she said. The little garden looked forlorn: even the thin drifts of snow settled in the empty flowerbeds were dirty, with the pawprints of defecating dogs. The hospital's cold white mass loomed out of the night with all the welcoming warmth of a state penitentiary.

Daniel's plan, for want of a better word, was to have Rajiv paged at the front desk. As long as they could just talk to Rajiv, even if only on the telephone, surely they would be able to convince him to introduce them to his supervisor. The chance of Redwhistle giving them any credence would be increased if they had a proper introduction from one of his star students. The only flaw – at least he hoped it was the only flaw – was that Rajiv might well be reluctant to risk his reputation with the professor by allowing some crackpot Californian student historian to get his foot in the door. What Rajiv might do on realising that Daniel had dragged along a wannabe Lois Lane from the local rag did not bear thinking about. On the other hand, nor did Therry's alternative plan of action. The idea of repeating his earlier masquerade, this time as a double act, sent a shiver down Daniel's spine.

Suddenly it seemed that their task was going to be a lot easier than Daniel had imagined. Just as they walked through the second set of double doors towards the reception desk, a nurse came running down the long corridor from the central lifts, chasing a tall man in a Burberry trenchcoat who was striding ahead of her, his eyes rooted to the floor in front of him. Daniel caught his breath as he heard the name she called: 'Dr Redwhistle, Dr Redwhistle, one moment please!'

The tall man stopped, with the precision of a Guards officer on parade, and lifted his head to look around him for the source of the call. The look on his face was black, as if he did not take kindly to being accosted. Daniel swallowed hard. So that was Redwhistle. He recognised him immediately: the tall consultant who had eyed him disparagingly while discussing golf handicaps in the lift.

What the hell! The chances that the man would recognise him were slight. Now he and Therry had got this far; there was nothing to be gained from backing out.

'Dr Redwhistle,' Daniel called. Now doubly irked, Redwhistle barked something at the nurse who had hailed him first, sending her scuttling off again down the corridor, and then turned towards Daniel with an expression that he might have reserved for cockroaches on the ward.

'Who are you? What do you want?'

'We're friends of Rajiv Mahendra,' Daniel spluttered, with Therry now close at his side. 'At least I am,' he added unnecessarily, though it seemed as if the man's stony face flinched for an instant. 'We have to talk to you. We know what's going on upstairs. On the fifth floor.'

If Redwhistle had looked for a moment like melting, he now froze over again and began walking forwards, not so much towards them as past them, heading for the door.

'I don't know what you're talking about,' he got out through clenched teeth. 'But if you're friends of Dr Mahendra –'

'Dr Redwhistle, you have to listen to us.' Daniel was

trying to hold the man's arm to delay his progress, an action which clearly annoyed the consultant intensely. 'Look, we know it's bubonic plague,' Daniel hissed at the man through clenched teeth. Redwhistle's eyebrows rose as his lips pursed. 'But it's not what you think,' Daniel continued blindly. 'It's not that simple.'

Therry thought she detected a glimpse of pure scorn in the man's eyes.

'For Christ's sake, man, it's the Black Death, isn't it?' Daniel was babbling now. The receptionist's head turned. Any moment now, Therry thought, she's going to be calling the security staff or at least a posse of burly hospital porters. Already there was an oriental man moving towards them purposefully from the waiting area, although he didn't look like any hospital porter Therry had ever come across. The dark suit he was wearing looked too expensive and his expression was hard to read. Therry felt his eyes flash across her like x-rays in an instant, both stripping her and seeing through her, and then focus back on the tussle between the eminent doctor and the distracted-looking young man with the American accent.

'Daniel,' she started. 'Perhaps we should just –'

But Daniel wasn't listening to her. 'Look, this is serious! It's the building site, Nether Ditchford. It's there, not Iran or wherever. It's the plague, the old one! They've dug it up! At least they may have. The fleas, they can survive! I know you might not want to hear this, but you have to . . .'

Redwhistle had stopped short, looking around him quickly, to gauge how much attention Daniel was drawing to them. A quick nod to the receptionist apparently reassured her. The oriental man in the dark suit had suddenly stopped about six feet from them with his head turned away, and was now tinkering with his watch as if suddenly realising he had failed to adjust it to this time zone. Slowly, deliberately, Redwhistle lifted Daniel's hand from his arm and released it.

'Young man,' he said, in a precisely articulated hiss. 'Believe me, I know just how serious this is. Just as I know that you have absolutely no idea what you are talking about. I don't know who you are but if you have anything to say to me, then kindly book an appointment with my secretary. Now if you don't mind –'

'No, wait!' Daniel was getting desperate. 'You don't understand.'

'*I* don't understand? I'm afraid it is you who do not understand. Now let me go.'

The anger in his voice and in his eyes took Daniel aback for an instant. And in that instant Redwhistle was gone, sweeping past Daniel and Therry and pushing through the twin sets of double doors out into the dark. His tormentors followed after him, helplessly.

'Wait!' Therry called, just for the sake of it. Her voice was lost in the cold wind that swept across the car park.

'Listen, for God's sake!' Daniel called, breaking into a run although he too had little hope that his words would have any effect. 'Rajiv Mahendra will vouch for us. You have to listen.'

Redwhistle stopped with a suddenness that caused Daniel to stop too. It was hard to discern, in the dark and with the sleet pelting their faces, just what expression was written on the features of the consultant.

'Really? In that case, I am afraid I have to inform you that Dr Mahendra is dead. He too was a victim of this unfortunate disease you seem to know so much about. If you were friends of his, as you say –' he paused to accentuate the brutality of the effect – 'then you might have known that.'

Daniel felt his jaw go slack. 'Why . . . ? How . . . ?'

But Redwhistle was gone. Therry watched them both. Daniel Warren remained standing there in the slanting sleet, silhouetted against the white neon of the car-park lights, paralysed like a rabbit who has glimpsed his onrushing fate and does not know what to do about it. Dr Simon Redwhistle marched off and disappeared incongruously into a low MG in the consultants' car park, slamming the door and firing the ignition into life.

At first it seemed Daniel barely noticed her when she clutched his arm, shivering in the wind, any more than he noticed the tiny pellets of ice that pelted his face. And then she turned and looked where he was looking, at the red tail lights of Redwhistle's car. Together they watched them circle the roundabout and vanish down the hill. And then there was nothing. Except the wind and the sleet, softening now into thick flakes of snow.

Chapter Thirty-Two

The King's Arms, Oxford; Monday 22
December, 6.00 p.m.

LATER, IN the Back Bar of the King's Arms once again, Daniel stumbled his way to the corner table which both of them now considered theirs and sat there like a man bereft, which was how he felt. Therry fetched drinks.

He was rubbing his face with his hands when she joined him at the table. She put the beer down in front of him. He lifted it, took a deep draught, set it down, then lifted it again almost immediately and took another.

'Hey, steady on!'

Daniel ignored her, and she took a long swig of her own. For a time they sat there in silence, while the bar bustled around them. While the world continued to spin. And carried them with it like reluctant passengers.

'I didn't know,' Daniel muttered at last. 'I just didn't know.'

Therry just nodded, not knowing whether he was talking to her or to himself.

'Did you hear me? I said I just didn't know.'

'Hey, come on, I heard you, I heard you.' She reached out a hand and put it on top of his. 'What is it, Dan, I mean Daniel, what's wrong? What didn't you know?'

His face twisted, ugly with raw emotion, grief contorting his muscles to make channels for unshed tears.

'That this would happen. That he would die. He

should never have gone back. Never have gone in there. It was just for me. Because I wanted to see.'

Therry was shaking her head.

'What are you talking about? It was Rajiv who diagnosed the plague in the first place, wasn't it? He had already been exposed.'

'Yes, but . . . but I made him go back.'

'Come on, he would have been treating this bloke anyhow. Wouldn't he?'

But Daniel wasn't listening.

'You don't understand. You see, I had to see how it looked. I had to . . . just had to . . .'

'Never mind. I understand.' She thought she did. There was a large element of the voyeur in every reporter's soul.

'No! No, you don't. It's . . . it's not what you think. That's what Rajiv thought too, at first. Gross. Just wanting to get in there and look at some guy suffering. I'm not that sort of ghoul. Really.'

Therry shrugged inwardly. Ghoulishness was part of her job description, but if Daniel wanted to tell her he was different, that was fine. It didn't change the fact that he had gone, though.

'I had to know what it was like, you see. Because of my mother.'

'Your mother the witch?'

'My mother the witch, yes.' The ghost of a sad smile flitted across his face for a second. 'The witch whose magic wasn't strong enough.'

'You've lost me.'

He shook his head. 'I lost her. It was in New Mexico, nearly seven years ago now. I was just a kid growing up, just beginning to understand what she had been trying to tell me all those years. We got a call at home from the chief of a Navajo tribe.'

'A Navajo? Your mum was a Native American?'

Daniel shook his head. 'No, but they'd heard of her,' he said. 'Down on one of the reservations out on the New Mexico–Nevada border. You get that? They'd heard of my mom! Heard she could heal people, had medicine better than the regular doctors. I guess they thought she was some sort of medicine woman . . .'

'A witch doctor.'

'I guess. It's sort of what she was really, I suppose. They said they needed help. Bad. They'd had an outbreak of this disease that no one could cure.'

Therry's eyes widened, anticipating what was coming.

Daniel simply nodded, as if it was obvious.

'In America?'

'Oh, don't look so surprised. I told you. Except in Europe, the plague's never really gone away. There are maybe a dozen cases a year in the United States, mostly among hunters. They catch it from the fleas that live on chipmunks or prairie dogs. It's only really found in the southwest, but if there's anywhere in the continental US where you stand a risk of catching plague, it's Navajo country. They're mostly isolated cases in areas of extremely low population; the patient either dies or sometimes recovers without infecting anyone else at all.

'My mother tried to tell him there was nothing she could do. But he was insistent. Said they'd had three young men die, boys really, about the same age as I was, fourteen or so. That clinched it for her, I think. Said she could only try. There were a few things that they hadn't known in Europe in the old days, things that probably wouldn't help but had to be worth trying. And if not, then at least she could persuade them to try the white men's drugs. She packed a bag that afternoon. Dad and I never saw her again.'

'Oh, Dan!' Therry squeezed his hand hard, watching the tears well up in his eyes.

'Turned out the new things weren't any better than the old things. Still can't beat this damn disease. It's always there, waiting. So when Rajiv . . . I had to . . . I had to stare it in the face, you see. Had to eyeball the bogeyman . . .' He looked down at the table. 'Guess I blinked.' And he put his head in his hands. 'And poor old Rajiv paid the price.'

'Shit.'

'What?'

'Shit happens. It's not your fault. You know that.'

'Therry!' They both turned at the sound of her name and Therry recognised, in the doorway to the Back Bar, the slightly confused-looking figure of Jack Denton pushing his way towards them with what looked like a sheet of photocopying paper in his hand.

'Here,' he said, handing it to her. 'After what you told me on the phone, the way they treated you and him, I thought you might want to see this.'

Therry took the paper, scanned it quickly, glanced up at him with a huge question mark on her face, then began reading it again.

'Henry's words. But Harkness's doing,' Jack said. 'Editor's "must". Virtually dictated the bloody thing.'

'Where's it going?'

'Where d'you think? Bottom of the front page.'

Therry nodded. Harkness's prime position for 'sensitive' stories. Just enough prominence not to appear trivial or lax, but not enough to appear sensationalist. Balance, he called it. No balls, she called it. Especially now.

It was a photocopy of a newspaper proof sheet with one story on it: a short one at that. For a newspaper that prided itself on its show-stopping banners on the front-page lead, there was no mistaking the message even in the downbeat headline. Therry sighed, and read aloud in a quiet monotone:

'Rare tropical disease claims 4 at JR2
'Two construction workers and a medical student have died of a rare tropical disease at the John Radcliffe Hospital in Headington, a hospital spokesman said yesterday.
'The construction workers, currently employed on new housing developments at Nether Ditchford, north Oxon, were believed to have contracted the disease, described as a form of lymphadentitis, while on overseas contract labour in Iran. The junior doctor, an overseas student from India, had been treating them.'

'What?' Daniel interrupted. 'He was from Leicester! The only time he'd been to India was –' He broke off.

'According to Dr Simon Redwhistle,' she continued with a shrug, 'professor of tropical medicine at Oxford University, this was an isolated occurrence and there was no risk to other patients or members of staff in the hospital. The medical student's death was caused by a lapse in normal precautionary measures, the student's own fault, but a regrettable result of his inexperience, Prof Redwhistle said. Supervision of junior doctors was being looked at within the limits allowed by current National Health Service staffing levels.
'Incidents like this showed how important it was for people travelling on holiday or especially working in foreign parts to take advice and get proper immunisation beforehand, Prof Redwhistle

said. "In the modern world, it is very easy for people to pick up a disease in one country and come back home before the symptoms have even materialised. I cannot stress strongly enough how important it is for people to get proper medical advice, particularly before travelling to parts of the world which do not have our standards of hygiene."

'None of the victims were local people.'

'That's it?'

'That's it,' said Jack, watching Therry for a reaction.

'That's very definitely it,' she said at last. 'In fact, in Mr Harkness's world, that last sentence says it all. Not local people, not our problem. I wonder . . .'

'What?' said Jack.

'I wonder who's pulling his strings.'

'Are you serious?'

'I don't know. Maybe. What do you know about him, Jack, this Redwhistle bloke?'

'The professor? Not much. There was a bit of gossip on the university beat when he got the job. A couple of years ago now. Apparently there was some other geezer the dons had their bets on, but Redwhistle just breezed in and got it. Supposed to have been doing important research or something. Come to think of it, there was a bit of fuss, I seem to recall, about him not even coming direct from another academic institution. But it might have been just bitchiness. You know how the old loves get it when their boy misses a plum job.'

'Hmm, I wonder.'

'Do you indeed, young Therry? Really got the bit between them for this one, haven't you? Tell you what, though, if it makes any difference I could ask one of my old mates in London, on the nationals, to have a trawl in their cuts and see if he can find anything of interest, a profile or something. Any use to you?'

'Would you, Jack? It might be a waste of time. Maybe you're right but I just find it aggravating. You should've seen the way this bloke treated us today! Telling Daniel here that his best friend's just died as if he was repeating a football score.'

'OK, love, see what I can do. I'll give old Burke a ring. Know Eamonn Burke?'

Therry shook her head. Daniel was staring at them blankly as if they had started speaking another language.

'Ah, well, before your time, I dare say. Used to be good, though, as good as they get. Then it all started to go wrong for him, marriage broke up and he got involved with some German bint. That ended up in tears too. But he still keeps a finger in the pie. See what he turns up. As you say, might be nothing, nothing at all. Who's for another drink, then? Drowning our sorrows, eh, as they say?'

'As they say.' Daniel sank the remainder of his pint and pushed the empty glass forward.

Therry looked at him, at those big green eyes, rubbed red but still moist. And wondered how long it would take before he would once again think the glass of life was half full.

None of them noticed the man perched on a stool at the bar, half hidden behind his copy of *The Times*, although it would not have taken a great detective to work out, from his dress and manner alone, that he was an unlikely regular among the donnish inhabitants of the KA Back Bar.

Harold Hammerstein glanced fleetingly at his Breitling watch to note the time the little party got up from the table and made their way through the heavy fug of the crowded public bar into the contrasting sharpness of the cold night. Extraordinary, he thought, the people you met in public bars. Just when he thought things were getting difficult. When he thought, for the first time, that he might – just possibly – have to abandon the whole business. Suddenly fortune handed him a gift on a plate. Proof, if any were needed, that luck was on the side of the angels. Even the angels of darkness.

Chapter Thirty-Three

North Oxford; Tuesday 23 December,
11.00 a.m.

'HERE, HOLD this!'
'What the . . . ?' Daniel Warren jumped as Therry grabbed his hand and set it on the steering wheel of the Range Rover just seconds after they turned off the Wolvercote roundabout. 'I can't steer like this! For Christ's sake, what are . . . ?'

'Just keep it straight. One second.'

Therry had arched her back in the driver's seat and hoisted up her flying jacket to reach into some pocket inside. A second later her right hand emerged holding a mobile phone, and her left brushed Daniel's away from the steering wheel, grabbing it again just in time to stop them drifting into the path of an oncoming car. The shocked driver parped angrily.

'Hello,' she barked into the phone. And then changed her tone radically: 'Oh, yes, that's right. From the *Oxford Post*. Good of you to ring. Yes, yes, I know what it's like at this time of year. Still, some of us got to work, eh?'

Daniel stared at her, with a weather eye on how she was coping steering single-handedly. Her sudden switch to an ingratiating tone amused him.

'Yes, that's right,' she continued, with an audible smile in her voice. 'For a roundup piece in the New Year.' A pause. 'Oh, certainly, very positive. Good for employment. Our editor's big on progress. Modernising

Britain and all that.' Despite himself, Daniel smiled; this was hypocrisy at a professional level.

Another pause. And then a sharp intake of breath and a low whistle. 'What? Really? That much difference? Yes, well, I suppose it would. Oh, yes, very good news. Particularly for the farmers. If there are any left . . . No, no, just a joke. Thank you very much for helping . . . Yes, don't worry, we'll make sure you get a credit.'

'*Yes!*' she exclaimed, closing the phone with a snap.

'What?' Daniel was curious. 'Do you want to tell me what any of that was about?'

'Yep.' She beamed. 'I do. A motive. That's what it's about.'

'A motive?'

'A motive. The best of all, a financial motive. That was FDD Sawyers, the estate agents. Banbury office. I'd called them first thing – before you'd shifted your sorry arse off the sofa – but there was no one there, this being Christmas and whatever. Left a message on the machine. Hadn't really expected them to get back. But that's underestimating the power of the press and the bastards' hunger for free publicity.'

'But what . . . ?'

'. . . did I want an estate agent for? To find out the price of land, what else? You remember the old boys talking in the pub? They said that bloke, the one who stormed out, stood to make a tiny packet.'

'Not so tiny, if I remember correctly.'

'Spot on. But they also said prices had gone up since he did the deal. I wondered just how much. So I asked Sawyers what the going rate was in north Oxfordshire for a piece of agricultural land these days. Well, what do you think?'

Daniel hadn't the faintest idea.

'Well, just a few years ago you were looking at nearly

£4,000 an acre. But what with mad-cow disease, cheap bacon imports and the whole bloody general crisis in British farming, it's gone right down the pan. According to Sawyers, its barely £2,300 to £2,500 these days.'

'So?'

'But what do you think it's worth if it's got planning permission?'

Daniel shrugged. He hated guessing games.

'£100,000, £150,000 even?' She saw she was getting no response. 'Well, that's what I reckoned, top end maybe. Turns out that given the pressure of development in the area, a piece of land with planning consent for high-density housing, on the edge of a picturesque village earmarked for expansion, with relatively easy access to main roads – all of which fits Ditchford – would be worth a cool million. Per acre.'

She paused to let the weight of her words sink in.

'And the builders reckon to make a hefty profit on top of that. It means Riggs-Mill got the bulk of that land up at Ditchford at a song. Our local farmer must be well pissed off.'

'Except that he still has a chunk to sell.'

'Absolutely. And they want it. In other words, both sides are deeply into this. Turning Ditchford into the new Milton Keynes of north Oxfordshire might be an ecological catastrophe and an unnecessary desecration of scarce rural landscape, but there is a little group who stand to make an absolute killing out of it.'

'You don't mean that literally.'

'Don't I?'

'Rajiv . . .'

Daniel and Therry had spent the previous evening drinking away his sorrows. After the pubs closed she had invited him back to Jericho, not really sure if she intended anything to come of it. But the poor bugger looked so miserable. And she was hardly thinking straight herself by that stage. They had shared a couple of glasses of cooking whisky, and then, just when it looked as if instinct might be triumphing over emotion and lust would win out over grief, he had keeled over on her sofa. For the best really, she had thought, half regretfully, covering him with a spare duvet.

The decision to drive back up to Ditchford – to what purpose neither was wholly sure – had been taken at some stage in the evening that neither properly remembered the next morning. They abided by it nonetheless. Somehow it was better than doing nothing.

'Rajiv was a casualty. All I'm saying is that there are people here who stand to lose a lot of money if anything goes wrong with this development. They're not an easy bunch to scare. They've already ridden roughshod over local protesters and environmentalist groups. When some hothead tried lying in front of one of the bulldozers, they came damn close to running over him.'

'You think this is a cover-up? That they honestly, really know that they've dug up plague bacteria and they're just hoping . . . hoping . . .'

'Hoping it'll go away? Sure. What other conclusion is there?'

Therry dropped the Range Rover into second gear as she swung it off the A3400 on to the secondary road that would take them into Ditchford. A few long-horned Jacob sheep in a field to the left ignored them as they pitched over the low brow of a hill. The horizon here dipped and rose again in the erratic pattern of the Cotswolds' northwestern edge. A few leafless trees stood like sentinels in lines that maybe marked the track of some long-uprooted hedgerow.

'That's where it happened.'

They had just come over the crest of the particular hill that afforded the best view down on St Peter's Alone. A thin grey veil of mist was drifting only a few feet above dark fields that showed patches of white frost in the deep ruts left by earth-moving machinery.

'Where what happened?'

'Where the bastards tried to run me off the road, of course,' she said, jerking a thumb backwards. 'I had stopped just over the brow of the hill to take a look –'

'I thought you said it was dark.'

'Ever heard of the moon? Anyway, I think I was sobering up. Beginning to realise I was wasting my time out here feeling sorry for myself just because a bloody story got spiked. And then suddenly here was this great one-eyed iron monster hurtling straight towards me and – shit!'

'What's the matter?'

'I've just realised. When I stopped, I turned out the lights. For the atmosphere. When I started up again to come down the hill, I don't think I turned them on again.'

'So they wouldn't have seen you?'

'No.' The word came out reluctantly.

'Especially given the hurry we assume they were in. And you say they had only one headlight working.'

'A crime in itself . . .'

'But hardly attempted murder.'

'No.' She conceded it grudgingly.

The pub car park was empty save for an elderly Jaguar XJ6, presumably the landlord's. Daniel thought the hanging sign no longer looked as comical as it had done, the ratlike fox's grin more of a sneer, the cartoon dogs just badly drawn. Maybe it was the lack of movement. There was no wind today, just a frozen stillness in the air.

There was no one at all at the bar, nor sitting on the high-backed settles. Without a fire roaring in the grate, the place looked a lot less welcoming than it had on Sunday. Daniel coughed and the big barman with the whiskers emerged from a back room and squinted at him quizzically.

'Uh, hi,' said Daniel, suddenly nervous. Therry was still in the car park, looking for her Ordnance Survey maps in the back of the Range Rover.

'Hello,' came the reply. There was a moment's awkward silence until it occurred to Daniel that he ought to order something. He gestured towards the Hook Norton tap.

'A pint, please.'

'Bitter?' said the barman, as if he doubted the order.

'Yes, please.' He quickly remembered that the big man's name was Frank and wondered if he ought to use it. British pub etiquette was ferociously complicated.

'Ah, and a pint of the amber nectar for the young lady, if I recall correctly.'

Daniel looked around to see Therry open the door behind him and beam her silly smile. Or perhaps not so silly. Something had clearly changed the barman's mood. Maybe he was just a sucker for a pretty face.

Frank set the drinks up on the bar and Therry clambered up on a stool. 'Nippy old day out there, isn't it?'

'You can say that all right, miss. Down to minus ten it was last night. Absolute brass monkeys, if you dont mind me sayin'.'

Therry laughed. Daniel smiled politely.

'Surprised to see you folks out here again. Had second thoughts about them houses, did you?'

Therry looked at Daniel, then back at Frank.

'Hardly. Not with what we've heard.'

'Oh, yes?' Frank had picked up a pint glass and begun polishing it.

'Bit of a to-do. I suppose it's all over the village.'

'What would that be then?'

'You don't mean you haven't heard? Two more of the site workers, so they say, gone down with this sickness, and a couple already dead. I'd have thought people would be pretty worried.'

Frank put down the glass and looked at them both in turn before settling his gaze on Therry. He was not smiling.

'I'm not sure I know what you mean.'

Therry set down a copy of that morning's *Post* in front of him, folded to display the story about the deaths. He read it slowly. And shrugged.

'Look 'ere, miss. I don't know what you know or think you know, but I don't know nothin' about no diseases, let alone this limphawhatchamacallit. All I know is that since you and 'im turned up on Sunday I've had nothing but grief about this bloody building business. It might be me and my big mouth, mind, what started it, riling Harry like that, but it's caused one hell of a barney around here and as far as I'm concerned, the less said about any of it, the better.'

'What do you mean, a barney? An argument? With Harry, the farmer? About the site?'

'I've told you, I don't want to talk about it.'

'What happened? It could be important.'

'So is my trade. Things are hard enough round here without people spreading stupid scare stories, let alone my best customers falling out with one another and rowing in the pub.'

'It's about the plague, isn't it? They know, don't they?'

'Bollocks the plague! It's about money. It's about

Harry making a bit out of flogging off his fields for a load of houses that no one else around 'ere wants. Bob, the bloke what runs this committee some of 'em have got up against the developers like –' (Therry remembered the man in the cap and waxed jacket who had seemed so well-informed and interested in their questions) 'well, he and Harry had a battle royal last night and both stormed out of the place saying they'd never be back. Right good for business, that was.'

'What were they saying?' Therry was pressing him too hard, Daniel thought. 'Don't you realise what's going on here? They could be covering up something that could endanger every man, woman and child in Ditchford. Just like it did hundreds of years ago.'

For a moment, Frank looked at her as if weighing up whether she was demented. Then he sighed. 'Bob was going on about something like that, maybe. I don't know. Harry kept trying to shut him up. Said he was just jealous and he would sell Lone Meadow too, see if he didn't. We would all be grateful in five years' time, he said, when business was booming and this place was full of customers. Right load of bollocks, it was. None of us wants money at the expense of our way of life. Except maybe Harry. Anyway he's probably done the deal by now. He picked up the bloke what owns the whole company from my car park not half an hour ago.'

'Here?'

'Yeah, the bloke's staying the night. That's his motor out back. Can't say I'd welcome him normally, but a customer's a customer. And whatever he gets up to, Mr Martindale's a gent.'

'Martindale?'

Frank grunted, as if he hadn't meant to mention the name.

'Where did they go?'

'Can't say they told me. Like I said, Harry won't even come in the door no more.'

'You must have some idea.'

'I should imagine they've gone back to Harry's place. Ridge Farm. Big place up at the end of the village on the Banbury Road. 'Though I can't see what it's got do with you,' he shouted as Therry disappeared through the door. Daniel, equally taken aback, gulped down the remnants of his pint and followed her.

Therry was already gunning the engine of the Range Rover into life as Daniel stumbled out. Come on! she waved to him impatiently. Doing up the toggles on his duffel coat against the cold, Daniel stopped just for a second to admire the sleek lines of the well-maintained old Jaguar. Whatever people thought about Mr Martindale's houses, there was no disputing his taste in cars. It was that deep wine-bottle colour that, for no reason Daniel had ever understood, was called British racing green.

On the back window ledge, behind the cream doehide headrests, lay a furled umbrella in bright colours. There were two stickers on the rear windscreen. One, showing a little map with some curious geographic adjustments, proclaimed that Mr Martindale was in favour of taking 'Britain Out of Europe'. The other, in gold on green that matched the car's paintwork, proclaimed his membership of Oatshill Golf Club. As he climbed into the Range Rover, Daniel wondered why it was that he found that name so familiar.

Chapter Thirty-Four

Upper Ditchford, Oxfordshire; Tuesday 23 December, 1.45 p.m.

THEY SPOTTED Ridge Farmhouse in a matter of minutes: a big, sprawling stone building about half a mile out of the village, set well back from the road down a long drive. A battered Mitsubishi Shogun stood in front of a Classical porch that Therry was on the verge of scorning as neo-Georgian when she realised it might well be genuine. Beyond the house they could see a clutter of tumbledown barns and what looked like a makeshift grain silo and some big, shiny objects that puzzled Daniel until Therry identified them as hay bales wrapped in black plastic. Two men were pacing up and down by the barn, presumably Harry and Martindale.

They took all this in on two swift passes, Therry turning the Range Rover around about a mile beyond the farm.

'I don't want to attract any attention,' she explained.

'I thought that was the whole point.'

'Are you kidding? We should just march in there and say, "Hi, guys, how's the Black Death?"'

'I thought we assumed they didn't know.'

'Now you are kidding. The only assumption we can make is that they are fully aware of what's happened and why and are doing their damnedest to make sure nobody else finds out.'

'But that doesn't make sense. That's a risk they can't

take. They have to find out. And do something about it, if it's true.'

'And that's not that easy, is it?'

Daniel shook his head. 'No. Not if they know anything about it. They'd need somebody like Gover advising them.'

And who was like Gover? Suddenly he had an image of himself sweating in the crowded elevator in the Radcliffe, afraid of being recognised as an impostor. The men talking glibly about handicaps – golf handicaps, as it had turned out. That was why Oatshill rang a bell. The course they had mentioned was Oatshill. And one of them, as he had recognised just the previous afternoon, minutes before the bastard had callously thrown the news of Rajiv's death at him, was Dr Simon Redwhistle. The fact that he and this Martindale guy belonged to the same golf club didn't necessarily mean they were in some sort of conspiracy together. Until now Daniel would have been surprised to find they even knew one another. All of a sudden it seemed incredible that he could have thought anything else.

'And you've only just put two and two together,' said Therry, turning the Range Rover down a narrow lane past a sign that warned it was 'unsuitable for heavy goods vehicles'. 'One more reason for trying to find out what the hell they're talking about in there.' About fifty yards further along she stopped and turned to Daniel. 'Hop out and open that gate, would you?'

'What?'

'The gate. It's a big metal thing with crossbars. Come on, Dan, I'm sure you have them in America too.'

'Oh, ha ha, but what are you –'

'Look, just get on with it, will you, or do I have to do it myself? We're wasting time.'

Daniel did as he was told, swinging the big aluminium

gate open. He was about to shut it again, but Therry leaned out of the driver's window and stopped him.

'No, leave it. I know it's not exactly the country code. But you never know; we may want to leave in a hurry.'

Still wondering what the hell she was up to, Daniel climbed back on board. Therry was fiddling with a little stumpy lever next to the gear stick. Daniel had noticed it before but had no idea of its purpose.

'I'm just putting it into low ratio,' Therry answered his unasked question. 'Gets better traction on rough terrain. We may need it across this field.'

Daniel nodded. As if he had the faintest idea what she was talking about.

Looking ahead of them, he could see what she meant about the terrain. Not only was the field entrance a mess of deep ruts, all frozen solid, but the rest of it stretched away downhill in a pattern of raised stripes, like a piece of old-fashioned upholstery on a geographical scale. 'Ridge and furrow. A great example,' he muttered.

'That what it's called? All I know is it can be a bloody pain to drive across. Either a roller-coaster or a valley straddle, depending on which way you want to go.'

'You realise it probably dates from the time of the Black Death?'

'What? This bumpy pattern?'

Daniel was clutching the handhold above his left shoulder as the vehicle pitched forwards.

'Yes, of course. It's the result of medieval strip farming: one-man bullock teams ploughing up the same little ribbon of land year after year, decade after decade, until in the end they had literally made their mark on the landscape. Most of them are protected, but that doesn't stop some of your greedy farmers from flattening the whole thing if they get the chance.'

'Well, we'll just have to assume our Harry hasn't had the chance yet.'

His head was being jerked back and forth as the Range Rover traversed the uneven surface, up and down across the ridges. Daniel wondered vaguely where exactly they were heading, and whether it would have been worse had the field been wet. It was the sort of landscape he imagined it would be very easy to get a car stuck in. No wonder people out here preferred four-by-fours. Ahead of them, forming the field's boundary, was a high bramble hedge that looked as if it too had been there for centuries. At their approach a lone male pheasant, which had somehow escaped the pre-Christmas shooting parties, scurried out from the hedgerow and then darted back into it again. Another lucky survivor. Therry brought the car to a halt in a furrow about two yards out from the hedge.

'There that should do it. At this angle, there's no chance they'll see us. Come on!'

Helplessly, Daniel followed her along the hedge until they came to a low stile, the crossbar of which had been broken in two. The hedge on either side was heavily overgrown.

'Look,' she said.

Daniel looked. Through the spiky branches they could see the side wall of the farmhouse, about a quarter of a mile away. In between were the two barns, the silo and a field full of Jersey cows. There were not two but three men looking out over the fields. From where they were, Daniel realised, they would have an excellent view of the church and the building site, with Melissa's Portakabin, the show home and the Riggs-Mill heraldic pennants on their flagpoles.

'Lord of all he surveys,' said Therry with obvious scorn in her voice.

'Which one?'

She shrugged. 'Both of them are bastards in my book. Come on. We've got to get closer.'

'What? Are you crazy? We're bound to be seen.'

'No, we're not. As long as you keep your head down. We can stick to the hay bales as far as the barn, and then crawl as far as seems safe. With a bit of luck we should be able to get within earshot of them. Their voices will carry further than they think.'

'What about the cattle?' asked Daniel warily, eyeing the big beasts, a couple of which had approached the hedge and were pulling with mixed success at a few tufts of withered grass.

'Extra cover,' Therry replied and slid over the stile, keeping an arm raised to avert the brambles. 'Try to be quiet and make as little disturbance as possible. We'll be fine. Wait and see.' Then, immediately breaking her own rule, she said 'Shit' loudly, and gave a little gasp.

'Are you OK?' Daniel asked in a stage whisper.

'Fucking farmers!'

Daniel looked down and saw barbed wire strung along the edge of the stile.

Therry was clutching her ankle, where a barb had ripped through her sock and torn a nasty gash in her leg. 'Never mind,' she muttered, pulling what looked like a well-used handkerchief from the pocket of her flying jacket and tying it in a makeshift bandage around the wound. 'Come on, let's get on with it!'

Not for the first time in their brief acquaintance, Daniel decided that Therry Moon was both an incurable optimist and quite mad. Nonetheless, he followed her as best he could.

The overgrown brambles, though they pricked abominably, provided excellent cover for crossing the stile.

Watching as one of the figures in the distance gesticulated in the direction of the village – he was probably talking about the pub, Daniel thought, damning the locals for failing to appreciate the benefits of bungalows – they sneaked, ducking low, out from the cover of the hedge to crouch behind the great black bulk of one of the plastic-wrapped bales. If the grazing cows were perturbed at having their living space invaded, they gave no sign of it.

'We'll split up,' Therry whispered. 'Less likely to be noticed than two of us moving at once. I'll take the route closest to the house.' She vaguely indicated a direction that would take her in a curve, mostly covered by wrapped bales, to the edge of the silo. 'You stick to the barn. And keep low once you get beyond the next bale.'

With that she was gone, ducking and darting. Within a few seconds she had disappeared from his sight.

Daniel sighed, as quietly as he could. He was not at all sure about this business. Playing commandos in a freezing field, possibly within half a mile of an infected plague pit, was not his idea of common sense. Besides, the light was already failing. Though that might be a good thing, he reflected, since it reduced their chances of being spotted. Even so, he doubted the likelihood of either of them getting within hearing range, but it was worth a try. Maybe.

Peering out from the side of the black plastic bale, he could see that they were not looking in his direction. In fact, it looked now as if they were arguing. One was making hand gestures. Daniel sucked in breath sharply. Of course! He might have guessed the identity of the third man: Dr Simon Redwhistle.

It was now or never. Daniel bent into a low crouch and scooted as far as the next bale, little more than a yard away. From there on in it would have to be snake-belly style, the way he remembered from those summer camps up around Lake Tahoe where his mother had sent him when they could still afford it.

The ground was cold and hard, the blades of grass more grey than green, and smelling of dried cow dung. The three men were still more than two hundred yards distant. The nearest he could get without being spotted, provided they stayed roughly where they were, was the edge of the barn. It was every bit as tumbledown as it had looked from the roadside: rusting sheets of corrugated iron hung down the sides, stopping some five feet short of the ground. It provided little more than basic cover for a few unwrapped hay bales (the traditional rectangular sort rather than these big black plastic doughnuts) and a few pieces of ancient-looking farm equipment whose use was a mystery to Daniel.

But if he could get there without being seen, he would stand a very good chance of catching a few snippets of conversation. If the men walked the other way, then it would have to be up to Therry. It was her idea anyway. But maybe, just maybe, they would let something slip, something that would enable him to nail them for God knows what – criminal negligence at least, conspiracy to commit murder at best. Somebody, he was determined, was going to have to pay for the death of Rajiv Mahendra. And if he could prove that old coot Redwhistle was complicit in some sort of skulduggery, so much the better.

Therry, meanwhile, was doing well. Or so she thought. She had easily been able to nip from one black bale to another for a distance of some two hundred yards, although the semicircular route she had decided on barely took her half the distance to the men. Even in this still air, where voices would carry, she reckoned she needed to be within a couple of dozen yards to make out what they were saying. But it was not impossible. There was a line of bales that led almost all the way to the silo, and next to the silo there was what looked like an old cattle trough.

A couple of minutes was all it took her to get within a few yards of her target. Face down, ignoring the cold and the stench of cattle urine, she had just made the cover of the trough, and noted with satisfaction that Harry and the man who had to be Martindale were talking loudly, apparently arguing. Then a dog barked, one of them broke off and gave an angry shout, and her heart sank.

'Oi! You there! Stop! What the hell!'

Her first reaction was to flatten herself into the foul-smelling earth. The shouts were receding: it was not her they had spotted. Oh, no! She risked a glance. What else? Dan, Dan, the history man, had cocked it up. As she might have expected. Why had she even suggested they both attempt to eavesdrop? Creeping forward to the front of the trough and peeking out beyond it, she could see Martindale striding briskly forwards. Harry was at least half a dozen paces in front of him, shouting loudly and brandishing a stout walking stick. The game was up. Dan had blown it. They would hear nothing now. The best they could hope for was that he would get away before they set the bloody dogs on him.

It was the cows that had done for Daniel. Or the fact that they weren't cows. No sooner had he begun his 'injun rattlesnake crawl' towards the cover of the barn than he heard heavy footsteps behind him and felt hot breath on the back of his neck. His first reaction was almost to wet himself. His second was to turn his head through ninety degrees. And he found himself staring into the great eye of an inquisitive Friesian bullock.

What was worse was when its pal started to nose its rear end, while the first pawed the ground with its hoof uncomfortably near Daniel's head. He did not know much about cattle. His experience of them was largely restricted to watching old episodes of *Rawhide* on television, and picking up a nice piece of fillet in a plastic tray at the supermarket. He had heard, worryingly, about British mad-cow disease, but that was all supposed to have been brought under control now. But one way or another, being menaced by half a ton of hamburger was a seriously worrying experience.

All he had to do, he thought, was to make a noise or a sudden movement. Anything like that was almost certain to drive the animal away. And equally certain to attract the attention of the two men he was trying to sneak up on. Then the decision was made for him.

A black and white dog, which Daniel, who had grown up thinking the classic English sheepdog was the sort who did walk-on roles in paint commercials, failed to recognise as a border collie, appeared from behind the corner of the barn, wondering what the bullock had found so interesting. Almost immediately it caught Daniel's scent and began to bark. The bullock panicked, lifting its head abruptly to toss it, and accidentally delivering a hefty blow to Daniel's backside. Then the big animal backed off. But the dog advanced, snarling.

There was only one option: retreat to the nearest hay bale. Hope against hope they wouldn't see him. But it was no hope at all. The shout of 'Stop!' came almost immediately. Shit! How stupid could you get? Stupid bloody business! Stupid bloody girl! Daniel turned and ran. The damn dog was snapping at his heels. A glance behind showed two of the men coming in his direction.

One of them was running, holding something in front of him. He hoped to hell it wasn't a gun. Farmers, he had heard, were among the few people in Britain who had them.

The bracken hedge was a good two hundred yards away. On his left, much closer, was a dry-stone wall. Better cover, but with no getaway car on the other side. The dog was running around in front of him now, darting back and forwards as if it were corralling sheep. It sprang forward to nip at his ankles. Ow! Daniel lashed out with a foot and caught the creature a glancing blow. It yelped – sparking another angry cry from the farmer in pursuit – then renewed its assault with a fresh frenzy.

Daniel changed direction, heading for the wall. At least it would halt the damn dog. But then what? Leg it as fast as he could beyond the next field. Hope he didn't get lost. And then somehow make it back to the pub. Hell's teeth! He hadn't counted on the cattle. Three or four of them were standing in the way. Snorting and pawing the earth, unnerved by the commotion. He looked back towards the hedge. The barking dog. The running man. Gaining on him fast now.

'Come back here! Now! I'm warning you!' It wasn't the voice of a man who wanted to listen to reason. Let alone sit down and hear why two crackpots were going to destroy his hopes of a fortune with some scaremongering story about the Black Death. If the man was trying to cover that up, then what would he stop at?

Only a couple of dozen yards now. If only the goddamn cattle would get to hell out of his way. And then they stampeded.

The crack split the grey afternoon air like a violent headache. Daniel half expected to fall to the ground, brought down by birdshot, grapeshot or whatever they used. Maybe with his leg blown off by a magnum cartridge. He had barely time to think, Christ, the bastard's actually shooting at me! before the four bullocks charged.

Straight past him. Heads held high. Snorting. Daniel stood rigid for a split second, then ran for his life. He reached the wall in seconds, tumbling painfully over it. Like a second-rate stuntman, he thought as he stumbled up, winded, bruised, fumbling for his glasses in the frozen mud. His foot found them first. Shit! He grabbed them in his hand and ran on. A glance over his shoulder revealed only a blurry image: grey, dark brown and green. He could hear the frustrated yelping of the dog, stranded on the other side of the wall, mooing cattle. The figure of a man, waving, was coming closer to the wall; and in the distance he could make out another, shouting unintelligibly. Whether it was instructions to his pursuer or to the herd of startled animals, Daniel neither knew nor cared.

Direction? Straight ahead was worst. He would still be in their sight. In their sights? And further from the car. From the village. But going back or circling round was not an option. Getting away from these nutcases was what mattered. He took an angle across the next field, heading for a bracken hedge that was obviously the continuation of the one they had come through. He was almost there when he heard another gunshot. And then another. This was serious.

So was the hedge. There was no stile. No obvious way through. And no way of clambering through a six-foot-high barrier of thorns that could have guarded Sleeping Beauty for a few centuries. Nothing to do but run the length of it, looking for a break or a thin patch, where he could scramble through without multiple lacerations. He didn't even dare to look back to see whether Harry was still chasing him, or whether he had decided to stop by the wall and take potshots until he brought him down.

Daniel was panting now. That's what you got for preferring the library to the gym. And then his foot caught on a tuft of matted grass and he went over on his ankle. It hurt badly. Ahead, however, the hedge was coming to an end, giving way to a thin wire about three feet off the ground. Thankfully, Daniel limped up to it.

He touched it and recoiled, crying out as a surge of electricity shot up his arm. What did these bastards think they were doing, wiring up the damn countryside? He thought he heard distant laughter. Better than gunshots. Avoiding touching the thing he threw his leg over, wincing as his damaged ankle took his weight. Hobbling, he ran on. He hardly dared look round to see whether anyone was still following him. Or aiming at him. If his pursuer had stopped at the wall, he would no longer be able to get a clear view. But if he was chasing, then it could only be a matter of minutes before an able-bodied countryman caught up with an unfit, limping academic.

There was a building in this field, a shed or a small barn. Daniel made for it. A bit obvious perhaps. If they were seriously looking for him, they would be bound to search it. But maybe, after all, they had just wanted to frighten him off. For all they knew, he was just an afternoon walker who had strayed off the footpaths. In which case, it was one hell of an overreaction to shoot at him. But then they hadn't hit him, had they? And that might have been deliberate, rather than poor marksmanship. So maybe they'd give up. Maybe they already had. In any case there was no way he could run any further with his ankle like this.

The door, a piece of rotting timber patched up with

sheets of hardboard, was hanging open, barely attached by its hinges. Daniel could see no one behind him.

He hobbled through the door, blinking to get used to the dark. And cursed himself again for not getting a British mobile phone with which he could have called Therry and got her to pick him up. Assuming, of course, that she had got back to the car.

He put his hand in his pocket and found his glasses. The frame was bent and one plastic lens was cracked. But with a bit of twisting, they were serviceable. Just about. He felt his way forward, looking for something he could lie down and hide behind. Just in case they did come looking. He reached out a hand and touched human flesh.

Chapter Thirty-Five

Ridgeway Farm, Upper Ditchford, Oxfordshire;
Tuesday 23 December, 4.03 p.m.

D ANIEL SCREAMED. Not just in shock but in pain, as his fingers were bent back almost at right angles to the palm of his hand, his legs were kicked from under him and his face was pushed into the dirt floor by a powerful hand which had enmeshed itself in his hair.

'Ssssh!' a man's voice said. Forcefully.

His hair was released. Straightening his battered spectacles as best he could, Daniel looked up. As his eyes adjusted to the low light, he realised that he had neglected an essential part of his national culture. Benny, for example, who had been his best buddy at Berkeley, or Greg, who ran the yacht club across the bay in Sausalito, would have known straight away just what they were facing. They would have known not only the make and the designation but also the bore, calibre and capacity for causing serious damage of the piece of weaponry pointed directly at his head.

To Daniel, it was simply a handgun. A big one, with a big round barrel that looked as if it fired slugs the size of beetles, Volkswagen Beetles. And it was approximately eight inches from his head. He didn't know whether to wet himself or say his prayers. Then, looking with some embarrassment at the front of his trousers, he realised he had already exhausted one option.

The man holding the gun was squatting on his haunches

beside him. He was dressed in English clothes. Archetypal English clothes, in fact: a deep-green, waxed cotton jacket with a rolled corduroy collar, open at the neck to reveal a hint of dark tartan lining. The sort of stuff the Prince of Wales and his young sons were depicted wearing on shooting expeditions, rather than the cheap synthetic fleeces Daniel had seen on most real English countryfolk.

But then this man wiping the muddy print of Daniel's palm from his cheek would not pass easily for an English country squire, no matter how much he might affect the apparel. Not unless the Cotswolds had been moved to the outskirts of Yokohama. The man rocking back and forward on his heels (brand-new Timberland walking boots), as he squatted before him and kept the handgun trained on Daniel's head, was unmistakably Asian, almost certainly Japanese, and strangely familiar.

'What are you doing?' he asked in an unexpectedly soft voice that seemed to Daniel remarkably free of any accent, until he realised that, to an Englishman, it would have matched his own. This guy was not like any American Japanese he knew: Hanji who ran the sushi bar in Mill Valley, Nikki with the lustrous jade eyes and ebony hair who'd been in his class at high school, or the overweight petrol attendant they all called Sumo Joe. Nor the businessmen you saw in downtown San Francisco or the tourist groups waiting for trams at Embarcadero. For a start, none of them carried guns.

This guy looked about forty, but fit and with steely eyes. Eyes, he realised with a jolt, that had last glared at him across the reading room of the science library. The question was the one Daniel should have been asking, he realised.

'Walking. In the fields. It's a free country, isn't it?'

The man showed no sign of considering that premise.

'I think you were running. Running away from some-body?'

Well, obviously, Daniel wanted to say. He had heard the gunshots, hadn't he? Unless – he almost bit his tongue – unless this guy was the one who had fired them. But why would he have . . . ?

'Did you shoot at me?'

It made sense, Daniel was telling himself. Some sort of sense. This man had a gun and showed every sign of being able to use it. Daniel had thought the shot had come from behind him. But had it? He couldn't be sure.

'I did not shoot at you. I thought a diversion would distract the men following you. There are always guns going off in the countryside. And I was curious.'

Daniel wanted to say that this was going all the wrong way. But he was hardly in a position to insist on asking the questions. Not with a piece of artillery pointed at his head.

'Curious? About me? Is there any chance of you putting that thing down?'

The man glanced at the weapon in his right hand as if he had forgotten he was holding it. He sat back on his heels, then stood up, stowing the gun inside a pocket of his waxed jacket, as if he had decided Daniel was no threat. Which unfortunately was wholly correct.

Daniel made to get up. The man put a hand down as if to help him. It turned out he had entirely the opposite intention.

'Just a minute, please,' he said, pulling Daniel halfway to his feet, then with a judicious shove landing him on his backside on the ground. 'What's your name, kid? What're you doing here?'

'Daniel. Daniel Warren.' He almost felt tempted to add the word 'sir'. 'I'm a student. At Oxford.'

'What do you study?'

'History.'

'What's your interest?' he said. 'Why were you trying to listen to those gentlemen's conversation without them seeing you?'

Daniel weighed up the odds of getting the answer right. The trouble was that he had no idea what this man wanted to hear, nor whose side, if any, he was on.

'It's the houses,' he said at last. 'In Ditchford. They're building on historical sites. A lot of people in the village are against it. I'm trying to help them.'

The man looked at him without expression for a full two minutes. Then, as if he had suddenly made a decision, he tilted his head slightly backwards.

'Are you? A history student naturally has an interest in conservation? Is that it?'

'More or less.'

'What's the more?'

'I'm doing a thesis. Specialising. In the Black Death.' Daniel bit his tongue, waiting to see what effect the words would have.

The man sucked his teeth and made a face as if he had just found something unpleasant stuck between them.

'How much do you know? About what's going on here, I mean?' Daniel asked.

'How much do *you* know?' he said. 'That's the question.'

That was when it hit Daniel that he should have recognised the type immediately. If only from the movies. This was a real-life yakuza. A Tokyo mobster. The English clothes had thrown him, when they should have been a pointer: expensive. The only problem with the analysis was that, at least according to the movies, falling into the hands of the yakuza was not a happy prospect for someone they might consider to know too much. The

248

irony was that he knew so little.

The man had gone to the doorway and taken a mobile phone from his pocket, but he seemed to have difficulty getting a signal. With a backward glance at Daniel, he moved out of the barn, his concentration momentarily at least on the phone screen. Then he pressed a few keys and began speaking. In Japanese.

Daniel realised it was his chance. The man was about twenty yards away from the door, occupied, the phone rather than a gun in his hand. He edged his way to the door, slipped outside into the grass, ignoring the pain in his ankle, and made a bolt for it.

At any minute he waited for a shout, or the gunshot that would bring him down without warning. Nothing. In the distance, several fields away, he could just make out the shape of a building which he thought might be the pub. He threw himself over a low dry-stone wall and, ducking down, limped the length of it. The second time that day he had been hobbling for his life!

Or was he? There was no sign of pursuit, no shout or shot behind him. With the pub now clearly in view, Daniel could not help risking a glance back and could just make out a slight figure still standing by the barn, maybe looking in his direction, maybe not. Perhaps, he told himself, you're not as important as you think.

As he clambered over a five-barred gate into the lane in front of the Fox and Hounds, he wondered whether he was important to anybody. The pub was closed. In darkness. Perhaps for another hour or so. He looked around to survey his bleak situation, and a set of headlights in the mid-distance, down by the church gate, flashed at him once. Therry Moon, in her battered Range Rover, had not let him down after all.

Chapter Thirty-Six

'NICE OF you to turn up,' Therry snapped as Daniel opened the car door. It was not the greeting he had been expecting.

'Listen –' he began, more angrily than he intended.

'Just get in, will you.'

He slammed the door behind him as Therry revved the engine, turning the vehicle through 360 degrees. Daniel was suddenly acutely aware of the state of his trousers. In the blast of the Range Rover's heater, they were beginning to give off an unmistakable acrid odour.

If she noticed, Therry gave no sign. She was leaning forward, peering out at the track her headlights blazed along the dark, narrow lane. Over the other fumes, Daniel thought he could smell a trace of whisky.

'Are you OK?' And then, hesitantly, 'Have you been drinking?'

'Do you have a problem with that?' she snapped in reply. 'I've got a headache. It happens. Sometimes the booze causes them, sometimes it's a cure. You want some, there's a hip flask in the side pocket. Where the hell were you anyway? Playing cowboys?'

Daniel breathed in deeply. 'You want to know?'

'Actually,' she cut him off before he could launch into his tale. 'Not right now, Dan, if you don't mind. We've got miles to cover and my concentration isn't quite up to it.' She proved the point by suddenly swerving violently to avoid something that Daniel couldn't see.

'Why are we in so much of a hurry?'

'We're going back to Oxford, where do you think?'

That wasn't what he had asked, Daniel thought. 'Sure, but why the rush?' he said.

Instead of replying, Therry leaned across and turned up the car radio. 'Listen,' she said.

If it had not been for the digital display, Daniel would have thought she had hit the wrong preset. What he was listening to did not sound like Therry's normal in-car listening choice, the local pop station FOX FM. For weeks now FOX had been driving Daniel mad, coming through the wall of his college room from the first-year undergraduate next door, an inane babble of jolly jingles, mindless disc-jockey banter and antiquated seasonal 'classics'. It was enough to destroy any supposed seasonal good will.

Overnight, however, it seemed the programming director had undergone a conversion. The music was soft and bitter-sweet, a lone boy chorister's voice unaccompanied save for the soft tones of a church organ in the background, singing an old carol that had always brought tears to Daniel's mother's eyes: 'Silent Night'. Daniel shivered as if there was suddenly something sinister in the very beauty of the music, a still small voice in the wilderness. *A voice*, he thought, *heard in Rama*: Rachel lamenting the loss of her children.

'There'll be another bulletin in a few minutes,' said Therry. 'Your damn plague's got loose. They've closed off the city.'

Chapter Thirty-Seven

The A3400, north of Oxford; Tuesday 23rd December, 6.30 p.m.

S NOW BEGAN to fall. The blizzard that had been threatening for the past two days, lurking in the thick cloud that lay over the country, a featureless void by day, by night a suffocating blanket. Now, as they passed the great iron gates of Blenheim Palace, heavy flakes settled on the windscreen, gently at first, leaving their familiar crystalline patterns for a second on the cold glass before the big rubber wipers brushed them away. More followed, and then more, forcing Therry to change the wiper frequency from occasional to regular, and then to fast.

Staring through the windscreen as the snow dashed towards them in the headlights, Daniel had the bizarre impression of being on the bridge in an early episode of *Star Trek*. Therry sat hunched forward over the steering wheel, eyes squinting as if to keep the snow out. They had passed most of the last six miles in silence. Daniel reached across and laid a hand on the back of Therry's neck, squeezing it gently, feeling the knotted tension in her muscles. She glanced towards him briefly and smiled, then turned her concentration back to the road.

Sensing a gap in her mood, he told her about the Japanese man who had been in the library and was now here, and with a gun. He had expected her to slam on the brakes and turn to stare at him in astonishment. Instead, he was the one to be shocked.

'Um-hm,' she said. 'I saw him at the hospital too.'

'What?'

'OK, it may not have been him. Maybe I'm just being racist, but most of the Japanese you see in Oxford are touring the colleges. There are students, of course, but not many middle-aged men making urgent enquiries at the Radcliffe in December.'

'You think?'

'I don't know what to think.' He could hear the fatigue in her voice. 'I think that I don't believe in coincidences any more.'

They passed Yarnton, once a rural village, now a dormitory suburb of Oxford strung out along the side of the dual carriageway: a line of identical houses with plastic Georgian pillars and net curtains. The English countryside had not so much been raped as imprisoned in a chastity belt: nature was something dirty, best covered up and never spoken of again.

A sign ahead indicated that they were just five miles from Oxford city centre. The first indication that all was not normal up ahead came as they approached the first in the series of roundabouts that marked the Oxford ring road. Traffic in the opposite direction was heavy, many drivers flashing their headlights at the oncoming cars, though Daniel could not tell what they were signalling. Then the road ahead of them snarled up. They inched their way around the roundabout and on towards the second, the junction with Oxford's ring road, here also a spur of the main A40. East led to the motorway and London, west towards the old market town of Witney. They were stuck behind a Toys 'R' Us truck and the traffic was hardly moving.

On the radio, the carol ended. There was a moment's

disconcerting silence and then a sober, calm male voice began speaking, sounding to Daniel like a BBC announcer in an old World War II film.

'Good evening. This is the Oxford city-council information service, broadcasting on all local radio stations. Following the declaration of a temporary emergency situation this afternoon, the city centre is closed to all traffic for the time being. Anyone heading for Oxford is advised that in most cases they will not be able to proceed beyond the city ring road, and should curtail their journey. There is no cause for alarm. The measures being taken are precautionary. But they are being rigidly enforced. Please assist the authorities and obey the instructions of police and other emergency services.'

There followed a long list of details of exactly which area of the city had been closed off. It did not, to Daniel's surprise, include most of the residential areas to the east of the city – Cowley, where the car factory was located, or the notorious Blackbird Leys housing estate. In fact, as far as he could tell, though his geography of the outer city was less than perfect, the so-called exclusion zone barely included the JR2 hospital out at Headington. It did, however, include the entire city centre, with a lesser restrictive zone apparently extending up the Banbury and Woodstock roads, the two Victorian arteries that stretched north of the city to meet the ring road at the junction now only yards ahead of them.

'Uh-oh,' said Therry. 'Here we go.'

As they approached the roundabout, they could see a line of policemen in Day-Glo lemon-yellow jackets strung out across the entrance to the Woodstock Road. In front of them a white patrol car was parked horizontally across the road, the lights on its roof flashing silently red and blue into the dark, illuminating the traffic that crawled towards them and, following the gesticulations of two officers standing out from the rest, obediently ploughed on around the roundabout, west to Witney or back out towards Woodstock again, or wherever people might go when they discovered themselves unexpectedly barred from their destination.

A few cars had pulled over to the roadside. Daniel noticed a man get out of one, as if to argue with the police. Almost instantaneously two officers emerged from the line and the man was quickly persuaded to enter his vehicle again and move off, reluctantly, towards Witney.

Daniel noticed that behind the police a strip of red and white tape, like the type used at crime scenes, was stretched across the road. The whole city of Oxford was being treated like a murder zone. Which was maybe what it was. Beyond, on the other side of the tape, Daniel could just make out several figures without the luminescent clothing, and the red tail lights of at least half a dozen vehicles. Apparently some cars were getting through.

Theirs, however, was unlikely to be one of them. 'Move along now!' The policeman's voice, amplified through an old-fashioned, hand-held battery megaphone, sounded unnaturally tinny. Big yellow signs proclaiming 'Diversion' and red ones announcing 'Road Closed' were set across the road in front of the police car, redeployed paraphernalia of routine roadworks.

Without warning, Therry swung the Range Rover to the left, as if she had been daydreaming and hadn't noticed that the road was blocked.

With the megaphone-wielding policeman almost under its wheels, the big vehicle lurched to a sudden halt. Daniel braced himself against the windscreen with his hands. Therry slumped forward in her seat, eyes closed, as if she did not want to see the red face of the extremely angry policeman gesticulating at her to lower her window. Daniel reached across and did it.

'Just what the hell do you think you're playing at? You nearly knocked me down!'

Daniel was about to attempt a reply when Therry, without opening her eyes or turning to face the officer, said simply, 'Sorry. I'm afraid I wasn't thinking.'

The man choked back his annoyance with a show of gruffness. 'All right, all right. But you can't turn down here. The city centre is closed.'

'Excuse me, officer, I don't think I can be hearing you right. You can't just close a city.'

The policeman sighed the deep, weary sigh of a man explaining the impossible for the umpteenth time.

'I'm afraid that's the way it is, miss. Sorry, you'll have to turn back.'

'Just a minute, officer.' Daniel recognised the danger signs in her precise delivery. 'I don't think you're hearing me: I live in Oxford. I'm going home.'

And with that she made a show of putting the Range Rover into gear. The policeman gave a quick glance back at the line of his colleagues, a glance he had obviously used before that afternoon, a glance that clearly said 'troublemaker'. Two of them began heading towards the car.

'I'm afraid that's not possible for the moment, miss. I understand your situation, but we've been told not to allow anybody, including residents, into the city for the moment. I believe it's for your own good.'

'Don't you tell me what's for my own good! I've told you, I'm on my way home. Now get those goons out of my way!'

The two policemen who had broken rank now positioned themselves in front of the Range Rover's bumper.

Daniel could not see their eyes beneath cap visors pulled low against the slanting snow, but from their stance he did not get the impression that they would accept being pushed around.

'This is ridiculous.' Therry revved the engine threateningly. The men in front were unmoved. The policeman at the window sighed exasperatedly.

'I'm very sorry, miss, but I'm not going to argue with you. If you'll turn into the car park of the Moat House Hotel, there's a representative of the emergency committee there. I know they're arranging accommodation for anyone who needs it tonight. With a bit of luck this'll all be over tomorrow and then we can all go home, eh?'

Some chance, Daniel thought, though he said nothing. In India, Rajiv had told him, a region struck by the plague might be isolated from the rest of the world for up to six weeks.

Therry's voice was rising in pitch and volume. 'This is outrageous! I'm a reporter. I have a right to get to my office. I need to know what's going on.' She was almost shouting now. 'You do not have the authority to do this.'

'Maybe not, miss, but *I* do.'

The new voice took both Daniel and Therry by surprise. The man who now spoke had arrived at the window without either of them noticing him. He was tall, or perhaps he just held himself that way, and dressed in a duffel coat with a beret on his head.

'Who are you?' Therry was not to be put down.

The new arrival tipped his hand to the beret. 'Colonel Hesketh, miss. Territorial Army.'

Suddenly Daniel understood. The dark men behind the police. The vehicles in the distance, down the inaccessible Woodstock Road.

'As of 1500 hours today,' the tall officer said, as if it were the most natural thing in the world,' central Oxford is under martial law.'

Chapter Thirty-Eight

Wolvercote roundabout, Oxford; Tuesday 23 December, 6.25 p.m.

A S THEY pulled away from the police line back into the traffic around the roundabout, Daniel looked back. The tall colonel had already melted into the background. A low profile. Orders given. Orders received.

The traffic was slow, three cars abreast. Daniel was resigned to the inevitable. They would turn into the car park of the Moat House, a grey slab of unimaginative architecture that made the brightly lit BP filling station across the road look an attractive place to spend the night. Judging by the number of motorists parked on its forecourt, more than a few others had felt the same. To his surprise, however, Therry ignored both.

The A40 east. Towards London? But Therry passed that turning too. Daniel thought with an inner groan, as they came full circle round the roundabout and again to the road into Oxford and the unflinching line of Day-Glo policemen, that she was going to take another crack at it.

But she didn't. She kept the car to the inside lane until they were a few dozen yards past the Woodstock Road and the police, then swung the nose out and pushed her way through the slow-moving traffic to the outside lane and into the little-used turning that led down to Wolvercote village.

'Where are we going?'

'What does it look like?'

'Wolvercote?'

'Brilliant!'

It was not said in a tone that invited a response.

The village green was only a few hundred yards from the roundabout, over a hump-backed bridge. Wolvercote's survival as a village was a lucky accident of topography. Trapped inside the ring road but semi-isolated from the urban sprawl by the ancient common land known as Port Meadow, it had not entirely escaped suburbanisation, but had retained at least the memory of a village identity. Daniel spotted a few bolt-on estates, but not many. The village had not been allowed to grow wholly organically, but at least it had not been force-fed on steroids.

At the end of the green, the lights of the Red Lion beamed welcomingly. But on closer inspection the door looked firmly shut, the curtains closed. If there was human warmth inside, they were excluded from it. Therry drove straight past, over another hump-backed bridge, crossing the second branch of the river which still defined the village frontiers, and swung right into the car park of the Trout Inn.

Daniel knew the Trout, but only slightly: a pub with an ancient history, fine buildings and a weir that squeezed the river water into a gushing torrent. The Trout was a tourist attraction masquerading as a rural inn: its clientele was drawn almost exclusively from visitors to the city. Wolvercote locals preferred the Red Lion. Nevertheless, its location was undeniably pretty in an Olde England chocolate-box sort of way. At least that was how it had seemed on Daniel's previous visit, when he and Rajiv had cycled up from college and eaten smoked-salmon sandwiches at one of the outside tables in early-autumn sunshine. They had sipped ale and watched the tame peacock parade up and down the terrace while a pair of swans backpedalled against the fierce current to stay stationary and gobble up crusts thrown by Japanese tourists wearing Burberry raincoats that shone in the sun.

Today, by stark and bitter contrast, it was closed, cold and silent. Because of the emergency? Or because of the season? Most publicans looked forward to a boom around Christmas. But out at the Trout? Maybe it only opened later in the evening. Daniel glanced at his watch: it was just gone 6.30. There was only one other car in the car park. The landlord's? The river water, murky and flecked with white foam, gushed over the weir faster than he remembered. Of the peacock and swans there was no sign.

Port Meadow, enclosed on the one side by the city and on the other by the ring road, extended flat and empty to a horizon lost from sight. The meadow was ancient common land, governed by rights, traditions and customs that dated back to the Iron Age. Somewhere out there, he had heard, there was even the remains of a Bronze Age tomb. People had been tramping across the meadow from Wolvercote to Oxford for centuries without number, certainly since well before the Black Death. In the fourteenth century, he told himself, they would have thought nothing of crossing it in the depths of winter. The winter of 1348–49 in particular. His mind's eye conjured up a vision of small figures wrapped in rags, straggling through the snow to escape the tide of pestilence, surveying the cloisters and halls of the university city. And suddenly, with the sinking feeling that accompanies overdue recognition of the inevitable, he realised why she had brought him there.

'Come on!' Therry shook him, opening her door to let a blast of freezing air into the car. And jumped out.

'Wait a minute,' said Daniel, pulling up the hood of his duffel coat as he clambered down from the Range Rover's high step. 'You're not . . . ?' Though of course he already knew she was. 'Where are we going?'

'We're going home. At least I am.'

'But –'

'But what?' She turned abruptly to face him, hands on hips, as she had done in the hospital corridor, her dirty-blonde hair blown back from her face. There was the same dogged determination on her face, except that now it looked lined, tired, as if she had aged ten years in the past two days.

'But why are we attempting to break the law to get into a city cordoned off because of a dangerous illness?'

'Because I've got a pussycat to feed! Because that's what makes us human.' As an afterthought she added, 'Besides, I'm a reporter.'

Resigned, Daniel shrugged. 'Do you know the way?'

'That way,' she said, turning towards the lightless bulk of the Trout. And then back towards him, with the ghost of a smile on her drawn features. 'First star on the right and straight ahead until morning.'

'Let's hope not,' said Daniel, looking up at the thickening snowfall from a sky that offered not the slightest glimpse of the heavens. 'What does that make us,' he added, 'Peter Pan and Wendy?'

'Maybe,' said Therry, holding out her hand towards him. 'As long as we're not the Lost Boys.'

Some twenty minutes after Therry and Daniel started out across Port Meadow, Jack Denton, sitting in the empty newsroom of the *Oxford Post*, clicked on the rotating envelope of his email programme. At least, he thought to himself, the damn thing no longer beeped. He was not entirely happy with the new technology, but keeping a job after the age of fifty was hard enough; giving the bastards an excuse to claim you couldn't keep up any more was just asking for it.

The mail folder expanded in front of him. There were three messages. One was from his nephew in Montreal, wishing him a happy Christmas. One assured him he could make a million dollars by copying the file and forwarding it to everyone on his mailing list while sending one dollar to the name at the top of the list; he binned it electronically. The third listed as its author <einstein@quickmail.co.uk> and Jack smiled, recognising the quixotic address of his old Fleet Street mate Eamonn Burke. Well, now, he thought, this could be interesting.

For the better part of half an hour he sat reading through the file sent him by Burke. Then he looked away, letting his eyes pan unseeingly across the empty room, the locked cubicle of John Harkness's fish-tank office with its coveted external window, beyond which the snow continued to fall thick and fast.

He turned once more to the screen, scrolling back to the top and running through it once again at speed until he got to the reference his mind had only just put into context. Amid all the background detail on Geoffrey Martindale, one salient fact stood out. This was something that did not concern the property developer at all; it concerned the university's professor of tropical medicine, one Dr Simon Redwhistle.

'Fuck me,' he said quietly. Then he lifted the telephone and began to dial.

Central Oxford is a surprisingly easy city to isolate. The medieval core, which contains most of the colleges as well as the shopping areas of Cornmarket and Westgate, is effectively self-contained. The great expanses of the richer colleges' privately owned land – Magdalen with its water meadows to the east and Christ Church Meadow running south to the river – provide natural barriers, as do the rivers and streams.

The busy little river that bubbles over the weir by the Trout Inn is locally named after the Egyptian goddess Isis, but it eventually broadens to become the Thames. In the flatland around Oxford the young Thames and its chief tributary, the Cherwell, twist and turn, breaking here and there into subsidiary waterways – the Hinksey stream and the Seacourt stream – which effectively isolate the long, thin north–south axis of the medieval city and its Victorian suburbs.

The operation to cordon off the city centre, which had begun at 2.00 p.m., was therefore remarkably simple in essence. In under an hour, the first units were in place. The police and army roadblock set up by the glorified traffic roundabout known as the Plain at the eastern end of Magdalen Bridge was as efficient a barrier to movement in and out of the city as the Royalist Artillery had been during the civil war of the 1640s, when a beleaguered King Charles I had made the city his capital, and royalist cannon stationed in Magdalen water meadow with a commanding aim on the bridge prevented a parliamentary advance from London. More than three hundred and fifty years later, the bridge is still the only link between the city's heart and the eastern suburbs. Similar checkpoints set up to the south, on Folly Bridge just beyond Christ Church and, for good measure to warn off those approaching, further south at the Hinksey roundabout, were equally effective, as was that to the west on the bridge at the far end of the Botley Road.

As soon as Daniel Warren and Therry Moon had been turned away from the main northern approach to the city along the Woodstock Road, Therry realised there would be no point in circling around and trying to drive in by another route. The idea that struck her as they passed the Wolvercote turning had, she told herself, been inspired. At least she hoped it had. It was the best chance they had got.

As a resident of Jericho, she liked to escape to Port Meadow in summertime. One of the few parcels of common land to escape the eighteenth-century enclosures by big landlords, the so-called meadow was the city's natural barrier all along the western side, cut off from housing by the railway. In summer it was a pleasant place for a leisurely two-pub stroll from the Trout down the river bank and over Fisher's Island to the Perch at Binsey. But in the depths of winter, in freezing fog, it was a bleak and inhospitable prospect. No one would be looking for two people walking across it. She hoped.

Yet before they had left the Trout Inn more than a hundred yards behind them, Daniel was convinced this was a bad idea. When he and Rajiv had come there in the early autumn, on seeing the spires of Oxford beckoning in the distance, they had been tempted to ditch the car and walk back across the meadow. Now, with heavily falling snow and visibility closing in to no more than a few dozen yards, it looked as inviting as a trek across the wastelands of Siberia. And here they were trying to get into the gulag, not escape from it. To make matters worse, Daniel's sprained ankle made him wince with pain every other step.

'Are you OK?' Therry had stopped a few yards ahead and was looking back at him.

Daniel limped up to her, wiping snowflakes from his eyes. 'Not exactly. My ankle hurts like hell.'

Therry sighed, but Daniel was not sure whether it was in sympathy or exasperation.

'What makes you so sure anyhow that we're not going to run into more police?'

'Out here? Look at it. The only place the police will be, if anywhere, is at the railway bridge which crosses into Jericho by Walton Well Road. But there's another bridge, a smaller one, just to the north of it. It leads over into some allotments that'll be abandoned at this time of year. The chances of anyone watching it are minimal.'

The chances of anyone seeing anything in the dark and snow were minimal, Daniel thought; about as minimal as the chances of their finding their way. The weather put him in mind of a peculiarly English Christmas carol he had recently become acquainted with: 'In the bleak midwinter, frosty wind made moan; earth stood cold as iron, water like a stone. Snow was falling, snow on snow. Snow on snow.' It was more like an ancient Saxon evocation of pagan Yule towards the end of the first millennium than a celebration of Christianity at the beginning of the third. Right now, however, watching the transformation of the barren, empty expanse of the meadow into an arctic wilderness, Daniel thought the words did not seem strange at all.

Out of the mist on their left, he could just make out the jagged shapes of obviously ecclesiastical ruins on the other side of the river. Godstow Nunnery, he supposed, an eerily romantic monument to Henry VIII's desire for divorce. The crumbling masonry and remnants of high Gothic arches now looked like the setting for a ghost story.

'Think about it,' Therry said. 'They're blocking the roads. That's all. Even with the army drafted in, they haven't got the manpower to put a ring all around Oxford. Besides, it just doesn't make sense. How many people do you know anyway who want to fight their way *into* an epidemic? If there's any police presence at all, it'll be to make sure people don't try to use the meadow to get *out*.'

'I've been thinking about that too,' said Daniel. 'How come there hasn't been any trouble? Why aren't there hordes of people trying to get out of the city? If this was America, there'd be a riot.'

'But this isn't America, not yet. Besides, it's Christmas, and all they've told people is to stay in their houses. That's all most of them were going to do anyway for the next forty-eight hours. All right, they've brought it forward a bit, but believe me, the great British public will find it a lot easier to stay in, turn on the telly and do what they're told. It's not as if anyone's going to starve: most of them will have got enough food stockpiled for Christmas to last them until February. Now come on, what else do you want to do? Stay out here all night? You can lean on me if it hurts that much.'

Daniel did, though only for a minute or two. It was quickly obvious that if he put any weight on her, she would fold under him. Underneath that hard-baked exterior, Therry Moon was not as tough as she looked. And Daniel found her vulnerability strangely reassuring. Not least because he was feeling intensely vulnerable himself.

For half an hour or so, they struggled on together, trying as best they could to keep to a straight line. The biggest danger, Daniel realised, was that with the limited visibility they would lose their sense of direction and keep walking in circles. He had long ago lost track of whether they were going in a straight line. With the river on one side of them and the railway line on the other, both converging at the meadow's southern end, Therry argued, they could hardly get irrevocably lost. Within another half an hour, she assured him, they would be home.

Daniel was not so sure. Particularly when the ground ahead of them began to ripple and move. They had somehow come back to the river bank, except that here it was not a bank, only a muddy shore where the snow-covered meadowland – not so much fell away as slid under the icy water. The river was wide here, much wider than back at the inn, at least fifty or sixty feet across. The landscape was Russian, not English: the Don in winter. On the other bank great spindly skeletons reached up into the low sky, bare trees with branching leafless arms, like desiccated ferns.

'The Binsey poplars,' said Therry. 'Shit! We've come too far west.' She looked up into the dark, snowy emptiness and shivered. What had begun as a light shower of snow adding a picturesque dusting across a drab landscape, was rapidly turning into a blizzard. The snow was blown into their faces, driven by biting winds that swept across the river from Farmoor and across Great Wytham Wood – J. R. R. Tolkien's sinister Mirkwood, when he had walked out here from his college rooms in Merton. But seldom on a night like this.

They turned away from the river, putting behind them the one identifiable landmark. Ahead, shapes seemed to move through the freezing fog. Once Daniel almost stepped into something warm and steaming, a pat of freshly dropped dung. In the invisible distance a soft, eerie lowing could be heard. Turning round, he just caught a glimpse of a shaggy head shaking itself free of snowflakes.

'Aberdeen Angus,' Therry explained.

'Who?'

Then there was a loud crack. For a split second Daniel thought he was being shot at again. And Therry stumbled and went down. Heavily. Pulling him down on top of her. For a moment, just a moment, he found himself lying with his face barely inches from hers, her mop of curly blonde hair unusually dark against the carpet of snow. At another time, in another situation, it could have been funny, romantic even: a tumble in the snow. But when Daniel looked into Therry's eyes, he saw only pain and anger. With herself and the world.

Daniel picked himself up. She remained sitting in the snow rubbing her ankle, a pink trace of blood now showing through her scrappy bandage. There was nothing in the featureless surroundings to indicate it but they had obviously wandered out on one of the patches of sodden marshland that in a typical wet English summer characterised Port Meadow. In this untypically cold English winter, however, it was frozen under the snow, or had been until the ice had cracked under their weight. They were lucky to have fallen to one side rather than straight through into the freezing water.

All of a sudden, Daniel felt immensely guilty. He was supposed to be the strong one: she should have been leaning on him. The snow swirling around them suddenly seemed menacing, as if it concealed dark spirits, wraiths circling them, forming and re-forming in different guises. Evil took various forms, his mother had told him, improbably, sitting on the beach at Stinson with the green Marin headland behind them and a sea of the purest Pacific blue washing the golden sands beneath the friendly Californian sun. Evil, she had told him, did not just lurk down dark New York alleyways, as it sometimes seemed in the movies, or in the hearts and minds of drug dealers, as he had learned at school. Evil could lurk anywhere: beneath a smart business suit or a policeman's uniform. In the mind of a woman with the face of an angel. Good was not to be taken for granted.

The universe was a perpetual battlefield in which

men and women were players, foot soldiers but rarely commanders. Disease was not an accident, any more than the cure. Even nature was not neutral. There were forces for good and forces for ill. That was why he had responded so instinctively to what Therry had dismissed as the ramblings of the old man in the pub two days ago. The man who – and he shivered – had read Gogol. Who understood about *Dead Souls*. And out there in the mist, in the dark, snow-filled clouds that had descended on Port Meadow, the dead souls were circling. Watching the game. He felt that he and Therry were the game. Walking towards the snare.

With a loud caw that startled him, a great black crow appeared out of the fog and settled a few yards away, eyeing them. Then it took wing again and was gone in a second. Therry gripped his arm and he pulled her up. She clung to him for a second, shivering, as if she too had sensed malignancy in the mist. Putting an arm around her, he felt her shake slightly, even within that thick leather jacket.

'Come on, then, kid. You can lean on me.'

He smiled down at her, doing his best to radiate a confidence he was far from feeling. But she did not smile back, just nodded. As if her morale were sapping rapidly into the night. In the corner of her eye he thought he noticed a tear. He swallowed hard and they began to move again, watching their footing now as best they could, though the thickening snow in front of them gave little indication of what lay beneath. Behind them, their footsteps were fading fast as the heavy flakes filled them.

'It can't be far,' said Therry quietly, as if she were no longer sure. But then she pointed. Ahead of them, off to the left, there was a subtle difference to the colour of the sky. Although it remained as featureless as ever, filled only with falling snow and Daniel's phantom imaginings, low on the invisible horizon the dull darkness was tinted a sickly yellow, like a patient in the early stages of jaundice: telltale evidence of the distant presence of sodium streetlights.

They hobbled towards them, encouraged by the knowledge that sooner or later the eerie primeval emptiness of the snow-covered meadow had to yield to the harsh edges of civilisation. That the grey bricks of Jericho would banish the spectres.

Then out of nowhere came a shrill warbling tone. Long, sharp and persistent, an unnatural sonic anomaly that pierced their eardrums. And then was gone. Letting go of Therry, Daniel spun round in search of whatever demon might emerge from the mist, although it was almost certainly already upon them. Then the noise repeated itself, weird, horrible and all of a sudden embarrassingly recognisable.

Therry stopped and unzipped the top of her flying jacket, reaching inside.

'Telephone,' she said.

Chapter Thirty-Nine

Port Meadow, Oxford; Tuesday 23 December, 7.20 p.m.

'THERRY, IS that you?'

'Jack! Shit!'

'What? Thanks! Nice thing to say to someone who's been looking after your interests. Where are you? Are you OK?'

She looked around her. Daniel was wiping his glasses free of frost. He looked cold and wet.

'We're, uh, fine,' she said. No point in going into details. There would be time enough for that later.

'Listen, you may have difficulties getting back into Oxford.'

'Really,' she said. Tell me about it, she thought.

'Look, you may not know this but I think – it's not official, mind, least not that I've heard, though God knows it's nearly impossible to get through to anyone, the lines are chocka, but anyway, the thing is . . .' Therry was willing him to get on with it, but she knew how Jack loved dragging out his revelations. 'I think they've declared martial law.'

Therry sighed. 'I know,' she said.

'You know? But how? Listen, where are you? You haven't said. I've got lots to tell you.'

'Never mind where I am, Jack, just get on with it, will you? We're freezing to death out here.'

'You're . . . ? Right, I mean, look, you know I got

that bloke in London to get on to your doctor friend, the one with the funny name who was such a bastard to your boyfriend.'

'He's not –' Therry was about to interrupt, but changed her mind. It was not worth the bother.

'What?'

'Nothing, go on,' she said, imagining Jack winking at his colleagues, delighted at finally 'penetrating', nudge, nudge, some detail of the ice maiden's private life. She did not picture him as he really was, alone in a darkened office, sitting staring at the only source of illumination, his computer screen.

'I don't know where to start. There's so much.'

'You could start by telling us what the hell's going on.'

On the other end of the line, there was a moment's silence. Jack was collecting his thoughts.

'Yes. Of course. They've had half a dozen cases of your mystery illness.'

'It's not a mystery, Jack, it's –'

'I know, I know. It's the Black Death.' There was a weariness to his voice. 'Whatever. Maybe it is, for all I know. Jesus, they're certainly taking it seriously enough.'

'So what about the new cases? Who? How? When? Tell me, Jack.'

'Two kids, it seems, were the vectors, if that's what they call them. They'd just come home from a party when this girl came over all funny, passed out on the floor and then came up coughing and spluttering. They called the ambulance and rushed her to the JR2 but she died within hours.'

'Oh, no!'

'Um. Nasty business. The bloke, her boyfriend, went into shock, then came out with symptoms himself, apparently. Told them about some geezer they'd met in the High Street who'd staggered out of a doorway looking for money and coughed all over them. It got the authorities moving all right: they rounded up every kid in the house they share, locked them all in an isolation ward. So far, all they'll confirm is that four more of them have symptoms. But I'm telling you, it has people scared shitless.'

'So much for old Harkness calling me a scaremonger, eh?'

'Don't even start! The old bugger's beside himself. Gone home in a funk. Hasn't even figured out what we're going to do for next week's paper. Probably still wants to run his precious Festive Quiz.'

'But how –?'

'Yeah, I know. How does some dead guy up at the JR2 wind up puking over party-goers in the High Street? Mind you, even that's more than the nationals know – and I haven't told them. I've had to take most of the phones here off the hook to stop them ringing. The hospital spokesman's tighter than a duck's arse on this one. Routing all calls to the same "emergency spokesman". And bugger-all use he is. Sounds like a military type: more used to giving instructions than answering questions. But I've got a theory.'

'You have?' Jack always did.

'Yeah, well, my copper mate down at St Aldate's nick – the one who told me about the geezer coughing on the kids – says he reckons it has to be the same bloke they found done in rather nastily down Magpie Lane. The PC who called it in thought he was a vagrant until he noticed the hospital pyjamas round his ankles. Within minutes the place was crawling with blokes in white suits. Carted the constable off an' all.'

'Crikey!' The other construction worker, Therry

thought. One of the pair brought in the night they nearly killed her.

'Listen, Moonbeam, I don't know what the fuck is going on. One minute you've got some cock-and-bull feature about the Black Death, and the next, it all starts coming true with bloody bells on. Anyway, I'm trying to help you. I only came in to check the email, but I think it may have been worth the effort. Listen to this.'

It was like Jack to drop a bombshell, knowing it, and then start gabbling. Therry heard him take a deep breath.

'Burke – my old Fleet Street mate, right? – trawled the cuts on our friend Martindale. He didn't come up with much beyond the fact that he has four or five companies, mostly in the construction business, is a bit of a playboy for a bloke his age, and used to hang around with a few of the less savoury characters in the last Tory government. Anyway, you'll see it all; I've forwarded it to you on the email. I'm assuming you've got that little laptop on you. No point in coming in to the office. But there's something else, something much more interesting, at least I think it might be . . .'

Therry couldn't take it all in. She could barely believe what she had already heard. This was a national story, for Christ's sake, There would be reporters clustering like flies on shit . . . Where? she suddenly wondered. If the city was shut down? Obviously, back at the Moat House motel outside Wolvercote. This ought to be her big break: all she had to do was get the story out, and one of the big boys would be bound to pay her a fortune. Maybe give her a staff job on the strength of it. Or even . . . Her head was whirling. She shivered violently.

'. . . and that was why the other candidates who were up for his present job were so pissed off . . .'

'What?' She realised she had no idea what Jack was rattling on about. Daniel was signalling to her to keep her voice down. The railway tracks and the houses beyond that marked the western edge of the city could not be far away. They still did not know if there would be police – or even army – patrolling the edge of town.

'Sorry, Jack.' She lowered her voice. 'I've got to go. What were you just saying?'

'I said that's why they were pissed off, because he was an outsider, came from a government job, not proper research, at least not pure enough for them.'

'Jack, Jack, wait a minute. Just who are we talking about here?'

'Who? Therry, have you been listening to a word I've said? Dr Simon bleeding Redwhistle, that's who. Your mad-scientist mate.'

'Jack, sorry, but just run me through the essentials again, will you?'

'There's only one essential. Where he worked before he came here. Immediately before.'

'And that was . . . ?'

'And that was,' Jack repeated with the laboured patience of an archangel repeating the annunciation to a slightly deaf Virgin Mary, 'the Defence Evaluation and Research Agency, usually abbreviated to DERA. At least that's what they've called themselves since 1995. But still better known as . . . ?' Infuriatingly, he made it a question.

'Yes, yes, yes, stop testing me! Better known as . . .' Therry dragged it out as if trawling her mental archives. In fact she hadn't a clue where or what DERA might be.

'Better known, for Christ's sake, as Porton Down.'

'Jesus Christ!' she exclaimed.

'That's what I said,' Jack replied laconically.

Then a movement of air in the empty office behind him made him turn his head.

*　　*　　*

Daniel stamped his feet to keep them from freezing, watching impatiently the bizarre sight of a woman standing still in a snowstorm talking on the telephone. It seemed insane to have stopped where they were, if she was right, so close to warmth and comfort. With relief he saw her click the phone closed. The expression on her face, however, did little to reassure him: stark frown lines were etched across her brow and she seemed to be staring beyond him into the empty freezing fog.

'What's the matter? Therry, are you all right?'

'Mmm? Sorry. No. Headache. It's just . . .' She looked down at the mobile phone in her hand as if there was something wrong with it.

It was not just the information that Jack had passed on to her, discomfiting and sinister though its implications were, but something more: the way he had abruptly told her about Redwhistle, like delivering a punchline to a joke, and then put the phone down. Her head was spinning.

'It's just that . . .' she began and then halted, unable to follow her own sentence to any sensible conclusion. 'I don't know. But somehow . . . there's something terribly wrong. I'll tell you later. Come on! Let's get out of this.'

The blizzard was abating, the snow no longer driving into their faces. It fell in thick, heavy flakes, like the snow in children's drawings, each blob adding to the last, building layers of white upon the ground. There were already drifts, in places up to a foot or more deep. They had been lucky to start their trek across the meadow when they did, Daniel realised; by now anyone out there would be wading through deep snow. In a day or two the meadow would be full of happy kids jumping into the snowdrifts and pelting one another with snowballs. Or maybe not. No, the truth was that there would be no children out there today and none tomorrow. There would be nobody outside at all. For the foreseeable future, the world was no longer safe.

On the edge of his vision, strange shapes began to appear, dappled grey and white like the world around them. Only their movement gave them away, and a soft muffled snort as first one, then the other, tossed a great head and exhaled a cloud of steaming breath. Creatures of myth come to guide them.

The ponies of Port Meadow lived as if wild together in a herd, though actually they were owned by Wolvercote commoners exercising their right to graze as they had done since the Middle Ages. Daniel thought they seemed bigger than ponies, and more beautiful. Unfettered, free spirits. The spirits of the meadow. Therry had seen them too and stopped. Her mind was elsewhere but her gaze, like Daniel's, was riveted to the two animals watching them back through the slowly falling snow.

Then the white pony snorted again and tossed its mane, sending a flurry of flakes into the air, and turned towards its dappled companion, rubbing its great neck down one side of the other animal's mane. The second responded, pushing back and tossing its own head. For a second Daniel thought that they were fighting, then realised that they were playing, displaying affection, having already dismissed the human intruders as harmless.

Horses, Daniel recalled, apparently repelled the otherwise indiscriminating *Yersinia pestis*. Maybe that was why they could play: for them the plague was less of an inconvenience than the blizzard. And in the end both would pass away. But watching the two animals as they turned and gambolled off across the snowdrifts, Daniel was unable to ascribe even a symbolic cynicism to them. They were messengers of hope, he told himself, and found himself believing it. It was what he wanted to believe.

Therry came up behind him and took his hand. 'Look,' she said quietly, as if wary of attracting attention. 'The bridge. We're almost there.'

Daniel looked. And saw through the gradually lightening snowfall, barely a hundred yards away, a long, thin wooden arch, as elegant as the curve of a longbow, rising out of the snow and disappearing into the dark. Like the rainbow, he thought, which the Vikings believed their gods crossed to get to earth.

'Where does it go to?' he asked.

'Aristotle Lane. On the other side of the railway tracks. Past some allotments on one side and a new housing development on the other. Takes us down into the back streets off the Woodstock Road, not far from the end of Walton Street . . .'

'Jericho.'

'You've got it.'

He smiled at the Americanism.

'So what are we waiting for?'

It took only a minute or so to reach the start of the little footbridge, which was barely wide enough for two people to cross at once. Therry crouched down and motioned to him to do likewise. He understood. It was unlikely, unless someone in authority had been a great deal more thorough than they anticipated, that there would be much of a police presence. The only regular users of Aristotle Lane were the allotment gardeners, rarely out in midwinter, even under normal circumstances.

Even so, Therry kept in a low crouch up to the halfway point on the bridge's steep arch where she could see the other side. She was just standing up and about to wave Daniel on when a figure entered the little pool of lamplight on the other side. Squeezing herself back down again, almost into the cold snow that had settled on the wooden slats of the bridge, she saw that it was indeed a policeman, though apparently only one, dressed in a long weatherproof cape. And, for the moment at least, he was not looking their way.

She motioned to Daniel to come forward, pressing a finger to her lips. The question was whether the policeman was actually supposed to be on duty there or had just wandered up from the main entrance to the meadow, several hundred yards further south, by the big bridge at the end of Walton Well Road. For the moment he showed no sign of going away. As they watched, he paced up and down, moving into and out of the circle of illumination cast by the solitary streetlight near the far end of the bridge.

'There's only one thing to do,' she whispered. 'Run for it.'

'Wha-at? Are you kidding? With my –'

Therry shushed him with a finger, then waited until the pacing policeman was at almost the maximum distance in his little routine.

'I know, I know,' she said, as quietly as possible. 'But he can't follow both of us, and with a bit of luck he might not even notice us at all. So far he hasn't even turned his head in this direction. Anyway, it's either that or wait here half the night, and I'm wrecked.'

Daniel nodded.

'All we have to do,' she continued, 'is get to the edge of the bridge and then slip into the allotment gardens. Make our way through them and out into the next street. If there's just one of him, he's hardly likely to chase us far.'

Daniel was dubious. But he did not see any immediate alternatives. The policeman had turned and was heading away from them again.

'Right,' said Therry. 'Let's go!'

Close behind her, cursing his aching ankle, Daniel ran at a crouch down the steep slope of the little bridge, almost sliding all the way and thankful that the snow dampened any noise they were making. At the end of the bridge they stopped for an instant, checking that the caped figure was still looking away from them, then dropped over the side of the bank into the allotments. Daniel landed heavily and only with difficulty managed to suppress a cry of pain, but was immediately on Therry's heels, crouched low and creeping through strange foliage that looked like miniature trees – only after bumping into several of them he realised it was the Christmas crop of Brussels sprouts. Talk about a turkey shoot! he thought, but just then a cry came from the road. They fell flat and held their breath.

Jack Denton had known there was something terribly wrong the minute he felt the movement behind him, like a breath of dank air on the back of his neck. But even as he turned, spinning round in his swivel chair to the left, he felt the phone taken out of his right hand and heard it replaced in the cradle as a ghostly white hand, stinking of rubber, closed over his eyes and nose, clamping his nostrils hard.

Instead of the intended angry protest, all his speech organs managed to produce as his lungs gulped for air was an incoherent strangled grunt, soon stifled as he felt his jaws stretched brutally open and something the size of a tennis ball stuffed into them. As soon as he could, he opened his eyes, only to find himself staring at a man in a face mask like a surgeon's, holding a latex-gloved finger to where his mouth presumably was and pointing the barrel of a large-calibre handgun directly at the middle of Jack Denton's forehead. Not a tennis ball, was his first thought as his eyes flickered downwards to the object choking him. It was red, and attached to a thick black rubber band that the gunman's other hand had brutally snapped over his head. Jack knew what it was all right. And he found it almost more frightening than the firearm pointing in his face. He had seen them in pornographic magazines. It was a bondage gag.

Part Three

Outbreak

(Come in under the shadow of this red rock),
And I will show you something different from either
Your shadow at morning striding behind you
Or your shadow at evening rising to meet you;
I will show you fear in a handful of dust.
                                        T. S. Eliot, *The Waste Land*

Chapter Forty

North Oxford; Tuesday 23 December,
7.30 p.m.

T HE GARGOYLES of Oxford do not inhabit only the stone guttering and battlements of the medieval colleges, where they were intended to ward off evil and warn of vices, Christian Europe's equivalent of the totem pole. They are also to be found adorning some of the more extravagant Victorian Gothic houses along the Woodstock and Banbury roads, perched high on gables or crenellated corners of these redbrick castles, designed to house dons in the days when academia was still considered respectable enough to command a proper salary.

The big house on the corner of Rawlinson Road and Woodstock Road was doubly blessed, or cursed, depending on your point of view. High up at the apex of the foremost of its three forward-facing gables, protruding from the brickwork and carved from a similarly coloured russet sandstone, squatted a malicious-looking pixie with pointed ears and a wicked grin. It was, in fact, a copy of the Lincoln Imp, an ancient gargoyle that hangs from one of the great pillars near the pulpit in that city's magnificent cathedral, and is thought by superstitious folk to have been responsible for much mischief over the centuries.

Most of the people who went in and out of the house regularly did not know that.

Certainly it had never crossed the mind of Neal Faversham on either of his two previous visits. But now, as he shook the snowflakes from his shoes and pushed open the door, inviting his companion to follow him, he glanced up and caught a sight of the imp grinning down at him. It was not the sort of omen he had been hoping for.

Most of the inhabitants of the Rawlinson Road house assumed it belonged to Trinity College. That was the college to which they belonged and it had provided them with this lodging. There were eight rooms that could be used as bed-sitting rooms, plus three bathrooms, as well as a large communal kitchen and a separate television room on the ground floor. Faversham and his companion ignored all of this, as they did the solitary graduate student who looked out apprehensively as they climbed the stairs.

Such comings and goings were not unusual, even if, at a time like this particularly, they could be disconcerting. Only six of the rooms had full-time inhabitants. The remaining two, it was understood, were kept back by the college from the general student letting pool to be used for putting up visiting academics or other guests of the Senior Common Room for whom there was not enough space in college. The house on Rawlinson Road had been a 'gift' to the college – on a lease with very specific covenants which had been precisely formulated by an 'old member' of Trinity employed in the legal department situated in the basement of one particular stone building on Millbank in London – but this detail had somehow been forgotten. Except by those who had the keys to the two unlet rooms. The popular idea of a 'safe house' as being an empty or secluded property, Faversham reflected briefly as he opened the door to the top-floor room, was a triumph of the romantic imagination over common sense.

'Sit down, please.' Faversham gestured to a couple of well-upholstered, if rather faded, armchairs and a sofa that looked as if it had come straight out of a 1989 Habitat catalogue. Which it had.

'Fancy a drink? I know I could do with one. I think we have some decent Scotch.' The former writing bureau which served as a drinks cabinet yielded a bottle of twelve-year-old Macallan. The other man, a tall, well-built African-American, shook his head, but let himself sink down on the sofa, sending up a small cloud of dust which made him grimace.

'So,' said Faversham, pouring himself a substantial measure which he sipped straight. 'It's not exactly what we had hoped for, is it?'

'Nope,' replied the man on the sofa in an accent that revealed origins somewhere south of the Mason-Dixon line. 'That's for sure. You've got yourself something of a situation here.'

With the city of Oxford closed off, half a dozen confirmed cases of a highly infectious lethal disease, most of the John Radcliffe Hospital transformed into a quarantine zone, and a killer on the loose, that, Neal Faversham thought, was putting it pretty mildly. Whoever said the English were the masters of understatement?

There was a gentle rap on the door. Faversham looked across at the American, glanced at his watch and said, 'Not before time.'

He opened the door and had to suppress a smile at the sight that greeted him: a middle-aged Japanese togged up in bottle-green corduroy and waxed cotton like an artist's impression of an English country squire just in from a day's shooting.

'Ah,' said the big American, leaping to his feet. 'Neal,

let me introduce my colleague Mujimo Takahashi, who runs a very special unit of Japan's National Public Safety Commission.'

Takahashi bowed politely. 'Mr Faversham. Good to see you again, Jerry.' Turning to Faversham directly, he explained, 'Mr Winner and I have cooperated on several occasions in the past.

'You must excuse my clothing, gentlemen,' he added, 'but I have been carrying out what you might call a little . . . field work.'

Faversham raised an eyebrow, then remembered his manners. 'Have a seat, Mr Takahashi. A drop of whisky, perhaps?'

'That would be most acceptable. Just a little water. Thank you.'

Faversham poured a large measure, topped up from a tap at a small sink in the corner, and handed it to Takahashi, who had unzipped his Barbour and sat down, looking somewhat uncomfortable, in one of the elderly armchairs.

'OK,' said Jerry Winner, sprawling back on the sofa. 'Why don't you fill us in on the little lady's background? Or should I say "the duchess" maybe, given that fancy title she used?'

Faversham snorted. 'Hardly. Though duchesses aren't what they used to be these days,' he muttered, leaning back against the bureau, toying with his whisky. 'I suppose you could call our Miranda something of a modern archetype. A classic case,' he explained for the benefit of his fellow whisky-drinker, who nodded appreciatively at the courtesy.

'Amanda Workington, to use her original name for the moment at least, was a bright, pretty schoolgirl from a middle-class south London family. Did well at school. Maths, French, German, even Russian, took music lessons, didn't go out much with the local boys. A bit backward in that respect maybe, to tell the truth. At her age half the little tarts in her class were probably dropping their knickers behind the bicycle sheds. But not our Amanda. Oh, no. She was a good kid, her mum's pride and joy. Her old man, a cabbie, had chucked in the towel by the time she was twelve: heart attack on the South Circular. Can't say I blame him.'

'Sorry?'

Faversham looked up. Clearly both his listeners had lost him.

'No, I'm sorry. It's the traffic. Londoner's in-joke. Digression. Doesn't matter. No. What did for Amanda was what I guess you might call Kate Moss syndrome. Too gorgeous for her own good. One Saturday afternoon she's out with her mum, trying on a couple of new summer frocks in Miss Selfridge, when this smarmy bloke comes along. Says he's a photographer. Don't they all?

'Says she's got a face in a million. Gets poor Amanda all in a tizz. Her mum, poor old dear, is thrilled to bits. Ought to have known better. Does now, I suppose.

'Anyway, this bloke's telling them that he knows the face of the future when he sees it, tells them young Amanda has the potential to be the first supermodel of the twenty-first century, Miss Millennium. All that stuff still sounded smart back then, remember. Promises her the earth. But doesn't mention the earthy bits.'

'Please?'

Faversham was shaking his head. He never could get the hang of speaking in what the Voice of America used to call 'special English': with all the curlicues knocked off.

'Never mind. What it all comes down to is he gives her a card with a smart address in the West End. List of names from Naomi Campbell to Cleopatra herself who're supposed to have passed through the books. Just drop in, he says. We'll do a shoot. Can't do any harm, can it, love? Ha, bloody ha.

'Amanda doesn't know. She's only fifteen, for Christ's sake. But her mum has pound signs revolving in her eyes. Means well, of course. Get young Amanda out of herself, etcetera.

'Anyhow, the long and short of it is that Amanda goes for it. The first time, Mum comes along too. Sits in the foyer. Nice and plush. Potted plants and all that. Signed photos from big names in the modelling world. Probably. Mum has to admit she's not too well up on who's who on the catwalks these days, but they all look the part. Well, they would, wouldn't they?

'Amanda comes out a different girl. Similar, but different. Got stars in her eyes too now, you see. Shows her mum the snaps when they get home. A contact sheet anyhow. That's when old Mumsie begins to get second thoughts. A bit revealing, these pictures, you see. Not exactly starkers, but certainly suggestive. Do models really need to lie back like that with their legs apart, in knee socks – particularly when she'd gone in wearing tights, purchased especially from Marks and Spencer for the occasion – clutching her skirt up to her crotch? Dodgy.'

He stopped and handed across a picture, clearly much enlarged and not from an original negative. Jerry Winner looked at it, frowned and passed it on to Takahashi, who took a large gulp of spirits and set the photograph down next to him. Within easy view, Faversham noted.

'But not definitely. You see, that was the problem. Now here's Amanda full of the brave new world that has such people in it. 'Don't be silly, Mum, it's just to sell the skirt.' Well, it's certainly selling something. There's a lot of sad bastards out there who would pay very good money for what's she's showing off. But that's another story. Or so she thinks.'

'Yes, but . . . where does this get us?'

'Sorry again. I'll come to the point. Despite Mrs Workington's reservations, Amanda goes up to the studio a couple more times, and comes home raving, with talk of a full-time contract and even – to smooth out any misgivings – a fistful of cash. Five hundred pounds sterling. In fifties. The size of note that people in Croydon don't see often. Not if they're in legitimate business, anyway. It doesn't exactly allay her mother's concerns, but it stops her pulling the plug. And there's the pity.'

'Because?'

'Because just before her last trip into town is the last time Mumsie sees her pretty baby. Six months down the line comes a postcard from Germany telling her not to worry. Fat chance. And that's it. From her mother's point of view. We, of course, know better.'

'Thanks to the BND, I believe.'

'Er, yes.' Faversham was annoyed but not surprised by the interruption. 'German intelligence notified us back in 1995 that the mob they were shadowing had a new bimbo in tow. Amazing, really, that she escaped the maw. Considering that the gang she'd fallen in with were in the full-time import-export business, shipping underage girls from all points east, Ukraine and Belarus mainly, to the piglet market behind Hamburg station.'

'Piglet?'

Faversham turned towards Takahashi, who had put down his empty whisky glass. The Englishman refilled it, lifted the photograph for a moment for another look at the seductively stretched-out schoolgirl on it, and replied, 'Actually "suckling pig" is the better translation. *Spannferkel* in German. That's what they call the kiddie-sex market that has really taken off since the fear of AIDS did serious damage to the trade of the old lags who used to hang out around the Reeperbahn. And the parasites who lived off them.

'Our Amanda might have ended up like the rest of them: dosed up and traumatised before she was old enough to vote. It was a close thing, but Amanda was something special. She caught the eye of the big boss, old Attila. Far from being put out like a welcome mat for visiting guests, she was elevated to queen of the harem. She was on the junk of course by then, shooting heroin like a supermodel. But nobody else dared touch her. Even had her own bodyguard, the *crème de la crème*, our friend HH himself.'

'Heil Hitler!'

'That's not funny. Nor appropriate, as you know.'

The American shrugged. 'Whatever,' he said.

Faversham shrugged back. And to think people thought the Brits were lumbered with stereotypes.

'The point is,' he continued, 'that we can imagine how pissed off our friend was when she did a runner. Remember, among the people we're dealing with, a bodyguard is not just protection but a jailer.'

'You said it, bud.'

'Indeed. Yet by 1998 Amanda was back in Britain. Not as Amanda Workington any more, but as the glamorous Miranda von Taxenbach, self-styled orphan of an obscure Austrian aristocratic family. Spoke perfect English – how about that? – but with a distinct accent, distinct enough to be sexy. One German diplomat who bumped into her – literally, I wouldn't be surprised – said that although her German was faultless, there was a lot more Hamburg than Vienna in it. She told him she'd travelled about a lot when young.'

'And who was paying for this new glamour?'

'I'm sure I can leave that to your imaginations. Some of her money may even have come from old Attila, he can be quite generous to his concubines, I believe. Whatever, it was enough to set herself up with a nice little pad in Islington, which is about the best place to start from these days if you want to get yourself a sugar daddy with a nice job in the government.'

'I thought all the nice jobs in your government went to nice men who only liked other nice men,' the American said. Faversham ignored him.

'Anyway, she gets asked to the right sort of parties, which is where she gets her claws into Charlie Fletcher, a rising star who has just been appointed junior minister. Within days of their meeting, she's shagging him silly and also his pal Geoffrey Martindale. Got the run of Denholm House, Martindale's country seat; got a nice new BMW Z3, which really pisses the hell out of his daughter, who's the only one that hates her guts.'

'Life's a bitch,' said the man on the sofa.

'More than one,' replied Faversham, whose relations with women were not on a high at that time. 'In the light of events, we have to assume that Martindale rather than the minister was her target. Always assuming she had one in the first place.'

'You seriously think there's any doubt about that?' Jerry Winner sounded incredulous.

'I'm always willing to keep an open mind. It is not impossible that she really was trying to get away from the mob but when they noticed she had ended up in circles that were particularly convenient, they decided to re-establish contact and ask a few favours.'

The American shook his head to convey that he found his British colleague's naivety charming but eccentric.

'I'm just saying it's possible. That's all. The way things turned out, it hardly looks as if she was doing what they wanted, does it?'

'I guess not.'

'Anyway, if it weren't for Mr Takahashi here and his boys, we could all have taken a lot longer to put this thing together.'

'Until your Mr Atkins, turned up croaking with black boils all over him, you guys didn't even know you had a problem,' the American put in.

The Japanese man nodded slightly.

'The fact that she was trying to deal with the Aum Shinri Kyo,' the American continued, 'seriously suggests to me that her little ladyship was experimenting with private enterprise. I think Mr Hammerstein's intervention can be treated as confirmation, don't you?'

Faversham could not deny it. 'But are we really saying that the only reason the deal collapsed was because they got to her first?'

The question had been directed at Takahashi. 'We had been monitoring the contacts of Aum Shinri Kyo cultists in the United States for some time,' he began. But the American, with a conspicuous lack of manners which both the others noted but affected not to, interupted and answered the question:

'We're saying that she blew it. Literally. And she knew it. She was shot up well before HH and his goons showed up. Couldn't shake her habit.'

'Her habit?'

'Sure as hell wasn't a nun's. Mind you, the forensics boys pretty well had to scrape their samples off the poolside. But what they got into their test tubes showed there was enough "horse" in her metabolism to saddle up the Seventh Cavalry.'

'You mean she killed her*self*?' Having seen the photographs of the remains, it was a possibility that had never crossed Faversham's mind.

The American shrugged. 'Let's just say she was pretty well anaesthetised when it happened. She knew these guys were coming for her, but I doubt she even noticed when they showed up.'

'But ... why did you bother ... ?' And then he realised.

'Because that was when Mr Takahashi here got on to us ...'

The Japanese man nodded in polite recognition.

'... and within the hour we had the place sealed off and crawling with guys in bio-containment suits wielding plastic bags and spatulas.'

Faversham let his disgust register on his face. 'You thought ...'

'If she was trying to peddle this stuff, she might have been in contact. We weren't taking chances.'

'And?'

The American shook his head. 'Negative. I guess dying twice over was enough for her.'

Neal Faversham had refilled his whisky glass, without thinking, and walked across to the mansard window which looked out on snow-dusted roof tiles and empty streets. Looking down at the sickly yellow pools of light shed on the pavements, he wondered how many chances he was taking. With how many lives?

Forty-One

*Jericho, Oxford; Tuesday 23 December,
7.40 p.m.*

PC JAMES Carrington, thirty-one, did not like to
admit it to himself, but he was scared. What scard
him most was the clothing he was wearing. There was
no danger, they had assured him, a warning rare enough
in itself to be intimidating, but the protective respiratory mask was a sensible precaution under the circumstances. The trouble was how little they went on to
say about what specifically the circumstances were. A
disease, potentially highly contagious, possibly airborne.
More detailed questions did not receive more detailed
answers.

So there he was, standing at the end of a dark lane on
the edge of the city in a snowstorm on the coldest night
of the year dressed like something out of *The Phantom
of the Opera* with a thick cape and the damn mask
that restricted his vision and allowed him to hear his
own breath circulating, as if there was forever someone
breathing down his neck. Sinister, it was; bloody sinister.
And he was on his own. True, he was only a couple
of hundred yards from the boys down at Walton Well
Road, one of whom was due to relieve him shortly; they
had arranged to swap over on a half-hourly basis. But
he couldn't see the point of any of it anyhow. They
had been told to warn people off, tell them that Port
Meadow was closed, just in case, he assumed, anybody

tried to leave the city by that route. Fat chance! Why would anyone want to wander out into a blizzard? And what was he going to do if they did? Shoot them with his finger? Oh, sure, they had said call on the radio if there was a problem. The truth was that nobody was expecting them to see a soul. The truth was that nobody knew what the fuck they were doing. There were no plans for implementing a state of emergency like this. Never had been. The orders had come from the top, they said, with hush-hush looks on their faces that suggested, wherever the top was, it was very far above them and even further above him. And then the military men had come in, from God knows where, not any regiment he recognised, and acting as if they owned the fucking place, quoting from some supposed civil-defence rulebook. What they were supposed to do in the event of a nuclear attack or a terrorist alert, something like that. Sullen police sergeants, even bloody inspectors, suddenly expected to jump to the order of some self-important squaddie. But they did, didn't they? In the end. Which just made the whole thing scarier too. Try as he might to muster some righteous indignation, some feeling of anger that would outweigh the other mounting considerations in his mind, PC Carrington could come to no other conclusion. Something serious was going down. Something that nobody in obvious authority had the faintest idea how to control.

And then he saw it. Heard it, more like. On the turn, as he swung round under the streetlight to pace back towards the bridge. A movement. A thud and a rustle of something moving on the bridge. Something that might have crossed it. From the other side. Coming in his direction. Damn this stupid gas-mask contraption! He wiped snow off the visor. Off to one side. Definitely.

'Oi!' he shouted. 'Stop!' Because that was the sort of

thing he normally shouted, on the rare occasions that he had cause to in uniform. And then, sensing that was inadequate, 'Who goes there?'

But there was nothing now. No sound. No obvious movement as he approached the bridge at a gentle trot. 'Never run into something you can't see, sonny,' they had told him at training college. He reached for his radio, and then hesitated a second. No point in looking silly, was there? No need to give the impression he had let himself be spooked. It could have been a fox, couldn't it? A big one. A badger breaking out of hibernation for some reason. Maybe. He had reached the foot of the bridge now and looked around him warily. On one side were the smart new flats, most windows lit, none open, curtains pulled as if to offer extra protection from the hostile world outside. On the other, were the allotments: dark, quiet. He shone his torch across them but lit up nothing other than snow-encrusted clumps of winter vegetables and shrivelled stalks. Awaiting infill development.

He looked down at his feet, at the marks in the snow on the bridge, looking for prints, hoping for animal tracks. Nothing. Well, nothing obvious. The snow had been disturbed all right, as if something – or someone – had rolled down it. He shone the torch beam further out along the bridge. Its wooden slats were protected by the solid side walls from the gusting drifts, and so the covering of snow was only slight. But there were marks all right. Marks that were definitely not animal tracks. Not, at this distance anyway, immediately identifiable as footprints either. But as like as not.

For a second time PC Carrington reached for his radio. On this occasion there was no doubt in his mind, as he played the broad beam of his torch once again across the quiet allotment gardens. He clicked open the frequency and, speaking in a quiet voice, gave the call sign to his colleagues at Walton Well. The voice of Dick Ebert came through, louder than he would have liked: 'What's up, Jimmy boy? Got a problem?'

He flicked down the volume and replied in the same self-consciously calm voice he had used a few seconds before.

'Not sure, Dick. But you'd better come down here and take a look at something. We might need backup.'

Chapter Forty-Two

Jericho, Oxford; Tuesday 23 December,
8.05 p.m.

THERRY AND Daniel hobbled into the front room
like the last couple standing in a Depression-era
dance marathon and flopped exhausted side by side on
a striped futon.

'Now what?' he wondered aloud. The close encounter
with the policeman on the bridge had shaken him, and
he was more than a little angry with himself, and with
her. They were behaving as if they were criminals, for
Christ's sake, rather than simply trying to get back home.
Her home. Whatever. In breach of martial law.

Therry was not answering, flat out on her back with
her eyes closed, her precious kitten curled up and purring
beside her. Daniel eased off his shoe and sock and
examined his offending ankle: it was swollen, but less
than he had imagined, certainly not the blackened, blue
and yellow joint he had been expecting to view, after
all the pain it had been causing him as they limped the
last few hundred yards across the meadow. Then, in a
relatively rare flash of common sense, he realised that
he was, as ever, being self-centred.

'Is there anything I can do?' he asked Therry.

'Hmm?' Her voice was hazy, as if she had already
dozed off. To Daniel, her face looked dramatically different from that of the cocky girl-power newshound he
had encountered only a couple of days ago. There were

lines on her brow. Lines that he thought made her look less arrogant and more interesting. And more tired. That, at least, he understood.

'My head hurts like hell. There's paracetamol some-where in the bathroom cabinet. Get them for me, would you?'

Daniel found his way into the bathroom, feeling more than a little self-conscious as he poked among her toiletries. A pale-blue plastic container almost fell out when he slid open the mirrored front of the cabinet. It held old lipsticks, makeup, packets of tampons, eyebrow tweezers. No paracetamol. Not since his mother had died, he realised, had he inhabited the same space as a woman. There was a curious, almost voyeuristic intimacy to sorting through the flotsam of someone else's private world.

'I can't find them,' he was forced to admit, poking his head back round the door.

'Hmm? Oh.' Therry hauled herself to her feet and pushed him out of the way. 'That's because you're not looking in the right place,' she said, retrieving a flat package of pills from somewhere on top of the cabinet. She staggered into the kitchen, popped a couple with a swig of water from the tap and began opening a tin of cat food. Tigger came running at the sound.

And then she stopped, half-opened tin in hand, as if the reality had suddenly punched her in the face.

'Tell me this isn't happening, Daniel,' she said.

'I wish I could.'

'But it's real, isn't it? It's out there. They've unleashed it. We've no idea, have we? What we do, I mean. You, me, any of us. No one has the faintest idea what the outcome of their actions might be.'

He held her eyes, but he had no answers. He was not even sure if he understood her question.

'So, come on then, tell me about this place that Redwhistle comes from – Portadown?'

She gave a little laugh, the ghost of humour flitting through the laden air, as she bent down and forked the cat food into a dish. 'I think you'll find Portadown's somewhere in Northern Ireland. Porton Down – two words – is very different. Very different indeed. The trouble is that is doesn't fit in. Doesn't fit in at all. Unless, as you guys say, we're in a whole different ball game. And maybe have been all along.

'Porton Down, eh . . . Porton Down.' She uttered the words like an incantation, an evil spell or a mantra, something that, once said, was supposed to have an immediate effect on the listener.

Daniel looked at her quizzically.

'You've never heard of it?'

'No,' he replied.

'What does it mean?'

'Back in the 1950s, Porton Down was probably the most highly classified place in Britain. More top-secret than Aldermaston.'

Daniel shot her another puzzled glance.

'The British nuclear-weapons facility. Our Los Alamos. Jeez, do they teach you Yanks nothing about other countries?'

Daniel shrugged. It hadn't really occurred to him that Britain had nuclear weapons.

'Porton Down was different. It was the nasty stuff. Set up back during World War I some time, allegedly after the Germans started using mustard gas on our boys in the trenches, though if you ask me, it was just that they got there first. Anyway, it became the main centre for the production of chemical and biological weapons.'

'You mean –'

She held up a hand. 'Wait a minute. I'm not saying

anything here. Not yet. Though I'm sure as hell thinking it. Porton Down supposedly stopped its research into biological weapons back in 1957 or thereabouts. Went over wholly to defence. Or so they say.'

'Who says?'

'MOD.'

Blank stare.

'Ministry of Defence. That's who they work for.'

'What are you saying?'

She shrugged. 'I don't know. I just don't know. I'm confused, Daniel. Confused.'

She reached over to a black leather bag beneath the desk. After a few seconds of fiddling with the catch, she extracted a preposterously orange and white translucent Macintosh laptop computer.

'Let's see what Jack sent through on the email.'

Even as she said it, she was disturbed again by the thought that Jack had finished their phone call uncharacteristically abruptly. She had tried ringing back but got only the answering machine on his desk. He had told her he had only nipped into the office for a few minutes, but on his home number too only the answering machine was picking up. And Jack was one of the few people she knew who still refused to have a mobile.

'Here we go,' she said as the Outlook Express window popped up. She clicked on the Receive All box and waited – for what seemed like an eternity. She had a headache; she hoped it wasn't one of the migraines that her mother suffered from. She had heard they were hereditary. She flicked her finger idly around the computer's trackpad. What the hell was making the thing so slow? There were apparently only five messages. Then, all of a sudden, it was done. She scanned the inbox, Daniel looking over her shoulder.

'Do you mind?' she said, feigning annoyance. 'Do you always read other people's mail?'

He looked flustered.

'Never mind. It's just the usual crap.'

It was too. A couple of electronic Christmas cards from friends eager to show off their mastery of the new medium, though she suspected it was an attempt to save money and not only on the postage. You want a card to hang on the wall? Print it out yourself. She trashed them.

And there, *there* was what she had been looking for. She realised why the download had been so slow: Jack's forwarded email, originated by his ex-colleague under the nickname 'Einstein', was a mammoth 11.2 megabytes of compressed information. She cursed quietly. Some of it was in plain text, but there was also a whole chunk of attachments, which, when she opened them, turned out to be scanned photocopies of old newspaper cuttings. She smiled to herself, despite the pain over her left eye: Jack's researcher employed a strange mix of old and new technology.

For the next half-hour, Therry and Daniel scanned the cuttings in electronic form. It would take too long to print them out, she had decided. And in any case, several of them were instantly dismissable: bits from society magazines, *Tatler* and *Hello!*. Not where she had expected to find references to the boring head of a building concern. On closer inspection, however, Geoffrey Martindale was not the focus of attention. Occasionally the text would refer to a rather dippy-looking young man in his company, referred to as the Rt Hon Charles Fletcher MP and later as a junior minister in John Major's government. But invariably the prime figure in the photographs was a stunning young woman with leggy, coltish good looks and a perpetual pout.

In earlier pictures she was not identified, but *Hello!* had nailed her down as the 'Countess Miranda von Taxenbach, one of the better connected of Europe's new glamorous young aristocrats'. Interesting, but hardly incriminating. Except possibly to Martindale's wife. But in the only reference to her, a short piece about a driving infringement two years ago which earned her a two-month suspension for doing 65 m.p.h. in a 30 m.p.h. area, she was described as 'estranged'.

Therry quickly found herself getting bored and sat back stroking the cat while Daniel trawled. As Jack had said, there was a great deal of stuff, but none of it was exactly riveting. Certainly not on a par with the revelation that Simon Redwhistle had arrived at Oxford straight from Porton Down. There was a cryptic comment typed in lower case at the bottom of the message. Therry had some difficulty deciding whether it had come from Jack or his friend Burke:

'check what foe say about cerberus'

'What do you make of that?' she asked Daniel.

'Search me. Rather quaint language, maybe. Who's the foe? Martindale and his companies?'

'And who or what is cerberus? Isn't that something mythological? Some kind of monster or something?'

Daniel nodded. 'A dog,' he said.

'A dog? With enemies? We can understand that, can't we, Tigger?' she said to the kitten on her lap.

'Well, not just any old dog. He was particularly fierce, had three heads and he guarded the entrance to hell.'

'Oh, great! So who was his foe and what did he have to say about him?'

But Daniel was shaking his head. 'Theseus was his foe, I guess. He killed the dog to get into the underworld and out again. But I'm damned if I can see the relevance to this Martindale guy.'

'I can. Look!'

On the screen was a cutting that they had hardly noticed, a short couple of paragraphs from the Lex column of the *Financial Times*. Therry read it aloud:

'Analysts have signally failed to remark on the recent turnaround in the fortunes of Cerberus, the troubled contracting concern headed by the colourful Geoffrey Martindale, following the award of several lucrative government contracts. Clearly the fact that Martindale is on first-name terms with several junior ministers, and one in particular, was not a factor.'

'It's called sarcasm,' she said. 'It's what we do best.'

'So Cerberus is a Martindale company. Do you think the guy who wrote this is the "foe"?'

'Could be. See if they have a website?'

'The *Financial Times*?'

'No, you dolt. Of course *they* do. I mean Cerberus. I'm going to fix us a drink. Don't know about you but I could murder a whisky.'

'Sure thing. Though I'm not sure you should, in the state you're in.'

'Listen to nanny! Look, Danny boy, let me worry about my health. I'm working on the anaesthetic principle.'

She disappeared into the kitchen, returning with a couple of whisky glasses, each containing enough, by Daniel's reckoning, to float a small navy. He showed her what he had found.

'Cerberus?' The name was written large across the screen, silver on a blue background, in a font that emulated steel girders.

'Mm-hmm, it's a security firm. Of sorts. Specialises in

secure storage. The website isn't as specific as it might be. Which I guess is a sort of statement of its own. They appear to be contractors. If you've got something you want looked after, whether it's a diamond vault or . . .'

'Of course.' It hit her like a minor revelation. 'That's what was on the shoulder flashes of those heavies up at the building site.'

Daniel shrugged. 'Makes sense, I suppose, that Martindale would subcontract to himself if he's in the security business too. It looks like our Mr Martindale is into synergies, as they say on Wall Street.'

'What do you mean?'

'Well, according to the limited info on their website –' Daniel scrolled down the screen – 'this Cerberus mob aren't your normal security guards, riding shotgun on armoured cars and that sort of thing. Their speciality is constructing and maintaining "secure facilities", by which I don't think they mean private jails, though they list HM Government as among their "satisfied customers".'

Therry was scratching her head. 'There's something that's escaping me here, and I just can't finger it – if it wasn't for this fucking headache . . . God, it's cold in here! I'm going to turn up the heating.'

Daniel gave her his best sympathetic smile, then looked back at the screen.

'There isn't much to go on here. I suppose if you're creating "secure facilities" you don't advertise where they are. The only one they mention is at somewhere called Sellafield –'

'Of course it is,' Therry burst in. 'Sellafield's the nuclear-waste reprocessing facility up in Cumbria. These guys must be the people who built the supposedly safe containment dump for spent fuels. Caused one hell of a fuss at the time. Nobody wanted it on their doorstep, not even the people who work at the plant. Got all the environmentalists going – Greenpeace, Friends of the Earth . . . Wait a minute! Give me that thing.'

Daniel allowed himself to be pushed aside and watched Therry's fingers fly over the keyboard, opening another browser window.

'What are you doing?'

'Searching. Alta Vista. It's just an idea. Linking Cerberus with Friends of the Earth. There, see what I mean?'

Daniel looked at the screen, seeing nothing beyond a long list of 'search enquiry returns'. And then suddenly the obscure became the blindingly obvious: 'Cerberus: FOE report into activities, March 2000'.

'I knew it!' Therry was triumphant. 'Not "foe" but "F-O-E", abbreviation for Friends of the Earth, though I suspect Martindale sees them as foes right enough. Look at this.'

Cerberus was obviously one of the environmentalists' pet hates. The screen filled with a diatribe against the company, condemning the Sellafield project and the whole of what it called the government's 'landfill and forget' policy towards disposing of nuclear waste. FOE listed the other sites on which Cerberus had been employed and included photographs and potted biographies of Martindale and several of the company's other top officials.

None of the names meant anything to Therry and Daniel. They looked, thought Therry, just like average middle-aged businessmen, and had average middle-class names – Trevor Hunt, Stephen Carbury, Michael McCormack, James Kirton – ordinary boring blokes in boring suits, smiling out of cyberspace as if they were advertising their CVs rather than appearing in a pressure group's rogues' gallery. She supposed that Friends of the Earth had somehow got access to a corporate public-relations dossier and replaced the text with their own.

'Wait!' Daniel seized her arm, stopping her scrolling down the list. 'I don't believe this!'

'What? Do you know one of these blokes or something?'

'Not exactly. But I do recognise one of them. Just about.'

The qualification was necessary. After all, the last time he had clapped eyes on Michael McCormack he had not been the complacent, self-confident man smiling at Daniel from the laptop screen. No, Cerberus's well-remunerated 'head of site safeguards', as the screen proclaimed him to be, had been lying in a hospital bed about to breathe his last. And the board next to his head had proclaimed him to be a building labourer by the name of Charlie Atkins.

Chapter Forty-Three

Jericho, Oxford; Tuesday 23 December,
8.30 p.m.

'BUT WHY? Why would he do it? I just don't see the point.'

Daniel lifted his hands in an empty gesture. He had no more idea than she did why a senior company executive would dress himself up as a building worker just before he was admitted to hospital with a serious illness. Unless, of course . . .

'Maybe he didn't.'

'Hmm?' Therry looked blank. She had drained her whisky faster than Daniel thought was good for her, and refilled it. He had barely touched his. She put a hand to her brow, but whether it was because she was concentrating or because her headache was worse, he had no idea.

'I mean, maybe he didn't. After all, it was someone else who brought him in and must have given the nurse his name.'

'But his clothes? Surely they would have –'

'I didn't see his clothes. Maybe he dressed casual. Maybe they have smartly dressed labourers. Maybe the sartorial standards of patients simply don't get questioned. Why should they? Anyway, maybe whoever brought him in changed his clothes first.'

'But why?'

'Why any of it? Unless, of course, somebody didn't want anyone to know his real identity.'

'But . . . but . . . it pointed us towards the building site. The connection to the plague, the Black Death, Nether Ditchford, Father Gray. The whole thing . . .'

'Precisely.'

'Jeez, Dan, my head hurts enough as it is. What are you trying to say here? That we've made the whole thing up? We're in a city in a virtual state of siege. What about the other worker who was brought in? The guys who tried to kill me, or didn't or whatever? It's not imaginary.'

'Isn't it? Look, if Redwhistle worked for your government at some biological-warfare place, and is linked to Martindale, and Atkins or McCormack – whatever his name is – was also involved in government work at so-called secure sites . . . I don't know but there's a link I don't like.'

'OK, I grant you it's weird. But let's not get carried away here. I mean, I'm the one you accused of inventing conspiracy theories. Look, we know what's going on. We've seen it! The guards. The trenches. The rats, for God's sake, the fucking rats. I agree that Redwhistle's Porton Down connection is spooky – I'm the one who brought that up, remember.'

Daniel thought that she wasn't exactly, but said nothing.

'But there's nothing linking him to Ditchford, and there's no reason to start imagining motives that aren't there. Especially when we don't need to. We've got the proof. It's money, Daniel, the most obvious motive in the world. This development site is worth a small fortune. All of a sudden they've discovered they've got a major problem on their hands in the form of a revived bacterium from over six hundred years ago. Something they didn't even think about until it was too late, because all the scientific evidence said it couldn't happen.'

'But –'

'But it can. It has. They tried to cover it up because they thought they could get away with one fatality, two, maybe even three, without anybody asking awkward questions, but now it's gone too far, way too far. There's going to be one hell of a row over this, a public inquiry. Somebody's going to want to know how this happened and whose heads are going to roll. And you know what? I'm going to tell them. Maybe not in the pages of the goddamn *Oxford Post*. Oh, no. But maybe in the *Sunday Times* or the *Daily Mail*. This is big time, Daniel. This is exclusive. World-beater stuff!'

'Yes, sure, maybe, but –'

'But, but, but.' Therry pushed the laptop aside and lay back on the futon. She felt cold, her head was aching and she was as tired as if she hadn't slept for days.

'Yes. No. Maybe. I don't know.' She threw him a guarded look and a quick, weary smile in rapid succession and let her head fall back again. 'Not now. I'm out of it. I'm just too wrecked to take any more of this on board at the moment.'

Daniel watched the tiredness in her eyes, watched the lids droop and sleep slip over her. He felt tired himself, but somehow, watching her drift off beside him, it was not exhaustion but peace that overcame him. And a relatively unknown quality of tenderness.

Two days earlier, imagining that he would have lain here next to her, in cosy proximity, with the effects of alcohol upon them, he would have foreseen only lust. But it was something more human, less animal, that controlled him now. To his own surprise, he felt no urge to possess her but rather as if he shared in her, and with her shared the world – with all its attendant ills. He felt a smile creep across his face, and recognised it as the smile of contentment. He moved his hand towards her forehead, to stroke it, to brush back the strands of hair that had fallen over it, but restrained himself. And then quietly, quickly, he bent his head and kissed her gently on the lips.

Her eyes opened and he pulled back in embarrassment and surprise. The expression on her face was unreadable. But he felt the weight of her arm upon his neck and his face pulled down close to hers, her other arm slipping around his waist, encircling him, folding him into her. Almost before he knew what he was doing, his hand was moving gently across her body, eliciting for a moment, he was sure of it, a tremble of pleasure. Sensing in her a mounting excitement, he began the accustomed ritual of edging her trousers over her hips, being alert for any muscular stiffening or other sign of recalcitrance.

Her buttocks rising, albeit ever so slightly, from the hard-packed wadding of the futon were an unmistakable signal. As was the soft moan that escaped her mouth, and the gentle yet insistent pressure of her arm around his neck. Beyond that she did nothing to aid him, did not wriggle her legs loose as the jeans slid down from thighs to calves.

His fingers brushed the downy surface of her thighs, flitted to the cotton-covered curls of her pubic mound and traced butterfly curves across the gentle silken swell of her lower belly. Her breathing came heavier. Almost, he thought, in a brief failure of self-confidence, as if she had fallen asleep and was dreaming. Putting forth the tip of his tongue to lick the sweet yet bitter salt of her cheek, he slipped first two fingers, then three and four, under the elastic rim of her underwear.

And then she cried out. Her body flinched, her legs squeezed together. His hand froze, like a criminal in a searchlight. And at that moment his blood froze too, as the nerves at the end of his fingers transmitted their unexpected signals to his reluctant brain.

Therry's eyes were now wide open in shock. She pulled away from him, supporting her upper body on her elbows and staring down, as he did, at the incriminating scene of aborted carnal knowledge. The sight of her jeans rumpled around her calves, her knickers halfway down her thighs, and her vulnerable nakedness gave way to the knowledge of something far more sinister. There, on the very fringe of her pelvic mound, where Daniel's hand had longed to cup and penetrate the soft warmth, the flesh of her thigh did not curve in as it should but bulged out. Bulged with swellings like subcutaneous eggs. Even by the low lamplight they appeared livid blue and black.

She pulled away from him, lurched clumsily to the bathroom and vomited copiously into the toilet bowl.

Chapter Forty-Four

*Magdalen College, Oxford; Tuesday 23
December, 8.30 p.m.*

IN THE darkness he walked alone. Along the little
cobbled path that crossed the quadrangle, and into
the gaping Gothic mouth of the cloister. He was late
– an unusual occurrence. The business with the old
journalist had taken longer than he expected. But it
had been worthwhile.

He had no interest in the pretty little girl reporter or
her gawky American boyfriend. But they had pointed
him in the right direction. It would, of course, only have
been a matter of time before he located Professor Simon
Redwhistle for himself. But he was never a man to turn
down short cuts.

Except, of course, when it came to sightseeing. The
walk though the empty streets from the offices of the
Oxford Post had been delightful. From the classical
splendour of Radcliffe Square he had turned right, passing under the 'bridge of sighs', a poor replica of the
Venetian original, and on along the ill-lit, echoing corridor past the windowless wall of New College and along
Queen's Lane with the medieval pinnacles of All Souls
against the night sky.

He was looking forward to a special musical performance in Magdalen Chapel this evening. Under the
circumstances one might have supposed it would be
cancelled, but the Dean of Divinity apparently felt that

it was the college's duty to provide spiritual uplift in times of trial. And the music was particularly apposite: a stripped-down rendition of Beethoven's magnificent *Missa Solemnis*, one of Harold Hammerstein's very favourite pieces of music. All too rarely performed, and almost never without the huge orchestra the half-deaf composer had intended. The choristers of Magdalen would perform it, the programme he had found on Denton's desk informed him, accompanied by just the chapel's magnificent organ and a string quartet. Interesting, he thought. Very interesting.

The chapel was less than half full. Hammerstein eased himself in through the great iron-studded oak door and found a place to stand, nodding in polite apology to the few who looked round and moved away, covering their mouths. He marvelled that there was anyone here at all.

He edged his way along the back wall with a view of the choir before looking back at what he knew was hanging above the entranceway, taking up almost a full wall of the chapel, some twelve feet from the ground: the only known contemporary copy of Leonardo da Vinci's *Last Supper*.

He had seen the original, of course, the fresco that adorned the refectory wall in the Convent of Santa Maria delle Grazie in Milan. This copy did not have the brushstrokes of the master, but it had his eye, his composition and most of all his vivid colours, undiluted by time and the fading of unsuitable pigments on porous plaster. In the low light of candles burning on great iron candelabra, there was the figure of Christ, surrounded by his apostles, self-obsessed even as their master prophesied his own betrayal and death. Above all, in green, leaning across the table in protest, the one man who, to Harold Hammerstein, more than any other summed up mankind's relation to its divinity: Judas Iscariot.

It was Iscariot who had performed the necessary sacrifice, had enabled the martyrdom – and the miracle. Without the crucifixion there would have been no resurrection. It was Iscariot, the despised, not Peter, the false prophet, who had performed the act that gave birth to the church. And paid the price. Was not Judas's the first and greatest confession?

As if shadowing his reflections, the sublime voices of the boy choristers in the depth of the candlelit nave soared into the most moving passage of the mass, the *miserere nobis*: Lord have mercy. *Agnus Dei qui tollis peccata mundi*, the Lamb of God, the sacrificial lamb, the most persistent symbol in the Book of Revelations, the 'lamb slain from the beginning of the world', the lamb of the Passover, whose blood daubed on the doorposts preserved the occupants from the visitation of the destroying angel. Hammerstein closed his eyes. For was not the destroying angel also an angel of the Lord? Doing his will.

He turned his gaze back to the great painting, thinking not about what it showed but what it did not: the one character missing from the tableau was the strumpet, the harlot who had dared to tempt the Son of God: surely the epitome of arrogant female sexuality. Mary Magdalen, *Saint* Mary Magdalen, for Christ's sake. Here in the candlelit darkness of the chapel, a fifteenth-century architectural jewel dedicated to a Jewish hooker, he thought, *Cherchez la femme. La femme fatale.* Seek and ye shall find. Harold Hammerstein had found his *femme* all right, and seen to it that the meeting was *fatale*. Flesh incarnate; flesh in carnage, the firepower-induced instantaneous transmutation of the human form. This is my flesh, this is my blood, take this in remembrance of

me. Harold would take with him to his grave the remembrance of the flesh and blood of the beautiful Miranda
splattered and steaming all over a freshly sprinkled
Miami lawn. But that's what you get, Miranda; render
unto Caesar the things that are Caesar's. Or take the
consequences, sweetheart.

Truth or consequences. Soon it would be time to
decide. He slipped out of the chapel and into the dark of
the cloisters, marvelling at the symmetry of the overhead
vaulting. You are forever the tourist, Hammerstein, he
told himself. Through the little archway at the end, and
in front of him, on the other side of four manicured
lawns, the great Classical façade of the New Buildings
confronted him with the clear-cut lines of the Age of
Reason.

He counted the windows. Three up; five in from the
left-hand side. A double set, he had been told. Through
rooms. Windows on to both front, for the view of the
Great Tower, and rear, for the rural illusion provided by
the trees of the Grove and the deer who grazed among
them. Fine. Very fine. In its way. He crossed quickly to
the colonnade, taking care to stay on the gravel path;
the lawns would show footprints in the frost.

There were eight staircases altogether, equally spaced
along the colonnade. With footsteps as light as Ariel's
he mounted the wooden stairs, avoiding the creaks.
Two rooms, or sets of rooms, on each floor. Three
proper floors with high ceilings, and one attic floor all
the way through connecting the top of each staircase.
Lined with small rooms: former servants' rooms, now
used by students, by the look of the jokey stickers on
a few doors. And the communal bathrooms, divided
into cubicles, probably only since the introduction of
female students. With little windows concealed behind
the parapet, to let in light but not protrude to spoil the

architectural lines. The rooms would be the same, he imagined. But one of these would do for now.

He was not certain how long it would be before the professor would return; if not tonight, almost certainly tomorrow. And Harold Hammerstein had that great faculty of the trained hunter: he could wait.

Through the open window of the little cubicle, he could hear the soaring notes of the requiem moving towards its climax. There was something endlessly fascinating about man's ability to rearrange in so many ways the basic words of the mass, words that, to him at least, had so much more potency for being retained in Latin. The vulgate, he had always believed, was for the vulgar. The old words, like the old rituals, were ingrained in the soul, from the times when as a child he had watched with awe the priest strike his breast with each *miserere nobis* and the final *dona nobis pacem*, give us peace. And of course the requiem, with its subtle variation on the text: *dona eis requiem, dona eis requiem sempiternam*. Give them rest, give them eternal rest.

Chapter Forty-Five

Jericho, Oxford; Wednesday 24 December, 9.00 a.m.

THE NEXT day the sun shone. As if there was nothing wrong with the world, and never had been. In the little house on Cardigan Street, Daniel Warren threw up the sash window, leaned out and was violently sick.

Through blurred eyes he could see the pastel blue of the Phoenix Picture Palace, piped around its pediment with sugar frosting, and the glint of sunlight on diamond icicles that hung from iced-up guttering around the higgledy-piggledy rooftops. The bitter bile that dripped from his chin formed a spreading yellow stain on the sparkling white snow below.

The taste in his mouth was rank and acid. His mind churned in sympathy with his guts, his thoughts twisting among curdled emotions. He had touched corruption, in its mortal sense. Desire had turned to disgust, then, out of horror at his instinctive reaction, into bitter self-loathing. For the first time he thought he knew what it meant to be sick to the soul.

He turned to look at the young woman lying curled up on the futon in the foetal position, her thick golden hair now lank and matted on her sweaty brow. How long had it been? How long did she have? Did she have any chance at all? And was it his fault? He fished in his pocket and found the remains of the tetracycline tablets Rajiv had given him. The tablets that had saved his life.

So far. Though they had not saved Rajiv. And now her? This silly girl with her ideas of conspiracy and cover-up. Dismissed by him with a scepticism which had turned out to be sillier still.

She was stirring. Or writhing? The bedclothes were tucked around her. He had fallen asleep in the chair. Fate had played a cruel trick on him again, he thought.

Therry opened an eye and then closed it. He wondered if she was trying to wish the world away. As he had.

'How do you feel?' he asked, wishing there was something else to say.

'Like death,' she replied, and then realised what she had said. 'Oh.' She pulled herself up, uncertainly, into a sitting position, shoulders against the low headboard, the duvet wrapped tight around her. 'I guess that about sums it up.'

Daniel's mouth fought for words that his brain failed to supply.

'Don't. Don't even try.' She shrugged. And he could see with palpable embarrassment her hand moving underneath the bedclothes, touching, feeling the private places where the sickness lurked. And grew.

'We . . . we should get you to the hospital. I'll ring the emergency number. Should have done it already. Don't know what we were thinking of. Weren't thinking, I guess.'

'Wait,' she called as his hand reached for the telephone. 'Don't.' Then she stopped as a convulsive shiver racked her body and her eyes closed.

Therry forced herself to open them and looked at him, a pathetic figure, thin, drawn, his hair mussed, his glasses grubby, skewed on his nose. In other circumstances it could have been comical. But before she could even think of forcing a smile, the pain across her temples began again, building persistently as if her head were clamped in a velvet-padded vice. Cold sweat dripped from her pores, trickling down the folds in her flesh. And a wave of nausea swept over her, part symptom and part psychological reaction to the feel of her own body. Not her own body, but the things growing within it. Like alien eggs.

The nausea of the night before hit her like a tidal wave. With a start she flung herself from the bed and stumbled to the bathroom, clutching the bedclothes clumsily around her, less out of modesty, she realised as she fell over the toilet bowl, than out of the desire to conceal her body's disfigurement. Daniel ran after her, making useless noises, halting only when she screamed at him. To get away. To leave her. She would be all right, she lied at the top of her voice. She wanted only to be rid of him. He understood, and withdrew.

Ten minutes later – a tenth of her lifetime it seemed; and how much of it remained? – she had regained a semblance of composure, despite the dire evidence of the bathroom mirror. She pushed open the door back into the bedroom, to find him not on the floor sobbing like a spoilt baby, as she had half expected, but sitting at the desk in the corner with her laptop computer open in front of him.

'I . . . I had to do something,' he stammered.

She just nodded. Clutching the duvet tighter around herself, she came round behind him, then moved back.

'I should keep a distance, I suppose.'

Instinctively – an instinct that for once made him do the right thing – he reached out to her and took hold of her hand. It was cold and clammy. Should he have realised earlier? But how?

'Come here. Don't be stupid. I'm either immune or these damn drugs have given me some sort of protection. Either way, it's too late for half-measures.'

She nodded, managing a half-smile.

'The bastards!' she said.

'It's my fault,' said Daniel, his head downcast, his voice sombre. 'I . . . I had the drugs. I kept taking them. I didn't think you needed to. I just didn't think. I guess at first I just didn't really believe it, that the thing was real. You . . . you must have caught it from me . . . I . . . I . . .'

'Hang on. That doesn't work. You shouldn't have been infectious if you hadn't contracted the disease yourself. The only possibility is that I came into contact with it independently. Up at Ditchford. The rats. Fleas. Proof that they must have been the carriers. The proof we were looking for. Though this is a hell of a way to find it.'

She shivered again, violently. 'In fact, this is going to be one hell of a story. If I live long enough to write it,' she added, after a long moment's silence.

Daniel looked up at her and gave her a smile that he hoped was one of encouragement. He wanted to say something to back it up, something reassuring, to tell her the worst wouldn't happen. But, in his experience, it all too often did.

Chapter Forty-Six

The John Radcliffe Hospital, Oxford; Wednesday 24 December, 10.00 a.m.

NURSING SISTER Annie Craig pulled the surgical gloves off her hands, leaned back against the boiling-hot radiator on the wall of Simon Redwhistle's empty office, and did the unthinkable: she lit up a cigarette. She felt drained, both physically and emotionally. She had never thought nursing would be a soft career option. She had been prepared to witness death and to experience tragedy. But not on this scale.

The top three floors of the hospital had been totally sealed off. Only two of the four lifts gave access and they had to be operated with a special key. Even so, all noncritical patients had been evacuated to other hospitals, outside the exclusion zone. None of the nursing staff who had come into contact with any of the plague patients were allowed to leave the JR2. They had all been given what they were told was a vaccine, but no one, it seemed, was even 100 per cent sure of that. Especially since they were advised to take daily doses of tetracycline as well. Meanwhile the JR2 had become an island of isolation within an isolation zone. No, not an island, she corrected herself: a concentration camp.

The whole of the fifth floor had been converted into dormitory accommodation. It would not be the first Christmas she had spent working in the hospital, but it would certainly be the least convivial. She just hoped to God it would not be the last.

How many of them were there now? she had to ask herself. More than a dozen dead, in less than twenty-four hours. She had never seen a disease with such frighteningly rapid mortality. The first girl had been wheezing like a ninety-year-old asthma-sufferer when they brought her in, her skin pale and blotchy, her eyes red and watering. Only four hours, according to her boyfriend, since some drunk in the street had sneezed all over her, spraying her with God knows what. But they knew what, all right. Only too well. She was dead before dawn. And the boyfriend was following her. Nurse Craig would not have believed it possible, had she not seen Rajiv go from a picture of health to a cold corpse practically overnight.

Watching Rajiv succumb had been the most frightening thing in her life. She was still not sure whether it was because she had cared for the lad, because the symptoms and speed of the disease were so atrocious, or because she realised it might happen to her next.

The top floor had been declared a total containment zone. Nursing and medical staff did not go into the wards now without full artificial respiration equipment. The hospital's internal air-filtration system had been switched off; the last thing they wanted was to circulate the reservoir of infection, legionnaire's-disease style. It was impossible to seal any of the hospital floors hermetically. But that did not mean they should not try.

The sixth floor was now a dormitory, male and female segregated, for those who had been in contact with the victims but had not yet exhibited symptoms. The 'departure lounge', one young houseman had taken to calling it. Black Death: black humour.

At the first sign of respiratory failure, the patient was reclassified on to a danger list and moved immediately into a private ward on the floor above. Only when the disease became full-blown were they moved out into the general population of the dying. The combination of containment and treatment was working, she had been told. The mortality rate was 'acceptable' and falling. It was still way above anything her training had ever led her to expect.

The ambulances had howled all night. Even before the first girl's body had been moved to the morgue, all the people who shared her student accommodation – many of them still drunk or hung over – had been rounded up and given ten minutes to pack a bag. There had been protests, arguments, fisticuffs with a male paramedic in one case. Only when they were told that their lives were potentially in serious danger did some agree to come. None in the end had refused outright. Which was just as well, one of the orderlies had told Annie, because Professor Redwhistle himself had told them not to take no for an answer. They had the backup to prove it – police squad cars at a discreet distance, their red and blue lights revolving.

The police had found, she heard via the same orderly, the body of 'patient X', the man who had escaped from the hospital. 'X', my arse, Annie Craig thought. Pirewski, that had been his name, the one who had done a runner virtually out from under her eyes. It was a train of thought with all sorts of complicated ramifications about responsibility that she preferred to avoid. She could never quite bring herself to be glad to hear of a death, but she found it very difficult to grieve over that one. Why he had fled, she had no idea. But the results were all too visible.

Those who had died were little more than kids. They should have had their whole lives in front of them. Instead they had been snuffed out horribly by a disease that was supposed to have been wiped out centuries ago. In Britain at least. Lymphawhatchamacallit might be what the professor and his acolytes wrote on their reports and in the dissertations they would produce afterwards – if any of them survived – but the symptoms of bubonic plague were hard to miss. And though the phrase 'Black Death' had been officially banned in the hastily isolated emergency wards, there was no way other than by amputating tongues that you could keep it out of the canteen. In the few brief minutes that anyone could snatch to take a bite.

Or take a smoke, she thought. Funny, wasn't it, she had remarked to Mary Clarke when they collapsed next to one another at one of the plastic-topped tables, how even in the midst of a deadly epidemic the no-smoking rule was considered sacrosanct. As if right now the risk of getting lung cancer wasn't the least of their worries.

Only Redwhistle was a chain-smoker, had been for years, and insisted therefore that his office was exempt from the ban. The whole room stank of stale smoke and was therefore probably the only place in the building where a harassed nurse could hope to snatch a few drags without being noticed or setting off smoke alarms. Annie inhaled deeply on her Benson and Hedges, one of the last packet she was carefully husbanding. Of course there was no vending machine in the hospital. A minute more and she would be gone, back into the fray. To minister to the dying.

And then the telephone rang. She closed her eyes in a vain attempt to deny its existence, deliberated for another ring on the option of leaving it to the answering machine and ducking out fast into the corridor, as if she had never been there. But the man was important, and so might the phone call be. After all, what would she have done, had she been passing the door and heard it ring, knowing there was no one inside? She would have gone in to pick it up, that's what she would have done. Wouldn't she? At any rate, it is what she did, answering like an automaton:

'Professor Redwhistle's phone.'

The voice on the other end was hoarse, frantic.

'Is he there?'

'If you mean the professor, he's very busy right now. You'll have to –'

'I have to speak with him. Now.'

'I'm sorry. There's an emergency. You'll have to –'

The voice on the other end of the line was raised suddenly. There was anger in it too, she thought, but an uncertain, self-conscious sort of anger.

'It's urgent. Tell him it's . . . tell him it's the friend of Rajiv Mahendra.'

Annie caught her breath involuntarily. 'Oh, are you –?' she began.

But before she could finish the question, the door opened and Redwhistle walked in, accompanied by a tall man in a blazer. She had seen this man twice with him in as many days – in a supposed total-exclusion zone. For a moment she thought the professor looked drained, pulling down the surgical mask from his face and drawing his hand over a deeply furrowed brow. But the look that he fixed on her, standing by his desk with his telephone in her hand, annihilated any illusion of empathy.

'Professor,' she began, instinctively covering the receiver with her hand, suddenly flustered for no reason. 'It's for you. He says it's urgent.' She made a face that said 'What isn't?' and added, 'He says he's a friend of Rajiv –'

But Redwhistle had already taken the phone out of her hand. 'Thank you, nurse, that will be all. They could do with an extra hand on 7c, I think.'

'Yes, of course.'

The bastard! As if she didn't know where they could do with an extra hand. They could all do with an extra hand. And extra arms and legs, come to that. She turned on her heel and closed the door behind her, tempted only for a second to hang on to hear the first words of the ensuing conversation.

But Redwhistle waited until he saw the door close and heard it click before he took his hand away from the receiver and spoke into it.

At the other end of the line, in the upstairs room in Jericho where Therry Moon lay rocking silently on the bed, Daniel Warren found it hard to suppress his anger at the way he had been left hanging on, listening to muffled incomprehensible voices. Then came the cold, crisp tone that said simply, 'Simon Redwhistle.'

Daniel breathed in. He felt like shouting at the man. But that was not the tactic he knew would work.

'My name is Daniel Warren. Rajiv Mahendra's friend. We met briefly outside the hospital.' When you all but spat in my face, he wanted to add.

'I know who you are,' came the immediate reply, with a directness that took Daniel aback.

'We know all about you,' he challenged.

'Do you indeed?'

'We have to talk. To meet. I have a sick girl here. Very sick. And . . . it's your fault.' The words came out without Daniel thinking about them. It was not what he had meant to say. It was not what he thought he meant. 'I mean we need . . .' he babbled.

'Stop right there, Mr Warren.' Redwhistle's voice was curtly authoritative. 'This is not a secure line. And I am sure you appreciate the need for security.'

'Security? Yes, I mean, no, wait a minute, what are you . . . ?'

'Give me your telephone number and I will call you back. Within five minutes. I promise.'

'What?' Daniel's mind was racing. What was the man playing at? Something had to be done about Therry, fast. How could he trust him to call back?

'The number, Mr Warren. Quickly.'

Daniel dictated it from the handset. 'Listen, Redwhistle, you have to –'

But whatever Simon Redwhistle had to do, he was not about to be told by Daniel Warren. The line went dead.

Daniel stood there staring dumbly at the phone as if its sudden silence indicated total collapse in global communications. But only moments later it came alive again in his hand. Daniel pressed 'talk' and heard Redwhistle's unmistakable tones, slightly less clearly than before.

'Mr Warren, I think perhaps it is time for us to meet again.'

Daniel was immediately taken aback. That was to have been his line.

'We know, I told you, we know,' he said, more lamely than he would have liked.

'Yes, so you keep saying. I don't know what you are talking about but –'

'About you. About Porton Down,' Daniel blurted out, hideously aware as he was doing so that he was giving the game away.

'About Por–?'

Daniel could not prevent himself from sneering as he heard what sounded like genuine surprise in the man's normally cool voice. But had he gone too far, and lost the element of surprise from a face-to-face meeting.

'Look, first things first, don't you think? You said your young friend was sick. What have you done about it?'

Daniel swallowed hard, then told the truth. 'Nothing.

Yet. We were going to . . .' Call the ambulance? Bury her in the back garden? Sit and sob their hearts out? Just what had they been going to do?

'How bad is she?'

'Bad. I think.'

'For God's sake, man, do more than just think. Is she wheezing? Coughing? How long ago did the chills start? Has she a headache?'

Daniel found himself describing Therry's symptoms and the progress of their appearance, mentally reclassifying the shivers she had spoken of as they crossed Port Meadow, and the first mention of her persistent headache, and tried to put them in a time context.

But all the time he was boiling inside. What the hell was he doing, expecting help from the man on the other end of the phone? For Daniel was convinced that Simon Redwhistle was not just part of a cover-up, involved in a cynical property scam that had gone seriously wrong. There was more to his relationship with Geoffrey Martindale than that. Somehow, he was sure of it, Redwhistle was responsible for the whole epidemic.

'Stop this! Wait a minute,' he began, though less certain than he sounded about what he wanted to say. 'This isn't how it's meant to be. This is your fault. All your fault. You know it is. You know it is. If she dies, the world will know about it, I can promise you.'

'And if she doesn't?'

'What do you mean? You bastard! You're threatening me.'

Redwhistle's voice was grave, with an urgency to it.

'Don't be ridiculous, man. Just listen and do what I say. There's an outside chance I may be able to save her life.'

Chapter Forty-Seven

*Central Oxford; Wednesday 24 December,
11.30 a.m.*

THE AIR was cold and unnaturally still. To Daniel
Warren's morbid mind, it might as well have been
the breath of corpses. As if the empty white streets had
been evacuated of not only people and sound but also
memories. And wrapped in a shroud.

In this sinister vacuum Daniel and Therry, determined
not to yield to incapacity until the last aching moment,
moved like ghosts with feet of lead, clinging to each
other. Down Beaumont Street they passed the Playhouse,
with its white-on-black 'Cancelled' banner across the
pantomime poster. There would be no *Little Red Riding
Hood* this year; the big bad wolf was out on the streets.
Invisible, silent and hungry for prey.

Even at the junction of Beaumont Street and Cornmarket, where pedestrians and cyclists fought a daily
battle with fume-belching buses, there was silence. The
quiet was deathly. A raucous cry made both of them
start. The caw of a crow. A big, black creature with
darting ebony eyes sat in the middle of the snow-covered
road, as if it were a winter wheatfield, and surveyed them
with disdain. They were not carrion. Not yet.

Cornmarket looked to yield more promising fodder
for such birds. On the steps of St Michael's the snow lay
clumped around the supine forms of two human bodies.
The tramps. The scum of the city, left to die in the gutter

and rot on the pavement. Until eventually their corpses were picked over by birds? And rats. Daniel shivered. Nothing attracted rats like a corpse. Nothing spread disease as efficiently as an itinerant population of rats, each one bearing its migrant population of the fleas that in turn carried *Yersinia pestis*, mankind's oldest, most lethal enemy.

He hugged Therry closer to him, wondering if it had been a mistake to try to walk. Every step clearly caused her pain. The way she moved with her legs apart, almost waddling, was tragicomic. Disease was no respecter of dignity. Were the tramps really dead, or just dead drunk? Daniel thought he saw movement. And then started back with a jolt as one of them raised his head, grinning the grin of the damned. An obscene leer from a dishevelled head dusted with snow. The tongue lolled. Daniel half lifted Therry off the ground to move them away, out of sight, out of range of this apparition.

He heard what sounded like a laugh, without humour in it, and hurried them on. Only when he was sure they were at least fifty yards away did he risk a glance back over his shoulder, prompted by a sudden noisy peal and an outbreak of voices into what under other circumstances he might have mistaken for drunken singing.

Both of the men had risen now, he saw, leaning on each other like lepers, each with a bottle in his hand and clanking them together like children playing with rubber swords until they smashed. He recognised the words, stolen from another time, yet lingering in the folk consciousness: 'Bring out your dead, bring out your dead, bring out your bread, a penny for the dead guy. Cheap at the price, mister, life's cheap at the price.' And Daniel ducked as a jagged bottleneck hurtled over their heads and smashed against the ancient stone of the Bodleian Library's back wall. Therry spasmed violently in Daniel's arms and he held her tight. He was almost carrying her now. Carrying her where? And why? Was Redwhistle lying about the chance of saving her? Why would he not be?

Onward they lurched. Through the absurd golden grandeur of Radcliffe Square with its soaring cupola and pinnacles traced with white against the blue sky, already losing its morning splendour to featureless grey. On down old New College Lane, past the ancient barn and the high defensive walls, to Queen's Lane and eventually Longwall Street. Daniel had his key to the little door set into the great wooden gate. They would attract no more attention than was absolutely necessary.

They had no idea.

Daniel closed the locket gate as silently as he could. Yet the click seemed to echo along Longwall Street almost as if he had shouted aloud. If anyone heard, they kept themselves to themselves. As one did, he reflected, in the time of plague.

A path led from St Swithun's Quad past the deer park to the great plane tree and on to the brown frozen lawns laid out in state before New Buildings. Over there, to the right, was Daniel's room, with its promise of normality: his things, his Californian clothes, all those trappings of another existence. And there beside it was the library window, the window he had looked out of to watch the shadow of dark clouds engulf the earth, the day before he had learned that normality was a lie.

He looked at Therry and squeezed her arm, and then glanced around at the ancient masonry that before had seemed so reassuring in its sense of continuity from the past, but now looked like so much crumbling stone trying in vain to cheat decay through endless restoration.

Quietly, as if they were afraid of being intercepted, which somehow, Daniel realised, he was, they made their way across the crunchy grass towards the colonnade. Somewhere up there, in room six on staircase number three, behind shuttered windows, there was a man who knew the answers, at least some of them. A man who, if Daniel was right, had a lot on his conscience.

Chapter Forty-Eight

Oxford; Wednesday 24 December, 11.56 a.m.

DR SIMON Redwhistle left the JR2 for the short drive to Magdalen a few minutes before noon, with Neal Faversham at his side. Outside the hospital the ambulances stood ready, more than a dozen of them. Several crew members in their paramedic green kicked pebbles in the snow. A surprising number smoked, the red glowing buts of their cigarettes the only sign of warmth in the freezing air.

The little MG was the only vehicle that moved. Roads normally clogged with traffic were empty and silent. Here and there police Land Rovers stood at strategic junctions, and behind them army vehicles, conspicuous in their camouflage. Backup on display. None of it necessary. Doors were closed, curtains drawn, blinds pulled. If there was anxiety, it was suppressed. A cross-section of the population of suburban England had turned its back on the world and was tucked up with silent fears and noisy television, the escapism for once wholly excusable.

Faversham was worried. The odds were not as good as he might have liked. He was playing a long shot, based on assumptions. That Hammerstein was circling. That he would close in as predicted. And that the trap would close upon him. His men were in place. Waiting and watching. The bait was in place.

*   *   *

By the time Daniel Warren reached the bottom of New Buildings staircase three, he was already imagining his own worst-case scenario. Therry Moon was hanging on him, barely suppressing cries of anguish with each move. With difficulty he coaxed her up the wooden stairs, their footfalls echoing loudly.

He had only just reached the third floor, and found Redwhistle's name painted in white on black above the door, when it opened, as if they had been expecting him to the precise minute.

'Bring her in,' said Redwhistle, as if he were supervising the delivery of a sack of groceries.

There were three other men in the room with him. Daniel had never seen two of them before, a tall, youthful black man and a middle-aged white man who looked like another don. The third, he recognised with a feeling of sinking inevitability, was the Japanese he had last seen pointing a gun in his face in a freezing barn.

'How the . . . ?'

'Never mind,' said Redwhistle abruptly. 'Lay her down there. On the daybed.'

Daniel blinked for a moment, then realised he meant an antique couch in genuine French Empire style. Napoleon had probably never sat upon it, but Wellington might have. Daniel looked around him at the dowdy college paintwork, a functional institutional veneer over exquisite panelling, at the antique clocks on the marble mantelpiece in their glass cases with brass rotating eight-day movements, and at the dark expanses of the windows on to the deer park three storeys below. As so often in the rooms of bachelor Oxford dons, the ensemble managed an improbable grandeur which was enhanced by the reflections in the burnished silver of an eighteenth-century mirror above the empty grate of the fireplace.

'Wait a minute. This is . . . how did she –? The plague in this girl is still at the bubonic stage. How did she become infected?'

'The rats, we assumed. Fleas from the rats, up at Nether Ditchford . . .' Daniel's voice tailed off as he realised how little what he was saying tallied with the allegations he wanted to make.

'Don't talk nonsense,' Redwhistle snapped. 'What the hell's this?' He was looking at the makeshift bandage Therry had tied around the cut on her leg. She had meant to change it, but in the circumstances it had been forgotten. Redwhistle was picking at it gingerly with a pair of scissors.

'Jesus Christ!' he said, pulling the thing away with the blades. 'Where the hell did you get this?'

Daniel felt his heart stop as he recognised, dirty, bloodied and tangled, the surgical mask he had worn on that fateful visit to the bedside of the man he thought was Charlie Atkins; the mask Therry had snatched from his face and thrust into a pocket. The same pocket where she had found it up at Ditchford and tied it round her leg, tied the plague bacillus on to an open wound. Without any idea what she was doing. And he had not even noticed. He gripped the side of the table for support.

'Never mind, never mind,' said Redwhistle. 'If anything, it means there is more of a chance. If she had the pneumonic form of the disease, it would have been much more serious. This will almost certainly stop it progressing.' He pulled up Therry's sleeve and exposed a thick vein in her arm, into which he prepared to inject a clear solution.

'Wait a moment!' Daniel shouted. 'How do I know I can trust you?'

'What alternative do you have?'

Daniel watched as the syringe emptied. The girl lying

on the antique bed gave not the slightest indication she had even felt the puncture wound. How fragile, Daniel thought, kneeling beside her and biting hard on his lower lip, how fragile we are!

The big black guy came over and laid a hand on Daniel's shoulder. 'Don't worry, kid, the doc here's a good man. He knows what he's doing.'

It was the wrong thing to say. All Daniel's emotions boiled over at once. The vision of the boils on Therry's groin, the memory of his mother's death alone and far away tending some similar sufferer, the thought of Rajiv keeling over and dying on duty. And yet these men could play God. That was what they had been doing, wasn't it? Wasn't it?

He spun round angrily, swinging the American's arm off him, flicking the man's jacket into the air and revealing a shoulder holster. All of a sudden Daniel saw what he had to do. He kneed the American in the crotch as hard as he could and, as the big man fell backwards, made a frantic grab for his gun.

He never got that far. A blow to the side of the head sent Daniel reeling headlong on to the carpet, his glasses knocked off. With a thrumming pain in his temples he could just make out the blurred image of the man he had taken to be an academic rubbing his knuckles only inches from his face.

'Don't even think of it, sonny,' said an impeccably English voice.

'Thanks, Neal.' The big American, Daniel noted, cautiously reaching for his spectacles, was nursing his groin with a wry expression on his face. 'But don't be too hard on him. The kid's a little upset.'

'I'm more than a *little* upset,' Daniel blurted. They could beat him to pulp if they wanted, but he had had enough. 'I want some answers,' he did his best to yell, but realised as the words came out that he was almost sobbing.

'Yes.' It was Redwhistle. He had kept well out of the way of the rough and tumble. 'And perhaps you are due some. Where would you like to start?'

Chapter Forty-Nine

New Buildings roof, Magdalen College, Oxford;
Wednesday 24 December, 12.30 p.m.

H E CRAWLED across the roof. Not because he had
no head for heights or was afraid he would lose
his footing. His boyhood in the mountains, not to mention his regular annual training in the *Schutzenverband*,
Switzerland's home guard, had seen to it that he
was as sure-footed as a mountain goat. No, Harold
Hammerstein crawled across the roof because he knew
that to stand up would make him a potential target.

For he had seen their trigger men, clumsily positioned in obvious places of supposed concealment in
the shadows of the cloister, in the dark corners of the
colonnade, in the windows of the little house down by
the mill stream at the edge of the college grounds. He
had overheard their poorly encrypted communications
and knew that two of them were disguised as porters
at the entrance lodge on the High Street, though the
college's great main gate was locked.

The one thing he had noticed was that they very
seldom looked up. Nonetheless, it would be foolish to
take unnecessary chances. Of course life was a game of
chance. But it was a game in which you could calculate
the odds, even if unfortunately they could not always
be rigged.

There was always the possibility that he was walking
into a trap. And he could not even be 100 per cent

certain that Redwhistle had what he was looking for. But he was pretty certain that he could persuade him to reveal where it was.

What mattered was that he was aware that they were waiting for him. That they had set up a dragnet, unaware that he was already at the centre of the web. That alone should be enough for him to reverse the polarity. And he had his insurance policy in place. He checked his watch and looked at the skies. The weather was closing in, but not too much.

Anyone who thought they could snare Harold Hammerstein so facilely was practising self-delusion. In this case it wasn't even practice; they were perfect. Even so, they would be watching the wall. He would have to be fast, he thought as he uncoiled the abseil cable and connected it to the stonework of the parapet. But he had the advantage of surprise.

Chapter Fifty

*Magdalen College, Oxford; Wednesday 24
December, 12.15 p.m.*

'IT'S NOT the Black Death, is it?' Daniel dragged out
the words wearily.

'That rather depends on what you mean.'

'Don't play games with me. You know what I mean.
This is not some bacteria that has lain dormant for
centuries, is it?'

'I thought Dr Gover had already told you that was
quite impossible.'

'Dr –?' Jesus! How long had these guys been monitoring them?

'It's artificial, isn't it? Some goddamn biological weapon
your mad scientists knocked up at this Porton Down
place? These guys are spooks, aren't they?' Daniel did
his best to gesture scornfully at the American and
the donnish-looking Englishman who had hit him so
unexpectedly hard.

Redwhistle followed his glance as if looking for
approval.

'These gentlemen whose acquaintance you decided to
make in such a physical manner, and Mr Takahashi here,
whom I believe you have already met, are indeed repre-
sentatives of the security services. It is an instance such as
this, I might add, that makes one glad of their existence.'

Daniel tried a sneer. 'Why? So you can protect some
goddamn evil fucking biological weapon?'

'It is a weapon.' Redwhistle's tone was as imperturbable as ever. 'But it's not one of ours. It's one of theirs.'

'Theirs?'

'Yes. The Russians. Incidentally, you were closer than you think about the Black Death. This little nasty is more closely related to it than anything seen anywhere else over the last half-millennium.'

'But they didn't dig it up. You said it wasn't –'

'And it isn't. But that does not mean it isn't closely related. Black rats were only the chief vector in western Europe. And that is not where the plague had its origin. Nor indeed where it continues to be endemic.'

'The east. China?'

'Not quite, although the Chinese are as keen to see this little business cleared up as the rest of us. I'm talking about Siberia. The Siberian marmot, to be precise. Something else I thought Dr Gover had told you. Probably the greatest reservoir of bubonic-plague bacteria in the world. Certainly the most thriving. For some reason the bacteria cause less ravages among marmots than any other species. Almost uniquely, in this case it does not decimate its primary host.'

'You mean?'

'I mean simply that the Russians – or the Soviets, as they still were in those days – had a ready-made supply of raw material. To go on from there, to culture it, grow enough to be able to use it as a weapon, was largely a matter of political will and moral vacuum.'

'So what the hell . . . ?'

'. . . is it doing here? We're looking after it. Or were. Not very well, I have to say. Believe me, I'm as upset about that as you are.'

'But you worked at Porton Down, the biological-weapons centre.'

'That's quite true, but as so often with you Americans

– sorry, Jerry –' the big American waved the comment away – 'it is not the whole truth. The DERA has other functions. Some of them, you may well be surprised to know, actually do concern defence. Yes, I was working on the potential of bubonic plague as a biological weapon. Not because we were producing it, but because we knew that they had it. We were working on a vaccine. Got there in the end too. The vaccine exists, as the people in this room will gratefully testify, but only in very limited quantities. It might have been possible, in the long term, with a great deal more money spent on research, to mass-produce it. But by then it was all over, you see, the Cold War. And it made a lot more sense to buy up the enemy's stockpile than to spend a fortune trying to provide protection against a peril that we could effectively eliminate.'

'We . . . you . . . we *bought* it *up*?'

'You, actually. Well, your government. Washington. Mine didn't have the money. Unfortunately yours didn't have the balls. Or the integrity.'

'Easy on there, professor,' the American said.

'So why's it here? I don't understand.'

'I do.' The voice, calm but weak, came from the form slumped on the daybed in the corner. Therry Moon had opened her eyes a fraction.

'We're the bloody left-luggage facility, aren't we, professor? The Yanks buy it but change their mind about destroying it, eh? Never know when a little biological nasty could come in useful. But easier if it can be kept abroad. In the hands of some patsy government who'll do what they're told and have an Official Secrets Act instead of a Freedom of Information Act, isn't that it?'

Redwhistle looked mildly embarrassed. 'It *was* during the life of the previous government.'

Daniel heard a snort behind him and then Therry fell

silent again. But even to him, it was all suddenly slotting together.

'Cerberus. The secure storage facility. Martindale.'

'Quite,' Redwhistle acknowledged. 'Geoffrey Martindale is a fool many times over. If he had half as many brain cells left as he thinks he has spermatozoa, the world would be a better and a safer place. But I am afraid that short of a revived eugenics programme we can neither legislate against the existence of the likes of him nor the excesses of their overactive libidos.'

'But the Ditchford connection? The building site? The trenches through the burial site?'

At the back of the room the American laughed. Daniel thought he noticed a glint even in the eyes of Mr Takahashi, who remained otherwise perfectly still and silent in his seat, as if he were nothing more than an invited spectator. Redwhistle, by contrast, looked exasperated.

'Forget Ditchford! I'm afraid the fact that another of Martindale's companies was building there is pure coincidence. Or was, until he had the panicky idea of using it to cover up where McCormack really worked. None of us – not even I – thought someone would dream up a totally off-the-wall connection to a fourteenth-century burial site and accidentally stumble on something perilously close to the truth.'

'You mean you didn't know about Ditchford?' Daniel wasn't sure whether to laugh or cry.

Redwhistle sighed. 'We are not historians. And there is no connection. Or only a very tenuous one. Yes, if I'd thought about it we would have done something else. But it didn't occur to us. Funny, isn't it?'

Hilarious, Daniel thought.

'But how did . . . I mean, what about Atkins? McCormack, I mean.'

'McCormack indeed!' sniffed the American at the back.

Redwhistle sighed, looking around the room briefly to see if anyone else was prepared to take over. The American was studying his shoes. Takahashi was looking at him with a keen interest, awaiting the next instalment.

'We tried to tell them –' Redwhistle nodded towards the American – 'those of us who were opposed to retaining the stuff. Tried to tell them it was too big a temptation. That it would attract other attention. And in the end it did. They wanted it back.'

'Who?'

'The Russians.'

'The Russian government?'

Redwhistle shrugged. 'The way things are going there these days, that could depend on a change in the weather as much as anything.'

'I'm sorry?'

'The Russian underground. The criminal mafia. The old communists, call them what you will. In this case it includes the former deputy minister of defence procurement, a man known as Attila, though he is neither a Hun nor a Hungarian. He not only knew the circumstances of the "disposal" deal but thought he didn't get "a fair price". I'm afraid the Russians have a very different idea of the free market, particularly when it comes to the second-hand market. Property is still theft, it seems, but only if it's their property that has been transferred – even quite legitimately and paid for – into other people's hands.

'They tried to get it back. A woman called Miranda was set up as a honey trap.'

'For Martindale?' Daniel thought he was beginning to get ahead of this.

347

'For Martindale. For the minister. For anyone who liked honey and could be useful, except that in theory they were the ones that were going to get stung.'

'Why "in theory"?'

'Because Miranda had other ideas. An independent-minded girl, you see. She favoured a little free enterprise. All the more so since it turned out that the important man was not Martindale but this McCormack, who had the easiest access to the Cerberus facility. And she fancied him. For real.'

'You mean they stole the bacteria?'

'They stole a vial of it. Of course they had no idea how to handle it. Martindale's company is a joke, as I'm afraid we have discovered to our cost. He only got the contract because he was in bed – metaphorically, though I wouldn't swear to it – with the former defence minister. His containment technology turns out to be about as successful as his underwear.

'As far as we can tell, McCormack had some sort of accident and got himself infected through a minor cut, rather like your young lady friend. They didn't know what they were dealing with. Thought it was just a liquid form of some sort of gas. Not wholly untrue, in a way. The Soviets' original evil idea had been to spray the stuff into the air – instant pneumonic plague, just inhale. That would have killed most unprotected, untreated people in a war zone within twenty-four hours. It is a particularly virulent strain. What no one expected, however, was for anyone to get exposed to it directly in a way which would manifest the classic bubonic symptoms.'

Daniel looked at the supine figure of Therry and wondered how much she was taking in.

'Yes,' Redwhistle continued, 'the fact that your young lady exposed herself to it is extremely unfortunate. On the other hand, if she had caught a full blast of the pneumonic variant, like those young people in the hospital now, she'd be lucky even to have lasted this long. You owe your own life, more than you know, to the swift actions of the late Dr Mahendra. Sadly, he was a lot less careful of himself, given his continued high exposure to the bacteria.'

Daniel closed his eyes. Typical of the good-natured, hard-working idiot; always thinking more of others than of himself.

'Miranda got greedy, however. Without really knowing what she had, she tried to double-cross her old chums. I suspect she didn't want to fall back under their influence. They have a very particular attitude towards their women. She tried to sell the stuff on her own. Made a meeting, in America, even. There's no lack of a market for lethal packages out there, you know. Aum Shinri Kyo were her first choice.'

Daniel's eyes shot to the man Redwhistle had named as Takahashi, the third member of the unholy trinity: the Brits, the CIA and the Japanese intelligence service.

'The people who injected poison gas into the Tokyo Metro?' Daniel said.

'Those are they,' replied Redwhistle. 'As I say, there's no shortage.'

'But what happened?'

'Let's just say that Aum Shinri Kyo were already under closer observation than they knew. Things were never going to work out for Miranda. She realised that things had gone wrong, that McCormack had got infected, that Mr Takahashi here was on her trail, and, more to the point as it turned out, so were her former colleagues.'

'What happened to her?'

'She died.'

'Murdered?'

'As good as.'

'I don't understand.'

'You don't need to.'

'So if McCormack died in hospital, why wasn't the bacteria contained there?'

'Yes, why indeed? A very good question. McCormack's partner here – a gentleman of Polish extraction, but you don't need to worry about that either – panicked and went back to the original dealers hoping to still make a quick profit, claiming he had nothing to do with her privateering. Unfortunately by then it was too late for him too.'

'What do you mean?'

'I mean that the people they are dealing with are not very good at cutting deals. They are better at cutting people, if you get my meaning. They are accustomed to getting their way.'

'But who are they?'

'We are assuming that there is only one of them in Oxford, but not one to be discounted. He is a very dangerous man. He almost certainly killed this Miranda woman. On Monday, in the streets of Oxford, he disposed of McCormack's accomplice – unfortunately not before he had passed on the disease – and I am very much afraid that last night he was responsible for the death of one of your young journalist friend's colleagues.'

Therry's eyes opened wide with horror. 'Jack! I thought – on the phone – he was there, in the office!'

The man called Neal intervened: 'What did you say to him?'

'No, he was telling me . . . about you.' She stared at Redwhistle accusingly. 'And I said . . . my last words were . . . that we would come here, to confront you.'

'And here you are,' Redwhistle said, but it was Neal he was talking to. 'Which may mean –'

'That we have taken the right precautions.'

'Let me get this straight,' Daniel burst in, 'you're telling us this is a Russian bacterial weapon derived from the original Black Death reservoir, that America bought the stuff from the Russians and now they want it back?'

'More or less.'

'Why on earth? Who on earth would use such a weapon? And surely the risks of it getting out of hand and spreading to the civilian population are enormous?'

'You're missing the point. That is just it. This was developed as a battlefield weapon but its real potential is against civilians. And its beauty – in a perverse way – is the fact that it is derived from a natural killer. In the right part of the world, it would be hard to prove that it was not just another natural catastrophe.'

'But who on earth . . . ?'

'Come, come, Mr Warren, are there no regimes you can imagine that might not exactly be distraught at a seriously depopulating disease taking hold of a particularly troublesome region?'

'My God! You mean this is a genocide weapon?'

'It has that potential.'

A vision of the unimaginable began to build itself in Daniel's mind. 'Russians . . . you mean . . . Chechnya?'

The tall man shrugged. 'It's certainly a possibility. Not something for the current Russian government perhaps, but as Professor Redwhistle said, so much over there depends on which the way the wind blows.'

Literally, Daniel thought with horror.

'There are, however, more immediate customers. We have reason to believe the people trying to get hold of this are doing so on behalf of certain elements in Belgrade.'

Daniel closed his eyes. It was all too easy to imagine.

'An outbreak of the Black Death in Kosovo would be a calamity that the Milosevic regime would be able to wash its hands of, but one that would quite quickly redress the nine-to-one balance in favour of the ethnic Albanians. Separatism would cease to be an issue.

'There would, of course, be an international outcry but no one could blame the Serbs for refusing to accept refugees from the stricken area. After all, as I think you've found out, a *cordon sanitaire* is precisely what the World Health Organisation and other international bodies prescribe. It is easy to imagine the smug smiles in Belgrade watching the Nato troops in the area having to enforce it.'

Overnight the liberators would become the jailers. With orders to shoot to kill.

'And then, of course, there are the Kurds in northern Iraq –'

At that moment the windows imploded and the air turned to acrid searing smoke.

Chapter Fifty-One

*Magdalen College, Oxford; Wednesday 24
December, 12.25 p.m.*

D ANIEL CAME to, gasping and choking for air with
his nose squashed against the thick pile of a Chinese
carpet. Grey-black smoke billowed around him, and his
ears screamed as if someone was taking a pile-driver
to his brain. Shards of silver mirror, glass, splinters
of wood and chunks of plaster were flying through
the smoke. Until the other day Daniel had never even
been close to a firearm being used. Now he was in no
doubt that he was cowering for his life beneath a spray
of lethal lead from a machine gun. Within seconds an
elegant eighteenth-century sitting room had been turned
into a twenty-first-century battleground.

The chair he had been forced on to was lying toppled
next to him. The man who looked like a don was
crouched behind the arm of the sofa, a pistol in his
hand, squinting into the thick billowing smoke. Why
Daniel wasn't dead, he wasn't sure. Keeping his head
down he looked around for Therry. The daybed was
empty, its upholstery covered with debris. He could just
make out a pair of legs beyond it, as if she had fallen off
the other side. Whether alive or dead he had no idea. In
the corner was a door, and he inched towards it. And
then the noise stopped.

The silence reverberated. His eardrums were still
vibrating from the pressure waves. Through the swirling

smoke, now gradually being sucked into the cold night air through the shattered windows, Daniel could just about make out a surreal figure: a shape in black with a face of featureless white. It was moving strangely, as if it was crippled and had too many limbs. And then he realised why. It was not one figure, but two. The thing without a face had its black-clad arm around the neck of the tweed-clad Dr Simon Redwhistle, his head twisting upwards, away from the gun barrel forced under his chin. The masked man was still holding an automatic weapon in his other hand, the other side of Redwhistle's waist, in a position that could deal death in an instant. In large helpings.

The big American, his own weapon back in his hand, was also crouched on the ground aiming at the apparition, or rather at his human shield. Only Takahashi, lying prone on the floor, showed no sign of being armed.

Then the figure said something into the ear of his captive. Through the clearing haze, Daniel saw Redwhistle shake his head. And saw the muzzle under his chin thrust violently upwards so that it looked as though, even without firing, the thing would soon force its way through the soft flesh of his gullet.

'Put it down, Hammerstein. Even if you kill him, there's no way out of here. The entire college and grounds are surrounded.'

Daniel glanced sideways at the source of the voice. It had that authoritarian-sounding British certainty to it, but the man Neal cowering behind the sofa, despite the gun in his hand, no longer looked as securely in command of the situation as he had a few minutes earlier. Was he serious?

The intruder did not even seem to consider the question. From behind the mask came a noise that could only be construed as approximating to laughter.

'*You* put 'em down,' he said, the words clearly enunciated through the muffling of the mask. 'Any of your jokers come through that door and you'll all be dead before he's wiped his feet on the mat. Get it? Good. Now get on your radio and pass it on.'

Nobody moved.

'*Don't* be so fucking stupid. Don't pretend you're not in radio link. I've been listening to your idiots for the past hour.'

And a brief spurt of gunfire thundered only a foot above their crouching heads, ripping into the damask curtain beyond. How many rounds did that thing fire a minute? A second? Daniel had heard that most modern automatic weapons could cut a man in half. The expression on the face of the man who had just tried to call the shots was anything but reassuring. Whatever he had planned, this wasn't it.

Neal lifted his left arm to his mouth and spoke into his cuff. Daniel thought he caught the words 'hostage situation'.

'Now you put your guns down. I said, now! Throw them into the middle of the floor. Quick.' The pistol muzzle buried itself even deeper in the soft flesh of Redwhistle's throat. Tiny choking noises emerged from the man's twisted lips.

Daniel watched with a mixture of relief and dismay as the two handguns fell together on the plaster-spattered Chinese rug.

Takahashi, lying on the ground, lifted himself slightly and raised his hands to say he was not armed. Daniel was disinclined to believe him, in the light of his experience at their last encounter. But there was no doubt that the Japanese man was not looking happy about it. He looked scared. Very scared.

'OK,' the man in the mask said. 'You know what I

want. Produce it and this is over. Fast.'

'You have to be joking,' the big American ventured. 'Like hell are we going to let you out of here with that little bottle. The genie inside it is not for your client.'

'Well, if you'd rather die!' To make the point, a staccato burst of regulated automatic fire reduced the sofa leg to matchwood only inches from the American's head.

'This is stalemate,' Neal called. 'And you know it.'

'It's nothing of the sort' came the terse, impatient reply. 'I can kill him and all of you in about ten seconds, then search the place. It's messier, less convenient and marginally riskier. But it's a small margin. Now get on with it. You! Up! Hands above your head!'

The automatic jerked in the American's direction. Slowly and carefully he stood up, raising his arms, putting them back as if to clasp them behind his head. Daniel noticed a slight movement of his hand at his collar, and then he fell, turning as he fell with his arm flung out. For a split second Daniel thought he saw a flicker of flame at the end of the man's finger. Then the thunder and lightning erupted simultaneously. Instinctively he closed his eyes for a microsecond. The microsecond in which Jerry Winner's right arm, shoulder and head were separated from the rest of his body.

Daniel was shaking. His groin was soaked and wet and warm and he was retching in small convulsive spasms. The air was warm and tinted with a pink spray. It reeked of hot black pudding, cordite and spilled bowels. Bright-red blood pumped out on the carpet where he was sure the mutilated torso still twitched. Useless and slightly ridiculous, a tiny thing like a child's toy gun from a Christmas cracker lay on the carpet.

Neal was swallowing hard, blood all down one side of his arm. His own or his colleague's, Daniel had no idea.

356

Only Redwhistle, still in the stranglehold of the masked intruder, and the Japanese man, gone a deathly shade of grey, had barely moved. The latter's eyes followed the smoking muzzle of the automatic as it turned through a tiny degree of arc to point at him.

'Your turn, Samurai Sam.'

Takahashi got to his feet. Slowly. Achingly slowly. For a moment Daniel thought that he too was about to play some heroic with a hidden weapon or martial-arts trick. He kept his arms out, his hands clearly visible at all times, as he moved towards the steel safe, which sat like a small, grey fridge against the wall next to the great Regency fireplace. Still watching the gunman, checking that his every step met with approval, he made to kneel, trying at the same time to avoid the jagged shards of glass.

'Slowly. Keep both hands visible.' The choking Redwhistle – crying, Daniel thought – was dragged sideways, giving his captor a clearer line of vision. In case there's a weapon in the safe, Daniel realised.

'I . . .' the Japanese man was stammering. 'I . . . I don't know the combination.'

'You,' Redwhistle's captor snarled in his ear. 'Tell him.'

Would he or wouldn't he? Surely he couldn't! Yet as the thought flickered from one neuron to another, Daniel was aware that, in the professor's place, he would already be blurting out whatever this evil bastard wanted. Anything that would make the nightmare go away. Even if he knew it was going somewhere else.

The gunman moved the pistol slightly from Redwhistle's throat. The professor tried to spit on the hand that held the gun, but all that, emerged was a thick trail of dribble. His chest was heaving beneath its Harris tweed jacket. The man's hyperventilating, Daniel thought. And then there was an explosion.

Daniel looked up, fully expecting to see the professor's head reduced to a bloody pulp. His first impression was that he was right. The head was still there, but lolling to one side and streaked with blood. And then, as a white shower of plaster dust fell from the ceiling, Daniel understood. The gun had been fired into the air a fraction of an inch from Redwhistle's head. It had blown away the lower half of his ear. The masked man's scream therefore was in his other ear: 'TELL HIM!'

From his own vantage point prostrate on the floor in a puddle of his own urine, Daniel was not at all surprised when Redwhistle did. And Takahashi, who had remained as immobile as a waxwork, turned the wheels as instructed. The little steel door swung open. And then he was standing up again, holding in his hands a receptacle that to Daniel, peering through his cracked spectacles from floor level at the far end of the room, looked like nothing so much as a small cafetiere, complete even with the metal framework. Except, of course, for the yellow skull-and-crossbones stencil. As for what it contained, it could have been bilgewater or homemade lemonade.

'Here. To me. Set it down. There. Now back off.'

Takahashi did as he was told.

Without relinquishing hold of the wreck of Redwhistle and without letting go of his Uzi automatic, Hammerstein used his thumb and third finger to extract a specially prepared padded black bag from his thigh zip pocket. Inserting the container into it required the full use of one hand. For a moment or two his only grip on Redwhistle was around the waist, with the hand holding the automatic. In the circumstances he judged the risk factor acceptable. As usual, he was right. He lifted the wrapped container, in its black bag like a funeral offering, and inserted it carefully over his shoulder into the small, also padded, rucksack. There had been enough stupid mistakes made with this stuff. He was not going to add to them.

The operation completed, he resumed his stranglehold on Redwhistle, motioning Takahashi back towards Daniel and then both of them into the corner, towards the bedroom door, where Therry lay. Or had lain – Daniel now noticed that she was gone. The bedroom door was ajar. All he could imagine was that she had not been hit, after all, and that she had somehow crawled out of harm's way. He uttered a silent prayer.

The four-legged beast of Hammerstein with Redwhistle by the throat advanced slowly, fastidiously avoiding the stinking mess of human debris. Faversham was ushered in front of them to open the door to the staircase.

'Tell them to withdraw,' Hammerstein told him. 'Down to the foot of the staircase.'

He did as he was told. Outside, on the landing, drawn by the gunfire, and mystified that their prey had somehow managed to outfox them, men with guns and hard, angry faces retreated sombrely. Hammerstein edged out the door and on to the staircase, and slowly, without relaxing his grip on his hostage or his potential spread of fire down the stairwell, he retreated. Upwards.

As soon as they realised what was going on, Faversham's men had moved quickly, with the minimum of commotion, up staircases one, two, four, five and six. They had been thwarted for the moment, but it was Hammerstein who was running into a trap. All the staircases linked up at the top corridor. There was no escape but the roof. And any attempt to repeat his abseiling antics would send him straight into the arms of the men in the deer park. If he got that far. Marksmen in the grove could pick out a man coming down a wall like a clay pipe in a fairground sideshow.

As long as they were expecting him. And now they had no excuse.

Within seconds of the gunfire in Redwhistle's room, marksmen stationed along the top corridor had targeted the top of staircase three, as best they could without moving directly into the target's line of sight. Redwhistle was important, the voice coming over their earphones said. He was to be saved – if possible.

Chapter Fifty-Two

*Magdalen College, Oxford; Wednesday
24 December, 12.38 p.m.*

IN THE instant that Harold Hammerstein backed out
the door, something flipped in Daniel Warren. He had
no idea what he was going to do, but he was damned if he
was going to let anyone threaten the lives of thousands
with the same horror he had seen visited on people he
loved. The miniature handgun that the American had
used in his attempt to take down Hammerstein still lay
by the corpse's outstretched hand. Daniel grabbed it and
ran for the door.

'Stop!' Takahashi called as Daniel rushed past him out
on the staircase. He didn't hear the rest. At that moment
no one could hear anything except for the unmistakable
whoop-whoop-whoop of a helicopter's rotor blades.

The machine descending out of the freezing night sky
was not just any helicopter, but one of the ultimate
machines of modern warfare: a Mikosoyan-28 gunship,
codennamed Havoc, the terror of Afghanistan, ex-Soviet
air force and now one of the bestsellers in Attila's
'catalogue'. It had been flown into the country at low
level, lights off, at night under the radar, flying at times
little more than forty feet above the ground, in brief
stints, no more than thirty minutes at a time, coming
in over the Welsh mountains. Using it today was a risk
– Attila had a buyer: somebody in Ireland interested
in 'contingency planning' – but the game at stake here

was worth more than even the Mi-28. And Attila had to admit it was one hell of a shop window.

Professor Simon Redwhistle might easily have died an untimely death at the hands of one of his fellow countrymen if not for the discipline of Neal Faversham's shock troops. They were dodging from doorway to doorway of student bedrooms along the sixth floor of New Buildings towards the top of staircase three when the dishevelled, bleeding form of the professor was almost catapulted into their line of fire.

'Don't shoot! Don't shoot!' he was screaming as the first two men, automatic pistols at the ready, dived towards him. Adeptly they pushed him behind them as they fell into a crouch, raking bullets across the line of little lavatory cubicles from which he had been expelled.

'No, no, no, for Christ's sake!' a distraught Redwhistle yelled out from behind and underneath them. 'Don't shoot *him*!'

Almost immediately another dozen armed men were posi-tioned at every conceivable vantage point around the square landing.

'He's gone out, sir. Through a toilet window. On to the roof.'

The observation was greeted by the commanding officer with a look reserved for statements of the blindingly obvious. The horrendous din of the Mi-28 hovering only feet above their heads made Hammerstein's intentions only too obvious.

'DO YOU HEAR ME?' Redwhistle bawled, grateful at least for now having a figure of obvious authority to address. 'Under no circumstances is he to be shot. The lunatic has taken out and is holding in his hand a glass vial of virulent *Yersinia pestis*, the Black Death, for God's sake. If he drops it or it is in any way damaged, the current medical emergency in this city will look like a case of the common cold.

'Tell your men to hold their fire. We have simply no alternative.'

In the ruins of Redwhistle's room on the third floor, Neal Faversham and Mujimo Takahashi, jointly monitoring events through their radio links, conferred briefly and made their decision. Only one option was left to them. Quickly all the armed men on the top floor were ordered down to ground level. Daniel Warren passed them on the way up. All around the grounds of Magdalen College, Neal Faversham's suddenly impotent warriors stood down. All except one.

On the roof, still below the parapet, Harold Hammerstein had waited until he was sure Redwhistle's warning had been understood. The Mi-28 hovering above had the firepower to take out half of Oxford, if it needed to, but its real advantage was its armour, solid enough to withstand direct hits by all but artillery. Hammerstein had calculated the risk of sniper fire. Knew he would be a target on the roof in the few moments it took him to get from the cover of the parapet to the lowered winch cable and be hauled up into the protecting steel belly of the great beast above. But as long as he had the vial and could threaten to drop it, he was certain no one would take the risk of bringing him down.

If he was wrong, of course, it would cost Attila a fortune; much more importantly, it would cost Harold Hammerstein his life. However, dispersing the content of that particular Pandora's box into the atmosphere would risk taking out a substantial part of the city's population within two days. Eighty, maybe ninety thousand lives thrown into the balance against the desire to take one. He knew the people he was dealing with. Their calculations were all too simple. That was their problem in dealing with people like himself; they knew he disregarded them. The idea of 'meet retaliation' was alien to him; nothing worked quite as well as the application of intolerable force.

He had known that ever since his first schooldays, in the little classroom in the Grindelwald valley, when Kurt, the boy who sat next to him and was one of those who teased him during playtime, had gone too far and begun prodding him with the sharp point of his compass. Young Harold had taken his own compass from his pencil case and, instead of prodding Kurt back, instead of poking him in the leg and causing him to squirm, as they had done to him, he had calmly, quickly and with a strength that surprised him skewered Kurt's index finger to the desktop.

They had sent him home from school, even recommended him for psychiatric study, but he had told his parents, the teachers and the doctor the honest truth, that he hadn't meant to, hadn't thought about it. And they believed him, because it had been true. But if he had not thought about it beforehand, he thought about it afterwards. And learned the lesson. He had fewer friends as a result of the incident. But no one ever teased him in the playground again. Curious, he thought, as he raised his head above the parapet, that that particular memory should come back to him now.

Daniel Warren, scared and yet determined, had only just managed to understand that Hammerstein had squeezed out of one of the little windows that led from the toilet cubicles on to the roof. Standing on one of the seats, he nervously tried to peer out. His only hope was to get one shot in. It had to work. He leaned out, caught a glimpse of the dark figure reaching up towards the huge ugly machine hovering above. And fired.

*   *   *

Erect and windblown, standing tall like the dark invincible angel of the night on the pinnacle of Solomon's temple, Harold Hammerstein exulted in the sense of power, the control over life and death that he held in the little flask in his hand, greater even than the power of the huge killing machine above him, which waited at his command to sweep him away. He was only momentarily distracted by the sudden flash from behind him. They wouldn't dare. And then his anger at the insolence gave way to laughter as his eye caught the telltale glint of a bullet ricocheting off the stone parapet more than six feet away. Incredible, he thought. Almost as incredible as the tiny red dot that had suddenly appeared on the flask in his hand. A tiny glowing dot, just like the mark made by a laser sight focusing on its target . . .

The explosion hurled Daniel Warren backwards, knocking his head against lavatory pipework. On the cloistered lawns below, heads rose in silent wonder at the cataclysm in the night sky. Hands flew up to protect faces against the flying glass from cracking windows. Leadwork melted and the golden stone glowed like the fire bursting all round it. The huge rotors scythed the air as the great beast shuddered, skewed and, erupting with its own internal furnace, smashed into the ancient parapet and fell in burning wreckage on the barren trees below.

Chapter Fifty-Three

Magdalen College, Oxford; Wednesday
24 December, 13.05 p.m.

In the central archway of the colonnade, beneath the great iron lamp, Neal Faversham rubbed his hands together against the cold, and watched as the first fire-fighters arrived to tackle the blazing debris of the Havoc gunship. Serious damage had also been caused to the top storey of the elegant Neoclassical building.

'Not exactly the most efficient way to solve our little problem, Mr Takahashi,' he said to the man who stood beside him.

'But more satisfactory than the alternative, you would agree.'

'Yes, I suppose so. You do realise, however, that normally we would frown most severely on a foreign government tampering with an operation on British soil.'

'Of course. But we were here by your invitation. And, in any case, what matters is the result, I think?'

Faversham gave a noncommittal grunt.

'I am afraid there was always a risk,' Takahashi continued, 'that if we attempted to draw him to us, he would escape. Even though they were not his immediate clients, nobody in Tokyo was prepared to take the risk that these bacteria could reach the Aum Shinri Kyo or any other fanatics of that type. Under the circumstances, therefore, it seemed wise to make a substitution. A compound of nitroglycerine seemed suitable. Even if he had got away with it, the results could have been most satisfactory.'

Faversham managed a smile. 'It is regrettable that you did not see fit to inform us, even a little earlier. Certain things might have been avoided. For one thing, Jerry Winner might not have been gunned down in front of my eyes.'

'Ah, yes, in front of my eyes too. I am very sorry. More sorry than you know. He was a friend. It was not anticipated that he would take unilateral action in that way.'

'As opposed to the unilateral action you took?'

Takahashi made no reply.

'Where, may I ask, is the vial?'

'It is being destroyed by my people. That was the intention, was it not, of both your government and the Americans? That supplies of such dangerous substances should not be stockpiled anywhere. Even for safekeeping.'

Faversham looked the Japanese man in the eye. 'I assume we can trust you, Mr Takahashi?'

Takahashi was unblinking. 'But of course. Trust is what good relations are all about, is it not?'

'Quite, Mr Takahashi. Quite.'

Epilogue

Date: 24 March 10:18:32 +0000
To: Daniel Warren <djhwar@histsci.mit.edu>
From: Therry Moon <moonshine@airwave.net>
Subject: all our yesterdays

Dear Daniel (I guess I should call you that now at least, since we both ended up in the lions' den) – sorry not to be in touch before now, but then considering the trouble I went to scouring the net to find what I am hoping is your email address, it's not so surprising, is it?

I guess they told you not to make contact. They told me the same thing. I just have a less literal brain. How's yours? They told me you got knocked out attempting to be a hero. I didn't believe them. Sorry.

It seems we were both lucky to survive the mayhem in Magdalen that night. Looking back, it's like some strange nightmare. Some of that is probably due to whatever drug Redwhistle pumped into me.

I barely even remember dragging myself across the carpet to the bedroom door – must have been some sort of primitive motor function like cockroaches refusing to die when you stomp on them. All I know is one minute I was expiring gracefully on an antique chaise longue, and the next I was chewing a rug with only a piece of wood between me and a real-life performance of *Terminator 2*.

They kept me in hospital for two weeks. At least I got out, which was more than can be said for some of the poor wretches in there. I was surprised you didn't visit. But they told me you'd gone 'home'.

It was only afterwards that I learned you hadn't exactly been given the option. Losing your Oxford fellowhip must have hurt, but getting a new teaching job at MIT is some consolation. I heard that the department was being sponsored by some big Japanese outfit.

You might not be totally surprised to hear that I gave up the idea of the big Fleet Street career-breaking scoops. Somehow scoops don't seem the same when you know someone else keeps hold of the ice cream. They made it pretty clear to me that there would not be much of an audience for my little story. We have ways over here, you know, of suppressing the truth.

The most insidious, of course, is self-censorship. Redwhistle – with his throat all red and bandages where his left ear used to be, he looked like Vincent van Gogh, but I didn't say; I wasn't sure if he'd see the joke – anyway, he made it quite clear how much I owed him. Which I suppose is true. He – and you – did save my life. I have to thank you for what you did for me. I got myself into the whole damn business. There was never anyone else to blame. Except of course for the bastards who were really responsible.

More to the point, they convinced me – as I guess they convinced you – that publicity would only increase the chances of something similar being attempted again. Next time they might get away with it.

The official figure for the plague outbreak in Oxford was 32 dead. All you can say is that it's less than the number that would have died in Kosovo, or Iraq. Or Chechnya. It seems the real disease is something in the human soul. That old geezer who used to live up the road from here in Stratford had something to say about it: 'and all our yesterdays have lighted fools the way to dusty death.'

I'm going to travel a bit, see the world, while there's

something worth seeing. There's precious little left in England. Who knows? Under other circumstances, you and I might have become better acquainted. But the circumstances were beyond our control.

Love, Therry
(with an 'h').

P.S.: For what it's worth, I drove up through Ditchford again the other day. The diggers had gone, of course. So had everything else. The Fox and Hounds has been renamed the Jolly Tinker. Not much support for foxhunting among the new inhabitants. I guess no one has told them the true history of Tinker's Field. The church is still there, of course, though you might not recognise it, set on the edge of a roundabout. The planners had built in a car park for it, which must have pleased the vicar, though it was empty when I passed. I thought I caught a glimpse of him, our latter-day Father Grey, in the queue for the McDonald's opposite. He seemed happy. I didn't stop. I couldn't bear it.

Perhaps the Black Death would have been better after all.

AUTHOR'S NOTE

The village of Nether Ditchford is an invention, but only in name. It represents many small communities in rural England. The name Ditchford in one form or another – Lower Ditchford, Ditchford Frary – was borne by several ancient villages listed in the Domesday Book in the north Cotswold counties of Oxfordshire, Gloucestershire and Warwickshire. In most cases, their site today is marked on Ordnance Survey maps with only the italic parentheses: (site of). The plague, subsequently known as the Black Death, which hit England late in 1348, took a terrible toll. Exact statistics are hard to come by, partly because of the scale of the disaster, but up to one third of the population is believed to have died.

In September 1999 a British veterinarians' conference was informed by a government expert that there had been a noted growth in the number of black rats in the country. It had to be assumed, he said, that they had come in aboard cargo ships from tropical countries. As a result, the conference was told, it was 'very possible' that bubonic plague could be reintroduced to Britain.

Scientists at DERA, the British government's Defence Evaluation and Research Agency at Porton Down, spent years working on a plague vaccine. They have, however, consistently denied that there was ever any intention to develop a biological weapon based on the bubonic-plague bacteria.

In June 2000 a group of children in Vladivostok,

Russia, con-tracted smallpox, a disease declared eradicated by the World Health Organisation twenty years earlier. It was subsequently revealed that they had been in contact with vials of the virus stockpiled 'for military purposes'. Russian authorities declined to comment on the safekeeping of other biological weapons manufactured by the former Soviet Union.

A NOTE ON THE AUTHOR

Peter Millar was born in Northern Ireland and educated at Magdalen College, Oxford. He is an award-winning journalist who writes for the *Sunday Times*, the *Financial Times*, the *Daily Mail* and the London *Evening Standard*. He has lived in Berlin, Moscow, Paris and Brussels and now lives in London and north Oxfordshire. He is married and has two children.

A NOTE ON THE TYPE

The text of this book is set in Linotype Sabon, named after the type founder, Jacques Sabon. It was designed by Jan Tschichold and jointly developed by Linotype, Monotype and Stempel, in response to a need for a typeface to be available in identical form for mechanical hot metal composition and hand composition using foundry type.

Tschichold based his design for Sabon roman on a fount engraved by Garamond, and Sabon italic on a fount by Granjon. It was first used in 1966 and has proved an enduring modern classic.